1

Castra Praetoria, Rome
Junius AD 61

Sempronius Densus, centurion of the third century, second cohort of the Praetorian Guard, idly spun a coin on the table top and spooned from his bowl a generous helping of lamb stew as he watched the shiny disc rotate fast enough to become a blur.

'I think our standard bearer is developing a twitch,' he murmured conversationally.

'Oh?' replied his counterpart, Claudius Faventinus, centurion of the fifth century, sliding his own bowl away and reaching for his cup of watered wine.

'There we were yesterday, full parade kit, marching from the camp to the grove on the Pincian for the festival, the emperor and all his entourage expected any time, and suddenly we find ourselves marching off up the Via Salaria out towards the wilds. If we'd kept marching we'd have been in Lucus Feronia by nightfall. Mordanticus swears blind he never gave the signal to turn, but the entire front two ranks say they saw the standard dip, and they reacted.

If I hadn't been paying attention and turned us round, we'd have been late. You know how Nero likes things like that.'

'Sounds to me like an omen. The gods are telling you something, Densus.'

'Like what?'

'Don't know. Go north? Leave Rome? Have a vacation? Dismiss your standard bearer?' Faventinus grinned.

'You're a veritable fountain of good ideas.'

From the widening of the other centurion's grin, Faventinus likely had a smutty suggestion lined up, but before he could deliver it, the two men turned at a familiar sound: outside the mess hall, the distinct clatter and click of men on guard snapping to attention. The two men turned, gazing at the large room's door, wondering who was coming to join them. The mess was restricted to the centurionate, a place in the Praetorian fortress where centurions, optios, standard bearers and musicians could congregate without having to deal with the lower, or higher, ranks, and the room was always busy, given the presence of more than three hundred men. Plus, the food was good, supplied as it was by civilian caterers rather than grudgingly pulled together by bored guardsmen.

The two men nearly fell over themselves in the sudden rush to stand, as a man in a senior officer's uniform appeared in the doorway. Such a thing was not only unexpected, but also, strictly speaking, impossible.

The tribune strode into the room as though he owned it, looked around briefly, taking in the décor with the same air as an artist peering into the bottom of a latrine, spotted other centurions standing to attention around the room, and then settled his gaze on Faventinus and Densus, and

TERRA
INCOGNITA

SIMON TURNEY

TERRA INCOGNITA

HEAD of ZEUS

An Aries Book

First published in the UK in 2024 by Head of Zeus,
part of Bloomsbury Publishing Plc

9 7 5 3 1 2 4 6 8

A catalogue record for this book is available from the British Library.

ISBN (HB): 9781804540367
ISBN (E): 9781804540343

Cover design: Simon Michele | Head of Zeus

Printed and bound in Great Britain by
CPI Group (UK) Ltd, Croydon CR0 4YY

Head of Zeus
First Floor East
5–8 Hardwick Street
London EC1R 4RG

WWW.HEADOFZEUS.COM

For Garry and Gill

PART 1

ROME, AD 61

Omnium Rerum Principia Parva Sunt.
The beginnings of all things are small.

Cicero

marched purposefully over to their table. Densus' chair slowly toppled backwards with a clatter as he straightened a little further. The tribune did not look impressed, and as he was not the commander of their own cohort, he was something of an unknown quantity. The two men remained silent, uncertain what had brought the officer to their mess and their table.

'Centurions Sempronius Densus and Claudius Faventinus?' the man said in a business-like manner.

'Yes, Tribune,' Densus replied, trying to keep the frown from his face and mostly succeeding.

'Outside,' the tribune said tersely, thumbing back at the door and turning sharply to march back outside. The two centurions looked at one another uncertainly, shrugged, and gathered their things from the table top, Densus tucking the coin back into his purse.

'Have you been naughty?' sniggered a centurion from the first cohort as they strode to the exit. Faventinus shot the man a scowl, and then they were out into the steaming sunshine of a dusty city summer. The men on guard beside the door were standing so rigidly at attention, Densus suspected he could fit a pilum up their arse without touching the sides. Other than the soldiers, the only person in view was the tribune, standing with his hands clasped behind his back. The door clattered shut behind the centurions, and the tribune glanced momentarily at the soldiers to either side.

'Go guard something else,' he told them, dismissing the pair with a flick of his hand.

The two soldiers looked at one another and then hurried off, glad to be away from a senior officer. The tribune's hands returned to their apparently accustomed place behind his back as he looked at the centurions. 'Which one of you is Densus?'

Sempronius Densus raised his hand. 'That would be me, Tribune.'

'I am told that you are in the unusual position of having not been recruited directly to the Guard, but transferred in from the legions? Specifically the Twenty-Second Deiotariana, in Aegyptus?'

Densus frowned. 'Yes, sir. From Nicopolis, by Alexandria. Served in the Twenty-Second for seven years as a duplicarius and four as a centurion.'

Nodding, the tribune turned to his friend. 'And Faventinus, you have ties to Africa? Experience there?'

Adding his own frown into the mix, the centurion straightened. 'Recruited directly in Rome, sir, but yes. My family have a wine concern in Uthina, sir, and warehouses and offices in Carthage. I've spent plenty of time out there.'

'Good,' the officer replied, unclasping his hands to tap his lip thoughtfully. 'I am to be granted a special commission by the emperor. I can say little about it yet, but I have been told to select two centuries of the Guard, and I need good men, preferably with some knowledge or experience of the southern fringes of the empire. Knowledge and experience of that sort is extremely hard to come by in the Guard, and so your names rather stand out. I shall be speaking to your own tribune to arrange a temporary transfer to my command. For now, I need you to put aside whatever duties you had for the rest of the day.'

Densus nodded. He'd nothing on now, having come off palace duties before noon, but Faventinus was shaking his head. 'With respect, sir, I have to take a detachment to the Navalia to meet the ship of Rubellius Plautus, returning from Baiae.'

'Not any more,' the tribune said, eyes narrowing. 'Someone else will go. The pair of you will meet me at the Porta Praetoria at the eighth hour. Do not be late by even a heartbeat, and attend in your best parade kit. One wrinkle or rust spot and I'll see you cleaning latrines in Germania for the rest of your career.'

Despite the tribune's abrupt attitude, Densus couldn't stop himself asking, 'Parade kit, sir?'

'We are to be briefed by the emperor himself. If you embarrass me, it will be the last thing you ever do as a soldier.'

The centurions blinked, nodding their understanding. The tribune gave them both a hard, warning look and then turned and marched off, hands going back to that clasped-behind-the-back position.

'What the fuck do you make of that?' Faventinus breathed once they were content the tribune was thoroughly out of earshot.

Densus looked up into the clear blue of the Roman summer, tinged slightly towards brown with the ever-present cloud of dung-dust that clung to the city for the hotter months. It was warm, but even now, at the height of its temperature, Rome had nothing on upper Aegyptus. Densus winced at the thought of taking his men somewhere like that. In these days of imperial grandeur it was rare for a member of the Guard to have any experience of warfare or the provinces at all, little skill beyond the training grounds and the palaces of the rich. What the lily-white glorified watchmen of his cohort would make of the southern deserts he could only imagine.

'A special mission for two centuries of Praetorians? And involving Africa and Aegyptus? Something's up. I'd always assumed that if the Guard were ever to be dragged into warfare it would be Germania or Britannia, where all the trouble is. I've not heard of any problems in the south. You?'

Faventinus shook his head. 'And the emperor himself? We've got half an hour. Best make sure there are no wrinkles in my dress tunic.'

The two men turned and strolled across the front of the mess hall, back towards the barracks of the second cohort, enjoying the warmth and the peace. High summer was by far the quietest time in the city, when the lack of wind and the seething sunshine combined to turn the detritus of the streets into that dusty cloud that filled Rome and sent the wealthy out to the coast and the countryside in search of clear air. It did make life in Rome a little unpleasant at times, but it also vastly reduced the workload for the Guard and resulted in a lot of free time.

'I didn't know you were drawn from the legions?' Faventinus said casually as they walked.

'Hmm? Oh, yeah. I kind of made a name for myself. Secured three decorations in the space of a year, which impressed the prefect enough that he mentioned me in dispatches to the emperor. Next thing I know I'm being offered a place in the Guard. A lower centurionate than the one I had out there, but a sight more prestigious and with a healthy pay increase. Couldn't turn it down.'

Faventinus smiled at that. No one in their right mind would refuse the pay rise between legionary and guardsman. And given the choice of a troublesome place in the provinces or a quiet duty in the capital, who would struggle to choose? 'So, what did you do to get decorated? I've been in the Guard fifteen years and managed to avoid all decorations.'

Densus snorted. 'Hard to achieve military glory walking around the streets in a toga and standing behind the emperor looking menacing, eh?' He laughed. 'Nothing really. Saw off some raiders at the quarries of Mons Claudianus, helped stop a small riot in Alexandria between the Greeks and the Jews, and caught another officer trying to sell grave goods from some pharaoh's tomb. The locals look rather hard on things like that.'

'You had an eventful time.'

'An eventful life is not something to actively seek, Claudius, believe me. Better to be quiet and unnoticed than draw attention through trouble.'

Faventinus could only nod at that. It was rare that the Praetorians were ever placed in a position of active service and danger. As they turned a corner, Densus sighed and rolled his eyes, pointing. Across the road, in front of the barracks, two musicians were engaged in a heated debate, their great curved horns propped against their legs.

'They're at it again. I wonder what's up this time.'

'Could be anything. Those two would argue over the colour of water.'

The centurions grinned as a cavalry musician, his short tuba horn over his shoulder, walked blithely past the pair, who immediately stopped arguing, hoisted their cornua into position, and then scurried along behind the oblivious cavalryman, taking a deep breath and pressing their lips to the mouthpieces of their instruments. The sudden twin blast of notes was discordant and deafening, and the poor cavalry musician almost leapt out of his skin before turning, wide-eyed, chest heaving rapidly. The two guard musicians, their argument forgotten, roared with laughter and turned, wandering away, shaking hands.

Densus smiled for a time, then turned to his friend. 'If we're to be sent to Africa, I might worry about this lot. No offence intended, Claudius, but most of the Guard would be more at home in a swimming pool than on a desert campaign.'

Faventinus nodded his agreement. 'I remember soldiers from the Third we used to see around Uthina. They always looked dirty, tired, and a little worried.'

As they separated to return to their own quarters and prepare, Densus mused on that last. 'Dirty, tired and a little worried' more or less described the eleven years of his life he had served in Aegyptus. It was a fascinating and heady place, but he wasn't convinced it was a place to which he longed to return, and most certainly not with two centuries of men whose most active duty in the last decade had been to stand still and not comment while the emperor had poisoned his step-brother at dinner.

What in Hades was Nero up to? Was he not content with a constant war of conquest in Britannia?

2

PALATINE HILL, ROME

Faventinus shuffled uncomfortably as he came to a halt in front of the great ornate doors of the palace, alongside the other officers. Whatever Densus might say about the martial quality of the Guard, no one could accuse them of weakness.

He could feel an itch somewhere beneath his left shoulder blade, but there was not a chance in Hades of getting to it to scratch. The itch was nestled beneath his white linen dress tunic, which sat in turn beneath a soft leather subarmalis tunic, worn to prevent the chafing of the ornate bronze breastplate he wore atop that, already preventing any hope of reaching the trouble spot. And that was without the heavy, white wool toga that sat draped across the top of it all, completing a garb that was in its entirety heavy enough to make any legionary gasp with effort.

He could feel the sweat trickling down his flesh beneath it all, a uniform far from suited to Rome's summer sunshine.

He adjusted the hang of the sword belted beneath the toga, a weapon of war for which only Praetorians could claim dispensation, protecting them from the laws of the city. Another drip of sweat formed on his eyebrow beneath the rim of his ornate, old-fashioned helmet.

Densus seemed to be suffering the same discomfort as his fellow centurion, but Faventinus had to give it to the tribune, who wore much the same garb, barring the stripe of rank on his toga: he seemed cool as a mountain stream, straight as a broom handle, and unsmiling as a tragedy mask.

Faventinus did *not* feel relaxed.

Also, his feet ached. He was wearing the boots he kept for parades, which, while shiny and clean, were still relatively new and tight and chafed in places, and the three men had been forced to walk the mile and a half from the camp, across the city, with an escort of guardsmen. With the combination of heavy, unwieldy togas and inflexible cuirasses, it was not possible to ride a horse, and was extraordinarily uncomfortable in a litter. As such, walking had been the only viable method of transport.

The palace doors opened before them, great oak affairs carved with scenes of luxury and decadence, studded with ornate bronze rivets, the handles great golden lions with rings hanging from their mouths. Other guardsmen on duty stood at attention to each side as the slaves pulled the great doors inwards, while the sixteen soldiers who had escorted them from the fortress waited patiently for the officers to enter so that they could sag and relax.

The three men waited quietly for a palace freedman in a white tunic bordered with gold decoration to approach, his kid-skin sandals slapping softly on the marble floor as he bowed his head in greeting, not quite lowering his eyes. Faventinus caught the look of disapproval in the tribune's eye before the man nodded in return. A man of the tribune's rank not being bowed to deeply by an ex-slave rankled, though there was little he could do to discipline a freedman of the emperor.

'If you would follow me, gentlemen,' the lackey said, still with his head lowered, then turned, straightened, and padded away into the palace.

The two centurions waited for the tribune to take the lead, which he did, marching after the freedman as though on parade, the nails on the soles of his boots clacking noisily on the marble with rhythmic pace. Faventinus and Densus followed, falling naturally into step with the practised ease of the career soldier, so that all three men made one collective set of footsteps.

Most men would marvel with every new doorway and room of this place, Faventinus mused as they walked. But then, most men did not spend half their life on duty in the place. The divine Tiberius had commissioned the palace after the death of the first great emperor, himself unwilling to live in the house of a normal patrician, no matter how large or well-appointed. The place was of a monstrous size, with a perfect layout, and decorated and furnished with a view to producing a palace unmatched across the world. Additions by Caligula and Claudius had only enhanced the hedonistic wonder of the place, and even now, Nero was adding his own stamp to the place, gaudier than the rest, but still screaming of wealth and power.

They marched through rooms filled with statues that each cost more than a centurion's lifetime pay, through the great garden with its ornate pool filled with fish native only to far and exotic lands, a gurgling fountain in the shape of a dancing satyr, and hedges and shrubs so neatly tended that there was not a hint of nature about them. As they progressed into the far wing of the palace, they encountered a great deal more activity, with slaves and freedmen hurrying this way and that, few of them offering any great deference to the officers in their midst. Palace staff were habitually used to important people, and were rarely expected to interrupt the emperor's business for such social niceties. There was also a greater number of guardsmen visible here. The combination of increased humanity spoke to the presence of the emperor in the vicinity, and the visitors were shown to the door of a grand room Faventinus knew to be Tiberius' grand summer dining room, a place greatly favoured by Nero for its view.

Their guide bade them wait, then slipped through the doors. There was a long pause, during which the waiting officers could hear nothing from within through the muffling doors and over the general hubbub of the palace. After a while, the door reopened and the freedman reappeared, bowing his head and gesturing for them to enter.

'Tribune Lucius Curtius Lupus of the Praetorian Guard,' a voice boomed from beside the door as the tribune stepped inside, and then continued as the two officers followed on. 'Centurions Sempronius Densus and Claudius Faventinus.'

The aroma of the room struck the visitors even as they approached the door, a heady mix of perfumes, spiced meats and fine wine – the unmistakable smell of wealth. Faventinus kept his face serene, gaze directly ahead, pace steady, though his eyes caught sight of the group of men already occupying the room and he ran them through his memory as the three approached.

Around the periphery of the room were a number of slaves: two waving great fans to help circulate the sultry air, which was at least clearer up here atop Rome's most exclusive hill, another playing a delicate melody on a set of pipes, others waiting beside a krater of mixed wine and water, prepared to serve anyone at a moment's notice. More perfumed and painted lackeys were simply standing around, waiting to be given an order. A naked girl leaning against a pillar watched the emperor carefully, awaiting the order to dance for Nero and his guests. Two guardsmen in white togas were unobtrusive, almost blending into the décor in shadowy corners.

But the centurion brushed the periphery aside, his attention on those men reclining on couches before the great apsidal window that looked out over the forum and across to the Capitol.

The emperor was dressed in his usual manner, more like a rich dilettante from Athens than an emperor in Rome, his tunic of purple and gold, a circlet in his gold-dusted hair, bangles and rings clinking and clattering on wrists and fingers. He was looking chubby these days, a product of his rich lifestyle, some way from the lean, handsome youth who had taken the throne a few years ago at the age of seventeen. The emperor's presence would stun or throw most people, of course, for there was a belief that to behold the emperor in the flesh was to risk losing one's sight due to his glorious aura, but men of the Guard, who were to be found in his presence most of their serving life, were a little more prosaic.

Most of the emperor's guests, though, came as something of a surprise even to Faventinus.

Not Seneca, of course. The old philosopher had been Nero's tutor and advisor for most of his life in the city. The portly, intense-looking old man was to be found in Nero's presence more often than anyone except the empress Poppaea. Beside Seneca, however, lounged his nephew, Lucan, who, if rumour were to be believed, had recently been the source of a number of rather insulting odes about the emperor that had drawn Nero's anger. If that were true, then whatever had drawn them all here was important enough that it overrode Nero and Lucan's current low-level quarrel. The next couch held the renowned officer Pliny, whose recent book on the use of the dart by cavalry had been the subject of some hilarity among the Praetorian horse guard who had blithely dismissed it as rubbish. The second to last couch held even more of a surprise, in the form of the Praetorian Prefect, Afranias Burrus. The last seat's occupant, Faventinus did not recognise, but the man had the tanned and weathered skin of a man from the south or the east, and the hard look of a military man.

'Great Caesar,' the tribune greeted the emperor, coming to a halt a respectable distance from the table, head bowed and gaze lowered, arms rigidly by his sides.

'Ah, tribune,' Nero drawled, though Faventinus noted with some interest how the emperor's eyes hardened as they fell upon the senior officer. There appeared to be some history between the pair, and not an entirely positive one. 'And these must be the two African officers you have selected for the task.'

'Sir,' bowed the tribune in confirmation.

'Good.' The emperor looked across at the two centurions, seemingly appraising them, then nodded. 'They have the look of hardened, experienced men. You chose well. Lions, rather than lambs.' His gaze returned to the tribune. 'We have been discussing the matter further and have made adjustments to the plan. Have you briefed your men?'

'Caesar?' put in Burrus, the Praetorian commander, 'you commanded the tribune not to speak of the matter outside the palace.'

'Of course,' Nero said with a smile. 'Of course I did.' He leaned back and gestured to one of the slaves, who hurried over with an ornate glass filled with rich wine for his emperor. Sipping it appreciatively, the most powerful man in the world's smile widened. 'The mission is no longer so restricted to the border region.' For the benefit of the uninformed centurions, he straightened to explain. 'It is my desire to add the contentious kingdom of Kush to the empire, and all the region of Aethiopia that sprawls to the south of Aegyptus and Libya.'

Faventinus blinked in surprise. Surely the man was not suggesting that two centuries of men could achieve such a conquest. He opened his mouth to explain a number of potential problems that leapt immediately to mind, and then clamped it shut again. Speaking in Nero's presence without invitation could be a career- or even life-changing decision.

'It is said,' Pliny put in, himself seemingly able to interrupt without fear, 'that while Aegyptus is the greatest source of grain and gold in the empire, the lands to the south, further up the Nile, also supply such goods in quantity.'

'The gold,' corrected the unknown tanned military man,

'not the grain. Aethiopia is less lush, but the mountains do contain a healthy stream of gold.'

'But also,' Seneca added, 'the lands of Aethiopia offer alternative paths to the sea and even to India without the need to rely upon the costly and difficult trade routes through Arabia and Parthia. There is certainly much to be gained by control of the region, financially.'

Nero, who looked faintly put out at having his discussion hijacked by his guests, cleared his throat. 'As such, it is only sensible to send a scouting mission beyond our borders. However, we have somewhat expanded upon our thinking. Any potential conquest of Aethiopia will require more than simply a better geographical knowledge of the bordering region. It will require preparation, understanding, and even the aid of the gods. So, rather than merely making contact with Kush and exploring the region, we have decided that you shall follow the great Nile to its source.'

Faventinus blinked again. His gaze slipped sidelong to Densus, a man who surely knew the great river. Densus had gone rather pale.

The tribune's eyes had narrowed. 'Caesar? Might I ask why?'

'Because,' Nero replied loftily, waving his glass around to emphasise his words, 'it is well known that the prosperity and even the life of both Aegyptus and Kush are entirely reliant upon the great river. As such, any attempt at controlling those lands will only be possible with the goodwill of the gods and spirits of the Nile. Rome has only ever launched one campaign against Kush and its success was... *questionable*, shall we say? As such, you will not only seek the source of the Nile, but you will carry with you appropriate sacrifices and offerings to the great river's spirits. You will buy their goodwill for Rome, and on your passage through Aethiopia, across which the Nile winds, you will also gather sufficient information to aid any military campaign I see fit to undertake in the coming years. A great task, of course, but also a remarkably simple one in design.'

Faventinus felt his spirits sinking. It *was* simple in design. So was suicide.

'I wonder, Cacsar,' mused the unknown soldier on the last couch, 'whether it might not be wise to assign the mission to the Twenty-Second, or the Third Cyrenaica, instead of the Guard. Both have been based in Aegyptus for decades, and have a more intimate knowledge of the region.'

'Both are *too* familiar with it,' Burrus, the Praetorian Prefect, countered with a scowl. 'It is not unknown for powers in control of the Nile to start to get ideas above their station. After all, that is why no one of senatorial rank can be assigned to the province. No, I think when the future of Rome's gold and grain trade are in question, it is better to leave the work in the hands of the emperor's own Guard.'

The soldier at the end threw Burrus a suspicious look, clearly unconvinced, but the others nodded their acceptance, and Nero smiled. 'It is agreed. Tribune, you will take two centuries and explore Aethiopia for me, locate the source of the Nile, and secure the gods' support with gifts, before returning with a wealth of information for us. You will leave as soon as you are ready, and with full access to the treasury to secure whatever you require for a successful journey.'

The emperor then glanced across at the tanned soldier, who was clearing his throat. 'Yes, Tiberius Julius Alexander?'

The man gave a wary smile. 'If I might suggest, Caesar, better that they do not depart until the kalends of the month after next. The Nile is currently flooded with the annual inundation, and the journey will be made longer and more difficult, for the current against them will be stronger. If they leave when I suggest, allowing a month by ship to Alexandria, they should arrive in early September, and the inundation will have receded sufficiently to make things much smoother, the current slower.'

Nero nodded, rolling his eyes. 'Very well,' he waved his hand negligently. 'Alexander knows the area better than most. You leave on the kalends of Augustus. I will have the rationalis of the Imperial coffers liaise with you over funding.' He looked across to the man called Alexander. 'Anything else they should know?'

'I can give them a full description of the journey as far as the third cataract, which is the furthest I have been personally, and I am fully familiar with the history of our relations with the Kushite kings, and their history with Aegyptus long before Rome's control, but that is perhaps a task for another time. The best source of information we have about what lies beyond Napata and the main cities of Kush remains the work of Herodotus. As such, I would recommend a thorough examination of the Greek scholar's writings before you consider setting foot in the place.' He turned to the three visitors. 'I gather one of you has some familiarity with Aegyptus?'

'Yes, sir,' Densus replied with a nod of the head.

'In what capacity?'

'As a centurion in the Twenty-Second Deiotariana.'

The man nodded with a smile. 'Then you of all people

are probably familiar with the tales of the wars with Kush. Where was the furthest you served?'

'At the quarries of Mons Claudianus in the eastern desert, sir, or at the fortress at Thebes.'

'And you speak Greek, probably with a local accent, yes?'

'I *did*, sir, though I've been back in Rome for years now. Probably lost my Aegyptian accent.'

Alexander brushed it off with a wave of his hand. 'It will be enough to see you as far as the cataracts. Always helps to have someone the locals might not think of as a foreigner. Once you pass south of Aegyptus, you might find things more difficult. The Kushites have a language all their own, and if you think the Aegyptians' native tongue is peculiar, it's nothing beside that of Kush. Some of them speak Greek, especially the traders, but not many, and from what I hear once you step outside the heart of their land, the languages all change again.'

Nero, who was starting to look distinctly bored at this more academic turn in the conversation, waved a hand. 'Such matters can be discussed later. For now, I think it is sufficient for these men to know what is being asked of them.' He turned back to the three Praetorians. 'You are dismissed. Go and prepare.'

The tribune bowed his head, while the centurions behind him saluted, and then the three slowly backed from the room, the door opening to permit egress. It was not done to turn one's back on the emperor, after all.

Outside, in the corridor, as the doors closed on the emperor and his guests, the tribune turned to his centurions. 'I shall visit the imperial library while we are here and speak to the master of the copyists. I think it would be useful to have a copy of Herodotus located and reproduced for the perusal of your men. While I do so, you will return to the fortress and assemble your men in the principia. Brief them on that with which we have been tasked, though let it be known that this is still not public knowledge, and I will personally have the hide of any man who gossips about the campaign.'

With that, the tribune turned and marched off.

Faventinus looked at Densus, who snorted. 'I give it an hour before it's all over the Castra Praetoria, and two more hours before every whore in the Subura has heard where we're going.'

'What *is* it with that man? He was uncomfortable.'

'The tribune? I worked that out when I heard his name and saw the way the emperor looked at him. You must have heard the rumours? I reckon it was Curtius Lupus who failed to kill the old empress with that collapsing ship?'

Faventinus broke out into a wide grin. That had been a ridiculous time. The emperor had forged some insane plan to have a ship collapse and sink while carrying his dreadful mother, and she had been the only survivor. It was said that the Praetorian officer who'd failed had been personally slapped by the emperor for his failure. No wonder the man was so uptight. He had a lot to prove, a lot for which to make amends.

'I don't know about *your* lot,' Faventinus sighed, 'but half my century are barely literate beyond basic orders and passwords. I wouldn't rely on them getting through a kids' "See Julius Run" text.'

'Then we'll have to read it to them, won't we,' laughed Densus.

3

CASTRA PRAETORIA, ROME
KALENDS OF JULIUS AD 61

Densus watched with a tight-lipped grimace that had
nothing to do with the smell. A latent, nose-hair-curling
odour of military manufacturing permeated every inch of
the place, a bitter mix of raw leather, oil, wet wool, furnace
soot and sweat. The fabricae – the fortress's workshops –
were probably his least favourite place in the entire Castra
Praetoria, perhaps even worse than the latrines, but the
place served a purpose this month. The fabricae sheds
tended to sit silent and unoccupied for three months in
the high summer, with work concentrated over the winter,
for no one relished the idea of hammering away next to
a furnace when the heat outside could fry an egg on the
pavement. So the fabricae had been the logical choice for
accommodating the better part of two hundred men out of
the way of the general life of the fortress.

And Densus had wanted privacy.

'This Herodotus bloke says you get winged serpents in

upper Aegyptus that fly across from Arabia,' one soldier murmured. 'Doesn't say whether they're dangerous.'

Another guardsman looked across at him. 'Sound bloody dangerous to me. It gets worse. This Dalion bloke says there are tribes with four legs who run as fast as horses, and a whole people with the heads of dogs who feed on other tribes. And there's more...'

Densus winced. What was the tribune thinking having all these copies distributed among the men? It was one thing to be told how many miles it was between towns, or where there were cataracts you couldn't sail past, but tales of monsters and danger seeping into the men's minds before they'd even departed their barracks was far from helpful. He took a deep breath and waved a hand at the pair. 'The whole dog-head thing is probably something to do with Anubis.'

'What's an Anubis, sir?'

Densus sighed. He alone, of every man in this room, had even set foot in the land for which they were bound. 'Anubis is a god of the dead in Aegyptus.' He realised his mistake even before he'd finished the sentence, as men all around the room began making warding signs and rubbing their phallic amulets for luck. Equating their dog-headed monsters with a god of the dead had not improved matters. 'Look, he's a god. Like Pluto. He's not going to lurk in the bushes when you go for a crap and leap out and eat your face.'

Still, the men did not look placated.

'You going to read the entrails, Urbicus?' one of them asked nervously, waving to his friend.

Densus glanced across at the man being addressed. Urbicus turned bloodshot eyes to the speaker. He'd been quiet as he read, which was unusual and could be either a good, or bad, sign. Urbicus was the unit's tesserarius, the third in command and the man in charge of watches and passwords, but he also played the role of priest for the entire cohort, which made him in practice almost as powerful as the centurions, even if he couldn't claim the same rank or authority. Certainly the men were as obedient to his word as to any officer.

Urbicus was an odd case. He drank too much, for sure. Never watered his wine, said that water was for bathing in, not drinking. And Densus had met some of the most superstitious people in the world back in his time in Aegyptus, where superstition and magic was part of everyday life, but Urbicus could give them a run for their money. Yet there was something about the man. Even when he was royally pissing Densus off, being bloody-minded and creepy, there was an aura about him as though the gods walked in his shadow.

Densus shivered.

'The centurionate have not sanctioned a reading,' the man said, flicking a glance at Densus.

'I've explained that. The tribune is planning a grand sacrifice and reading on behalf of the whole expedition at the end of the month. He's arranged for a renowned haruspex from Dodona to perform it for him. He's not keen on us having our own sacrifices. Says it detracts from the status of his own one.'

'You mean he's worried we'll find out what a nightmare we're in for, sir,' another soldier snorted. 'Doesn't want us to hear the truth from our own.'

'Stow that attitude, Plautus,' the centurion barked. 'I'm

being very accommodating this month, given what we're all facing, but let's not forget etiquette here. I don't want to have to write any of you up.'

No one said anything in the short silence that followed, but Densus had the distinct impression that his men were weighing up whether being disciplined would be worth it if it meant being removed from the mission. He tried not to note the look Urbicus was throwing his way, which was insolent and sour enough to piss off most centurions. Densus knew when not to poke the coiled asp, though.

'Forget your dog-headed monsters,' came a familiar voice, 'and your men with no heads and eyes in their chest.'

He turned to see Faventinus standing a few paces behind him.

'Isn't the world dangerous enough without populating the shadows with monsters?' the other centurion went on. 'If I were you, I'd concentrate on worrying about starvation, heat sickness, scorpions, ague, snakes and all the other hazards of desert travel.'

'Thanks a fucking lot,' hissed Densus out of the corner of his mouth, noting with dismay the fresh worry flooding across the faces of his men.

'Better to have them focusing on real dangers than imaginary ones, eh?' his friend replied quietly.

'I was trying not to focus on the dangers at all.'

His gaze caught that of Flaccus, his optio and second in command, who'd been reading out a few passages of Herodotus to those men whose own literary skills left something to be desired. Flaccus caught the look and nodded, then straightened, snapping closed the tablet from which he'd been reading, and grinning. 'Of course,' the junior officer said in a loud voice, 'men like Herodotus only focus on things that interest scholars.'

There was a murmur of uncertainty around the room, and Flaccus shrugged, grasping his staff of office and sweeping it around him, encompassing the room. 'Not once in all this has the old Greek fool mentioned the huge amounts of gold that pour from the rocks in Aegyptus and Aethiopia. A year's pay in a day's prospecting, some say.'

The mood seemed to lighten a little, and Densus made a mental note to buy his optio a number of drinks next time they got to a caupona.

'And what about the whores?' Flaccus laughed. 'All those pretty girls you chase in the subura, and the not-so-pretty ones in your case, Vocula,' he winked, causing a ripple of laughter and one irritated red face. 'That make-up they all wear, the black eyes and all that. Where do you think that came from? Yes, Aegyptus, home of the whore. You've all seen the statues of Cleopatra, or those of Isis? The Aegyptians know how to breed a good-looking woman. And don't worry about starvation. We can load up on a decade's worth of supplies. You know most of Rome's grain comes from there, and the harvest will have been gathered only a few months when we get there. There'll be food galore. And they make beer, too.'

Small pockets of banter had broken out now, men looking up from their serious texts and laughing with one another about what awaited them. Densus heaved a sigh of relief. Half the effort of this campaign was going to be keeping everyone content enough not to mutiny before they even arrived. He frowned and turned.

'What brings you here?'

Faventinus' own smile slid away as he held out a wooden tablet case. Densus took it and opened it, running his eyes down the words scratched in the wax in a tight, neat style with a flourish at the end of every line.

'What's this?'

'This,' his friend said with a sour look, 'is the list our dear tribune put together for his journey. Sent it to me to arrange.'

Densus blinked, then looked down at the list again. 'Is he fucking mad?'

'Certainly looks that way.'

'Who takes a chef and a hair-stylist with them on campaign?'

'Someone who has no idea what he's up against.'

'He wants his own covered wagon? And one of the good ones with the new suspension?'

'At least he got *that* right. Last thing I'd want to do is rattle across the rocky deserts of Africa in a wagon with poor suspension.'

Densus turned, lip wrinkling, to see the grin his friend wore. 'That's not going to happen for a start. He can ride a horse and enjoy it.'

'You going to tell him that?'

Densus shook his head. 'I'm going to pay a visit to the quartermaster. Neither the armicustos nor the praefectus fabrum is going to sanction most of what's on this list, and I'll make sure they put black marks against all the most stupid stuff. Then we can go back to the tribune and tell him we tried but the prefects wouldn't have it. You know what they're like. The more he goes back and demands, the more they'll refuse, and he can't outrank them.'

Faventinus chuckled. 'I like your thinking. Blame the administration. But let's give it a few days. I'm putting together our own list for the journey at the moment, and I don't want the tribune's idiocy to put the quartermasters off helping us. I know we have free hand in the treasury, but if we can get good quality stuff straight from stores, it saves time and effort.'

Densus nodded. It made sense. 'That reminds me. We need to get to the Graecostadium and buy every strong-backed slave they have.'

'Oh? Can we not just rely on the carts?'

'And who's going to load and unload the carts every time we change ship or set up camp? I want my boys concentrating on the job at hand, not bitching about carrying tent sections. How many slaves did Terrentius get for his little trip to Apollinaris?'

'Ten. He put in a requisition for twenty, but they allowed him ten. He complained, but I note he came back with all his men intact and well anyway.'

'We need at least two score. And if we want two score, we need to put in an order for twice that. On the bright side, that one can go straight to the imperial treasury without passing our own prefects.'

Faventinus grinned. 'I wonder if I can re-outfit myself on the treasury. I could do with some new boots.'

4

CASTRA PRAETORIA, ROME
SEVENTH DAY BEFORE THE KALENDS OF AUGUSTUS AD 61

The wide space before the headquarters building at the heart of the Praetorian fortress was thronged. The two centuries of men commanded by Faventinus and Densus stood in full parade kit in ordered lines and columns, as perfect as they always were in full view of the emperor, gleaming steel and bronze, white tunics and cloaks, and blue and gold shields glowing in the morning sun. But as well as those two centuries of men and their officers out front, and the small gathering of luminaries at the centre of events, the occasion had drawn most of those men in the fortress without duties to attend to, and so guardsmen, officers, even the odd tribune and prefect, stood around the edge watching. Most were in their off-duty tunics, looking cool and relaxed compared with the fully armoured centuries standing at attention and sweating their bollocks off.

Three altars had been erected in the open space, brought out of the headquarters shrine for the occasion, and the ornate blocks with their delicate epigraphy sat in the gleaming sun, two hundred offerings piled atop them, from gold coins to honey cakes to rich, rare incense, all steeped in the rich wines that had been poured on each to seek the favour of the gods.

Three altars. Jove, Minerva and Mars. Not the Capitoline trinity, but a different trinity of gods whose very names were synonymous with war. The gods of the Roman campaign. Each deity's favour sought by scores of worried men.

And then there was the tribune's offering. His was to be the *bloody* sacrifice.

It was, Faventinus had to admit, quite the most handsome ram he had ever seen in such a ceremony. Clearly Tribune Curtius Lupus had spared no expense on this. A ram like that was not to be found in an ordinary farmer's flock, but was from a special breeder, grown for the pure whiteness of its wool and the perfection of its curved horns, for its impressive size and powerful bleat. As the victima was led forth by two of the priest's bare-chested attendants in their crimson skirts, Faventinus marvelled again. The animal's horns were tipped with solid gold, its head covered with a harness of gold chain to which were appended garlands of laurel, rosemary, and roses of three colours.

Silence fell across the square now, even the odd murmur and shuffling of feet among the incidental witnesses at the edge halting. Far off down the street, at the gate, the musician steadfastly kept his instrument over his shoulder and his mouth shut. Even the blowing of the watch times would halt for this.

Then the one permitted sound started up as the young flautist began a haunting melody that washed across all present like a sacred wave. The animal made little noise, a good sign, as it was brought to the front, near the main altar that was the focus of the ceremony.

The tribune stood straight and silent, proud and noble, his cloak pulled up over his head in the form of a hood in the traditional manner for the Roman rite. Beside him, another attendant hurried forth with a bronze bowl, and the priest carefully washed his hands in the bowl, drying them on a proffered towel. The same process was repeated for the tribune, the bare-chested attendants not required to do so, having ritually cleansed before bringing the animal forth. Another attendant moved about with a bronze vessel, sprinkling pure water all around the space.

'Great Vesta, keeper of hearth and home, whose sacred flame we here echo, we greet you,' the tribune called, his voice clear and strong. At a nod, his own attendant poured a small quantity of rich wine into the dish atop the altar. Another dropped some herbs into the huge, glowing brazier, making it hiss and throw forth sparks and smoke. 'Sacred Janus, who sees all beginnings and endings, we greet you.' Another offering given, this time of wheat.

Now, two more of the attendants appeared from the rear of the tableau, one carrying the sacred knife, the other a bronze bowl. The dish, containing mola salsa, a mix of the precious first-harvested wheat and of sea-water brine, was dripped onto the head of the animal, which shook and grunted, dancing a little, nervous at the sudden contact. Still, to the relief of all, it settled again quickly, and even remained still as the priest took the knife and then ran the blade on its flat edge along the animal's spine from head to tail.

The priest, head covered with his own garment, held up both hands now, knife in one, and began to chant his prayers, and Faventinus had to admit the man was a showman. The tribune had spared no expense to get the best for this. As if to illustrate that fact, the haruspex, a famed man in the east and brought from Dodona at eye-watering cost, stepped forward and joined the rest near the animal.

'Great Jove, Father of Rome, master of gods, grant us your favour. These men go forth to widen the reach of Rome and to bring your light to dark corners of the world. Strike down with your mighty thunderbolts those who would stand in our way.'

His voice had begun low, melodic, but had changed as he spoke so that as he finished, it was strong and booming. Had it not been for the requirement of silence for the rites, Faventinus was under no illusion that the men would have roared.

'Wise Minerva,' the man went on, 'patron of heroes, grant us your spear to carve a path into fearsome foes, and hold forth your shield to keep safe the brave men of Rome.'

Again, from low to high, a showman plying his trade.

'Mighty Mars, God of War, grant these men your spirit and strength in the coming days and watch over them as they take the gleaming edge of Roman power into the unknown.'

The priest reached the end of his prayers, his voice apexing at rapturous heights, drawing all eyes, and suddenly the deed was upon them. The attendants gripped the animal tight, holding its gilded horns and its torso, as another of their number brought down the sacred hammer onto the ram's forehead, stunning it in one heavy blow. As it slumped, the other attendants jerked its head back, ovine eyes gazing up to the Olympian gods, and the priest stepped forward and drew the blade across the animal's throat with the practised ease of experience. The man was good. He managed to cut through pipes and veins and step back smoothly without a single drop of blood staining his clothing. Indeed, so good was every man there that as the attendants stepped back, the blood sheeting from the animal barely touched any of them, mostly flowing into the gutters and then off to the drains.

The beast shook for a while, and then fell still, the flow of blood from the throat wound slowing, and finally the haruspex now approached, taking centre stage. This man clearly had no qualms about becoming soaked in blood, for even as the animal's essence continued to trickle and pool, the man walked across the crimson lake in his soft sandals, then knelt in it as he took his own knife and began to saw at the animal's gut. With an indescribable sound, the creature's innards slopped out onto the stonework, and the haruspex looked into the viscera, a frown of intense concentration on his face.

He began to saw between parts and move them around, and the attendants crouched beside him with bronze bowls. As he worked, he lifted pieces of offal in blood-soaked hands and dropped them into the bowls, whereupon the attendants carried them across to the brazier, one at a time, casting them into the coals where they hissed and spat, sending meaty smoke up to the delectation of the gods.

Finally, the man waved away the last attendant. He rose. His face was inscrutable, strange. He lifted a wobbling, glistening red thing in his hands, showed it to the tribune and the priest, and then held it aloft.

'The beast's liver is small,' he announced, eastern-accented voice neutral, giving away nothing.

'But it is exquisitely formed,' the tribune added, giving the man a hard look.

'That it is,' the priest put in, pursing his lips. 'Perhaps a second reading? A stray bird or a man's sneeze may have nullified this one.'

'No one sneezed,' the tribune barked, glaring at the priest. 'Everything is as it should be. The animal was pure; its liver is healthy and delicate.'

'And small,' reminded the haruspex, receiving the latest in the tribune's barrage of glares.

'Tell us,' the tribune said.

The fortune teller straightened and cleared his throat. 'There is no bad omen, for the liver is of good quality, though it is of a diminished scale for a beast this size. I foresee success in your endeavours, but I see that your mission will not unfold as you expect. There will be surprises, shocks, difficulties, and all is not as it seems. The success might not be all for which you had hoped.'

Once more, Tribune Lupus gave his expensive haruspex a look that could wither plants and then turned with a straight face to the gathering.

'The mission will be a success,' he announced, and to everyone's relief, the priest and the haruspex both nodded their agreement. All around, the silence now broken, the men laughed and joked in relieved voices. The officiant had pronounced a prediction of success and all powers were in accord. Any shadow cast upon it could not overturn a basic prediction of success.

'What do you make of that?' Faventinus murmured to his optio, who stood nearby, sweating in the sun.

'I don't know, sir. The lads seem happy, and I guess when nothing's bad, it has to be good. Just…'

Faventinus followed the man's gaze to where Urbicus, the unit's own priest, stood. Urbicus had overseen the bloodless offerings on the three altars before the main event, and still stood with his cloak over his head in ritual manner, the only soldier of theirs attending without his helmet. Urbicus did not look happy. Whatever the tribune had pronounced, and no matter how reassured the men were, none of it seemed to have touched Urbicus, who stood like an island of ill omen in a sea of relief. The man's gaze rose slowly, and Faventinus found himself following suit, looking up as the victimatii began their work of carrying away the sacrificial carcass to carve up for the ritual banquet.

Two crows circled lazily overhead and then, the moment Faventinus looked at them, they turned and flapped off over the headquarters and out of sight. The centurion looked back at Urbicus and was surprised to see that he had gone pale. He studied the man for a short time, and then saw his lips moving. The centurion was no great reader of lips, but he thought he could see Urbicus repeating the word 'north' over and over.

Faventinus had no idea what that meant, but it certainly didn't look good.

5

Portus Augusti, Ostia
Kalends of Augustus ad 61

Sempronius Densus narrowed his eyes and sucked in warm, salty air through his teeth before marching across the dock, fists clenched at his side. Two guardsmen from his century stood halfway between the grain wagon and their ship, snarling curses at one another, while the sacks of grain they had dropped sat between them on the dusty flags, split and gradually issuing a steady stream of grain with multiple hissing noises.

'Attention!' he bellowed.

The two men, training overcoming their argument, snapped straight and silent in a heartbeat.

'You're both fined one week's pay.'

The guardsmen blinked.

'But this prick started it, sir, tripping me up,' one pleaded, a tall man with a hooked nose.

'If lazy bastards like you would walk *around* people instead of trying to walk *through* them, it wouldn't happen,' barked the other soldier.

'Shut the fuck up, the pair of you, and pick those sacks up, before a week's fine becomes a month.'

The men frowned and looked down. 'But the sacks are split, sir?'

'And every moment you morons argue, another meal leaks out onto the stone. Snap to it.'

The men leapt a little at his sharp tone and dropped to the sacks, their quarrel totally forgotten as they tried to stem the flow of the precious supplies, and lift the sacks again. Densus watched them for a moment, then stepped back and turned to take in the scene. Everything else seemed to be going smoothly, or at least as smoothly as any operation like this could hope to go.

One entire side of the port was given over solely to their imminent departure, by order of the emperor. Ten wide-bellied actuaria transports wallowed in the water, bumping gently against the dock, tied tight, their boarding ramps scraping an inch or two back and forth with the waves. Each bore a pennant fluttering from the prow with the scorpion image of the Praetorian Guard, a warning to all shipping that these vessels had priority on the water, empire-wide. The ships were perhaps half loaded now, sitting at various levels in the water, though their loads should be equal in the end, and so those depths would level out by nightfall.

Slaves and soldiers alike hurried this way and that, loading supplies from the carts that had brought them from Rome, or from cargo barges that had docked nearby. The slaves had been given the bulk of the worst jobs, of course, but Densus and his fellow centurion had made the unpopular decision to set the guardsmen to work alongside them, in order to speed up the process. The various officers marched this way and that among the organised chaos, maintaining control. The overpowering smell, a mix of brine and fish, filled the air to bursting point, seemingly seeping even into one's pores, the din of the work only heightened by the cacophony of the gulls that almost filled the sky.

And this was only part of the supplies. The foodstuffs being loaded this afternoon were simply to feed the centuries, the slaves and the ships' crews on the month-long voyage to Aegyptus. Then, upon disembarkation at Alexandria, they would collect carts and fresh supplies to see them to the very edge of empire. Had their expedition been given more notice, orders would have been sent to Aegyptus and all would have been made ready in advance, but as it was they would just have to work things out when they got there. It would be good practice for when they were further from civilisation, after all. At Syene, the last notable city under Rome's control, they would make their next supply halt, which should see them as far as Meroë, the capital of the Kushite empire, where the next chance would be. After that, no one knew, but the plan was at least acceptable to beyond the boundaries of Rome.

Along at the northern end of the docks, towards the great harbour wall that marched out into the water, Densus could see merchant vessels loading and unloading, ships of various designs and sizes, from all over the empire.

He returned to watching his men, now and then catching sight of Faventinus haranguing his own unit as they went about their work. All should be ready today, despite butter-fingered idiots and unexpected cock-ups. The rest of the day would be filled with loading and preparing, and the expedition proper would begin with the morning tide.

They had originally planned to be at sea by this morning, but several days ago the plan had changed, departure put back by one day. Poppaea Sabina, Nero's new obsession, had been due to sail from her villa near Pompeii to be at the emperor's side for her birthday, and woe betide any man, of any rank, who stood between the emperor and his woman. Thus the ten ships of their own flotilla had been kept at sea until Poppaea's ship had docked and she had been transferred to a carriage bound for the city.

What had intrigued Densus was that her ship, a fast liburna, of the sort used by couriers, freshly painted and fully crewed, had not departed again after disgorging its precious cargo. Instead, it had moved a dozen ship-lengths along the dock and then moored once more beside the hastily raised signs marking this half of the port as out of bounds for general traffic. It had made room for the fleet, who had finally and with much relief docked and readied to take on their cargo, but only just.

His eyes slid to that ship. It had stayed there, insolently right on the edge of the restricted area, neither loading nor unloading. He'd considered going over to enquire, but half a dozen marines of the Misenum fleet kept anyone away from the ship, among their number a centurion. In the eyes of the Praetorians, even the most junior centurion of the Guard should outrank the most senior one in the navy, but in practice the two services were sufficiently separated that the marines would never acknowledge that. Much as with the legions, the navy distrusted and resented the Guard, believing them soft and overpaid. He was unlikely to be met with friendly helpfulness.

A shout drew his attention, and he turned back to

another of the transports, where a line of slaves was busy carrying heavy grain sacks. He rolled his eyes. A soldier had grasped the breast of one of the slave women as she worked, and a small fight had broken out about ownership of the girl and the impropriety of groping another man's property. He clenched his teeth in irritation, grateful when a moment later Flaccus, his optio, marched across to the men, tore them apart and gave each of them a hefty clout with the bronze knob on the end of his staff. He reminded them, none too gently, that all the slaves were the property of the Guard, and therefore of the emperor, and if any man wanted to claim ownership they simply had to wander back to the palace and ask Nero for his slaves.

Further movement caught his eye, and he looked round to see that Urbicus had gathered about him a small crowd of men as he looked up, cloak pulled up over his head priest-style, and pointed at the shapes the birds were making in the sky. Densus felt his spirits sag once more as the men paying attention to their priest suddenly looked back down and began murmuring prayers and grasping their various amulets for good luck. He sighed. He didn't need the innards of an animal, or the flight of birds, to tell him there was a good chance this mission would be a total disaster.

As if the gods were not crapping on him from a lofty enough height already, a brief fanfare announced the arrival of the tribune at that moment. As the senior officer's covered carriage rattled in through the gate and onto the flagged surface of the dock, every man at work, from centurion to slave, suddenly stopped their arguments and comments and bent to their work in efficient silence. Even Urbicus pulled down his cloak and picked up a wooden crate of vegetables from the top of the stack, marching them over to the nearest ship.

Densus frowned to see that the tribune's vehicle was not alone. His richly appointed carriage was being followed by five wagons, each with a cover, and which were clearly part of his retinue, for they followed him in a line across the port.

At least one of Densus' questions was answered then, for the tribune's carriage, far from approaching any of the other officers, made straight for the sleek liburna that had brought Poppaea from the south. That explained why it had not yet departed. In a way, it irked Densus that the officer considered himself so far above his men that he would have his own luxury transport to Aegyptus, but on the other hand it also meant that the man would not be travelling with them, which would make life a lot easier. In his opinion, and that of the centurionate in general, if tribunes would stay in their houses and lounge around in baths and leave the business of soldiering to the centurions, things would be a damn sight more efficient all round.

The line of wagons trundled to a halt close to the marines standing guard around the liburna, and as the centurion in his blue tunic stepped forward, the tribune alighted from his carriage, the two meeting and exchanging words, unheard from across the dock. The marine officer saluted, and moments later more men were scurrying down the ramp from the ship and heading for the wagons.

Densus squinted into the bright light, between toiling soldiers and slaves, his eyes widening at what he saw. The vehicles' drivers and their mates were beginning to unload all the wagons that had followed the tribune's carriage, and a steady pile of the most impractical things began to grow. A solid oak table as long as a man is tall, a luxurious accubitum – a couch of gilt wood and crimson velvet, a set of shelves, a chest of scrolls in neat cases. The centurion shook his head in disbelief as the marines and sailors began to carry the goods across the dock and up into the liburna. There was a brief disaster as a wicker cage containing a dozen birds fell and the door snapped open, two of the animals flying free before the men could shut it once more and pick it up. Two elegant, long-haired hounds were brought from the carriage by a shapely slave in a diaphanous gown of pale green.

'What the fuck does he think we're doing?' Faventinus murmured, suddenly coming to a halt beside him.

Densus sighed. 'I think he sees it as a vacation. I vetoed half that stuff with the help of the quartermaster section. He must have gone out and bought it privately. And some of that shit wasn't even on the list. We could do without having to feed his *dogs*.'

'If he thinks I'm going to wear out my men carrying his furniture across Aegyptus, he's got another thing coming.'

'With any luck, he's going to travel separately from us all the way.'

Behind them, there was the thud of a heavy sack hitting stone, followed by the hiss of escaping grain.

Densus sighed.

PART 2

EGYPT, AD 61

εστι δὲ καὶ ἐν ἀμμώδει τόπῳ σφόδρα ὥσθ᾽ ὑπ᾽ ἀνέμων θῖνας ἄμμων σωρεύεσθαι, ὑφ᾽ ὧν αἱ σφίγγες αἱ μὲν καὶ μέχρι κεφαλῆς ἑωρῶντο ὑφ᾽ ἡμῶν κατακεχωσμέναι αἱ δ᾽ ἡμιφανεῖς ἐξ ὧν εἰκάζειν παρῆν τὸν κίνδυνον, εἰ τῷ βαδίζοντι πρὸς τὸ ἱερὸν λαῖλαψ ἐπιπέσοι

a place so sandy that dunes are heaped up by the winds; and by these some of the sphinxes which I saw were buried to the head, others only half-visible

Strabo, *Geography*

6

ALEXANDRIA

NINTH DAY BEFORE THE KALENDS OF SEPTEMBER AD 61

'If you don't step aside,' Faventinus said quietly but with more than an edge of menace, 'you'll be regretting it for the rest of the month, from your hospital bed.'

The legionary's eyes hardened. 'I'd have thought a punch-up would be beneath *your* sort, *sir*,' the soldier replied with breath-taking insolence.

Faventinus wasn't sure whether the man meant officers or Praetorians by that, but he was at the end of his patience either way. 'Listen, lad. I'm a centurion. It's beneath me to go around thumping arseholes. That's why I have people to do it for me.' Without needing to snap his fingers, the familiar bulk of Gallo, his second in command, appeared by his side.

'I, on the other hand,' Gallo said with a fierce smile, 'am an optio, which means I outrank piss-streaks like you, but I'm not important enough to have to worry about fighting in the street.'

'Now listen, you...' began the legionary, wagging a finger at them. He got no further, as Gallo's hand shot out, gripping that wavering digit and snapping it to an unnatural angle.

The legionary shrieked in shock and pain, dropping his shield as his other hand came up to gingerly touch his wounded finger. His wide, panicked eyes rose to meet those of his assailant. 'You can't do that,' he gasped.

'Bet you nine more fingers I can.'

'What is the meaning of this?' barked an imperious and very familiar tone.

Without even bothering to look across to the approaching tribune, Faventinus shrugged. 'All sorted, sir. The soldier here seemed to think this dock was solely for the prefect's own barge. Maybe he didn't see our insignia.'

There was a moment's odd silence as the tribune seemed to weigh up the argument, then he stepped into view, nodding. 'Ordinarily, soldier, you would be quite correct. This is the prefect's private dock. However, since we are here by direct command of the emperor, our mandate outranks that of even the Prefect of Aegyptus.' He looked across to Faventinus, a question in his eyes.

'The port's clogged, sir,' he explained. 'We've had to use any space we could find to berth. The official who came out in a boat to see us told us it would be three days before there would be room for our ten ships. We decided that wasn't good enough, so we took matters into our own hands.'

'Quite right,' the tribune said. 'I will clear this up with Prefect Julius Vestinus straight away.' He turned back to the injured legionary. 'Go and find your medicus and have that set, and we'll say no more about this.'

The soldier stared, and for a moment looked as though

he might argue, but while he might feel he could cheek a centurion from another force, a tribune was just a step too high. He saluted, regretting it with his odd-angled finger, and then hurried off, gathering up his shield as he left.

'Try not to provoke the local garrisons,' the tribune said as soon as the man was gone.

'He deserved that, sir.'

'I have no doubt. But we could do with the goodwill of the local legions and auxilia as we resupply and prepare to travel upriver. You know that the legions already envy us. Let's try to remain their friends. Try not to cause a fuss.'

Faventinus saluted, not entirely trusting himself to reply.

'Ah good,' the tribune said, all business now, 'here comes your friend.'

A quick glance around revealed Sempronius Densus striding across the dock from the distant berth he'd found for his own vessel. As the man came to a halt with a salute for their commander, the tribune nodded with satisfaction. 'Walk with me.'

He turned sharply and began to march away from the water towards the huddle of buildings that marked the offices of the harbour. Faventinus gave a quick wave at his optio. 'Have the men bring any remaining supplies off the ship and gather ready. I'll be back when I know where we're going next.' As the man nodded, the centurion turned and followed his commander.

'I have been anxiously awaiting your arrival,' the tribune said. 'I have been in Alexandria for five days now, and was beginning to become vexed with the delay.'

Faventinus had to bite down on an acidic comment comparing the relative speeds of single courier ships and convoys of heavy troops transports. Besides, they had actually made very impressive time, and had docked five whole days ahead of schedule. Instead he nodded quietly, catching sight of Densus rolling his eyes.

The tribune harrumphed. 'I have secured a compound dockside, in which I have stored my own preparations for the journey.' He pointed across to a stockaded area with two of the tribune's bodyguard watching the gate. 'The prefect has already granted me four carts, the most he can spare, and I have begun to gather supplies for the journey. We have yet to load them aboard, for I thought to wait for you, first. Given the busyness of the main harbour, I have managed to find us a place on the dock of the inland lake on the far side of the city. I have ten river barges moored there ready, as well as a galley for myself.'

Faventinus glanced sideward again. If his friend's eyes rolled much more, they might roll out of his head.

'I am told that the lake to the south of the city is connected to the Nile,' the tribune put in.

Densus nodded, eyes now focused. 'The Mareotis Lake, sir. It's connected to the Canopic Nile by a canal which limits traffic, and is a little too small for large traders and warships. Good enough for our purposes though, sir, since the grain barges use it, and we'll be in those same barges.'

'Good. Very well. I need to visit the prefect once again, and then I must get up to date with my campaign record, lest I find myself lacking in detail to supply upon our return. Accommodation for the men has been arranged by the prefect in the form of bunk houses at the lake port. When you report to the harbour guards there, they will show you to our accommodation and ship berths. While I am absent this afternoon, however, you should use your time arranging for all further goods we need for the journey, and transporting all our extant supplies from here to the ships at the lake port.' He thrust out a hand holding a sealed scroll case. 'This is your authorisation to charge any goods to the provincial treasury, confirmed by the procurator. As soon as we are fully prepared, I wish to depart. The earlier we move south, the better. I trust you will be careful in the transport of my own goods from port to port?'

'Of course, sir.'

The tribune gave them a nod and then marched off, leaving the two men standing alone in the midst of the busy harbour.

'Prick,' said Densus, with feeling.

'Quite. Where do we secure everything we need? You know this place.'

Densus shrugged. 'Plenty of places to get stuff. I presume you agree that four wagons is pitiful and we need plenty more. If the prefect can't give us them, we'll have to buy them privately and charge them to his treasury.'

Faventinus grinned. 'I'm sure that'll please him. Yes, more than four. How many? Eight?'

'Ten, I reckon, since we have ten barges, one wagon per boat. And twenty-eight oxen, two for each cart and a bunch in reserve against injury.'

His friend nodded. 'And we need to pick up as much food as we can carry. Should be easy what with the harvest just passed. Water too? Or can we drink river water?'

'I wouldn't recommend it. Most of the time you'll find a croc between you and the water, and if you *do* get to drink it you'll probably be pissing out of your arse for a week.'

Faventinus snorted. 'If this place is anything like the southern parts of Africa Proconsularis, we'll need a lot of water. I'm thinking at least two of the wagons purely for water.'

'Probably three. Right. If the tribune's chosen common Nile barges, they should be adequate at least, and ten wagons will do us. You and I can take a trip to the warehouse district and talk directly to the traders there, while the lads bring everything ashore and prep it for transport to the lake port.'

The two men first strode across to the compound. The two men on duty there challenged them, but in moments they were inside.

'The fool's still planning to take half a domus full of furniture with him. Look at that lot.'

Three wagons sat in the centre of the compound, surrounded by piles of rich, expensive junk. Faventinus' gaze swept across the gathered rubbish and fell upon the shape of a fourth cart sitting over by the stockade, filled from side to side and front to back with large amphorae. 'Wine, you think?'

'Or garum. Either way I'm not carrying that lot upriver. Come on. Let's go back.'

In a trice they were back near the ships. The ten vessels were moored in scattered positions around the harbour, but already the men of the two centuries, as well as their slaves, were hauling goods from their ships to a central place where they were being stockpiled under the careful gaze of Flaccus. The unloading would be faster and easier than the loading had been, for the majority of the foodstuffs had been consumed on the voyage. As they neared the growing pile of goods, Densus called to his optio.

'We're going to find more vehicles so we can move all this to a different harbour on the other side of the city, where the tribune's got us some ships and bunk houses. While we're gone, have this lot shifted to that stockade over there. I want all our stuff gathered with the tribune's gear, and sorted and categorised so we can move it quickly.'

Faventinus gestured and interrupted. 'But before you let any of the men in there, go with a dozen slaves. There's a cart full of amphorae. I don't care what they're filled with, it won't be water. Unload the whole fucking lot, and get rid of them. I don't want the men getting funny ideas and drinking a cart load of wine before we leave.'

Flaccus nodded, and, satisfied, the two centurions moved away. Leaving the men to their labours under the direction of the optios, Faventinus allowed his friend to lead him out into the city. Densus had served here for years, and even though he'd been back in Rome a while, clearly his memory was still good, for he led them with ease through the crowded streets. Faventinus looked about himself as they walked. In some ways, the place was so familiar, and in others so very different.

The temperature and the environment in general were similar to the land of his youth out in Africa, the port city of Carthage, with the same ambient dry heat soothed by the sea breeze that left the unwary unconcerned, and with sunburn. The mudbrick and white plaster everywhere was familiar too, as well as the markets and their smells. But that was where the similarity ended. Everything here had a strangely exotic, ancient feel, the people slightly swarthier and often with shaved heads or black-rimmed eyes. And the architecture was totally alien, all painted temples of great square construction with columns shaped like plant stalks, and titanic statues of long-dead kings with funny hats.

He was starting to enjoy himself for the first time. As Densus led him round, pointing out sights here and there, they passed the steps of a monumental temple, and he stopped suddenly, pointing up at the statues flanking the stair. The left one was of a woman with some sort of grand headdress on, but it was the other that had attracted his attention. The creature seemed to be a well-muscled man, for the most part, though in place of his head was a dog head with gleaming eyes.

'Shit. Look at that. Dog-headed men.'

Densus snorted. 'It's Anubis. A local god.'

'Whatever you do, don't let Urbicus see that.'

This made his friend chuckle. 'You should see Sobek, then.' With no further elucidation, he marched on. The next two hours were less heady and exotic, as Densus took them to the warehouse district and located a number of traders. Deals were struck for meat, vegetables, grain and water, for carts, oxen, horses, for light local linens suitable for the weather, each trade sealed with the guarantee of payment direct from the treasury with no delay or argument. They paid a little over the odds each time in order to have the bulk of the goods delivered directly to the lake port at sunset, and the wagons and animals to the main port, saving the two men having to attempt to lead vehicles through the streets. With two hours of light left before the sun set, they returned to their men to find that the wagons and animals had been delivered in good time, and the optios had had the foresight to begin loading the various goods. As such, by the time the centurions entered the compound, all was ready for transport. Faventinus noted with a dry smile the huge pile of pottery shards in one corner, next to a lake of rich wine and pungent fish sauce that had been unceremoniously tipped out. The tribune's food was going to be drier than he'd like on this trip.

As the sun started its inevitable descent, and lamps and torches guttered into golden life around the city, the two centuries of Praetorians with ten loaded carts and spare animals began to make their way across Alexandria. It was something of a relief to get away from the harbour, which remained ridiculously busy even at dusk, though the relief was brief. Night-time did not clear the streets of the city, nor reduce the noise and activity. It just changed it slightly so that it was less mercantile and more rowdy. As such, leading a column of wagons through the place would have been practically impossible for civilians, and it was only the escort of armoured men, bristling with implements of war and with hard expressions, that kept the streets relatively accessible for them.

It took around an hour to reach the smaller port that opened out onto Lake Mareotis and the first leg of their journey proper. This harbour was considerably less packed and busy than the main port, dealing as it did solely with internal traffic, and the main bulk of grain shipments had already left for Rome over the past month. Thus it took only moments for them to be directed to two recently emptied grain warehouses in a line of twenty-four that had been made up as bunk houses for the accommodation of ship crews. The goods that had been delivered by the various traders over the past hour, and which were still sporadically arriving, had been piled in those same warehouses for convenience, which suited the centurions. It was too late in the day now, as the last golden glimpse of the sun vanished in the west, to begin unloading the carts, and so a quick exchange saw the opening of a third warehouse, into which the vehicles could be driven and left with an eight-man guard for the night.

It was as half the men entered the bunk rooms with relieved groans, and the others, under the centurions' watchful eye, began to move the laden carts to the warehouse, that the tribune appeared, riding a white mare he had apparently acquired from somewhere. In the officer's wake came a number of slaves, servants and functionaries, led by his accensus – his secretary – carrying a stack of wooden tablet cases.

The tribune crossed the open ground and came to a halt close to the two centurions.

'What in Jove's name is all of *that*?'

'Our wagons and supplies, sir,' Densus frowned, as Faventinus looked past the officer and noted with weary wariness yet another wagon in his retinue.

'Too many,' the tribune barked. 'Too slow. We will move like an army on campaign.'

'We *are* an army on campaign, sir.'

The tribune's lip began to twitch. 'No. We are a unit of explorers on imperial business in the world of barbaricum. We need to be able to move light and fast. I fully intend to have documented the source of the river and bought the goodwill of its spirits by Saturnalia. I shall be most put out if we are not back in Alexandria by spring, and Rome by summer.'

Faventinus blinked in surprise, and looked across at

Densus, who was shaking his head. 'Sir, we have thousands of miles to travel, through desert and, if rumours are true, swamps and jungles. This is not going to be a speedy trip. It will be a long and gruelling journey, and all care has to be paid to our transport and supplies, unless we wish to disappear without trace.'

'Nonsense,' the tribune sniffed. 'We are within Roman lands as far as the cataracts, and can call upon support throughout. From there we will be in Kushite lands, and the treaty that has held good with them for much of a century will see us supplied and supported there and beyond.'

'Sir,' Densus said, drawing himself up defensively, 'if you chose me for my local knowledge and understanding of the lands we are moving through, then I must humbly submit that my opinion is of the highest value in any planning.'

The tribune's eyes narrowed as he seemed to consider this. He might well have argued, Faventinus thought, but the emperor himself had told him to assign such men, and it might not be healthy for the man's career to ignore such things. In the end, the tribune straightened. 'Very well, but I expect all efficiency and speed. I will brook no delays beyond the unavoidable. Since you are clogging the port with your endless farm traffic, you can take our new addition in with them,' he commanded, gesturing at the wagon.

'Sir, we already have ten vehicles for ten ships, as well as the animals. Another wagon will not fit, unless you can secure an eleventh ship.'

The man's lip twitch returned with a vengeance. 'Then you can take the goods from it and stow them with those in the other ten.' His tone dropped to a conspiratorial hiss. 'Only assign the most trusted of men, though.'

'Sir?'

'These are valuables. Gifts for the Kushite king from the Prefect of Aegyptus. The prefect wishes to strengthen the alliance we currently enjoy. He has warned us in the most base terms not to start a war with his southern neighbours.'

'Despite the fact that's exactly the purpose of our journey,' Densus snorted.

The tribune fixed him with a hard look. 'Until the emperor declares war and the fetials have thrown their crimson spears, there is no guarantee that such a war will ever happen. Therefore, for now we are to maintain the best possible relations with Kush. Have the goods stowed and make sure none of your thieving men get their grubby hands on my valuables.'

As the tribune rode off towards the house that had been put aside for him, Densus glared at his back. 'I'd like to get my hands on *his* valuables, and squeeze until they go grey.'

'He might be right, though,' Faventinus said. 'We're not here to conquer, but to explore.'

'Never trust the Kushites,' Densus replied. '*Never*. The moment Rome drew troops away from here to deal with Arabia, they sacked half of Aegyptus. The treaty holds, but they've been gradually taking control of lands towards Syene for the last fifty years. One day they'll come again. Their kings and queens live for conquest. They owned all of Aegyptus for centuries, and I reckon they still consider it theirs. Just watch them, and make sure you're always armed.'

'You paint a very encouraging picture of what's to come.'

'Trouble. Trouble's to come.'

7

BABYLON FORTRESS

SIXTH DAY BEFORE THE KALENDS OF SEPTEMBER AD 61

'I'm still impressed,' Faventinus said, looking out over the water.

Densus smiled. People unfamiliar with the Nile usually were. Sailing here was a totally different proposition from the Tiber or the Rhodanus, or almost any other river. Ships coming downriver to the coast could generally rely on a strong current taking them north without great need for oars. Normally, that would mean struggles against the current going the other way. Not so the Nile. The coastal winds blew strong up the river to the south, and the river's surface was calm enough and broad enough to allow the use of sails and tacking to maintain more or less the same pace upriver as down. That was only one of the ways in which the Nile was unique.

They had moved as fast as transport would allow, by the tribune's orders, sailing all day, and stopping only for eight hours overnight, a pace achievable without the need for oarsmen to rest. Thus they had made the one-hundred-and-seventy-mile journey from the lake harbour to Babylon, the first Roman installation upriver, in just three days.

Faventinus, along with almost everyone else, had goggled at this new world as they travelled. It had been years since Densus had made the trip, but he had done so often enough in the old days that it was remarkably familiar.

'It's so green,' Faventinus had said that afternoon. 'I always thought Aegyptus would be brown and dusty.'

'That will come soon enough,' Densus had sighed to his friend. 'This is the delta. It's kept green and lush by all the channels of the Nile. And most of the way to Ambo or Syene it'll be green enough along the water edge, but one look further inland and you'll see what awaits us.'

And now, here at powerful Babylon, they were finally leaving the delta, and that barren golden brown of the desert was closing in.

'How many pyramids are there?' Faventinus asked, pointing out from the boat's prow, across the river, to where three great peaks in a row pointed to a sky that had already begun to take on that rich purple of evening. It was a good question. Densus had no idea. Once you got used to having pyramids around, you sort of stopped noticing them.

'Dunno. I think there were about a hundred and fifty kings, but not all of them had pyramids.'

'They make the two in Rome look pathetic. And that big lion thing...'

'The sphinx.'

'That's bloody impressive, too.'

It was. It really was.

'I don't know about animal-headed men,' Urbicus

grumbled from close by, pointing at the great monument, 'but it looks like they have man-headed animals.'

Shouts from another of the barges drew their idle gaze, and they looked across to see the tribune tottering unsteadily down the ramp to the small dock constructed to serve the fort. There was only sufficient room at the dockside for the one vessel, and the others remained moored a little further out into the channel, the ropes for their anchors almost at full stretch.

The fort had been constructed in the days of Augustus to control the canal that connected the Nile with the Arabian Gulf, and was well enough established these days that a settlement had grown up to the north, along the riverbank. The tribune had made the decision to impose himself upon the garrison commander for the night, requesting accommodation within the fort. The man would complain bitterly as soon as he was out of the tribune's earshot, of course, but he would not refuse a man of such rank, and so the tribune would have relative luxury, at least for one night.

Tribune Curtius Lupus had been less than impressed with the decision to stay aboard the barges and sleep afloat during the two nights since Alexandria. He had expected to be putting ashore each night, the men making camp, setting up his nice comfy tent and carrying all his furniture inside to make it a home away from home. He had only argued against staying aboard until three crocodiles emerged from the riverside reeds, slit-eyes flicking lazily as they took in the barge full of men like a glutton at a banquet. He'd quickly gone quiet and agreed to staying aboard.

Now, though, with a fort's walls and a comfortable bed

on offer, he was going to take advantage of the opportunity. Densus smiled drily as he watched a man stumble down the ramp behind the commander, carrying a chair, and then turned his attention to the other boats.

One of the barges was still moving, and drifted closer, slowing as it came alongside, and Densus looked over to see his optio, Flaccus, leaning into the prow.

'Sir.'

'Optio.'

'I think you should allow shore parties, sir.'

Densus shook his head. 'Not likely.'

'Sir, we don't have to camp, but the men are starting to get more than a little twitchy. They've not left their boats in three days. Small shore parties, one at a time, for an hour or so, might be allowable.' He pointed off towards the civil settlement, and Densus looked that way to see small groups of natives with carts moving their way. Traders, presumably. He sucked on his teeth, weighing the options.

'Personally, I think we could do with seeing what the traders have,' Faventinus urged.

'Alright,' Densus conceded, warily. 'Once the tribune's ship leaves the dock, we'll put in and check it out. If it's safe enough we'll do it, one boat at a time, but not the slaves, so a single tent party of men will have to stay aboard to watch them. Double pay for those who volunteer to stay.'

That would mean around twenty men at a time ashore, and if they landed at the dock and moved straight inland, keeping their wits about them, they should be fine. He and Faventinus would go first, to assess the dangers.

By the time the more accessible of the tribune's goods had been carried ashore and ferried off towards the fort that would be his home for the night, that barge had pulled back out to anchor in the channel, away from the crocodile-strewn riverbank. At Densus' order, their own vessel moved to take its place.

'Right, lads,' he said, as the boat bumped against the dock and the sailors threw around ropes and collected the boarding ramp, 'listen up. This place is full of dangers. I don't care about tricky merchants, local criminals and the like, and there's nothing you can really do about scorpions, but snakes here can be deadly and quick, and there are as many crocodiles as there are people at this time of year. Every man keeps a hand on his sword at all times, and keep your eyes all around you. Never be complacent. As long as you're alert and sensible, we should have no problems. We leave in single file and move off inland. It's two hundred paces to the fort gate, and I want you to assemble halfway. The further you are from the water's edge, the less the danger. Crocs mostly attack from the water or the bank. Then we'll move off to meet these traders. You can have half an hour with them, then, on my double whistle, everyone assembles back at the meeting point and we return to the boat. Got it?' A ripple of affirmative murmurs arose from the boat, and as soon as the plank was run out, Densus led the way, leaving Faventinus to bring up the rear.

Despite his familiarity with this land, it still made his heart jump as he crossed the ramp to the dockside and looked down to see two ridged, wriggling shapes in the water beneath. The magnificent, terrifying animals were so brazen, hanging around underneath the plank in the hope that a meal would slip and fall from it. He'd seen men fall foul of the Nile's most infamous denizens before, and didn't want a repeat of that grizzly display. They had a long way to go, and he didn't want to lose precious men so early.

There was a flourish of relief as he reached the dockside and began to move away inland. The dock was just thirty paces long, formed of rough ancient stones concreted into place, devoid of life, for the soldiers were all inside the fort, and even as he began to walk towards the walls ahead, he could see movement in his peripheral vision, creatures wading through the reeds at both ends of the dock, evil yellow eyes glinting for a moment before they closed and the creatures slunk away.

'Shit,' breathed a soldier a few paces behind him, and, glancing over his shoulder, Densus saw the man looking both ways repeatedly, knuckles white as they gripped the hilt of the sword at his side. Densus turned back and marched on. He could see crocs to either side, at a distance, keeping pace with this mobile meal, scuttling from one piece of undergrowth to the next.

Once he judged he was halfway to the gate of the fort, now closed, having admitted the tribune and all his rubbish, Densus came to a halt, the men beginning to form on his position, each one as they arrived looking around nervously. All hands were on weapons, most men with one on sword and the other on dagger. Good. Let them be nervous. Nervousness was the key to survival at times like this.

He gradually watched the men arrive, including Urbicus, who had managed to acquire a jar of wine from somewhere and was taking swigs from it as he walked. Strictly speaking, Densus should discipline the man and remove the wine, since he was on duty. Practically, if hitting the bottle was the worst Urbicus got here, Densus could live with that.

At least the man wasn't spelling out doom for the lot of them right now. By the time Faventinus arrived, bringing up the rear, two other distinct groups had also formed. A hundred paces north, close to the corner of the fort wall, the various traders, prostitutes and mobile bars, had created a small village of stands. The carts from which they unloaded their wares stood nearby, but it did not escape Densus' notice that the mercenary guards retained by the merchants were guarding neither the stalls nor the carts, but were standing in a protective cordon, watching the reeds and the undergrowth carefully. The other group was of the animals for which they were watching. Crocs had gathered all around them, keeping a reasonable distance, occasionally snapping at one another.

'Remember: safety and attention, and back on two whistles,' he said, and with that, he moved off towards the merchants. Faventinus caught up with him as they walked.

'Weren't you laying that on a bit thick? The crocodiles are keeping their distance.'

Densus snorted. 'They don't run far, but when they do, they'll run faster than you.'

This seemed to shut his fellow centurion up, and Faventinus' hand dropped to his sword hilt like the others. Still, in short order they managed to reach the small temporary village of merchants' stalls, and Densus led the way, looking them over, perusing their wares. He was entirely unsurprised to find that the majority of it was extremely overpriced tourist rubbish. He passed the models of pharaonic statues, replica obelisks, lamps in the shape of pyramids and scrolls of native magic spells. He rolled his eyes to see Urbicus buying Aegyptian charms, though the man was shrewd enough to haggle merchant down to a reasonable price first.

The centurion's eyes lit up as he saw a trestle covered with jars of powders and balms and baskets of leaves and spices. He hurried over, and Faventinus followed, intrigued. He looked over the table, but none of the items were named, and many were very similar looking. He could not see the ones he wanted, and so gestured to the merchant.

'Do you have Artemisia?' he asked the man in Greek, with just a tiny local accent.

The trader grinned, and reached out, indicating a basket full of spiky-looking green leaves.

'How much?'

The man held up a small pouch of rough jute material with a straggly drawstring. 'Nine tetradrachm,' the man said, shaking the pouch.

'For nine tetradrachm,' Densus snorted, 'I would want a sack full.'

'How much you got, soldier?'

Densus leaned closer. 'You and I both know that if I shopped around, I could get that whole basket for seven tetra. But our time is limited by the presence of reptiles that would like to eat us, and I don't have the patience to haggle down to the inevitable end. I'll give you eight for the basket, and we'll pretend we argued over the price for half an hour.'

The man gave a soft chuckle. 'Alright, soldier. Deal. But you're no fun.'

'So my last girlfriend used to say,' Densus retorted as he fished in his purse and located eight silver coins, handing them over. The man simply took the coins, lifted the basket of green leaves and passed them over to him. He took the container and nestled it carefully in the crook of his arm.

As they left and moved on to another stall, Faventinus pointed to the basket. 'Food seasoning?'

'Hardly. Upriver there's another lake, called Ephiom, and it forms a lot of stagnant pools. You get so many bugs there, it's like being in a cloud with wings, and when they bite you, there's a bloody good chance of you getting any one of a dozen illnesses. I've seen men delusional, fevered, fountaining fluids from every orifice, and even dying from what those bugs carry. But they don't like Artemisia. You can crush it and rub it on your skin to keep the bugs away, and chewing it can help build your resistance to the illnesses too. I already picked up a small sack of it in Alexandria, but whenever I see it, I'll buy it. It'll pay off in the end, believe me.'

'Wouldn't it be easier just to avoid this lake?'

'You've heard the stories and read the accounts. Swamps further up the Nile. I'm willing to bet they house the same sort of illness-bugs as Ephiom does. As of the morning, I'm going to start issuing a leaf to each man every day to chew.'

Faventinus sighed. 'Deserts, dangerous Kushites, hungry predators, and now disease-carrying bugs? What a land.'

Densus merely snorted, and went back to perusing the stalls. Over the following quarter hour, he bought a new straw hat, a spare scarf of soft white linen, two small skins of thick pomegranate wine, and a bag of assorted fresh fruit. Every stall visited, and satisfied with his haul, he returned to his starting point, blew two sharp blasts on his whistle, and then led the way, moving back slowly towards their muster point, keeping slow in order to allow the others to catch up.

With Faventinus close by, he reached the place where they had gathered upon leaving the boat, keeping an eye on the landscape around them, then turning and looking back at the line of men hurrying back from the traders to assemble.

He saw the danger when it was too late. Two of the men who were returning were walking side by side, sauntering as though out for a morning stroll, each with their arms folded around a small pile of wares they'd purchased. Intent on their conversation, they had totally failed to notice that they had drifted away from the line of men, who, equally buoyant from their expedition, thought nothing of the straying.

Densus shouted a warning, but he knew it was no good. The two men had come a little too close to the reedy undergrowth that marched all the way down to the water. Guardsmen looked up sharply at their commander's shout, and then turned and looked back, just in time to see the attack.

The crocodile, a large example even among some of the giants in the region, emerged from the reeds at an astonishing speed, a single lunge that sent it forward an entire body length in one bound. Its jaws closed on the nearest soldier's lower leg, a line of curved fangs sinking into calf and shin until they almost met, kept apart solely by the bone. The man screamed, his armful of gains scattering across the ground. Before he could do anything, draw his blade, shout for help, or attempt to reach down, the whole thing was over. The croc, a massive ridged shape, was gone back into the thick reeds, dragging the screaming soldier by the leg. To his mate's credit, he almost went after him. The second soldier, eyes bulging with horror, threw away his own shopping and reached down, yanking his sword from its sheath, eyes on the quivering reeds. But ready as he was, he did not follow, which, to Densus' mind, made the man at least sane.

The soldiers all started paying a lot more attention to the undergrowth as they now half jogged, half sprinted, back to the muster point, where they formed up, weapons out, eyes on their surroundings at all times.

A series of crunches and blood-curdling wails issued from the depths of the undergrowth, though there was nothing to see, and by the time everyone was gathered, the screaming had stopped and the reeds were still once more. Densus could still see shapes moving at the edge of his vision, and the last of the light was failing now, the purple of evening folding into the black of night. He looked at the men gathered around him.

'Back to the boat. Quick, but keep it tight and stay together. Watch the reeds,' he added, somewhat redundantly, given that every man's eyes had been doing just that since the moment the soldier had vanished.

As they made their way back to the dock and then, with some relief, up the ramp and into the boat, Faventinus cleared his throat. 'I presume that's the end of merchant visits?'

Densus just gave his friend a look, and then shouted the order to push away from the dock and seek anchorage out in the water.

8

MEMPHIS

FIFTH DAY BEFORE THE KALENDS OF SEPTEMBER AD 61

It had been a quiet and subdued day since their fateful night at Babylon. The men had slept aboard once more, and with no argument over the denial of further shore visits. Prayers were said for the lost man, Bibula, and every boat set a rotating shift of four men on watch throughout the hours of darkness. That had been strictly unnecessary in Densus' opinion, for he'd never known of a crocodile attack a flotilla like that, but the men were on edge, so he did not want to intervene – to rock the boat, as it were.

This morning, as they'd prepared for departure and the tribune returned from his comfortable night in the fort, the commander had been appraised of events, and had let loose with a long, barbed diatribe against the two centurions on the subject of not taking care of their men. The pair had taken the rant stony-faced and without comment, but as soon as the tribune was back on his own boat, they had speculated about a number of potential species that might play a part in the man's genetics, much to the amusement of other troops within earshot.

It had been just fifteen miles upriver to Memphis, and they had not planned to stop here, but as they had prepared to set off this morning, Urbicus had cornered the two centurions.

'We need to stop at Memphis.'

'Why?'

'I spoke to a stall holder last night. He sold me a number of charms and two spells, but he also told me of the place. Memphis is named after a goddess.'

'So?'

'So, sir, Memphis is the daughter of Neilos, the god of the Nile. Her husband is a son of Jupiter. Accordingly, she has a temple in the city named for her. We must visit her temple and give gifts. We must appease the Nile.'

Densus was not remotely inclined to argue. He'd only ever been to Memphis once, years earlier, a place full of temples and more superstition even than most Aegyptians, but it made sense. The place had been the capital of the ancient kingdom for thousands of years, and was still one of the biggest cities on the Nile, and a stop there could serve more than one purpose, for the acquisition of more Artemisia if nothing else. Furthermore, even had he not agreed with the importance of giving offerings to the daughter of the great river, he felt sure the rest of the men could do with something to lift their mood. It had not taken long to persuade the tribune.

And so here they were, a little after noon, docked at the ancient capital. Due to the sheer size of the place, the river-side harbour was huge, and could easily accommodate all eleven of their boats. The orders were passed around. Half the boats would go ashore immediately, Densus' century, along with the tribune, Centurion Faventinus, and Urbicus, for clear reasons. They would visit the goddess's temple and pay homage, then stay ashore for two hours before returning to the boats so that Faventinus' century could do the same.

'Watch your purses here, and stay together, in groups of at least four,' Densus warned them as they disembarked.

'Sir?'

'It's a busy city, full of thieves and murderers, just like Rome, but while you *know* Rome, you *don't* know Memphis, so stay sharp and look out for one another. When we're done at the temple, you have two hours, and then back to the boats.'

'What about crocs, sir?' someone called, raising the spectre once more of the previous night.

'No crocs around here. Too built-up. All walls and paving. No reeds and mud for them to hide in. You're safe tonight... from crocs, at least.'

And with that advice, they disembarked.

'Any military presence here, centurion?' the tribune asked, with a thoughtful expression, as they walked across the dock.

Densus nodded. Undoubtedly the commander spied another opportunity for a comfy night. 'Every nome of Aegyptus has a strategos in charge, sir, answering to the prefect back in Alexandria. The one here is more powerful than most, because this city and nome is one of the most important. He lives in an old pharaoh's palace at the north wall, and he's got half a cohort of auxiliaries based in a compound there, too.'

'A palace implies plenty of room,' the tribune said in a satisfied tone. 'Once we have visited this temple, we shall pay a visit to this strategos. I am not at all sure what his rank equates to in Rome, but we carry the authority of the emperor himself. After their ordeal of last night, the men could do with a real rest. Two men shall be chosen to remain guard for each boat, and for the rest I will secure accommodation at the palace and military compound. Shore leave in the town will be granted in shifts.'

Densus nodded in surprise. It was more or less what he would have commanded, which seemed strange, coming from the tribune. Perhaps there was at least an element of common sense about the man, even if it was usually buried under pomposity.

'I'll offer enhanced rations and a pay bonus for any man who decides to stay and guard the boats.'

'Good.'

Densus gestured to one of the dock's many workers and asked the location of the temple of Memphis, which sparked a long and confusing conversation before he managed to explain he was referring to the deity and not the city. The man finally gave him a short list of directions, and with that, they were off, marching into the town. Densus accompanied the tribune at the fore, along with Faventinus and Urbicus. Flaccus, Densus' optio, herded the men from their boats and sent them off after the quartet of officers, bringing up the rear himself and leaving his counterpart, Optio Gallo, to keep charge of the other century.

Memphis was a sizeable city, if not on a par with Alexandria, though the two were very different. Where the great port city on the coast was filled with temples and statues of gods and brightly coloured wall hieroglyphics, it also carried the definitive stamp of the Macedonians who had built the city, and had populated it as kings and gods for three centuries. Memphis, though, was all Aegyptian, with architecture and imagery that stretched back millennia, and no sign of Greek or Roman culture had even woven its way into the cracks. Memphis was truly ancient.

It was also very busy. And the locals here seemed to pay less deference to their Roman masters than the people of the north. The column of soldiers was required to more or less force its way through the crowds in the wide thorough-fares and squares of the city. The local gods were on display everywhere, both humans of a surprising variety of skin colours, and human bodies with the heads of various animals.

Memphis smelled of a roughly equal mix of dung and incense. The one thing that struck even Densus, though, as a man familiar with the province, was the temples. There seemed to be more here than in most places, and of greater size and complexity than anything north of Thebes. Every corner turned revealed a new and impressive temple complex, with its grand decorative pylon, obelisks, statues and massive carvings of gods and kings. The entire column stopped briefly at the entrance to one temple, where the pylon gate was flanked by twin statues of such an enormous scale that it hurt the neck to look up at them for protracted periods. They moved on, impressed at the pair of statues, each taller by far than any other in the empire. Moreover, the main street itself marched away from the water between lines of ram-headed sphynxes on plinths. With the apparent lack of dangerous predators this time, the men were looking around with fascination as they marched.

At the end of the main street, Densus collared someone and checked his directions. Route confirmed, they followed a few more streets until they found the temple of Memphis. It was, to the centurion's mind, somewhat underwhelming. Given that the city itself was named for this goddess, he'd expected more than a small and relatively plain structure with an unimpressive pylon, sandwiched between two much larger buildings, and cast into shadow by one of them.

As they approached the gate, it occurred to Densus that despite all his time in this land, he'd only ever been in a temple as a common visitor, never with a need to invoke the god there. He actually had no idea how you went about it, for there were no altars or great divine statues inside to which you could libate. He waved the tesserarius forward.

'You speak Greek, Urbicus?'

'Enough to order food,' the man replied, frowning.

'Alright, you go ahead. You have more authority in this place than we do.'

The priest frowned, but nodded and took the lead, a move that made the tribune's lip twitch in distaste. They waited quietly at the pylon gate, as the life of Memphis went on around them, watching Urbicus ambling slowly into the temple's small precinct, looking distinctly unsure. Densus saw a priest, distinctive with his shaven head and white pleated skirt, and carrying a long, gilded staff, cut across the compound to intercept the man. There was a brief, intense exchange between the two, and then Urbicus turned and wandered back to the entrance.

'There is an offertory chamber over by the north wall,' he said, pointing at a dark doorway in a squat, golden-brown stone building. 'There the public can make their devotions, and ask the goddess for her goodwill. The cult statue itself is apparently held in some sort of magic boat in a sacred cella at the centre, where oracles are given and the true spirit of the goddess lives. Problem is, that part is for priests only. I've managed to argue my way in, but they won't let anyone else enter.'

'Have they any idea who I am?' Tribune Curtius Lupus demanded haughtily.

'Sir,' Densus leaned towards him, 'it is understood that the priesthood here is but an arm of the pharaoh himself, which is Nero. These men are not just priests, they carry the authority of the emperor every bit as much as we do. Even the Prefect of Aegyptus himself wouldn't interfere with the priesthood.'

The tribune turned an irritated look on him, battling for an argument he could use, but apparently failing entirely to find one. In the end, he nodded tersely. 'Then we give our offerings separately.' He turned back to Urbicus. 'But I want you, soldier, to meet with this goddess, ask for her protection along the length of her father's river, and seek an oracle's predictions.'

'Yes, sir,' nodded Urbicus. 'And when you give your offerings, you consume all the food and drinks yourself, so that the goddess can take their essence. And there must be incense burning.' Satisfied he had imparted all critical information, he turned and marched back across the square to where the local priest was waiting for him.

As the two men trotted off towards the complex at the heart of the place, the tribune gave the order and eighty-five men moved into the compound in double file, like a glinting steel serpent. All eyes turned to the spectacle, but the officers kept their mind on their purpose. At the doorway of the squat building they peered in to see a room almost dark, but for the trapezium of golden light shed by the doorway. Blinking into the gloom, a single shape resolved. A table of stone, standing on four drum-like legs. The rest of the room was empty, the walls covered with carved images and hieroglyphics. Taking the initiative, Densus turned to the waiting crowd.

'The room is not large, so the tribune, Centurion Faventinus and I will go first. Then you take turns in groups of ten. When everyone has given something and put forward their prayer, congregate in the middle of the compound.'

With that, he led the way.

The room was oddly cold, after the steaming heat of the sunny day. Densus did a little tour around the walls first as the other two approached the altar. The pictures were as indecipherable as ever, though a female figure with some sort of feathered hat and a staff was likely a representation of the goddess. One thing he'd never even begun to get the hang of in all his time here was their writing. Giving up any hope of interpreting the walls, he joined the others at the offering table. Faventinus was already removing two small sachets of myrrh, ironically bought at great expense from a merchant who had acquired it via a tortuous route from the very Aethiopia for which they were bound. The table surface was carved like the walls, showing a pharaoh of old making an offering of grain to the goddess and being given in return a flail. Marks on the stone indicated where previous offerings had taken place, and so the centurion burned his incense on a discoloured spot where it had happened before. Faventinus then undid the thong on a rather bulbous pouch at his belt and with some difficulty produced a small melon. He looked at it, frowned for a moment, shrugged, then smacked it on the edge of the altar three times until it broke open. He then stood and ate the melon, chewing at its soft innards with some gusto after the dry heat of the day.

Densus smiled. He himself had one of those skins of pomegranate wine at his belt, which he now freed and began to drink, one hand reverently held on the altar to aid the goddess in finding the essence of the wine as it slid down his gullet.

By the time he had finished, and Faventinus had left six well-chewed melon rinds on the table, the tribune was frowning. He produced two golden coins and tossed them onto the surface, murmured his prayer, then left the room.

'Forgot his fruit,' grinned Faventinus.

Densus chuckled. 'Well, maybe the goddess likes gold. Or maybe she'll be good to us and shit on him.'

'I like the sound of that,' his friend laughed. The pair then sent their own prayers to the goddess and followed the tribune out, leaving the incense burning for the rest of the offerings. The next ten men entered to make their own devotions, and the tribune wandered away to one side of the compound, into the shadow of the wall, out of the sun, where he stood alone. The centurions enjoyed the warmth and passed their time with gentle jokes, as group after group of guardsmen entered the building and then left, their offerings made and prayers said.

Densus was beginning to feel distinctly hazy. The wine had been a lot stronger than he'd expected, and consumed the way it was, he couldn't mix it with water. The alcohol and the heat combined were making him a little wobbly and a little sleepy, and he realised suddenly, after a while, that the last group was returning to join them, and Faventinus had been talking to him unheard for a while. He gave his friend a smile that he hoped suggested he'd been listening, and the soldiers gathered, waiting. Finally, the tribune wandered over. 'When your priest returns, we will make for the palace. The men can go about their business in town for a time while we secure space for the night. I think—'

He stopped talking as the two centurions turned away from him. Urbicus had reappeared from the inner sanctuary of the goddess and was marching at speed across the compound. Densus was about to shout him over and enquire, when his slightly blurred eyes picked out a detail that sobered him a little. The tesserarius was white as a swan's back, eyes twitching with fear. He was actually shaking slightly. As the man approached, Densus waved at him.

'Urbicus?'

But the tesserarius was in no mood to talk, apparently. He walked straight through the gathering, the guardsmen scattering out of his way, and never even slowed, marching on away from them all, towards the pylon gate that would lead him from the temple complex.

'Urbicus?' Densus called again at the man's back.

'Soldier, get here *now*,' barked the tribune. The call had no impact. Urbicus continued to march away from both them and the temple, at pace.

'I will have your *hide*,' shouted the tribune furiously.

'Let him go, sir.'

Curtius Lupus' angry gaze snapped from the retreating soldier to the centurion, losing none of its fire. 'What?'

'Sir, whatever he saw or heard, it's hit him hard. Urbicus knows the workings of these things better than any of us. I'll have Flaccus follow him and make sure he gets safely back to the boats.'

'I *will* not be ignored,' snarled the tribune.

'Sir, he's a priest. In this place, he is the voice of the emperor. I won't order him back, and I think it would be a bad idea for you to do it.'

Lupus' lip danced with that twitch again as he wrestled with the idea that a common soldier could somehow outrank him in any circumstance. Finally, he narrowed his eyes at Densus. '*You* go. You follow him and find out what has driven the man mad. And if the explanation is insufficient, I will have *both* your hides.'

Grateful to leave the situation, Densus nodded and hurried away, leaving Faventinus to deal with the angry officer as they went to visit the local strategos.

His head was thumping as he darted between the great pylons and out into the city. He may have temporarily sobered up when Urbicus appeared, but the heat and the activity were still driving the heady wine through his veins. At the gate, he looked this way and that until he spotted the figure of Urbicus lurching away between the crowds. Densus broke into a jog, running to catch up.

Twice, he lost sight of the man, each time catching him once more as they hurried through the busy streets. Finally, he saw the tesserarius turn down a darkened alleyway and followed, closing on him. He caught Urbicus a short way along in the shadows, grabbing him by the arm and turning him. Urbicus fought him for a moment, but in heartbeats Densus had him pressed against a wall, cursing the wine that fogged his mind and was making his temples thump.

'What happened?' he demanded.

Urbicus' eyes were almost spinning, so wild were they. 'No real altar,' the man gasped.

'What?'

'No Roman temple. Nowhere to find *our* gods.'

'What happened, Urbicus?' he repeated, shaking the man in his grip.

Urbicus' eyes focused on him for the first time. 'We are not meant to find the source. *No* man is, Densus. It's not a thing for humans.'

'Oh, come on,' the centurion snorted, but what he saw in the priest-tesserarius' eyes pulled the rug of his certainty out from under him.

'We'll not find it, Densus. And the more we try, the more we'll lose. The more we'll suffer. Better for you to persuade the tribune to turn round now. We need to go home. If we try to reach the source, there will eventually be no one left to tell Nero what we found.'

'What else did you see?' the centurion asked, quietly. He didn't like what he was hearing, for sure, but it should not be enough to make Urbicus react the way he had. The man looked as though he'd seen the restless undead.

'Nothing. Just...' the man began, looking for a moment as though he had something important to say, but he shook his head again. 'Nothing.'

Densus sagged. 'Whatever the fuck you heard, you know how it is with gods. It always needs to be interpreted. Maybe you're wrong.'

Urbicus just shook his head.

'Well,' Densus said with a weary smile, 'I am already half cut, as drunk as I've been in months. On the way here, I saw a bar. The tribune and the others will be busy for at least the next two hours. What say we go there and I try and get the other half cut, and you try to catch up?'

The priest gave him an odd look, which broke slowly into a wary smile.

'I'll drink to that.'

9

LAST DAY OF AUGUSTUS AD 61

Faventinus leaned closer and cupped his hands around his mouth.

'I said we need a spare oar. One of ours was cracked and is going to break soon. You got a spare?'

Densus shook his head and held up his hands in bafflement, unable to hear his fellow centurion over the noises of the boats and the many oars. Sighing, Faventinus gestured to the boat's skipper. 'Take us closer.'

The man frowned. He didn't like getting anywhere near close enough to entangle two sets of oars, as the centurion well knew from their days of travel. Still, Faventinus was the boss, and so the boat turned, angling across the current and making for the other officer's vessel.

'I said—' he began, as the two vessels came close enough almost for the oars to touch, but stopped mid-sentence as he was thrown from his feet and smacked into the boat's rail, scrabbling to not slide under an oar bench as the vessel tipped dangerously to one side.

As he scrambled to pull himself back up, he looked about, alert and worried. Men were shouting, and not just the ones on this boat. The vessel was leaning at a strange angle. They'd hit something, but what? There could hardly be rocks sticking up in the middle of the Nile, and the ever-present crocodiles were never to be found out in the open water near boats.

The vessel came back down to the water with a huge bang, sheets of water hurtling out to either side in massive waves. Men fell from seats, losing control of their oars, others, who had risen, were pitched over the side and into the water. The boat rocked and shook, drifting. The oars had met those of Densus' boat, and the two vessels were linked together, even as this one bounced and rolled.

'What the fuck was that?'

Whatever it was struck again. The first time, the boat had been moving fast when it hit something. This time, it was drifting, and instead the something had hit the boat. The entire vessel left the water for a moment, then the aft rose and continued to climb as the prow smashed back into the river, sending water over everyone.

Faventinus, who'd been at the boat's side, was thrown, and totally unable to stop himself. He hurtled over the side, bouncing painfully on several of the flailing oars. Jupiter, or possibly Neptune, was clearly watching over him, for while other men were dropping into the water like screaming stones, he bounced from the oars of his own boat and landed extremely painfully on the bank of oars of Densus' boat, which was rocking gently but had become disentangled the moment the second blow had struck.

Men were shouting, pointing, some were moving to the

far side of the vessel, one sitting hugging his knees, rocking back and forth on his oar bench. Faventinus could feel himself slipping on the oars. Death was but a heartbeat away for, despite the heat, the centurions had opted for wearing their chain armour and medal harnesses at all times, as befitted their rank. A chain shirt and deep water could be a deadly combination. But even as he slid from the bank of oars, his foot dipping into the water, hands were on him, grabbing, pulling, straining, and he was yanked clear of the river and dragged into the boat.

He still couldn't quite make out any details of all the yelling and screaming, and he'd yet to find out what had happened, but for the moment he contented himself with recovering from his fall, and rose in this second boat which was *not* leaping around like a dolphin, clutching bruised ribs as he came to his feet beside Densus, and stared.

The boat he had been on had smashed back down to the water after the second blow, but a third had come, and this time, the entire stern section had been damaged, timbers cracked and split. As he watched in shock, a giant, smooth rock seemed to surface for a moment beneath the vessel, and those split and broken timbers finally gave, the entire stern breaking free and falling away into the water. The boat was finished, and he noted with passing dismay the entire supply section stored there drop into the water, along with a cart and several bellowing animals.

The men were everywhere. Maybe eight or nine remained clinging for dear life in the spinning and bucking vessel, holding on to benches and ropes, a mix of native sailors, slaves and Praetorian passengers, all distinctions lost amid the brotherhood of terror. The rest were in the water. Most had opted for light kit, leaving their armour in the pack, a situation the officers had allowed because of the constant heat, and their lack of chain shirts was the only thing that had saved most of them thus far. They were swimming like mad, and with panicked lack of focus, scattering in every direction as fast as their arms and legs could pull them, the importance of getting away from the disaster taking precedence over any chosen destination.

'What the fuck?'

Densus, next to him, swaying with the boat, pointed.

'Water horse!'

'What?'

'Hippopotamus. Look.'

The stricken boat, now split into two distinct pieces, dropped back into the river, and what Faventinus had thought to be a smooth grey rock now reared, a head attached to one end coming up and out of the water, sending a crown of white droplets in every direction. Any other time, had he seen such a creature, he might have labelled it comical. It was enormously fat and bulbous, with funny little ears, a massive, peculiarly shaped nose, and an impossibly wide jaw. It was truly a funny-looking creature. But in the current circumstances, two things struck him beyond the comedic angle. The first was the size, for this thing was greater than any ox, and closing on the size of the elephants he had seen brought from the south to Carthage, bound for the entertainment circuits of Rome. The second was that, when that huge mouth opened, the four great teeth in it were each the size of a man's forearm.

'Shit.'

If he'd still harboured any image of the thing as funny,

that was ripped from him in the next moment, as the creature caught one of the struggling men falling from the ruined boat into the water. The man howled in panic as he slid into that mouth, the great head rising so that he slipped deeper towards its throat. He was struggling to free himself, and Faventinus could still see his top half, chest, head and arms, as he tried to grab the slippery tooth and prevent being swallowed.

Then, with an enormous splash, the creature disappeared beneath the surface, leaving great circular waves as evidence of its passing.

'Pila,' bellowed Densus, next to him, throwing out a pointing finger.

Faventinus looked about in simple shock. The remnants of the ruined boat were sinking fast, bits of timber and various pieces of kit bobbing up to the surface. One of the oxen was trying to swim, but was tiring fast. Men were still scattering in every direction in panic. Other boats had decided that coming to help went above and beyond a Praetorian's duty right now, and were moving towards the far bank as they passed, giving the disaster a wide berth. The centurion could hardly blame them. He'd have done the same. Besides, the lead boat held the tribune, and it would have been he who sent them out of danger.

Without warning, and with a massive splash, the creature reappeared above the water, sending white drops out once more in a cloud. Faventinus again saw with horror the top half of the creature's victim, but now that torso and arms were falling free of the mouth to land in the water, separated from the pelvis and legs that remained somewhere inside the creature. By some miracle of nightmare, the half man was still alive, screaming as his intestines unwound with the current, drifting away from him downriver.

Men were reaching the side of the boat around him now, each hefting a pilum taken from the stores.

'Loose at will,' Densus bellowed, and the men began to hurl their pila at the creature. The heavy javelins arced out with varying success. Many fell short, splashing into the water, the result of a combination of nerves and lack of recent practice. Only by the greatest of fortune did none of those misses accidentally strike one of the panicked, desperate swimmers. Three, though, struck the creature.

Faventinus felt hope then, for a moment, until he realised that all the missiles had done was to annoy it. As the hippopotamus turned in the water to face the threat, the pila simply fell away, leaving almost inconsequential red tears in the immense grey hide.

'More,' Densus bellowed.

The creature was distracted from coming after its attackers, though, as it found one of the terrified survivors swimming in the way. Faventinus watched in fresh horror as those great jaws opened, and then both it and the swimmer vanished beneath the surface.

Slowly, the ripples disappeared and the boat they occupied stopped rocking. The ox had drifted so far downriver that it was just a vanishing shape now. Soaked and white-faced men were climbing aboard this boat, helped in by soldiers and sailors alike, while others stood at the rail, wide eyes on the deceptively calm surface as they continued to grip raised javelins, ready.

A scream drew Faventinus' attention and he turned to see the next disaster unfolding. Some of the survivors of the attack had made it to the riverbank, only to discover that it harboured yet more of the crocodiles that occupied such places all up the Nile. Howling in pain and panic, a man was dragged straight back into the river from which he'd just climbed, exhausted, disappearing from view, his fate eloquently revealed as a red cloud emerged on the surface, drifting with the current.

All along the bank, men panicked, realising they were trapped. Already tiring, they faced either the open river, beneath which the great monster lurked unseen, or the bank with its seething mass of teeth and wicked yellow eyes.

Faventinus shivered.

When the creature reappeared, he nearly shat himself, for it had approached their boat beneath the surface, and suddenly reared from the water, only just beyond the oars. Densus did not have to give the order this time, for even as men climbed aboard or struggled to cling to the projecting oars, others flung their pila. This time the majority struck home, their target close enough to be hard to miss. Given the proximity, the blows were not only more accurate, but also carried more power, and the shafts slammed deep, puncturing that great grey hide and carving through meat and bone, lodging there.

The creature reared in pain, bristling with projecting and hanging shafts, wounded now. When it smashed down into the river, scattering broken pila into the water, it struck the oars, sending the boat rocking madly this way and that, drifting back towards the shore. Faventinus had to fight to keep his footing once more, and Densus was slammed against the boat's side before he recovered. Another couple of men toppled into the water with shocked cries. The thing was gone again, but now blood showed in the river, and shattered pilum shafts spoke of weapons lodged in it.

Everyone watched now, eyes sharp. The officers didn't even spare the time to look back across at the bank, where the crocodiles were making neat work of those men who were too exhausted to swim any further and had taken their chances on the shore. Another armful of pila were brought from the stores at the stern and distributed among the men at the rail.

Faventinus prayed silently that the creature hadn't gone underneath the boat. He'd already seen the result of such a thing once, and had no wish to repeat the experience. Much to his relief, when the creature surfaced once more, it was further away. It was making eerie noises that could only be an expression of pain, for its hide was bloody and torn, and the stubby remnants of broken pila jutted from all over. More struck it now, as the men desperately tried to finish the creature off.

The hippo screeched and thrashed, its porcupine-hide of wood-and-iron shafts shivering this way and that. The last few men still in open water were now climbing aboard Densus' boat. The rest of the flotilla had carefully passed the entire scene close to the far bank and had slowed a little upriver, watching carefully. The near bank was a grisly scene of reptilian meal-time.

The hippopotamus gave one last great cry and then slumped on its side, slowly submerging beneath the surface like an echo of the boat it had killed. For a long time, Faventinus and the men around him stared at the slowly diminishing ripples in the river until they faded away and all evidence had gone. Things were deceptively calm. There were no more shouts or screams on the boat, just the tense silence of held breath as every man waited, unconvinced it was over. Those who had reached the riverbank had all gone, and those in open water had finally drowned if they hadn't reached Densus' boat. An entire cart, a boat, two oxen and enough supplies for days on end, lay at the bottom of the river. Even the blood had now dissipated with the current, washed downstream.

An eerie silence reigned.

'Is it gone?'

'I would say so,' Densus replied, shakily. Then he turned to the men in the boat. 'Pila away. Everyone find their place. Survivors of the other boat secure a position for now until we stop for the night.'

'Don't stop *too* soon,' Faventinus urged, still watching the calm water.

A distant noise drew their eyes, as another hippo breached the surface a few hundred paces downstream.

'Jove, they're everywhere.'

Densus nodded and threw out a hand. 'Row. Get us back with the others. Fast, now.'

In moments the boat was lurching forward upstream, every hand bent to the oars with fresh urgency, the pace the fastest since they had left Alexandria. Every oar stroke they managed to put between them and the distant grey monster allowed Faventinus to calm his breath and recover.

As they neared the other boats, which had slowed to allow them to catch up, he looked across at his fellow centurion. 'And I thought the crocodiles were the problem.'

Densus sagged. 'Hippo attacks are not as common. You

actually have to come near them. But they're a lot more bloody dangerous when you do. That was just bad luck.'

'I'm still not sure what happened. Did we hit it, or did it attack us?'

'From what I saw, I'd say it was under the surface. They do that. They spend a lot of time underwater. Your boat must have gone over the top of it and clonked it. They'll happily attack individuals and small groups, but they usually leave boats alone. I think you gave it a headache.'

'Any way we can avoid a repeat of that?'

'Only by leaving the boats and slogging south by land, through the desert.'

'Fabulous.' Faventinus sighed as he looked about the boat. 'We've lost a tenth of our supplies, two oxen, and one of the wagons. That's a lot. But the loss of men is the worst problem.'

Densus nodded. 'By my count you've lost fifteen guardsmen, as well as a handful of slaves and most of a boat crew.'

'And we're still inside the bloody empire. That's ridiculous. How close are we to the border?'

'The administration recognises the first cataract as the edge for now. That's at least twelve days away. And the further south we go, the less civilised it will get.'

'I have no idea why even a dreamer like the emperor would want this place, let alone the bits outside it.'

'Grain and gold,' Densus replied. 'You know that.'

Faventinus nodded wearily and went back to watching the calm river slide past. The rest of the day's journey passed without incident, though with a constant background tension throughout. That evening the decision as to whether to stay aboard or to put ashore for the night was easier than usual. No one wanted to stay on the river. The boats put to shore, and the few men with bows loosed a score of arrows into the bank, sending the ever-present crocodilian inhabitants scattering to either side or into the water. Having cleared a small area, men armed and armoured themselves and stepped ashore to create a cordon with blades bared, keeping any danger at bay. The boats were unloaded and tied up, for the men would need to be redistributed for the next stage, and a small camp was set up a safe distance from the water and its watchful reptiles.

It took a number of hours for sleep to claim Faventinus.

10

THEBES

THE EIGHTH DAY OF SEPTEMBER AD 61

Eight days. Eight days of every man on every boat watching the water nervously, waiting for it to erupt and throw forth a great grey monster. That it had failed to do so had not done much to calm the men. It did not help that even though no such creature surged from the water to attack them, they could see the things now and then, off in the distance, either in the water or in the rich, silty farmland to either side.

Even though it was severely stretching the term to call Thebes civilisation, Densus was as relieved as everyone else to reach the place, the capital of one of the larger and more influential nomes in the province. Densus had been here a handful of times during his service in the Twenty-Second, and the place never changed. A thriving native town with narrow streets and mudbrick housing, filled with shouting people, howling animals and the smell of hot dry dung and pungent spices, it had a small neighbourhood of Roman buildings tacked on the edge, as though an afterthought. The whole place clustered around two great temples, linked by an avenue of sphynxes, which formed the heart of Thebes, and which stood so high and mighty they dwarfed the town around them. Several small docks served the place, but the visitors utilised the one near the large temple, for it was there that the Roman fort sat, squat and brown, close to the temple's pylon gate.

'What do you know of the unit?' the tribune asked, rubbing his chin as his slave gave the ornate bronze helmet a last polish and flicked a hand through the white crest to neaten it up.

Densus shrugged. 'The Cohors Facundi. Like most of the southern border cohorts, they're more native than Roman. They don't even particularly like their fellow auxilia, and they don't trust the legions at all. It remains to be seen what they make of the Guard, but I doubt they'll be enthusiastic.'

'They will do as ordered. We carry the emperor's authority.'

Densus nodded thoughtfully. 'Actually that might carry some weight even here. To the Aegyptians, the emperor is Pharaoh, and Pharaoh is god. This lot probably think of Nero more as a pharaoh than an emperor anyway.'

'I shall lead the way.'

'I would let scouts do that, sir.'

'Nonsense.' Curtius Lupus settled his gleaming helmet into position, tied the thong at the chin, and marched off along a road bordered by many ram-headed sphynxes on podia. He managed about twenty paces before the native merchants pounced, seeing a rich visitor. Fortunately, anticipating this, Densus had waved Faventinus and the others forward, and before a third merchant could touch the tribune with grubby hands, the escort were there, shouting in rough Greek, forcing the merchants back, away from the senior officer. Lupus gave Densus a narrow-eyed look that suggested this was all his fault, and then marched on, soldiers scurrying ahead to make sure his way stayed clear. His secretary, personal slave, and two other attendants hurried on in his wake.

Densus rolled his eyes at his friend as the two centurions strode on to catch up. The fort was a small example, and like most of the forts in southern Aegyptus, was constructed of mudbrick. Everything here was brown, from the river to the ground, to the buildings, to the people. Only by looking up into the blue could you escape the brown, and with a sun that blinding, you didn't do that too often. The unit, like most cohorts, had a strength on paper of five hundred men. However, also like most cohorts, between retirees and deaths that had yet to be replaced, the sick-list, and various deserters, imprisoned criminals and corrupt record-fudging, the manpower in practice would not hit more than four hundred. Given that Cohors Facundi had the responsibility of policing most of the nome and garrisoning other fortlets, they would be lucky to have as many as two hundred men at a time in Thebes, hence the reduced size of the fort.

'Poor garrisoning,' the tribune rumbled as they approached. Indeed, the walls seemed to be entirely devoid of guards, barring a single man in a chain shirt and a plain grey tunic, standing above the closed gate, leaning on a spear. Densus could feel the tribune's disapproval at the man's slovenly stance and the fact that he remained so, even as a senior officer approached him.

'Stand to,' Lupus barked as they neared the gate.

The man failed to do so, though he did reach up and

brush hair from his eyes. 'Who goes there?' he asked in a thick local accent.

'Lucius Curtius Lupus, Tribune, Praetorian Guard, direct from Rome, and these are my officers and men.'

If he had been expecting that revelation to see the man shoot upright to attention, he was sadly disappointed. The man remained slouched, and nodded. 'Business?'

'With your commander.'

The man paused for an insolent heartbeat, then turned, looking back down into the fort. 'Heron? Get the gate and send someone to wake the chief.'

The tribune was positively vibrating with irritation, and Densus took a step forward and cleared his throat. 'Might I suggest something, sir?'

'What?'

'Don't try and interfere with them. I know they don't look like soldiers, but they're going to be hard enough work without putting them on the defensive straight away. No matter what authority we carry, they know the area and the stores, and if they feel like being uncooperative, it could add days to our journey.'

Lupus looked for a time as though he would argue, though he finally nodded, still irritated. 'Very well. But upon our return, my reports in both Alexandria and Rome shall be far from favourable.'

Densus nodded. He suspected the Prefect of Aegyptus wouldn't give a shit about the tribune's opinion, and the Cohors Facundi even less so. In a place like this, units that had gone partially native and understood the land were worth far more than a gleaming cohort of clueless soldiers.

The gate was opened, and the visitors entered the Thebes

fort at a march, Lupus looking around with clear distaste at the dusty ground, the water butts, the low, mudbrick buildings and the small corral of camels watching him with suspicious eyes. The soldier who'd opened the gate, unarmoured and just wearing a belted grey tunic with a sword at his side, shut it behind them and then scurried past, heading for the largest building, which would be the headquarters.

Of other life there was no visible sign, but there were murmurs of life emerging from the darkened open doorways of some of the buildings. They reached the headquarters and entered the open door, just the three officers and the tribune's slaves, leaving their escort outside. The place was not grand. No forehall, or crosshall, no statue of Mars or the emperor. In fact, the small courtyard building had just the square with the colonnaded walkway around the edge and three doors at the far end, each open, each dark. As they crossed to one in the wake of Heron, Densus glanced into the shrine of the standards. It was empty.

He winced as they entered the commander's office. The prefect of the Cohors Facundi was seated, his chair tipped back against the wall, feet up and crossed on the desk in front of him. He wore a grey tunic like his men, though with a decorative stripe to denote his rank. His colouring would have seen him lost among locals, his hair cut short and thinning on top, a beard curled and oiled at his chin. He wore a surprising amount of jewellery.

Curtius Lupus actually made a small gagging noise as he bit down on the urge to order the man to his feet. Rank here made little difference, and Densus couldn't imagine anything the tribune might say that would send the commander hurtling to his feet.

'Speak,' the man said in a weary tone, stifling a yawn.

'We are passing through, heading south on an imperial commission to locate the source of the river and secure the goodwill of its spirits, with a view to potential expansion into Kush,' the tribune announced. 'We have two centuries of Praetorians, along with sundry support and guides.'

'Congratulations,' was all the man said in a bored drawl.

'We suffered an attack by hippopotamus a few days ago, and lost an entire barge, along with a vehicle, beasts of burden and a substantial portion of the supplies for our journey.'

'Ah.'

'Indeed. I am seeking to resupply in preparation for the next leg, taking us beyond Syene and into Kushite lands.'

'I have few supplies.'

'*That*, I can believe,' Lupus said with a wrinkled lip, looking around. 'But it is within your power as local garrison to commandeer what you need. We require one cart, preferably with good suspension, at least two oxen of solid health and strength, obedient to the whip, foodstuffs and sundry supplies for a score of men for at least eight days, and a number of replacement items of arms and armour, as well as other kit.'

'Hear that, Heron?' the commander said with a smile, looking past them at the man who'd escorted them. 'Perhaps you could also have the moon brought here and put it on a stick for the man?'

Densus winced at that, and could feel the anger building in the tribune. 'Perhaps the commander would like to verify your authority, sir?' he asked, meaningfully.

There was a pause and then finally the tribune thrust

out a hand behind him, snapping his fingers. His secretary slapped their orders into his palm, which he then held out to the prefect, taking a step forward. The commander took the scroll case and opened it, noting the broken seal as he did so. He slid out the contents and perused them briefly.

'Signed and sealed by Epaphroditus on behalf of the emperor,' he mused. Then, he reached up and interlaced his fingers behind his head. 'I can do you two lazy oxen, a cart that shakes the bones more with every mile, basic grain and a few veg, and whatever sundry pickings you can find knocking around in the fort fabrica.'

The tribune's eyes narrowed dangerously, but the man simply gave a bored smile. 'Without your orders, I'd have kept all that here. I am stretching my hospitality. If you wish more than I offer, then it will require me making official requests, having a local census carried out to locate appropriate goods, sending to other forts for equipment, and so on. Most visitors would have sent ahead and this could have been done before your arrival. If you wish to remain in Thebes, I will begin having those arrangements made. Otherwise I offer you all we have to give.'

Densus clenched his teeth, hoping the tribune wasn't going to be obstinate enough to argue. Finally, Lupus nodded. 'Thank you. That is acceptable. You can deliver it...'

'Your men can pick them up from the fort before dusk,' the prefect interrupted. 'And now I must return to my afternoon nap. In this climate it becomes a necessity. I recommend you do the same.'

And with that, he leaned back and closed his eyes. Curtius

Lupus glared at him for a while, unseen, and then the three men turned and left the building.

'See that all he promised is delivered,' the tribune said, tersely, and marched off, men flocking protectively to his side at Densus' signal.

'That could have gone worse.'

'Why are tribunes always clueless?' Faventinus snorted.

'I think it's the weight of the posh, decorative helmets. Presses hard on their brain.'

The two men chuckled, as Densus waved his soldier over. 'Take a friend and look through the fort fabrica. Take some chalk and mark anything we might need. We'll pick it up at sunset.'

The soldier saluted and hurried off. A weird, warbling cry drew their attention, and on the way back towards the gate, the two men paused at the door of yet another low, mudbrick building, from which the call had come. They looked inside, and confirmed that the place was some sort of hospital. An orderly in the usual grey tunic was mopping the brow of a man in a bed, and a smell of sweat and unpleasantness wafted their way. The man in the bed had stopped crying out and was now burbling as he tossed and turned. The orderly sensed the presence of the two officers and turned to the doorway.

'Swamp fever,' he said, in thickly accented Greek. 'Stay out.'

The centurions needed no further advice and returned to 'fresh' air with gusto. Prompted by the reminder, as all was set in motion, the two men found a local merchant nearby and bought from him all the Artemisia he had available. Then they returned and made camp near the dock. At dusk, as agreed, soldiers headed to the fort and collected a rather poor cart, two very poor oxen, some uninspiring foods, and a collection of shabby replacement kit from the fort stores.

As Densus was passing a camp fire, the men settling down for their evening meal, he saw Urbicus standing with a sneer, holding up a cloak he'd received as a replacement from the fort. A hole in the area of the lower back was stained with old blood. The priest huffed unhappily, made several warding signs against ill fortune, and tossed the thing into the fire.

'Never mind,' Faventinus said by his shoulder. 'Five more days to Syene.'

11

SYENE

TWO DAYS BEFORE THE IDES OF SEPTEMBER AD 61

'So where do we put in?' Faventinus asked. The place was complex, with settlements on both banks of the river, which was wide enough here to play host to a number of large islands that seemed to also be packed with buildings.

'Elephantine,' Densus replied from the next boat, as though the one word explained everything.

They had passed the local Roman military presence some five or six miles ago on the west bank. The tribune was in no hurry to repeat their experience in Thebes, for undoubtedly the garrison commander of Syene would be every bit as irritating and uncooperative as the former. He had decided to take the financial hit, and deal with civilian sources in the city for resupply. Densus, as the only man who had ever been here, was now their leader.

The man was having his boat steer towards a particularly large island in the centre of the river. Faventinus' attention was momentarily distracted as the capsarius, the century's medic, handed him an Artemisia leaf. It had become a daily routine for every man since Thebes, where the centurions had first seen the fever at work. He took the leaf and tucked it in his mouth, lip curling at the bitterness as he ground it between his teeth and then swallowed, feeling the unpleasant foliage slip all the way down. It would be worth it, if it held off what they'd seen in Thebes.

By the time he concentrated on their destination again, he could make the connection. Elephantine. The island was full of clustered houses, temples and other structures, but along the shoreline, the walls rested behind or upon huge rounded grey rocks that did indeed faintly resemble elephants in the water.

Densus leaned from his own prow with hands cupped around his mouth and began to bellow commands. Six of the nine remaining boats were to pass by the island and put ashore at the landing before the cataract, while the craft carrying the three senior officers would land at Elephantine.

Faventinus watched as Densus directed his pilot towards a dock on the island, and the vessels of the other centurion and the tribune followed suit.

'Busy,' Faventinus noted as the boat was tied up and the ramp run out. The island was thronged with people going about their business, as well as carts and animals, several markets having sprung up in open spaces.

'I've only been once,' Densus replied, 'but it's probably always this busy. It's the first port on the navigable river after the cataracts. Trade routes come here from Kush, but also from across the eastern and western deserts, from ports on the sea that trade with India, and nomadic caravans. There are few things you can't get in Syene for a price.'

'Eight-man escort only,' Faventinus announced loudly so that his voice carried across the three boats. More than that would be trouble in such a busy place. Besides, the idea was not to actually acquire supplies here, but purchase them and arrange delivery to the cataract, where it could all be loaded into the carts for the next leg of the journey.

Moments later, while Densus and the tribune stood on the dock, deep in discussion, Faventinus gestured to one tent party of guardsmen, who disembarked and formed an honour guard, the centurion joining the other two officers on the dock to complete the shore party. Led by Densus once more, they moved into the crowded island. Not far from the dock, the first of the numerous markets filled an open space between the high compound walls of a temple, and a row of public buildings. The place reeked of spices and exotic foods, and Faventinus looked around with fascination. Large wicker cages held brightly coloured birds of many species, small, ugly monkeys, snakes, and so much more. Camels were tied up with price signs around their necks, jugs and jars, bowls and sacks, and a surprising number of stalls stacked high with ivory tusks.

He kept largely quiet and at the back as Densus moved from stall to stall, looking for what they needed, Faventinus only chiming in occasionally with an opinion on required quantity and quality, content to let his friend handle most of the deals. Indeed, the tribune did much the same, though the senior officer seemed to shun involvement, largely to stay away from everything and not let anything touch him. He held an expression of distaste throughout. It was only as Densus struck up a conversation with one particular merchant that Faventinus started to pay more attention.

'Source?' the merchant replied in Greek, but with such a thick, peculiar accent that it was rather hard to understand even to a Greek speaker. 'No. Not see source. River massive long. But I go many south. *Many* south. Where river swamp, yes?'

Faventinus leaned in to listen. They had read ancient accounts of the swamps far upriver, but it was different to actually speak to someone who'd been there.

'You have been to the swamps on the Nile?' Densus pressed, careful to annunciate every word clearly and avoid contractions.

'See swamp yes. Many swamp. Never go. Too much.'

'Are they crossable? The river still navigable?'

'Navible?'

'Can you still use a boat?' Densus clarified, miming his words as he spoke.

'Boat? Yes. Small boat. *Many* small.' The man mimed the same as Densus but tiny, with a suggestion that just one man sat in it.

'Well that's a relief,' Densus sighed. 'At least we have a little more knowledge.' He turned back to the merchant. 'Where do you go if you do not cross the swamp?'

The man seemed to think about this for a time, then nodded as he understood. 'Near swamp pay ivory. Many ivory.'

'You buy ivory there?'

'Yes. No go jungle. Or swamp. Here to Kemet-land, or east trade road.'

'Trade road?'

'Swamp town. Road go east much mile. Half month to sea and India men.'

At this, the tribune's ears pricked and he took a step closer. 'From the swamps there is a trade route to the eastern sea? That would be to the south of known Aethiopia. Such a route could be invaluable to us. It would allow Rome to stop using the expensive trade routes across Arabia, and remove all need for negotiations with Parthia. That trade route alone would make our expedition worthwhile. I shall consider its discovery and location our secondary objective after the river's source.'

Faventinus nodded, though he was in two minds about it himself. He was sure the tribune was right about the value of the place, but their current mission was going to be hard enough without adding new places to their route. He stepped back again, then, and let Densus go to work once more. The centurion bought goods from the merchant, and when the tribune made veiled complaints about high prices, Densus pointed out just how valuable the man's information could be, and noted that any inflated price had therefore been made worthwhile.

It took an hour or so to secure the purchase of two more good oxen to replace the half-dead creatures they'd taken from Thebes, and replacement food and supplies. All requirements would be delivered to the dock at the cataract before sunset. As such, they returned to the boats directly, preparing to join the others upriver. It was only as the tribune's boat pulled away, with him on board, that Faventinus heard the argument from Densus. Disembarking once more, he hurried over to the other centurion's boat.

'What's up?'

'Fucking Urbicus. He's gone ashore with six other

soldiers. I swear that man is going to get a good hiding the next time he disobeys orders.'

Faventinus nodded. Urbicus might be a junior officer, and out here, in this place and with their remit, his role as unit priest gave him a certain heightened authority, but he was definitely starting to overreach his rank. 'Come on. He won't be hard to find, I reckon.' He turned to his own boat and told them to follow the tribune to the cataract. Then, he and Densus crossed the dock.

'You're going to have to start clamping down on him,' Faventinus said.

'It's not that simple,' Densus replied. 'He knows his gods, and the men follow him like a rulebook. And to be honest, I'm not sure I disagree with him. Back at Memphis, he told me that no man is meant to find the river's source, and that the longer we look, the more we'll lose. Since then we've lost one boat to a hippo, and we haven't even left the Roman province yet. He's a pain in the arse, but I'm more on his side than on the tribune's.'

Faventinus nodded. That was a seductive viewpoint. 'But we've given our oath to eagle, prefect and emperor, on the altars of Mars and Apollo. And this mission isn't the tribune's. It's the emperor's. I might be inclined to argue with Curtius Lupus, but Nero is another matter. Come on.'

With a grumbling Densus, he climbed the sloping street, looking this way and that.

It was not hard to find Urbicus, but only because he was not alone, and had become something of a centre of attention. Over by the great carved pylon of a temple, Urbicus was gathered with his friends, a crowd of locals around them, watching with interest. The priest was chanting something, but it was hard to hear what it was, over a deafening metallic rattle.

As they closed, and made their way through the crowd, the source of the noise became clear. Urbicus had a cloak on, with folds pulled up over his head in priestly fashion. He was standing at a trio of Roman altars that had been placed outside the temple gate, incense burning on all three as he wafted his hands this way and that through the smoke, forming patterns as he chanted. The six men with him each had a sistrum, the bronze rattles that the Aegyptians used for rituals, which had become surprisingly common in Rome over the past few decades, and which they shook madly.

'Warding off bad luck, I think,' Densus noted.

As they closed on the small group of soldiers, as if sensing them even through the back of his head, Urbicus turned, hands lowering, chant trailing away.

'I make exceptions for you, Tesserarius,' Densus told Urbicus. 'Because of what you are. But it would at least be courteous to ask permission before you desert your post. As for the rest of you, you have no such distinction. We gave specific orders to stay aboard. You are all on half rations and on latrine duties for three days.' A series of groans arose at that, but Densus, hard-eyed, levelled an accusatory finger. 'One word from any of you, and I'll remind you just how much shit you can get in for disobeying an order. Now get back to the boat, the lot of you.'

They scurried away, Urbicus at their rear. He paused as he reached the centurions, lowering his cloak once more. 'My visit was a good choice to make. These are the temples of the Elephantine trinity, of Khnum, of Satet, of Anuket, each a god or goddess of the great river and its cataracts. Were we not sent here with orders to secure the favour of those very gods?'

That was hard to argue with, though Faventinus could see his friend fighting the urge to do so anyway. As Densus marched the priest back to the boat, Faventinus lingered for but a moment, glancing at the three stone blocks. Roman altars placed to add to the nature of this place, honouring the Nymphs of Aegyptus, Nilus himself, and Volturnus, the gods and spirits of rivers. All three had been set up by someone called Ulyxes in days long past. Faventinus nodded his satisfaction. Urbicus may be a pain in the arse, but perhaps they should *all* have been here, doing the gods honour.

Before hurrying away to follow the others, Faventinus also dropped a small offering on each altar.

12

FIRST CATARACT, SYENE

Densus looked about with a mix of satisfaction and nerves. He'd been here only once, but nothing had changed, and everything had worked out perfectly. They had managed to secure everything they needed, the boats were already largely unloaded, as the golden light began to sink lower, casting long shadows across the river, and the camp for the night was already set. The men had been relieved, with no need to raise ramparts, for so busy was this junction of trade routes that the area near the start of the cataract played host to a dozen walled compounds of different sizes that could be hired out by passing merchant caravans. The largest currently housed two centuries of Praetorians and their support staff, animals and vehicles. All that would be required for the night was a few men on guard duty.

His nerves came from the fact that this was the end of his own experience. He knew a little of what lay upriver, from others, but this place was the furthest south he had ever been. From here, the world would be truly unknown land.

The place was organised chaos. Faventinus had taken charge of the carts, which was a relief, and was currently overseeing the unloading of the last two boats and the transfer of their goods across to the compound, where they were being carefully distributed among the carts. He was being thorough. Not only was each cart packed with even weight and bulk, but also the various supplies had been divided so that the loss of another vehicle would not result in the critical absence of any one thing. Faventinus was good. Such was the value of having the scion of a merchant empire doing the organising.

Over near the river, where the first rocky rapids turned the water white and impassable, his optio, Flaccus, was drilling the horsemen. The tribune had decided against hiring native scouts for the next section of the journey. It was, in his opinion, an unnecessary expense. They were moving from Roman lands into the territory of the Kushites, who had been allies for a century, and their route was simple, dictated by following the river. As such, no native guide would be required. Still, Densus had made sure to buy six horses of reasonable quality. He'd then picked out from the two centuries six men who claimed to have some riding experience and assigned them as scouts, vanguard and rearguard. Two would advance a mile ahead of the column, two just in front, and two bringing up the rear at a distance of eight hundred paces.

Those men had complained bitterly when they had been handed pairs of braccae, the knee-length breeches worn by northerners and some of the units based up there. It was, they said, far too hot to wear barbarian trousers under their tunics. Still, they had done as ordered. By the end of the first day's ride, they would be grateful. Bare thighs in a saddle were not something to contemplate easily, especially in burning heat and among ever-present sand.

Currently those six men were busily riding in circles, and practising, under the watchful eye of Flaccus, whose parents owned a horse-breeding centre in Campania.

Less satisfactory was the sight of the tribune's own little caravan. Three wagons full of comforts and luxuries that, had he the authority, Densus would tip into the Nile and replace with water and grain. The impressive campaign tent for the senior officer was still packed away on one of them, for the tribune was housed for tonight in a waystation, like a small and poorly appointed mansio. It would be the last time he would find such comfort until at least Meroë, the Kushite capital.

Densus strolled past the two centuries' musicians and stifled a smile at the sight. The two men had picked up a native harp and a long, narrow pipe, and were alternating the two, attempting to play military commands through them and then collapsing into shuddering heaps of laughter at the result. At least someone was feeling positive about their work.

A lot of the men had acquired bits and pieces from local merchants. A small trade post served the gathering and embarkation point by the cataract, and the two centurions had allowed their men to visit in groups throughout the afternoon... with one exception. The tent at the highest point, on the edge of the trade post, remained closed and unvisited, by order of the tribune. When the woman had arrived in the mid-afternoon, with her guards and attendants, and the tent raised, her identity had been sought among the traders. She was described as a seer from some tribe out of the desert, and that had been enough for the tribune. The last thing he wanted, he'd said, was some mumbo-jumbo woman from the desert filling his men's heads with pessimism.

And that was why, as Densus turned and spotted Urbicus striding in that direction, he cut across to intercept.

'Not a chance,' he said, as he came close.

Urbicus stopped, turned. 'Sir?' His voice was slightly slurred. Densus' gaze dropped to the almost empty wine jar swinging idly from the man's fingers.

'I know where you're going. Tribune's orders, though. No one visits the seer woman.'

Urbicus' brow rose quizzically. 'Yet she comes out of the desert to the southwest. The very direction we're heading in. Aren't you the least bit curious? And if not about what she might have to tell us of our own journey, about her actual practical knowledge about the lands we're about to cross?'

For a moment, Densus wavered. It was a very good point. But the last person he would send to question her was Urbicus, even when he was sober, let alone drunk.

'I agree. And that's why *I'm* going to visit her. You get back to the men and tell them how much Mars and Minerva value them and will look after them on the journey.'

Urbicus' eyes narrowed, but even he, argumentative as he was, would not easily ignore an order from a tribune. In the end he nodded. 'You'll tell me? Later?'

'I might. Go on.'

He waited until Urbicus was all the way back to the compound gate, and then turned and marched off in the direction of the square black tent atop the slope. He was almost there when Faventinus caught up with him.

'You know that's forbidden, right?'

'I think we could argue a case for the officers. What if she has useful information?'

'You don't have to sell it to me,' his friend laughed. 'Just to the tribune. Come on, then.'

Densus felt uneasy, and that uneasiness only heightened when, as they approached the dark tent, the door was opened from within by an unseen hand. He held his breath as he stepped inside. The interior was almost black, especially when Faventinus followed him in and the tent door closed behind them with, again, no hand apparently involved.

It took a while for his eyes to adjust. The only light in the tent came from an aperture at the roof's apex, where the poles that formed the tent's shape, met and were tied. The hole was perhaps two feet across and showed the deep purple sky of evening.

'Sit,' said a voice in thick Greek.

'We come—'

'Sit,' it said again. Now, Densus could just make out the shape of a figure seated on a cushion at the far side of the tent. The floor was made up of mats and pillows and, not knowing what else to do, Densus dropped to a cross-legged position amid them. Beside him, Faventinus did the same.

'We wanted—'

'Wait.'

This time, he did not need to be told a second time. Instead, he simply sat in silence, occasionally looking back and forth between Faventinus beside him, and the figure opposite that was slowly coming into better focus. It did not help that the woman was ebony skinned and wearing a dark-coloured robe. She bore gold jewellery as was made clear by the occasional glint as she moved.

Gradually, the purple light through the roof aperture gave way to black, with the pinprick white of stars quickly becoming visible. Night fell fast this far south. Outside, in the distance, Densus could hear the horsemen putting away their mounts for the night and returning to their mates for dinner. He could hear the general life of camp, and the far noisier general life of Syene. He heard the two musicians blowing the watch. Still the two centurions sat in silence and near darkness. It was just as he was about to rise and make his excuses to leave, that the woman spoke.

'You go journey.'

'Yes.' Well that much was obvious. Why else was anyone here with wagons and horses?

'You seek know?'

'We do.'

'Stone,' she said suddenly in a commanding tone, and an ebony-skinned youth who'd been crouched at the edge of the tent, unseen in the darkness, suddenly unfolded and rose, hurrying across. He passed her what appeared to be a bag made out of some small animal's hide, with the nubs of four small limbs and a neck still showing. She took it and began to murmur in a barely audible tone and in some odd language. She then lifted the bag and turned it upside down, emptying its contents onto the mat between them.

Seven smooth, round stones scattered and rolled to a stop. There was an odd silence.

'Is good bad.'

Densus frowned. 'What?'

'See stone. See sky? Good.'

The centurion, brow still creased, looked carefully at the stones, and then looked up through the hole. He blinked. The stones were in almost exactly the same pattern as the stars that were visible above. There were slight differences, but it was close enough to see.

'Well, I'll be a fucking donkey's bollocks,' Faventinus breathed next to him. 'How did she do that?'

'I'm not sure I want to know. But she says it's good, so I'm going to walk away happy with that.'

'She also said "good bad",' Faventinus added.

'Shape,' the woman said. 'Shape bad.'

Seven stones. He couldn't make out any particular shape. Unless he thought the two closest were a leg. That would make the two closest to Faventinus another leg. At a push, the other three could be a body of two pieces with a single stone head. It *could* be an animal. Even so it could be any one of a thousand animals, and that was assuming there were two more legs unseen on the far side.

'Is Fisi.'

Faventinus looked over at him, questioning. 'No idea,' he said with a shrug.

'Fisi. Fisi,' she repeated, making shapes with her hands that looked like they might be suggesting a dog of some kind.

'And Fisi is bad?'

'Fisi bad.'

Good bad. Great. Good because it echoed the stars, but bad because it resembled a mutt.

'You win,' she said.

This took Densus a while. He mulled it over, then hazarded 'Are you saying that our journey will succeed?'

'Yes. You win.'

He sagged a little. That was the first time he'd heard anything positive.

'But...'

He sat up again. 'What?'

'You wish *not* win.'

'What?'

'Many time before win, you want not.'

'Shit,' Faventinus breathed. 'We're going to succeed, but we'll wish we didn't many times. Great.'

'Still better than that crap Urbicus has been spouting,' Densus reminded his friend.

'True.'

'Go now,' the woman said. 'End.'

As she did so, two more figures unfolded from the shadow at the edge of the tent and crossed to the middle. One placed an empty bowl in front of them, while the original attendant retrieved the stones. The other new arrival proffered the centurions something each. Densus took the knife, a small iron thing, shorter than his own forearm, with a plain hilt shaped like an I, and a truly curved blade that became almost a hook at the end. Unintelligible symbols seemed to have been scratched into the blade. It was a peculiar thing. He glanced across at Faventinus, who was turning a small scarab amulet over and over, frowning at it.

'Pay the woman,' Densus said, as he fished out several gold coins and dropped them, tinkling, into the empty bowl. Faventinus followed suit, and the two men bowed their heads to the woman, then rose and left the tent. Densus had toyed briefly with the idea of pressing her for geographical information, but given her stilted Greek, he feared the conversation would be long and difficult, and probably not all that informative.

'What did you make of that?' Faventinus whispered as they made their way back to the compound.

'I don't know. Maybe not hugely positive, but better than we've heard before. Let's get settled for the night. Tomorrow we leave the empire as we know it.'

'At least you got a knife,' his friend complained as they walked. 'All I got was a stone insect.'

PART 3

KUSH, AD 61

Nam Timosthenes, classium Philadelphi praefectus, sine mensura dierum LX a Syene Meroen iter prodidit, Eratosthenes DCXXV

Timosthenes, commander of the fleets of Philadelphus, without giving any other estimate as to the distance, says that Meroë is sixty days' journey from Syene, while Eratosthenes states that the distance is six hundred and twenty-five miles

Pliny, *Natural History*

13

PSELCHIS
IDES OF SEPTEMBER AD 61

Somehow, Faventinus had expected the edge of the empire to be more inspiring. Oh, it wasn't the end, per se. The empire had no permanent edge. Any border was merely a temporary line until a new campaign of conquest could bring into the empire the lands beyond it. But advances had generally reached specific lines, well-defined militarily. In Germania, the Rhenus River was just such a border. The same with the Danubius in Pannonia and Thrace. In Africa, where he came from, the southern border was this nebulous thing, because the habitable world simply petered out into hostile desert, which was its own natural boundary. Even up in Britannia, from what he understood, successive governors were advancing the line of control and fortifying it as they went.

The land beyond Rome here looked exactly the same. In fact, Faventinus had turned this way and that a few times, looking north and south along the river, and both directions looked so damn similar, it took him a moment to work out which was which. No sign. No river. No clear border. Just a fort that wasn't a Roman one anyway. The last garrison south in the Roman world occupied a place called Pselchis, which had all the hallmarks of being either an ancient Aegyptian fortress, or possibly a Kushite one. It was under Roman control, but it did not look at all Roman.

Densus had said that the line of forts and settlements along the river and the cataracts until they reached Napata, over five hundred miles away, had all been Kushite and Aegyptian, control of the region swinging this way and that until the ill-fated attempted invasion of Kush almost a century ago. Then an official border had been drawn, but since then Rome had abandoned most of the forts along the line as pointless installations, falling back to Pselchis as the frontier. Until a new conquest was attempted. And with the information they brought back, Nero could do just that, and hopefully with a little more success than the last time.

'I don't like the look of this,' the Tribune mused, shading his eyes with his hand and peering at the fort of Pselchis through squinting eyes.

'Sir?'

'Centurion Sempronius Densus, you know these people. Are they Kushites?'

Now, Faventinus focused on the place. As the silhouetted figures came into view, he decided he would have asked the same question. The men on the walls of Pselchis wore white linen robes, long and flowing, with long, wide sleeves, their heads covered with some sort of cloth, skin dark and leathery, no helmet or shield or armour, as they leaned on spears from which tassels and feathers fluttered. Their tunics were belted with brightly coloured material.

'Sir,' Densus replied, 'I've never actually seen a Kushite, barring the odd merchant that had come north. I've never been south of Syene.'

The tribune grunted in reply and then, after a long silence, heaved in a breath and tucked his thumbs in his belt. 'Lead on.'

Densus looked across, and Faventinus nodded, then gestured for an honour guard of eight men to join them. Adjusting the hang of their belts and scabbards and brushing off the worst of the dust, the three officers approached the gate as the column sat still around the wagons, taking the latest water break. As they neared the fort, the gate swung open. Two more of the men in long linen robes appeared to admit them, and then stepped back into the shadows.

A new figure, similarly dressed, appeared from inside the fort and met them as they reached the gate. He bowed his head, hands at his side.

'Tribune?' he greeted the senior officer in perfect Greek but with a heavy local accent.

Faventinus felt tentative hope. Perhaps these were not potentially hostile Kushites after all, if they recognised a tribune from his uniform.

'I wish to speak to your commander.'

The man bowed his head again, gestured for them to follow, and then strode off into the fort. There was nothing Roman about the interior. The clusters of buildings inside were of ancient mudbrick construction, low and heavy, with many windows, like much of the civil architecture of the region. The building to which they were escorted sat on the far side of the fortress, overlooking the river, with the fort wall as one side of the structure. It was a single large room, with an alcove off to the edge, and a man sat inside, in the shade, picking at a plate of fruit with distaste. The fear that they were already in foreign lands evaporated at the realisation that the bald, wizened man wore the creased and stained striped tunic of an auxiliary prefect. These men were Romans, whatever they looked like.

'Prefect,' Curtius Lupus said, unable to keep the disapproval from his tone, his lip twitching.

'Tribune. Have a seat.'

'I shall stand, thank you. We do not intend to impose on your command.'

'I had hoped you were the relief,' the man said with a sigh. 'If you are not here to take control, then why *are* you here?'

The tribune, still clearly fighting to keep calm at the way a slovenly border commander was addressing him, straightened. 'We are leading an expedition into Kush and beyond, to identify critical trade routes, secure the goodwill of the great river's spirits, and to assess the military and political situation in Kush and Aethiopia, with a view to potential annexation.'

The prefect sat up suddenly, interested. 'Annex, you say?'

'Yes.'

'For the love of Venus, that might mean I could get out of this armpit of a garrison. To somewhere with latrines and running water. You have my attention. What do you need?'

'Just whatever you know about the lands ahead. You are the last Roman intelligence, and I use the word loosely, in the south.'

The man either missed the insult, or didn't care, for he nodded. 'Trade is still reasonable. Kushite caravans, as well as other traders from beyond their lands, pass by every ten or twelve days one way or the other, attending markets at Syene. It has dropped off this past few months, though, due to increased nomad raids in the region.'

'Raids?'

'Yes. There are several tribes that occupy the local mountains, the most active being the Blemmyes. They have been known to attack weaker caravans, but they have become more adventurous and more active recently. My scouts tell me that a number of Kushite garrisons upriver have withdrawn, and I suspect their absence is what has allowed the raiders to become so bold.'

'Why have they withdrawn?'

The prefect shrugged. 'They didn't leave us notes. The last caravan I spoke to told me that Nebmaatre is still king at Meroë, and he has always held true to our treaty. There are hints of tension back in Kush, from what I hear, but as long as Nebmaatre is in power, there should be no reason to fear a change in policy.'

The two centurions looked at one another. Withdrawal of troops from the border suggested a strengthening of the military at the heart of the kingdom, and things like that were not done without reason. *Something* was happening, though they couldn't yet guess what.

'Could there be a rival in Kush? Civil war, perhaps?'

The prefect pursed his lips, then sucked his teeth. 'The Kushites are always hard to fathom, hard to predict. Nebmaatre has two senior generals, but I doubt either would be powerful enough to threaten the king. Besides, his sister, the Kandake, is more powerful than either of them. I think Nebmaatre still has supreme authority.'

He hooked a parchment from the pile on his desk and slid it towards them, indicating a series of hieroglyphics at the bottom. 'Nebmaatre's name, still appended to trade documents.'

The tribune nodded. 'Alright. Go on.'

'Heading upriver, there are Kushite forts at Bohón, just before the second cataract, and Semna before the third. Just after that is the Kushite town of Kerma with its own fortress. Those are the ones that were still occupied eight days ago when I last had scouts out. There are maybe half a dozen other smaller installations that have been abandoned recently. I cannot say whether those three are still garrisoned, but at least Kerma should be occupied, being a civil settlement also. The next major place you'll come to is Napata, which is their big religious sanctuary. From Napata, you're in solid Kushite land all the way to the capital. From there, it's four hundred miles by the river, or two hundred in a straight line across the desert, but don't even try that unless you have locals with you.'

'Thank you,' the tribune said in a business-like tone.

'No. Thank *you*,' the prefect replied. 'If you can gather intelligence that leads to conquest, it means I can leave this shithole and go home.'

'We shall take no more of your time. There is sufficient daylight to see us seven or eight miles south today.'

The tribune straightened, saluted, and marched from the room. Faventinus made to follow, but Densus gestured to the prefect. 'Do you have a medical section?'

'We've got a medic, if that's enough?'

Densus nodded and turned to Faventinus. 'Given how fast we're consuming Artemisia, it might be worth seeing if their medic has some. Otherwise it'll be Kerma or Napata, I guess.'

'Find him in the building to the left of the gate,' the prefect said, then leaned back with a strange smile. The two centurions left the room. The tribune was already crossing the fort, back towards the gate with their escort. The pair hurried to catch up, then explained their intent to the tribune and veered off towards that building.

As they neared, a wave of some pungent aroma wafted across them. Faventinus coughed and gagged. 'What in Hades is that?'

'Dunno. Come on.'

They strode through the cloud of sweet-spicy-gross smell and into the doorway, where it intensified into something you could almost chew on. After a moment to adjust to the dim light, Faventinus took in the building's interior with shocked fascination. The place looked more like one of the Aegyptian temples, inside, than a fort. The walls were painted with hieroglyphics and pictures of gods and men performing tasks. A soldier in one of those long white linen robes was at work, with the body of a man on the table before him.

Faventinus gagged, eyes wide, as he realised the victim's torso lay open and largely hollow. What had come out of the hole was now in a number of jars on a second, smaller, table, as evidenced by the gore and viscera around the vessels' lips. Even now, the man was stuffing what looked like flowers and straw into the body.

'What the fuck is he doing?'

'Mummification,' Densus replied quietly. 'Local custom for the dead.'

'Gods, but these people *needed* Rome to come and save them from themselves!'

'Bloody good job we didn't bring Urbicus or the other lads in here,' Densus said, pointing at the wall. Faventinus followed the gesture and saw the image: a weird picture as the god of the dead used a set of scales to weigh a human heart against a feather. It was the god himself, though, that mattered. Anubis, again, the black-dog-headed god.

Faventinus shivered.

14

SECOND CATARACT
THREE DAYS AFTER THE IDES OF SEPTEMBER AD 61

'No idea what the place is called,' Densus admitted. They were now outside all his experience, and he knew little more than any of the others.

The solid mudbrick fortress sat by the Nile, walls reaching out to the water, though to protect no dock, for here was the second cataract, and the river, for over a mile, turned into a mass of narrow channels, often of white, rushing water, between rocky outcroppings and small islands. No ship had ever passed from Syene up this stretch of the river. Any vessel beyond a one-man fishing boat would be impossible, and such a vessel would be dangerous to pilot in these waters.

The fortress was not dissimilar to that at Pselchis, both in scale and in construction, its singular northern gate flanked by great block towers and protected by a series of shallow ditches and mudbrick walls, designed to prevent a siege.

'It seems odd to find an empty fortress, do you not think?'

the tribune mused as they stood on a low rise and peered at the installation, while the column crawled slowly forward behind them.

'I guess it's possible that Kush has left a buffer zone, a no-man's land between the two peoples. Perhaps this fortress is left empty to give plenty of room between them and the Pselchis garrison, to prevent accidental clashes and incidents?' Faventinus chewed his lip in thought.

'Possibly,' Densus mused, 'though everything I ever heard about the Kushites suggests they're more direct and proactive than that. And territorial, too. For them to leave an empty region seems strange.'

'Then we need to check the place out thoroughly,' the tribune announced. 'I was in half a mind anyway,' he added, causing a dozen unspoken jokes to leap to the centurion's tongue, 'to check the stores and see if there is anything useful we can commandeer. See to it. Centurion Faventinus, you and your men will bring the column close to the fortress gate and stop there until we decide whether there is anything of value. Centurion Densus, you will take your men into the fortress and search it thoroughly. I shall spend my time perusing what detail we have of the lands ahead. Find me and report when you are finished.'

Densus saluted, turned, rolled his eyes at Faventinus, who grinned, and then waved to Flaccus, his optio, giving their standard signal to fall the men in. In mere moments, Flaccus had the century moving away from the column. Densus watched them with interest. They were six men down now, since that incident with the hippo, though Faventinus' century had fared worse. Seventy-four guardsmen, plus musicians, officers and signallers. They moved with professional competence, though the more dangers they encountered, and the further from recognisable civilisation they came, the more the confidence of the Praetorians abraded.

Part of it, he knew, was their very nature. Yes, the Praetorian Guard were the elite in the empire. They were the best equipped, and nominally the best trained soldiers of Rome. But there was an unspoken problem with that. For all their training, they were not really a combat unit. The Guard had never served in wars, even when they had accompanied an emperor into the warzone. Not once had Praetorians been called to battle. Their skills were there in case the battle ever came to Rome, to the emperor's door. And so, for all their training, their experience was pitiful. Densus had fought in the sand and the dust and the blood with the legion, and he knew deep in his heart that one veteran legionary was worth far more, somewhere like this, than a well-trained guardsman.

The other problem was that the Guard were drawn almost exclusively from Latium and the regions around Rome, from good families of long-standing Roman blood. This meant that all they really knew was Latium and Rome, and their experience of the hardships to be found in some of the lands on the fringe of the empire was utterly non-existent.

In short, on paper they were the best. In practice, they were hopelessly unsuited to this mission.

Which made it all the more impressive that they had weathered the nightmares so far with the professionalism and aplomb that they had. That they were still marching with chins high was, to Densus, nothing short of miraculous.

He smiled. He'd make proper soldiers out of them on this journey, and when they got home, the rest of the Guard would quake beside them. As they fell in before him, Densus looked around. Faventinus had disappeared to attend to the wagons and his own men, while the tribune had his small personal entourage setting up an awning on four pila, with a campaign stool beneath it so that he could sit in relative comfort and read the records of the lands ahead. The centurion turned back to the men.

'We are to search the fortress. I want you to note anything that seems out of place or noteworthy. I want you to identify any stores that might be of value to us, their nature and location, so that we can retrieve them once the place has been thoroughly searched. Actually, I anticipate little of value. The place appears deserted, but you never know. As we move in, I will call off your numbers by contubernium, and assign you a section of the fortress to search. Right. Minerva watch your hides, and off we go.'

With that, he turned and marched off towards the gap in the outer defences. The century followed on close behind, four abreast in perfect time, signaller and musician alongside them, as well as their tesserarius, Milo, with the optio as always bringing up the rear, where he could keep an eye on them.

Densus strode on through the gap in those outer defences, noting that they had not been cleared of drifting sand in many years, and seemed to be entirely abandoned. Likely the long peace between Rome and Kush had rendered them largely unimportant.

The sense that this place had been abandoned only increased as they came closer. It had been clear even from a distance that no figures stood guard on the walls, but inside the peripheral defences, and closer to the entrance towers, he could now see that the great gate stood wide open and unmanned. It was impossible to tell from the ground how recent any activity had been, for mere hours with even the slightest breeze set the sand scudding and covering any tracks or disturbances.

The body, therefore, took him entirely by surprise. His hand shot up, halting the men behind him as he came to a stop, head whipping this way and that, looking into every crevice, dip or nook, checking for unseen trouble. Nothing seemed to be moving, and if anything was hiding in a shadow, it was doing it extremely well. Motioning for the men to stay put, he stalked forward slower now, careful, hand going to the hilt of his sword as he neared the gateway, stepping between the great solid towers. A quick glance to either side was an uncomfortable reminder that both towers were pierced by row after row of narrow dark apertures, through any of which an arrow could issue at any moment.

Then he was at the shape on the ground and looking down. He'd never seen a Kushite warrior, but he'd met a few mercenary guards protecting merchants as they came to Aegyptus to trade, and the similarity with the thing on the ground was clear. Which made it almost certain that this fortress had, after all, been garrisoned by Kush.

The warrior had a white tunic and pleated skirt, surrounded by a thick hide girdle, all of which were now discoloured and matted with dust and blood. His feet were shod in simple sandals, and a strangely curved sword and animal hide shield lay close by, apparently unused. What had adorned his head would remain a mystery, though, for that head was gone, the neck no more than a meaty stump with a jagged wound, the gore dried and coated with more dust and sand. Gingerly, Densus lifted a foot, first prodding the body, then testing the dusty stain by the neck, with his toe.

The result put him further on edge. The body was soft but cold, yet remained uncorrupted. From his long experience of bodies in the army, that suggested the man had been dead for at least a day, but no more than three. Whatever had happened here was recent enough that it had been happening at the very moment that Densus and the others had been at Pselchis, learning about this place. He shivered.

Rather than call them on, he returned to his men. That no arrows came suggested that the aggressor was long gone, but he was not a man to take unnecessary risks. As he walked, another thing occurred to him. There had been no other wounds on the body, and the weapons had been unused. The man had been taken by surprise, and his head removed, before he could fight. That suggested either that he'd known his attacker, or that the killer had been swift and unseen, moving like an assassin in the night. Neither possibility was a pleasant thought.

'Someone attacked this place and did for the Kushites here,' he said as he reached the others. 'Looks like it happened a few days ago, so they're probably gone, but while we search, I want all units to stay together and be alert. Whether this is an internal Kushite trouble, or the work of nomad bandits, let's try not to get involved. Come on.'

They moved forward into the gate, slower now, a touch

of nervous tension hovering in the air. As they passed the body, every pair of eyes dipped to take it in, and the tension grew. Inside, the fortress proved to be comprised of two concentric walls, a square within a square, the gateway to the inner fortress directly ahead. He gestured to the first two contubernia, tent parties of eight men.

'Outer compound: two groups, left and right. Secure the open space, then move into the wall passages and rooms and check them systematically. Once you're done and you're happy the outer fortress is secure, return to this point and wait for the rest of us.'

He then led them into the second gate. He did not bother to check the two headless bodies in the shadowy opening here. Their resemblance to the one outside made it obvious they had been part of the same attack. As they moved into the inner fortress, it became clear that this place had once been a thriving garrison. Dozens of buildings crowded the great square, though a thoroughfare led between them, inviting the Romans somewhere. Densus could see another, postern, gate off to the left, near the riverbank, and sure enough another road led off that way a few moments later. The place was eerily quiet, and here and there a headless body announced that the occupants of the place's heart had fared no better than the guards at the walls and gates.

This had not been an assault. This had been a massacre. Densus looked about, and began to throw out gestures, assigning roles. 'Third and fourth contubernia, secure the inner fortress walls, check everywhere. Fifth contubernia, to the river gate and check beyond it. Sixth and seventh, start searching the building left of this road, eighth and ninth the right side.' That left just two men, who had lost the rest of their tent party to the hippo attack. 'The rest of you, with me.'

As his men scurried off to their assigned tasks, Densus marched on along that roadway, accompanied by two unassigned guardsmen, musician, standard bearer, tesserarius and optio.

'Where are we going?' Flaccus murmured, eyes darting from one body to another around the street.

'There has to be some sort of headquarters, and it's probably at the middle, where this road leads.'

Sure enough, a large building came into view moments later, sitting at the junction of several such roads, higher quality than those around it, with its own defensive wall. As they reached the structure, it became clear that this place had formed a last stand against the attacker. Everywhere else, the bodies had been swiftly and efficiently beheaded. Here, the bodies bore brutal wounds, making it clear that they had fought to the last. The damage to the door said that the enemy had had to force entry. Densus noted in passing that hieroglyphics carved beside the door included the name of the king, Nebmaatre, that he'd seen on that parchment back in Pselchis.

Inside, the place was filled with bodies, and the smell was somewhat intense, even without putrefaction having yet set in. As they moved from room to room, Densus' feeling that this entire place would hold little of value was borne out. Apart from the bodies, the place was empty. He found the corpse of what had to have been the commander, slumped in a chair, again headless, but what was left was better dressed than the others. Marks suggested he'd been decked out in jewellery, which was now gone.

'This place is a mausoleum,' Venator, the musician, murmured in distaste.

Densus just nodded. 'I think we can safely say there's no reason to linger here. The place is dead. We should move on.'

'What happened, though?' Flaccus put in. 'If it was some sort of civil war, why would both sides take the heads of the other. And if it was raiders, why are there none of their bodies?'

Again, just a nod. That question had occurred to him too. Either way, it boded ill for the next leg of their journey. 'Let's get back to the inner gate and call the search off.'

Leading the others, they left the charnel house once more, forging their way down the street fast, approaching the gate of the inner fortress. As they moved, Densus spotted what appeared to be a granary, from its similarity to Aegyptian ones further north. A quick glance inside proved it to be empty, further confirming his opinion of the place, and in moments they were back at the inner gate. At a gesture from Densus, Venator lifted the great curved buccina horn to his lips and blew the recall. As they stood waiting, every fifty heartbeats, another contubernium of men appeared from a side street or an aperture in the walls. When there was only one missing, and they had waited a little longer, a sinking feeling settled into Densus. He had the musician blow the recall again, and checked his men, identifying which unit had yet to return. Just as he worked out that it was the party sent to the river gate, they finally put in an appearance, hurrying up along a narrow road. His relief was short-lived, though, as he realised that seven of them seemed to be carrying the eighth.

His suspicion was confirmed a moment later as the ashen-faced men came to a halt, carrying the headless body of their comrade.

'What the fuck happened? I told everyone to stay together.'

'We were, sir,' their leader said in a quavering tone. 'Ancus was bringing up the rear. He was maybe two paces behind the next man. We stopped moving, turned, and there was his body about twenty paces back, already dead. Never saw or heard a thing. One moment he was with us, next he was dead. I'm starting to see how this massive fuck-up happened, sir.'

Densus nodded sombrely. He didn't like this one bit.

'Keep together, and watch the rear and each other until we're back with the column.'

And when they got back and he had to report to the tribune, he would make sure to change the column's organisation now. He wanted plenty of scouts and outriders. This was no civil war, and the attackers had not been other Kushites.

Something else was at work.

15

SECOND CATARACT

They had gone little more than a mile beyond that fort, when the scouts returned.

Faventinus looked back and forth.

The column had changed. The tribune had been rather scathing, suggesting that no native creatures would stand a chance against Rome's elite, yet Densus had been so persuasive that the man had eventually submitted, and the column had reorganised. Now, each century had taken one side, with Densus' men on the left and Faventinus' century on the right. The scouts were to ride ahead, still, but to circle back into sight every quarter hour so that their ongoing existence could be noted. Furthermore, some of the more athletic men had been allowed to stay out of armour and had been sent ahead, just within sight, as a light and fast vanguard. The rest, all in front, alongside and behind the carts, had been ordered to don their armour once more and wear it at all times, as well as helmets and shields. It was cripplingly hot in these conditions, but if even half of what Densus had said was true, no one wanted to become the next victim of the head-takers. Finally, a small unit was following on, again just within sight of the column.

It was the best they could do. There had even been the idle suggestion of arming the slaves, but no one wanted to risk sparking a new Spartacus war, and so that had been brushed aside... for now.

Then this.

The scouts looked worried as they approached the column, which made Faventinus tense as he hurried out ahead with Densus and the tribune to meet them.

'Report,' Curtius Lupus barked, face straight and hard. Faventinus silently mused on the fact that perhaps some people weren't bright enough to experience fear, and he wondered if the tribune might be one such man.

'I think we've found your missing head, sir,' the rider said, shakily.

The tribune, eyes narrowing, turned and gestured. 'Halt the column. The officers and I will go ahead.'

Curtius Lupus, of course, had his own horse, which he sometimes used, other times travelling in a covered cart with his steed tethered behind. The two centurions, though, marched with their men, and so now had to commandeer two of the scouts' horses to ride ahead with the tribune.

As he cantered away, Faventinus looked back to the now-halted column, the squat, brown shape of the fortress still visible back along the river, looming like a mausoleum, an analogy he'd heard from the musician more than once since they'd returned.

They did not have to go far. Just a little way ahead of the column, they rounded a low dune from which protruded rocky lumps, and the Nile came into view once more in the distance, but it was what stood beyond the dune that captured their attention. Twenty-one poles rose from the sand in a neat line, like some triumphal parade, each decorated with a head. Twenty of them were clearly those of victims from the fort, livor mortis having pulled what blood remained in the heads down into the chin and neck, which had become discoloured, while the rest of the head remained waxy pale.

Ancus, though, was clear, for his head, though pale, was still fresh and clean, looking as though it had only just stepped away from the body for a moment. It was odd to see the serene look on his face. Faventinus would have expected open-mouthed horror and agony. He reasoned that the attack had been so fast, the guardsman hadn't had time to react, even facially.

'Shit.'

'Who is responsible for all of this?' the tribune demanded.

Faventinus shrugged. This was far outside his area of knowledge.

'Nomadic raiders is my guess,' Densus replied. 'Possibly the Blemmyes. I've heard stories of them taking heads. They've not really been much trouble for a long time. Rome's peace with Kush has allowed us all to keep control of the region. Something's changed in Kush, though, and this, I think, is the result. The Blemmyes have become confident enough to overwhelm an entire garrison in their fort and sack the place, taking everything of value.'

'And how long are we at risk from these Blemmyes?'

Now, Densus also shrugged. 'Possibly all the way to Napata in Kush. Depends how much control King

Nebmaatre is currently managing to exert over his northern reaches.'

'Then we must forge on south. Let us return to the column and get moving. The further south we can get before sunset the better.'

Faventinus waved a hand. 'Best we get rid of these first, sir.'

'Why?'

'Sir, the men are already nervous enough, without parading them past a line of heads, including one of their own. Let's not feed their anxiety, eh?'

Curtius Lupus frowned. 'Then get rid of the soldier's head. Your men should not care about a few dead barbarians.'

Faventinus sighed. No matter whose the heads were, their presence would send shivers through the men who passed them. 'I think we need to bury them all, sir.'

The tribune harrumphed. 'I will not waste precious travelling time. If you wish to bury them, be my guest, but I return to the column to get it moving. You have until then.'

With that, he gestured to the scout, and the two of them rode off back towards the carts. Faventinus and Densus shared a look. They would have too little time to bury twenty-one heads before the column reached them, and so they worked fast, ripping the grisly totems from their poles, running around the rocky outcropping and dumping them in the lee, out of sight. Once the heads were all gone, they returned and plucked the sticks from the ground, carrying them away and adding them to the funereal pile. They had just kicked and pushed the sand around to hide the bloodstains beneath the latest head and the holes from the poles, when the lead elements of the column appeared. They mounted and rejoined the force a moment later as though nothing had happened, the entire column marching on, oblivious, past the site.

For the rest of the afternoon, Faventinus found himself watching the lands to east and west and, as they came to a halt with the setting sun, his nerves were no better than they'd been while hiding the heads.

He found Densus standing looking south, in their direction of travel, and stopped beside him, clasping his hands behind his back. The men were busy raising a temporary rampart of low sandy banks and installing a fence of sharpened sudis stakes from the carts. They'd not bothered with full defences thus far, but recent events had changed things.

'They'll come for us, won't they?' he said.

Densus stood still and silent for a while, then nodded slowly. 'I reckon so. Even armed as we are, we're an easier prospect than that fortress back there. If they weren't worried about *that* place, they won't be concerned about *us*. And with all these carts we look like the mother of all merchant caravans. We're a clear target.'

'I've been thinking,' Faventinus said.

'Dangerous stuff for an officer.'

'Ha ha. Seriously. I don't think there's danger to the west. These attacks are coming from the east. The Blemmyes are coming out from there.'

Densus turned. 'How'd you figure that?'

'Firstly, from what I hear, all there is to the west is desert trade routes, but to the east is all the lands between the Nile and the coast, with Roman quarries back north, and native gold-mining settlements further south. It's more conducive to life.'

'I guess.'

'But more importantly, it was down by the river gate that your man died. I think they're already aware of us. Watching us. Sizing us up. I think they'd left a man on watch at the fort when they went back across the river, and he took a head because the opportunity presented itself. I don't think he was supposed to. It's too much warning for us. They came from the east, across the river. Think about it. The fort was at a cataract, where they can move from rock to rock and island to island. They could cross there, and they'd be straight at the small river gate, which is a lot less defensive than the main one. We were still passing that long cataract when we found the heads. I reckon they moved along the river and are using the cataracts to cross back and forth at will.'

'We're at another cataract now,' Densus pointed out, turning east, towards the river.

'I know. I reckon we're in as much danger right now as we have been since that fucking hippo.'

'What can we do other than fortify?'

Faventinus took a breath. 'Be more prepared and aware than the garrison was. They didn't know the Blemmyes were coming. We do. It was the surprise that saw them brought down before they could properly fight back. I reckon they'll come tonight, once they think we're asleep.'

'So have the men pretend to sleep, and in their armour?'

'Exactly. And have two of our best, most alert men posted in hiding places down by the bank, along the cataract. If the enemy pass them, they can call a warning. You and I can give them our whistles. We'll all hear them. We'll have warning, and the men will be ready.'

'Agreed. What do we run by the tribune?'

'Nothing. He's oblivious now. If they don't come, we lose nothing. If they do, we're better off with him cowering in his tent than trying to take control of the situation.'

Densus grinned. 'I like your thinking. Let's pass the word through the junior officers, keep things as quiet as possible, so the Blemmyes don't spot anything out of order.'

As they passed back through the hastily raised defences, a figure bore down on them from one side. In the failing light, it took Faventinus a moment to recognise him as the capsarius of his friend's century. His own combat medic was close behind, the two men who formed the entire medical team for the expedition wearing looks of purpose.

'What is it?' he asked as the men fell in beside them.

'I'm afraid it looks like we've contracted a case of swamp fever.'

'Two,' corrected the other capsarius.

'Swamp fever?' Faventinus frowned. 'But we're in a desert with a free-flowing river. There's no swamp for hundreds of miles.'

Densus turned to him. 'There was swamp fever in Thebes, remember? Maybe we picked it up there? I should have asked how they got it. Probably came upriver from Lake Ephiom. Whatever the case, we have it.' He turned to the medics. 'Is it catching?'

The man shrugged. 'It's not something I've ever come across in Rome. I read about the symptoms and what little there was about it before we came, and then in Alexandria. I don't *think* it can be passed on, but I can't say for certain, and after all, our men got it somewhere. What I do know is that both the men who have it, one from each century, are already starting to become properly feverish.'

'What's the prognosis?'

The other medic snorted. 'Roll dice. Toss a coin. Neither of us have ever treated this. I'm hoping it's going to be alright. I've commandeered a bunch of the Artemisia and we'll do what we can with that. Under normal circumstances I'd recommend they be given a sick wagon and be sent back to the nearest allied post. But that's three days back through dangerous land, and I don't think the tribune will sign off on losing a cart and an escort for the sick, sir.'

'I think you're right,' Faventinus noted. 'We'll just have to take them with us and hope. Keep them separated from the rest, just in case. The second water cart has a bit of space. Put them on there for the time being and we'll reassess the situation if they get any better or worse.' He sighed. 'Looks like chewing on Artemisia does nothing after all.'

'Or it's doing so that's limited the illness to just two men,' noted Densus.

'True. Let's keep that up, then. Come on, let's pass around word of the plan for the night.'

16

MINOR CATARACT

FIVE DAYS AFTER THE IDES OF SEPTEMBER AD 61

A scream jerked Densus' eyes wide open in an instant. Damn it. What now?

The Praetorians had spent that first night after the fort sleeping in short shifts, with most of the column awake and prepared for an attack. Faventinus had been so convinced, and convincing, that there had been little doubt among them that the attack would come. So, when the sun came up the next morning, and nothing had happened, it was almost more of a shock than a surprise attack would have been. They had moved on south, upriver, the next day, and had fortified their camp for the night, just as they had earlier. They had been a little more relaxed though. They were away from the cataracts for a time, and so the danger had diminished. They still had watchers out, of course, and two men with whistles down by the shore. But the lack of easy access, combined with the slight improvement in confidence brought about by an uneventful night, had loosened their tension. They still slept in shifts, but more of them at a time, and the sleeps were longer ones.

Now, the second night on, they maintained the careful vigil, but inevitably the level of fear and alertness had waned. They were by another cataract now, though this was one of the many minor ones that presented but a short obstacle, and had seemed less of a threat. Indeed, even as Densus shot to his feet, he realised it had been a scream and not a whistle blast, which suggested no one had come across the cataract.

And yet... a scream.

Bursting, fully clothed and fully armed, from his tent, he looked this way and that. Clearly the rest of the camp had only had the same amount of warning, as other men were appearing, blearily, through their tent doors, including Faventinus across the way. Of the tribune, nothing could yet be seen. Densus closed his eyes and tried to place the scream. It had, he believed, come from upriver, at the southern side of the camp, which was where the tents of his own century were largely based. As Faventinus hurried out to join him, Densus turned and made for a gap between the tents, from which men were emerging.

He was nearing the defences when a familiar sound whispered through the air, and he had but a moment to throw himself to one side before an arrow thrummed through the space he had just occupied and disappeared through the leather side of a tent.

From the cursing, it sounded as though Faventinus had done the same in the other direction.

They rose once more, and Densus darted from tent to tent, trying to stay covered from the rampart direction. He reached the last one, and ducked out and back just in time to avoid being given an impressive piercing. Moving to peer carefully around the edge, he noted that the southern rampart was empty, undefended.

Shit.

Either they had come across the cataract and silenced the pickets there, or Faventinus had been wrong and they'd come from elsewhere. Whatever the case, they had waited two more days until security had relaxed a little, and *then* struck, the devious bastards.

'What is the meaning of this?' demanded an officious voice. Densus turned again, to see the tribune marching towards them. Was the man mad? An arrow missed the senior officer by only about two feet and thudded into a stack of shields. Ignoring it with either impressive bravery or breath-taking stupidity, or possibly both, the tribune marched out into the open. Densus found himself running to join his commander. He couldn't let the men see him cower while the tribune marched into danger. His authority would evaporate in an instant.

As they neared the rampart, with arrows coming through the night like dark stars shooting through the sky, he spotted one of the rampart's defenders lying out in the open some ten feet from the broken fence, head gone.

Beyond him, two black shapes were dragging another Praetorian away into the darkness, their prisoner screaming in panic and trying to fight to free himself as he was taken.

'Retrieve that man,' bellowed the tribune, pointing out into the darkness at the disappearing soldier.

'On me,' Densus shouted, sword in hand, and ran for a

part of the stake fence that had been neatly dismantled. By the time he leapt the low sandbank and was out into the open, a dozen men were at his heel, including Faventinus.

They raced into the darkness, and the folly of the pursuit was brought home as an arrow thudded into the soldier by Densus' left shoulder, who disappeared with a squawk, to be replaced by another white-eyed, fearful man.

Densus only saw the body when it was too late. Running blindly into the darkness, he'd been lucky not to fall earlier, but when he did, it was because he tripped over the body of the man who'd been dragged away. From the blood, it was clear that they'd tried to hastily take his head, but decided there wasn't time, and settled for cutting his throat, deep. Densus hit the sand, hard, and rolled. By the time he was up, the others were past him.

He could hear the sounds of a scuffle, and as he rose to his feet, he realised the arrows had stopped coming. Looking back, he could see that the Praetorian force was now largely gathered at the rampart, prepared for a fight, the tribune commanding. He turned. He couldn't see further into the darkness, and moved forward slowly, gingerly.

He almost fell over the next body, this one another guardsman, head still where it should be, but with an arrow jutting from his chest. He blew the recall on his whistle. It had been utterly foolish to give chase in the dark anyway, and it had only been an instinctive reaction to the tribune's order that had made him do it. Now, his men were out there in the dark, wandering around blind, with the enemy somewhere nearby.

His men started to drift back to him, looking nervous. Six men in all answered the whistle, as well as Faventinus, thank the gods. With the two already downed by arrows, that meant that four were lost somewhere out there in the darkness. If they'd not come to the whistle now, it meant they weren't coming. He'd wasted six men trying to save one, and had even failed in that.

He pointed for the others to return to the camp, and Faventinus fell in beside him, nursing a deep scratch on his arm, presumably from an arrow. 'Nothing,' the man said. 'We found nothing. No one. They just disappeared. And I reckon they took some of us with them.'

They marched back towards the tribune, who stood, stony-faced, at the gap in the rampart.

'What was this all about?' Densus sighed.

Faventinus shrugged. 'Maybe they came across the next cataract ahead and lay in wait?'

That made sense, of course, but it wasn't what he meant.

'No, I mean, why such a short and flighty attack? If they managed to do what they did at the fort, they could probably have overrun us here. So why didn't they?'

'Because we were more prepared.'

'Were we?' Densus mused. 'I doubt it. This was like a probing attack. As though they were testing our strength, our readiness...'

The thought clearly struck him and Faventinus at the same time, for they turned to look at one another, the words coming out in unison.

'Or a *decoy*.'

With a string of blistering curses, the two centurions ran now, outpacing their men. The tribune shouted something officious and demanding at them, but they both ignored him and ran past. The camp was almost empty. The men had all gathered at the south rampart to see what was happening and prepare to help if possible.

It came as no surprise when they closed on the north rampart to find no men on guard there, the whole length empty, and a large section of the defensive stakes removed. It came as no surprise, either, to find that where the raiders had hit at the north, silent and unseen as they made a lot of noise on the far side, was also where the carts were gathered.

By the time the tribune arrived at the scene with his escort, the two centurions had confirmed the worst.

'Report!'

'The attack on the south was a feint to draw all our attention. While we were there, they hit the north. They took out all our guards, dismantled the fence, and raided the wagons. They've emptied three whole vehicles, totally unseen. We've lost days and days' worth of food and water, spare weapons and more.'

'How?'

Densus pointed at the churned sand. 'Those tracks are horses and camels, and quite a few of them. I reckon they threw whatever was close into bags, slung them across their animals and rode away before we noticed what had happened.'

The tribune had gone a funny colour. 'Have your men mount up and chase them down. I want those supplies.'

Densus shook his head. 'I advise against that, sir. Look what happened when we gave chase to the south. We lost another six men. If we follow them north, I suspect no pursuer will return from the hunt. These people are natives. They know this land and how to survive in it. We don't. We'll never find them, and we'll all die trying.'

The tribune was almost shaking with anger, but even as he did, the sense in Densus' words was sinking in, and he began to nod slowly. Finally, he straightened. 'Will we still have sufficient supplies to reach Napata?'

Densus pursed his lips. 'Probably, sir. It all depends on Kerma now. That's two hundred miles away, yet, but we should have enough supplies to get there. The question is whether Kerma is still a thriving town where we can resupply, or another empty graveyard. If the latter, we might be in trouble.'

'Then we should preserve food and drink as best we can, and pray hard,' the tribune said quietly. 'Have the defences manned once more and repaired. Have an inventory run on the wagons so that we can adjust our supply usage appropriately, and redistribute the vehicles.'

Densus saluted. As the tribune stalked away, looking unhappy, Densus' gaze rose past the figure and spotted an even less welcome sight. Urbicus and his small group of disciples stood in a cluster near the animal corral. That did not bode well, and so Densus gestured to his fellow centurion and the two of them strode over to the priest and his cronies. They all had their sistrum rattles out, but fortunately the men were bright enough not to shake them and draw too much attention.

The whole group went silent as the two officers approached, and there was an unseen kerfuffle at the centre. As Densus reached them and gestured for them to part, the group opened up. Urbicus had a stick in his hand, and clearly something had been hastily drawn on the ground, but then rubbed out quickly with a number of boots.

'Alright, what's going on?'

Urbicus took a step forward. 'This is only the first step on our descent to Tartarus, centurion,' he said.

'Bollocks.'

'You know I'm right. Before I retired tonight, I saw an owl in the late sky. It circled three times and then flew off north, back towards Rome. The omens are not good.'

Densus snorted. 'The owl is a bird sacred to Minerva, to wisdom and war, and to Rome. This has to be a *good* omen, man.'

'Do you not know your Ovid, centurion? On Ascalaphus? "He became the vilest bird, a messenger of grief; the lazy owl, sad omen to mankind". He became the familiar bird of Hades in the underworld. A *good* omen you say?'

Densus' eyes narrowed. 'I'd not had you pegged for a poetry fan, Urbicus. And I think you need to lay off the fucking wine. It's sending you round the bend. Now disperse back to your tents and get some sleep. I reckon we'll need to be well rested in the coming days.'

Grumbling, the priest and his friends moved away. Densus spent a long moment looking at the sand where they'd stood, but he couldn't make out what it was they'd drawn and rubbed out. With any luck it was just prayers, magical symbols and the like. One thing was certain: the time was coming when there would be a confrontation with Urbicus. The man was getting more influential and audacious as time went on.

'Of course, he's right,' Faventinus muttered once they were alone.

'What?'

'Oh, I don't mean about the owl. But about being on the

slippery slope to Tartarus. I can see that with my own eyes, without a priest's help.'

Densus rolled his eyes. 'Not you too?'

'Oh, I'm not going to cause issues or demand we turn back or anything. We have a duty to the emperor, the eagle and the tribune. We have a job to do. But I'm starting to think we will be very, very lucky ever to see Rome again. What was it the seer said? We could succeed, but to do so we'd wish we hadn't many times.'

Densus sighed. 'Just help me assign burial details and guard duties and then run this inventory. And then you can help me *"redistribute"* the wine ration before we crash.'

17

SOMEWHERE BY THE NILE
SIX DAYS AFTER THE IDES OF SEPTEMBER AD 61

The shouts halted the column, and Faventinus heaved yet another sigh. He gestured for the musicians to send the signal out to the scouts and vanguard to stop, as he turned and jogged back along the line, no mean feat in armour in such temperatures. He was going to have lost a great deal of weight by the time they returned. *If* they returned.

'What is it?' he shouted to the small group of guardsmen and slaves gathered around the rearmost cart. Beyond the scene, the rear-guard had fanned out, hands on hilts, eyes on the horizon in every direction. Since the night raid, the last drops of good nature seemed to have sapped from the men, to be replaced by gloomy wariness.

One of the soldiers pointed. As the centurion neared the wagon, he could see one of the slaves with his hand pressed against one of the water barrels. Even though he pressed hard, water was still oozing out around his palm and between his fingers. The cart around the barrel was soaked, and there was a small puddle of gloopy sand beneath the vehicle.

'How?'

The soldier pointed now at the slave, whose eyes widened in panic. 'He found it.'

Faventinus looked at the slave. 'Speak.'

'It just started, master. Just sprung a leak as the cart moved.'

The centurion sighed. 'Just an unfortunate accident, then. It was probably weakened when we moved the barrels yesterday. One or two were dropped quite hard, I noticed. Then all it would take is a nasty bounce when a wheel hit a rock. Unfortunate, but quite explainable.'

'That it is,' said another voice, coming up from behind, and Faventinus closed his eyes and rubbed his temple.

'Stop seeing signs in everything.'

Urbicus gave him a dark look. 'That is my job, Centurion.'

'Can you try not to do your job so well. This is just an accident.'

'This is a warning. Everything we see now is a warning. Look around you. Look at that rock,' he added, pointing.

Faventinus did so. A jagged dark rock emerging from the sand and grit, just like every other rock in this bloody awful land. 'What?'

'It is clearly an owl.'

'It's clearly a *rock*. That's all. It doesn't even look like an owl.'

'You are becoming blinded to the realities of our fate by your rigid oath of service.'

'You took that same oath, Urbicus. Need I remind you of the penalty for a guardsman breaking said oath?'

'Can it be worse than the penalty we face anyway?'

'Listen—'

'No, Centurion. *You* listen. You know logistics—'

Faventinus began to argue, but to his amazement and frustration, Urbicus continued to talk over the top of him, louder.

'You know logistics and strategy. You can command. But you do not know the will of the gods as I do. I have seen things, Claudius Faventinus, things that made me shudder. I have been told we must fail, by the gods of this land and of this river.' Faventinus was making threats now, louder, but Urbicus simply raised his voice again and shouted over the top. 'AND I TELL YOU NOW, THE RIVER WILL KILL US ALL BEFORE MEROË UNLESS WE FEED HER.'

Faventinus stopped speaking, eyes bulging, partly at what he was hearing, partly at the audacity of the man shouting over his centurion, and partly at the sight of Densus and the tribune approaching with angry expressions.

'Feed the river?' the tribune demanded. 'What are you suggesting, soldier?'

'The Nile needs a sacrifice, sir,' Urbicus said, voice returning to a lower level as he turned to the tribune.

'It may have escaped your notice, tesserarius, that we have no animals with us. Other than the beasts of burden, of course, which we cannot spare. Indeed, I would be loath to spare even a sheaf of wheat given our short supplies.'

'A sacrifice need not be a base animal,' Urbicus said, his tone darkening again.

'You cannot be suggesting *human* sacrifice?' the tribune said, brow creasing in surprise.

'Perhaps by offering one of us to the river, we can buy

the lives of all the others,' Urbicus said in oddly reasonable tones. 'Is it too much to give one to save many?'

'Human sacrifice is a thing of barbarism,' the tribune barked. 'It is as un-Roman as anything in this world. Perhaps the Getae or the Carthaginians might consider such a thing, but we are civilised.'

Urbicus' lip twitched. 'Tell that to the mothers who drown deformed babies to appease the gods, sir. Tell that to the Greeks and Gauls buried alive in the Forum Boarium when the city was in danger. Tell that to Marcus Curtius, throwing himself into the chasm to save Rome.'

The tribune's eyes bulged, not so much at the content of the statement, but at being spoken to thus by a junior officer. As he wound himself up to rant, finger coming out pointing, Faventinus grabbed Urbicus and turned him round. 'Spurious, Urbicus. Such babies are not classed as human, *or* Roman, the burials in the forum were before the law banning sacrifice, and Curtius was the brave choice of one man to save his city. This is the final word, Urbicus: there will be no sacrifice. There will be no more *talk* of sacrifice. And the next time I hear you stirring up the men's nerves with your omens, I personally will jam my foot so far up your arse you will taste the hobnails.'

Urbicus looked for a moment as though he were about to speak. Faventinus fixed him with a look. 'And you will remember to whom you are talking, and respect the chain of command. It's been years since I had to flog a soldier for insubordination, but I'll do it if I have to, and that will bring with it a reduction in rank and removal from any offices. Bear that in mind while you slink off and stay out of my sight for the rest of the day.'

With that dismissal, Urbicus threw one last unpleasant look at Faventinus and wandered off along the column. The tribune, still practically vibrating with fury, paused only long enough to twitch at Faventinus, glare at the departing tesserarius' back, and clench and unclench his fists a few times, and then marched off back to his horse.

Faventinus turned to the current disaster. 'That barrel's had it. Keep your hand on it and stem the flow as long as you can. Turn the barrel and use it. Fill every available flask, jar, skin and bottle, and then mouths with what's left. Then dump the barrel and we'll move on.'

When he turned back, Densus was beside him. 'Nice job in keeping that under control. The tribune was about to order an execution, I think.'

'And he might have been right to,' Faventinus sighed. 'Urbicus is becoming a problem.' He gestured along the column to where the tesserarius had fallen back into line, and a dozen of his cronies were glaring back towards the centurions. 'His discontent is spreading to his friends, and the number of men listening to him grows by the day. It takes a lot to make a unit mutiny, I know, but we're slowly getting closer.'

'If it gets too bad, we're either going to have to remove him or mollify him.'

'Kicking him out of his office will only turn him into a martyr,' Faventinus said. 'Then the whole bloody century will be with him. That's not an option. And while he's a pain in the arse, he's not entirely wrong, and he *does* know the gods better than us. That's why he is what he is.'

'Then we'll mollify him. We've got more than enough vehicles for the supplies now. We'll abandon one cart and use the ox for a sacrifice. I'll have to persuade the tribune, but it can be done. I reckon we wait and see, though. Your threat might have done the job anyway.'

Faventinus looked forward, to the gathering of glowering looks aimed at him. Somehow, he doubted that.

18

MINOR CATARACT

SIX DAYS BEFORE THE KALENDS OF OCTOBER AD 61

'So we have three cases now?'

Faventinus nodded. 'A new one reported this afternoon. He was put with the other two.'

Densus sighed. 'I wish we knew more about it. We've not been anywhere swampy. Unless maybe you can catch it with all the eddies and slow waters of the cataracts. Or, maybe he caught it from the other two before we isolated them. Or even caught it at Thebes and it's taken longer to show on him.'

Faventinus sagged a little. 'The capsarii said much the same. All they can do is treat it and hope. On a brighter note, they have said flatly that they've seen no more deterioration of the other two, and are tentatively suggesting there may even be an improvement there.'

'Good. It's nice to hear something positive for a change.'

Although Densus had already decided on one positive. It had been five days since the night attack, and there had been no further hint of trouble from that quarter. No tracks, no heads, no fortresses full of corpses, and no blood-curdling screams in the middle of the night. That in itself – the absence of a negative – had to be considered a positive. And now they were maybe twelve or thirteen days from Napata and the supposed safety of Kush itself, where the nomads did not raid. As long as Kush was still a friend...

He swatted at a bug that was lazily circling his head with a high-pitched whining sound. These bugs were getting more prevalent at the moment, but that, he reasoned, was because of the cataract. Here there was more vegetation and pools of eddying water, so bugs were more likely than out in the dry and hot stretches.

'The rate we're going through Artemisia leaves, we're going to have to try and find some in Kerma in a few days, or at least in Napata.'

Densus was about to reply with a noncommittal something when he paused. 'Did you hear that?'

As Faventinus leaned forward and cupped a hand to his ear, Densus rose and crossed to the door of his tent. A distant commotion was clearly audible. Urgent shouts, though no screams and no whistles or signals.

'Come on,' he said, fastening his sword belt around his middle as he ran out into the darkness, looking this way and that.

The camp was quiet, barring the gentle lowing of the cattle over in their pen, the whispering murmur of the slaves, talking quietly so that they woke no one, and the distant sound of the river with its endless rocks.

Then a fresh cluster of shouts came. Again, urgent. Worried. Frightened. Yet no call to arms. It was coming from the river edge of the camp. For a moment, he wondered whether someone had fallen foul of the crocodiles, but the army had managed to shoo them all away with pila when they set up camp, and the beasts had gathered on the opposite shore, out of reach. With men ready to throw pointed iron at them, it was doubtful they'd sneaked back in the hope of a swift meal.

Some thirty paces from the water's edge, they reached the camp's fence of sharpened stakes. The men were no longer on guard there, and the gateway was open, though the men were visible, for they had moved to the riverbank. Densus tried to control his anger at men abandoning their posts. In the current circumstances, they were close by, and something apparently important had drawn them. He was learning to give the men more leeway here than he would in Rome.

As the two centurions pounded across the sand down to the water, the cause of the shouting became apparent, and Densus blinked in surprise.

Urbicus was in the water, maybe a third of the way across the river. Due to the cataract, parts of this stretch were only chest deep, but the priest had found one of the deeper parts, as evidenced by the fact that he was treading water and circling his arms to stay afloat.

The soldiers by the bank were, to a man, exhorting him to come back. Some, likely those disciples of his, were almost begging, tears in their eyes, horror on their faces. Others looked more irritated or at least concerned.

'What is going on?' Densus demanded.

A soldier turned, noticing the officers for the first time. 'Sir, it's Urbicus. He's in the water.'

Very helpful.

Closer now, Densus could see that the priest was naked, or at least perhaps wearing a loincloth somewhere under the surface, but he was at least naked to the waist.

'Urbicus, what the fuck are you doing?' he shouted. 'Swim back here now.'

The priest turned slowly, languidly, in the water, to face the centurion. 'How can you ask me to come back, when it was you who has caused this?' the man said.

'What?'

'The whole world and all its gods have told us repeatedly that this quest is doomed. That to proceed will bring only pain and loss. Yet still we press on. How many men have we lost already, centurion? Ten? Twelve? How many more will die to monsters in the water or assassins crossing it in the dark. With every mile we travel, the Nile finds more horrors to set against us.'

Densus held up his hands. 'The Kushites worship the Nile, just like the Aegyptians, Urbicus. When we get to Kerma, to Napata, to Meroë, we will give great offerings. For now, we have a chance to get south to somewhere more civilised. You're being a fool.'

'On the contrary, centurion, I may be the only one here seeing things clearly. The Nile wants blood. The Nile wants sacrifice. I told you this days ago, yet on we march into the maw of Cerberus. Well, if you must march into a nightmare, the sacrifice must be made. Thus, I give myself, like Marcus Curtius in his crevasse. I give myself to the great river, and die in the hope that my sacrifice will allow you all to live long enough to come to your senses and turn around.'

Densus ground his teeth, then wagged a finger. 'I was

planning on speaking to the tribune. We can give an ox as sacrifice. You don't have to do this.'

'But I do. Do you not understand? Do you remember Memphis? When I went into the temple and you chased me down. Remember what I said?'

Densus thought back. 'If I remember rightly, you said we weren't meant to find the source.'

'Yes. But maybe it was *me*. Maybe I misunderstood, and it was just *me* who wasn't meant to find the source.'

'Urbicus—'

'No. I give myself slowly to the black. To an end.'

Densus hadn't realised that there was a blade in the man's swirling hand until it came up, glinting. A short knife for peeling fruit, it flashed again once as it lanced into his wrist, and then he was cutting, grunting with the pain and effort, carving a line up his wrist. In the darkness, Densus couldn't make out any difference between the black water and the dark blood flowing into it, but it had to be coming out in a fair torrent. He wanted to shout again, but there was no point. Clearly Urbicus was not going to come back. The man truly believed the only thing he could do was offer himself to the gods of the Nile. As the centurions watched in dismay, the priest changed hands with the knife, blood sheeting down as he lifted it and repeated the procedure on his other wrist.

'Silent. Dark. Peaceful.'

But he was wrong. Densus winced as he saw the various shapes slithering from the far shore, sliding silently into the water, converging on a spot mid-channel. There would be nothing peaceful about this sacrifice, no matter what Urbicus intended.

'Swim, man,' Densus shouted, and now, all along the bank, the men had seen the crocs and were shouting warnings. One man, identified as one of Urbicus' cadre by the rattling sistrum in his hand, began to wade out into the water, but others were quickly at his back, grabbing him, pulling him to safety on dry land.

Finally, the warnings seemed to get through to the priest, and he turned, seeing the tell-tale 'V' shapes in the water that spoke of creatures moving at speed just beneath the surface. All priestly serenity disappeared then from Urbicus' face. He began to shout in desperation, though his strength was ebbing, and all that came out were broken croaks and whimpers. Suddenly, he began to swim, but it was hopeless. He managed a single stroke, and then half a second one before his strength gave up, the blood-loss far too heavy now to allow him even a chance. He disappeared beneath the surface for a moment, then reappeared, coughing and choking, weak arms windmilling.

The first attack went entirely unseen. For a moment, Urbicus was flailing, panicking, then suddenly he was gone, as something gripped his ankle and pulled hard. For a few heartbeats the riverside fell entirely silent, as nothing stirred, barring the ripples in the water that marked the last position of the priest.

Then, suddenly, he re-emerged, and seemed to have recovered sufficient strength to scream, though the scream began as bubbles and choking. But he kept rising, and as he fully surfaced, the horrible reason became apparent. Two of the crocodiles were fighting over their meal. Each had tight hold of one leg in their powerful jaws, and between them they were almost pulling Urbicus apart. With a small fountain of blood and a horrifying scream, the priest vanished beneath the surface again.

They waited, but the longer they waited now, the less likely any reappearance became. Once they had waited long enough that no man could have survived, Densus cleared his throat. In the silence, a single sistrum gave a desultory jingle.

'Alright, everyone back to the camp. There are plenty of other crocs out there who feel cheated out of a snack.'

The men slowly began to file away from the riverbank, heading back to the gateway between the stake fences. As Densus turned, he realised that quite a crowd had grown at the rampart, watching from a slight distance, including the tribune who stood, arms folded, looking not at all unhappy at the loss of the troublesome priest.

One of the men must have made an off-colour joke, for as they returned to the camp, one of Urbicus' disciples with a sistrum gave another guardsman a resounding punch in the gut, then thumped him on the head as he bent over, gasping.

'Remember that Urbicus gave his own life that we could live a little longer. Have some fucking respect.'

The cultist spat at the huffing man and then marched off with his friends. Densus sighed and leaned a little closer to Faventinus. 'Remember what you said about making him a martyr? I think he did it to himself. Somehow, I think our Urbicus troubles have only just started.'

'You mean all his friends? I'm sure we can change their minds.'

'What we need,' Densus said, 'is a new chosen priest, and one a little more amenable. What do you think?'

'My optio's an eminently practical man. I reckon he'd be good. We might even be able to undo all the trouble Urbicus caused.'

'Let's take it to the boss.'

Striding past the muttering crowd of acolytes of Urbicus, the two centurions made for the command tent, where they could see the tribune entering. Approaching, nodding to the two men on guard, Densus reached up and rapped on the wooden pole. After a short pause, a tired voice bade them enter.

The tribune was busy removing his boots, sitting on the ridiculously ornate bed that took a full quarter of an hour to load and unload from the carts every day. He looked up.

'Yes?'

'Sir, Urbicus' demise has opened up an opportunity.'

'Oh?'

'The unit is without a priest. Now, I know that unit priests are all unofficial, unpaid, and purely an internal position, voted by the men, but they put a lot of stock in it. We feel that going on without a priest might play into the hands of those men already hanging on Urbicus' words.'

'I agree. Go on.'

'So, we think it would be good to elect a new priest, and one who could help bring the men back around?'

'Again, agreed. You have a candidate in mind?'

Faventinus chipped in now. 'We were thinking of my optio, Gallo. He's a pragmati—'

'Gallo?' snorted a frowning tribune. 'That man who tells filthy jokes about Vestal Virgins, and who does crude impressions of the emperor at his latrine?'

Densus found it hard not to grin. 'That's the one, sir.'

'Absolutely not.'

The two centurions shared a look, both crestfallen at the sudden and adamant refusal. 'Sir?'

'The man dishonours the gods with his jokes. You cannot possibly consider him for a priest. It would be sacrilege of the highest order. No. *I* shall take his place.'

Densus felt a huge pit opening up beneath him, and winced. 'Surely, sir, your duties as senior officer would keep you too busy.'

'You think I am unaware of the centurionate's opinion of senior officers? That we are elaborate figureheads at best? I am aware that the general running of the unit comes down to the two of you, both on campaign and in battle. I am here to make policy decisions, the really difficult choices, and to lay out overall strategy. I am perfectly capable of playing both roles.'

'But surely a military priesthood is beneath—' began Faventinus.

'Nonsense. A full decade ago, I was initiated into the College of Augures. In actual fact, since the priesthood is for life, I am already officially and legitimately a priest, as is logged in the records of the Tabularium in Rome. It is decided. I should have replaced the difficult man many days ago, had I thought of it. Now, however, I will assume his duties. Before departure tomorrow, call a general muster. I will address the men.'

Densus looked across helplessly at Faventinus, but his fellow centurion had that same look of panic. He could think of absolutely no argument against it, and the longer he said nothing, the more uncomfortable things became and the less possible it was to argue.

In the end, he saluted and the two men rose, nodding goodnight to the tribune and exiting the tent.

'Why didn't you do something to stop that?' Faventinus demanded as they marched away into the camp.

'Me? I didn't even see your lips move.'

The two men sighed. 'I have a feeling we just swapped a vulture for a wolf.' Densus scratched his head. 'No good will come of this.'

'But he has at least been a priest. One of the augures. You never know, it might work out.'

Densus was shaking his head, though. He couldn't see that.

They split up then, returning to their own tents, where Densus spent one of the less comfortable nights of his career, plagued by dreams of drowning, of being eaten by crocodiles, and for some reason of angry dwarves, though he couldn't work that one out. The morning dawned just like any other, steaming hot and bright blue above a world that was brown-gold and dusty.

There had been no other incidents during the night, and for a brief moment, he felt an odd hint of positivity until his memory supplied him with what had happened last night. He sagged, then, and grumbled and complained as he raked his hair neater, decided he could get away without a shave for another day, and then pulled on his uniform and armour. Fully kitted out, he emerged from his tent into the boiling world. To his dismay, he could already see that the tribune's slaves had constructed a temporary podium off to one side of the camp and cleared the area before it. The tribune was serious, then.

Densus actually had little to do, for Faventinus was

already up and had spread word of the muster. Instead, he wandered down to the riverbank once again while the camp prepared. Three men stood on guard at the rampart, pila in hand, ready to oust any approaching crocodile. The river looked peaceful, grand, calm, languid, even inviting. A long way from how it had looked last night.

One particularly large boulder some five paces from the water had been newly worked. Either during the night or early in the morning, someone had crudely carved the shape of an owl on it, and penned a brief epitaph to the priest. Despite his urge to kick the damn thing, Densus left it alone, and wandered back into the camp just as the call resounded for the muster.

The men were still assembling when Densus reached the cleared area. The tribune was standing next to the podium with his servants, and Faventinus, who was nodding at whatever he was hearing, though his face did not suggest full agreement.

Lines of guardsmen stood silent, in full kit, a rare sight these days, gleaming in the sun as they sweated their bollocks off for the edification of the man before them. Densus walked around the edge and approached the other officers. The optios, standard bearers, musicians, and the one remaining tesserarius, stood before the platform like a consul's lictors.

'Ah, good,' the tribune said. 'When I finish, I shall read the omens, and then I shall expect support from my officers, encouraging the men to feel cheered and uplifted.'

Densus nodded, despite catching the look on Faventinus' face. He then moved to take a position on the far side. Once the lines of men were in place, silent and still, the tribune stepped up onto the platform, flanked by the two centurions.

'Good morning, men of the third and fifth centuries, second cohort of the emperor's famed Praetorian Guard.'

Densus had to admit it was a good opening move. They'd been out here so long now that there was a certain amount of 'going native' already, and the men had probably never felt less like Praetorians than now. To remind them of their pride and their duty together might even help break the spell Urbicus had cast.

'The day dawns mournful for the loss of a man who was not only Praetorian, and an officer, but also beloved of the gods.'

Densus wondered whether everyone else heard the faint hint of strain then as the tribune paid honourable service to a man he would happily have sent to meet the gods personally over the preceding days.

'Given that at the very heart of our mission, granted by the blessed emperor Nero Claudius Caesar Augustus Germanicus, is the need to commune with, and seek the blessing of, the gods of the Nile, it is imperative that we proceed only if we boast a priest among our number. As such, it is my great honour to present myself to you in that role. As a member of the College of the Augures in Rome, I have great experience in interpreting signs and omens, and a close relationship with the gods of the state. From this point on, I shall lead any rites or services required.'

He paused, perhaps expecting applause. What he received was uncomfortable silence. Bracing himself anyway, the tribune went on.

'Hark. Am I alone in hearing the song of birds?'

Yes, thought Densus for a moment, but then he had to admit that he did hear something. It was hard to hear over the water, but the hooting, honking and rasping of ducks was more and more audible as he listened.

'And what do I hear?'

'Ducks,' snorted an unenthusiastic voice from the crowd. Densus scanned the ranks, trying to see who had spoken so, but could not identify the man. The tribune, however, seemed to take what was clearly sarcasm as encouragement.

'Ducks,' the officer called. 'The content and lively sound of ducks. And those of you who have studied the sciences of the beasts of field, stream and air, will know that ducks and geese are of the same blood. Geese, who are sacred to Juno, who saved Rome from the Gauls. And ducks are their cousins, which tells us that ducks can only be a good creature, sacred and noble.'

'I step in their sacred and noble shit from time to time,' someone else called.

This time Densus was ready, and took note of the culprit for a clip round the ear later.

'That the duck, sacred cousin of the goose, can be content upon the Nile, even with great predators around, humbles us. It reminds us that we are the greatest predator in the world, not just men, but Romans! No one escapes us, and we *fear* no one. And we shall follow their example and be content with our lot, even here, in this harsh and dangerous world. Juno watches over us, be certain of it. The omens for our journey through Kush are good.'

He probably expected a roar of agreement and support. He probably expected more than an uncomfortable silence and another wag covering his mouth so that the stifled word 'bollocks' seemed to come from nowhere.

Densus just could not think of what to say. Cheering seemed facile, but the tribune expected support. He looked past the frowning officer to Faventinus, wondering what his fellow centurion planned. Then he saw that his friend had paled and remained silent, looking up into the sky. Densus lifted his own gaze and it took but a moment to see what Faventinus was looking at. A large, mottled owl was circling above the camp in wide, lazy circuits. His heart jumped. An Indian merchant in Alexandria years ago had spent a whole evening in a bar trying to explain to him the idea of reincarnation, and to persuade him of its reality. He'd never really considered it until now, when he could not shake the notion that the bird circling above them was somehow Urbicus reborn. That an owl was even out in the bright morning seemed strange, after all.

He was just wondering how he could possibly put a positive spin on this when the owl stopped circling. In a heartbeat the great bird, graceful and powerful, was plummeting towards the earth. The animal disappeared from sight over towards the east side of the camp, and for a moment Densus wondered what was happening. Then, in disastrous glory, he found out, at the same time as everyone else. The owl reappeared, climbing into the air, leaving a spray of water in its wake, a small, juvenile duck struggling in its claws.

Even the tribune looked dumbfounded now, wondering what to say. Having so lauded the ducks, and with Urbicus' villainisation of the owl present across the camp, it would be near impossible to present what had just happened in front of everyone as anything other than an omen of disaster.

The spell was broken by a man who could have been today's priest, as Optio Gallo shaded his eyes, watched the two birds climb, and cleared his throat.

'Fuck me. Looks like the omens call for duck for breakfast.'

19

FIVE DAYS BEFORE THE KALENDS OF OCTOBER AD 61

It seemed that every day brought a new trouble. Faventinus sighed. 'Has the tribune been told yet?'

'No, sir. I came straight to you.'

'Good. Leave it like that.'

Belting on his sword, he opened the tent doorway to that eerie mauve light of a desert pre-dawn. The camp was silent and still, most of the men asleep, the only noise the rush of nearby river water and the murmur of the animals in their corral. With the soldier leading the way, Faventinus ducked between lines of tents, and approached the northern rampart.

The three guards were all sat together by the gate, the century's capsarius at work on them.

Damn it. At least they were alive. He hurried over. 'How are they?'

'Bumps on the head. I'm a little worried about Libanius

over there. They hit him harder than the other two, and I fear they may have cracked his skull.'

'Can't you tell?'

'I'm only a capsarius, sir, not a medicus. Patch 'em up and ship 'em out. Even if it is cracked, he'll probably recover, but there's always a risk of complications. I'd like to have him travel in a cart, but not with the fever victims, for obvious reasons.'

'That should not be an issue, now the supplies are much lower.'

'So are the carts,' said the soldier who'd brought him here.

'What?'

'They took two.'

Faventinus sighed and rubbed his head. 'So, how many slaves have gone?'

'Twenty-six, sir.'

'Shit, that's a lot. That means we still have twenty-two, yes?'

The soldier nodded. 'Though seven of them are injured, some quite badly. It appears they had a bit of a disagreement.'

'I'm going to have trouble from the tribune for this.'

It had happened hours ago, obviously. Roughly half the slaves had finally had enough. They were treated relatively well, as slaves go, but they were as aware of the dangers they were walking into as the Guard, and *they* had not taken an oath to keep going. They'd faced crocs, hippos, beheading raiders, and yesterday the omens had been clear and appalling. The slaves had argued, and almost half of them had risked the punishment of crucifixion, or scourging, to do a runner. They'd sneaked up on the rampart guards from behind and knocked them out, then taken two carts and presumably the animals to pull them. A thought struck him.

'I take it they stole supplies, too?'

'Yes, sir. They were very efficient. Took sufficient to see them back to Roman land, no more.'

Faventinus nodded. 'Travelling light. I'll bet they took the best animals, too. Of course, the slaves have done all the loading, unloading and transport, and looked after the animals. They knew what to go for.'

A bellow of anger resounded, back among the tents, and Faventinus took a deep breath. Someone had told the tribune. He'd hoped to be able to break the news himself, but he was too late. He pointed at the soldier who'd summoned him. 'Get some mates and do an inventory of supplies and animals. I want to know exactly what we have left.'

He then looked around. The tribune was on his way, but he had a few moments' grace. He crossed to the fence where two men were guarding the remaining slaves. Leaning on the fence, he waved to the forlorn gathering.

'Right. Here's the deal. You lot have earned my respect for not running with your mates. More than that, for trying to fight and stop them. I know you didn't alert anyone, but I also know how you'd have been treated then. As such, I will prevent any punishment coming your way. And beyond that, from now on, you all get the same rations and allotments as the Guardsmen. You're facing the same perils, so you get the same chance. And lastly, any man who reaches the end of the journey with us will walk free and with a purse of coins to show for it. Well done.'

Leaving the slaves wide-eyed and looking to one another with fresh hope, he turned to see the tribune marching towards him. One of the slave guards coughed. 'Are you really going to give them our water and food?'

Faventinus leaned close and replied in a low whisper. 'If you still want them here tomorrow to carry your supplies, yes.'

With that, he turned and hurried off to intercept the tribune.

'Our slaves have escaped?' the man snapped.

'Roughly half, sir. They've been gone for hours. The men they overcame will live, and they've only taken sufficient supplies to reach Pselchis or Syene. The rest of the slaves fought to stop them, but dared not shout to wake others, for fear of being lumped in with the fugitives.'

'They'll struggle on crosses for this.'

'No, sir. That's not a good idea. The slaves still here were obedient. They need to be rewarded, not punished. Besides, I've already told them what they'll get.'

The tribune frowned. It was sensible, but he clearly didn't like having the decisions taken out of his hands. 'What is your plan for retrieving the runaways?'

'I don't have one, sir.'

'Then let me clarify for you. Have all the horses rounded up and give them to light-armed soldiers. They will chase down the runaways, retrieve the carts and supplies, and leave the villains bound and naked to die in the desert.'

Faventinus winced as he shook his head. 'We can't do that either, sir.'

'Why not?' snapped the tribune.

'Sir, they have several hours' head start. We'll lose the best part of a day trying to retrieve them, and we don't have a day's supplies to waste. Every loaf of bread and jar of water is precious, now. We can't afford to chase after them. Besides, that would mean sending our men back through territory preyed on by head-takers, which would be foolish. We have to leave them and take the loss.'

The tribune fumed impotently, stomping back and forth, those fists clenching repeatedly again. The problem was that Faventinus was right. They had lost a great deal, but to do anything about it would risk losing even more. In the end, he stomped off back towards his tent, and Faventinus turned to see the first golden ray of sun appear over the rocks on the far side of the river.

Another day in paradise...

20

KERMA
KALENDS OF OCTOBER AD 61

It had been a tense six-day journey. Almost all optimism and humour had vanished from the column now, with the exception of the slaves, who had new reason to feel hopeful with their improved conditions and promise of a future. The soldiers, however, were looking forward only to a nebulous doom announced by an owl and a duck.

Worse still, by the third day after the slaves' departure, supplies had become thin enough that the entire column went onto half rations, further irritating the soldiers, who were now sharing those rations equally with the remaining slaves. By the time the scouts called back that what must be Kerma had been spotted ahead, the officers were to a man worrying about dwindling supplies, and how long the men could last without dropping to quarter rations.

'Halt the column,' Densus called, thrusting a hand into the air to signal everyone.

As the scouts gathered, their horses snorting and pawing at the ground, and the column slowly ground to a halt, carts coming closer together as they did so, the tribune came cantering up on his horse.

'Why have we stopped?'

Densus could not help but note the sour glares the men threw at the tribune's back as he rode past. Trouble was brewing there now, too. He pulled his attention back to the officer with difficulty. 'Sir, Kerma is just beyond those trees.'

'And that is where we are going, Centurion.'

'Sir, given recent events and our uncertainty as to the political situation in Kush, it would seem prudent to halt the column under guard and take a small, well-armed group into the town first, to check how the land lies.'

The tribune paused, considering the matter, and looked as though he were about to disagree, but then deflated a little and nodded. 'Perhaps you're right.' He turned and signalled to Faventinus, back along the line. 'Stay with the carts and keep them safe, while we move into Kerma and take stock of the situation.'

Faventinus saluted and turned to organise his men, and Densus signalled two contubernia of men to step forward. Along with them came his optio, standard bearer and musician, but he waved them back. Marching into a foreign town with Roman military pomp may well cause an entirely adverse reaction, after all.

A quarter of an hour later they were past the trees and bearing down on Kerma. It was clear to Densus that this place was not Aegyptian. Despite the presence of a huge temple of the same sort as was to be found in the north, sitting at the heart of this place, everything else seemed to be different. In addition to the rectangular mudbrick houses that were familiar, there were a large number of circular structures of varying sizes, odd compounds and long structures, a tangled web of streets. The strangest thing, though, was the walls. In the centurion's fairly broad experience, a town was either fortified, strong ramparts surrounding it with regular access gates, or not fortified, with no ramparts at all. And, of course, there were occasional important places where a palace complex or the like was fortified *within* a town. Kerma, however, was a perplexing mass of ramparts, some parts of the town seemingly undefended and open to the desert, while other parts of varying sizes had their own high mudbrick walls, separating them from other parts of the town. In some ways, it seemed Kerma was lots of walled districts, loosely gathered together as a whole. At least, to their relief, the place was not abandoned.

Which was not to say that everything looked normal.

Densus had seen towns all over Aegyptus and Libya, across Italia and even in Crete, and the one thing that they had in common was that they were full of people. Kerma was not. There were figures in the streets, and the buildings were clearly occupied, but the population was sparse, not even a quarter of the number of people Densus would expect to see in a place this size.

'Quiet,' mused the tribune as they moved between two great curved mudbrick walls and into the town without apparently passing through a gate.

'*Too* quiet. I don't like it, sir.'

'You must work with it, anyway, Centurion. We need supplies.'

'And a little more insight, too, I think.'

The street led into the heart of the place, past a large,

square house and a small cluster of round huts, and the two people they came across on the way gave surprised looks at the approaching military and turned into side streets, disappearing from view.

'There,' Densus said, pointing ahead. 'That looks like a merchant's warehouse.'

It had to be. A large building stood with wide doors open as several carts were unloading sacks and huge jars into it. With a nod from the tribune, they moved towards the building. One man there stood apart from the work, hands on hips, watching his goods moving with an air of authority. He was dressed in slightly finer clothes, and if he was not the merchant, then he had to be a senior factor in the man's business. For a moment, Densus regretted the fact that his fellow centurion was back with the convoy. Faventinus came from a mercantile background, and had proved several times on their journey that he knew what he was doing when negotiating with merchants. Still, while they were almost devoid of supplies, the Roman column continued to be well supplied with coin, and so they could afford a little price rise if necessary.

He approached the man and noted with a sigh that the tribune had dismounted and was striding along close by.

'Do you speak my tongue?' he asked the waiting man in slow and carefully pronounced Greek.

The man frowned.

'Little.'

'We have a column of men travelling from Rome to your capital in Meroë, and raiders cost us critical supplies. Can you help restock us for the journey upriver?'

The man gave him a helpless look and shrugged.

'Need food and water,' he simplified, miming eating and drinking, and pointing to the others.

The man nodded slowly and gestured for them to wait. He disappeared inside for a moment, and then returned with a slightly lighter-skinned man, who looked surprised to see them. The man then broke into a wide smile.

'Hello, Caesar. What you know? You speak this goodly, yes?'

'Thank the gods. We need to resupply. Much food and water. Enough for maybe a hundred and seventy men for however long it takes to travel the river to Meroë.'

The man took this in slowly, shaking his head more and more as Densus spoke. When he'd stopped, the man replied. 'Supply too small. No boss in town give many supply. You go Napata?'

Densus nodded. 'Yes. Napata on the way to Meroë.'

'We give many supply to Napata, yes?'

'Thank you, yes.'

The centurion turned to see the tribune looking confused, trying to pick through the weird, thickly accented Greek. 'I believe he's saying nowhere in town has enough supplies to see us to Meroë, but he can give us enough to get to Napata, and I presume we can pick up more there.'

'Good. Arrange it.'

After a short exchange, the man went over to pass the deal on to the merchant, who nodded and then disappeared inside to make arrangements. While he was gone, the smiling translator stood idle, and as the tribune mooched around nearby, looking bored, Densus gestured to the man.

'Why is the town so quiet?'

The smile vanished in an instant. 'Not talk. You fine. You happy. Buy supply and go Napata, yes?'

Densus nodded, though he could feel the hair standing up on the back of his neck. There was something going on, and even the friendly and talkative interpreter was not willing to tell them what it was. Still, he seemed content they would be safe, and that they'd get to Napata, and for now that would have to be enough. A short while later, the merchant returned, and the deal was finalised. They would bring five carts to the warehouse and load. When this was passed on to the tribune, he was content, and he and half the men returned to the caravan to make the arrangements there. Densus, however, said he needed to check something out in town.

In a perfect world, he would have gone alone. A man learns more on his own than with an escort of guards, usually, but there was still a strong element of danger in this utterly alien world, and he would have been foolish to do so on this occasion. Consequently, he was backed by eight armed men as he moved further into the town.

He wanted to know what was going on.

Unfortunately, the further into town he went, the less likely it seemed he was going to find out. A few merchants appeared content enough to make contact with the strangers, though each shut down quickly when it turned out that no transactions were likely, and no one was happy to discuss anything about the town, the population or the wider political landscape. The majority of ordinary folk melted away into alleys and doorways at the sight of the Romans, and the few who warily passed them, in a wide arc, made it clear that they did not, or perhaps *would* not, speak Greek.

Half an hour later, when he returned to the warehouse, where the carts were already being loaded and the gold changing hands, he had learned not a single word from anyone in the town, though one sight had given him pause for thought, and seemed to confirm that something was going on, under the surface of this place.

On some official building in the centre, he had again seen the sequence of hieroglyphics he now knew to be the name of Nebmaatre, King of Kush. This time, though, someone had put some effort into trying to scratch the whole damn thing out, just like they'd done with Caligula's name in Rome.

What were they walking into?

21

NAPATA

FIVE DAYS BEFORE THE IDES OF OCTOBER AD 61

'What's the date?' Gallo asked as they wearily approached the next stop. Faventinus told him, and the optio took on a thoughtful look. 'That means we've been gone from Rome just short of two and a half months, one and a half of them on the Nile. It *feels* like it's been forever.'

'I know what you mean. Still, at least you're seeing exotic places and eating exotic foods.'

'And getting bitten and stung by exotic creatures,' Gallo added wryly. 'But I know what you mean. Most members of the Guard never get beyond Rome, or the imperial villas on the coast. Not sure that this is an improvement, mind.'

Faventinus excavated some bitter seed from the corner of his mouth, left lodged there since the noon meal. For ten days they had followed the Nile upstream from Kerma, relying on the supplies they'd picked up there. The foodstuffs had been enough to see them on their journey without having to ration the men, which was a relief, but apart from the grain to make bread, the rest had been rather adventurous. Language barriers had prevented identification of most of the supplies. The cart and oxen were easy enough, and the grain and water, but meats, vegetables, fruit and seasonings were all an unknown quantity, as well as what Faventinus speculatively called fish, but may actually have been other meat, or even some weird vegetable product. Consequently, every meal had been an adventure, and approached with a mix of fascination and trepidation. On the whole they had been good, though on one or two occasions they had clearly chosen the wrong ingredients in combination and the meal had been either bland or eye-watering.

He looked ahead to the city. Perhaps Napata would supply them with more identifiable goods.

This place was infamous in Roman-controlled Aegyptus, the site of the main struggle in the last war with Kush, some eighty-odd years ago. The Roman army had largely burned and dismantled the place, given its importance as the main religious centre of the kingdom. It had clearly been fully rebuilt, for it was thriving now. The town, centred around a cluster of temples beneath a great mountain, was a damn sight busier than Kerma had been, which was something of a relief. Even Densus, who'd been tense of late, looked happier. Of course, he'd served his time with the Twenty-Second, which had something of a history here, being the legion that had taken Napata from the warrior queen, a story the centurion had told them one night on the voyage to Alexandria.

'This place,' the tribune said, 'should have an official Kushite commander. It is, I understand, the second most important settlement after Meroë. Hopefully that means not only better information, but less of a language difficulty. We shall follow the same process as at Kerma. The wagons can wait here.'

Densus cleared his throat. 'Take Faventinus in with you, sir. He can get better deals with traders, and we need to start keeping an eye on funds now.'

The tribune nodded. 'Very well. Densus, you keep the column in order. Faventinus and two tent parties with me.'

With that, he rode off towards the city, at a slow pace to allow those on foot to keep up. Faventinus and the sixteen chosen men followed on, traipsing through the omnipresent dust. A small collection of tombs lay scattered among the sands to the northwest of the city's wall, and all eyes turned to watch them warily as they approached the gate. The pyramids here were different from those in Aegyptus, Faventinus was interested to see. Considerably smaller, they were also sharper and narrower, with pylons, similar to those of Aegyptian temples, attached.

The city walls were of relatively recent construction, presumably another victim of Rome's wrath the better part of a century ago. The two men standing guard at the gate were Faventinus' first look at a living, breathing Kushite warrior, and he took them in, appraising them at a glance. Very dark skinned, like all their people, the men were well-built, with impressive musculature. Sandaled feet and bare legs below a pleated blue kilt, tied with a scarf-like belt, into which was tucked a sword that looked not entirely unlike a slightly smaller version of a Roman gladius. Powerful arms with bronze armlets around the biceps, their torsos covered with sleeveless tunics of white linen, over their shoulders simple bows and sizeable quivers full of arrows. Hair short, black and tightly curled with a leather thong around the brow that kept a linen veil in place over the back of the neck. They were not heavily armoured, but he would be willing to bet they were well-trained with both weapons and, lightly attired as they were, would not suffer with the heat and would be fast moving and lithe. In short, they would be the perfect warrior for their environment, while Faventinus was not at all sure how Rome's elite Imperial Guard would fare in battle in this sort of land.

He rather hoped he wouldn't have to find out.

At least they did not appear unwelcome here. The guards bowed as they approached, and made no attempt to block the gate. Faventinus nodded back to them as the tribune came to a halt. In slow Greek, he asked 'Where will I find your commander?'

The two guards frowned, and there was a short exchange between the pair, before one spoke in very broken Greek.

'Big wall. Mid. Long road.'

He pointed straight ahead, and the tribune bowed his head in thanks. As they moved into Napata, the impression that it was more fully occupied than Kerma was borne out. It felt like a proper city. Whatever was going on downriver did not seem to have affected the sacred city, yet.

It was not hard to find their goal. 'Big wall' turned out to mean a large structure at the middle of the town, directly at the end of this road. Two similar guards stood by the door to the building, which was covered in hieroglyphics and pictures. As they closed on it, Faventinus searched the carvings and was relieved to find the symbols that represented the Kushite king, and more so to discover they were intact, after what Densus had found in Kerma.

'I need to see your commander,' the tribune announced, and in response, one of the guards, who apparently had a better command of the language, moved inside. He returned a few moments later, and gestured to the door.

'Faventinus and two men with me.' The tribune slid from the saddle and handed his reins to one of the men, then strode into the doorway, with the other three at his back. The inside was stygian and musty, after the dry brightness of the Kushite day. They were directed by other men inside, to a room occupied by three men. Two were dressed in a similar manner to the soldiers outside; the third in a flowing garment of blue was sat on a simple chair with a small table beside him, bearing a cup.

'Rome comes,' the man said in good Greek. 'Should I cheer? The last time Rome came, they burned our temples.'

His face was unreadable, showing no hint of anger, but no sign of a smile either. The tribune pulled himself up to full height and folded his arms.

'The last time Rome came, we came to punish the queen for invading Aegyptus. This time, we are friends, or so I believe.'

'Friends do not often bring soldiers to one another's house,' the man, presumably a general of some sort, countered.

'We are not here for war, but for knowledge.'

This seemed to intrigue the man, who leaned forward, cupping his chin in his hand. 'Go on.'

'The emperor commands us to trace the great river to its source and there to honour the gods and spirits of the Nile, and in our passage to learn what we can of the lands beyond our reach, for all knowledge makes trade and treaty easier.'

Faventinus nodded to himself. It was well-spoken. Curtius Lupus might be a liability in many ways, but when it came to oratory and high politics, he was much better made for it than most of the Guard.

'This,' the Kushite said, 'is true word. You seek then to pass through our lands on your journey?'

'We do. We would avail ourselves of the goodwill of Kush, given the strength of the treaty between our peoples.'

The man was silent for a few moments, apparently sizing them up. Then he leaned back in his chair and crossed his arms. 'If it is knowledge you seek, you will find it in Meroë. There, the king has priests and wise men, learned in many things. In the name of the treaty with your emperor, I extend the hospitality of Kush. We will resupply your wagons and give you comfortable accommodation for the night, and then see you safely to Meroë.'

Faventinus found himself wondering how the man knew they had more men and wagons.

'Might I ask how long the journey to Meroë is?' he asked.

The tribune frowned at him, but the Kushite sucked his lip for a moment. 'Eleven days if your men move at good pace.'

The centurion's brow creased in thought. 'That is remarkable.'

The tribune nodded. 'How is that possible? I have the journey at an estimated three hundred and fifty miles.'

Finally, the Kushite smiled. 'It is a long journey, following the river. But there is a trade road through the desert that cuts the loop off, and takes you directly to the capital from here. Half the distance at most.'

Faventinus felt his stomach flutter at that. 'Is it a good route? Safe? Wells and oases?'

'You know the desert?'

'I was brought up in a place not dissimilar, far to the west. I have seen the desert and its trade roads. Only those who know the land can use them, for only *they* know in the shifting sands where the water is to be found.'

The officer laughed now. 'A Roman who knows the desert. A wonder, I am sure. Yes, the route is safe and well-used. There are even garrisons in places.'

The tribune took a step closer. 'Tell us what is happening in Kush.'

For just a moment, Faventinus saw a flicker of surprise in the local's eye, before he feigned ignorance and shrugged. 'I do not understand.'

'Yes you do. Your military has been pulled back south and weakened near the border with Rome. Your king's name seems to be unpopular in some areas, and the people there will not speak of it. If there is a threat to the peace with Rome, I need to know.'

The man gave a slight sigh. 'It is nothing that need concern you. A small internal issue. A disagreement in the palace. The military moves to lend its support to the king's authority, but both parties have Rome's friendship in mind.'

'I would like to know more.'

'It is not my place to speak of it, though when you meet the king and his court, I suspect all will become clear. You are, I say again, in no danger, unless *you* pose a danger to *us*. Otherwise, accept our friendship, our aid, and pass through on your way without issue.'

Faventinus listened to the conversation as the tribune and the Kushite general hammered out their deal. He was not going to be of the value here that Densus had suspected.

Here there would be no haggling with local merchants, just an ordered resupply with the help of the native military.

As the others talked, Faventinus found himself pondering their journey. Meroë sounded dangerous. A 'disagreement in the palace' sounded a lot like factions at court, and that could easily boil over into civil war. Someone was powerful enough that the king's name was being erased in outlying fortresses and the troops removed to somewhere. His mind, wandering, meandered through the history of this place as related over wine by Densus, and something occurred to him. As the conversation hit a lull once more, he gestured to the general.

'Do I not remember hearing that Kush has queens? Not just consorts, but women rulers. And warriors. Yet, you have a king now?'

Again, for just a moment he saw a flash of something in the man's eyes before it was covered over once more.

'Kush has a king. Always a king. But when the king dies, rule passes through the highest ranking woman in the dynasty, to her eldest son. Succession is always through a queen. And if the son is not yet old enough to rule, the queen, the Kandake, will rule *for* him. Your armies have met one such queen,' he added pointedly.

Faventinus nodded, and the answer clicked into place. Only one person in Kush, then, could realistically be powerful enough to oppose the king, and wield sufficient authority that the kingdom would still respect them.

It was only when they were on their own again, leaving the building to bring the column into Napata for the night and for resupply, that Faventinus revealed his concerns to the tribune.

'When we reach Meroë, sir, be very wary of the king's sister.'

'What?'

'The tribune at Pselchis told us that the Kandake in Meroë was more powerful than any general. I will be most surprised if it is not she who moves to oppose the king.'

'You are talking about civil war, Centurion.'

'Yes. Let's hope we can be through Kush and gone before it erupts.'

22

DESERT

MID OCTOBER AD 61

The men had thought they were acclimatised. Densus had tried once or twice to explain that thus far they'd had it easy, but this had been blown off as rubbish even by the gloomiest of men. The past few days, trawling along the desert trail, though, had brought his words back to them and hammered them home. Even on their worst days, so far, the men had not experienced the most intense heat these lands had to offer, for they had travelled alongside the widest river in the world all the time, its flowing water and the faint wind that blew along it enough to take the edge off the heat. They had thought they were hot. Now they knew what hot was. Densus had been prepared. He'd followed the desert trails to the quarries of Mons Claudianus in his time, and knew what the place could be like once you got away from the river. Of course, this was hotter than even he was used to. So far south, the sun seared the land that little bit more than it did in Aegyptus, the reason, he presumed, for the darker skin of the people here.

And then there was the terrain. Most of the men were from Rome or its surroundings. When you said the word 'desert' to them, they pictured the beach near Sperlonga, their image infected with romantic notions of mirages and nomad camps with sultry, pliant women. What they were getting was rather different. For one thing, beaches were generally flat. The desert trail from Napata to Meroë, on the other hand, dipped and bucked like a ship in a stormy sea, with the way made perilous by scree slopes, jagged rocks protruding from the path, deep sandy pits and steep drops.

Add to that the snakes and scorpions, and it was truly a place to test the mettle of any man. On the bright side, the men were no longer worried about hippos, crocs, and head-taking lunatics. Just making it past the next rise seemed to be enough to worry over. Densus was probably the only one fretting more about their destination than the journey. The revelations of Kerma and Napata did not sit well. Even if what was going on in Kush was an internal matter, there was little chance of passing Romans not being caught up in it somehow.

After the first day's travel, the only one of their Kushite guides who spoke anything like comprehensible Greek had asked why they were all wearing metal armour. Didn't they feel the heat? Faventinus had explained to him that they'd gone with light kit early on, but meetings with Blemmyes raiders had seen them arm up ready ever since.

'No Blemmyes here, Caesar,' the man had said. 'Too far south.'

No matter how often they told these people their names or ranks, they seemed incapable of referring to any Roman, from tribune to slave, as anything other than Caesar.

And so, after that first day, they'd compacted their supplies and opened up an entire cart, into which went every man's armour, helmet, shield and pilum. The men travelled in tunics and sword belts now, those with straw hats wearing them, the others having torn up their cloaks and used them as bandanas to cover their heads from the sun, and to hold back the eternally pouring sweat.

In short, they were changing again, adapting. The tribune clearly didn't like it, but he could go ram it up his arse, unless he wanted men dropping dead every half mile. The men were doing what they had to, in order to survive this place, and Densus would never discipline a man for that. Notably, a day later, the tribune started wearing only his tunic and a crimson felt hat, and he had slaves to fan him as he slept.

Densus had noticed two other changes in the Praetorians, though, since Napata. Firstly, they no longer carried that air of condemned men. They were no longer doom-laden, for the simple effort of survival had stopped most of them even thinking about what lay ahead. Meroë lay ahead, and Meroë meant the river, shade and cold fruit. Right now, men would eat each other to be there.

The other change was physical, rather than mental. Two months of this had changed them. He'd never have thought of his men as pasty and pale, but they had been compared with what they were now, which was heavily tanned and wiry-muscled men with bodies the colour and texture of saddle leather. They were being tested, physically, and were rising to the challenge. And that meant that they could survive further, and adapt more. Right now, they more resembled the men of the Twenty-Second, veterans of several hard campaigns, than the emperor's pampered Guard on the Palatine. If all else went bad, perhaps some good things had come out of this, after all.

By the end of that first day, they had two more men come down with the fever, which had been an increasing concern, and they'd been added to the sick cart. But the next few days across the desert had seen a marked improvement in the original two, and there seemed little doubt they were now healing. And if they could survive it, then so could the others. It was not the death sentence it had first appeared, perhaps due to the Artemisia, and perhaps to the capsarii who looked after them. And since leaving the river and moving out into the dry desert, there had been no more cases, which further supported the idea that it was being around the eddying waters of the cataracts that had caused it.

When they'd departed Napata, Densus had been a touch concerned to see only a small emergency supply of water added to the carts, but he'd soon understood. The trails the desert traders used were older than the gods, and men had been using them since the days Achilles and Hector had walked the world. The trails were precious, and known to few, and that was because they moved from well to well. The desert might be sand and rock, and dust, and things that wanted to kill you, but here and there there was access to water, coming from deep down. Occasionally this was noticeable because trees and vegetation managed to grow around the water source, but as often as not there was no sign, and no one could have guessed until their guides pulled a wooden cover or a pegged sheet aside and revealed the life-giving spring.

And so they moved every few hours from one water source to another along the trail, which would be easy to miss if you didn't know it by heart.

It came as something of a surprise, at the end of the sixth day, when they rounded a rocky bluff and a building sat awaiting them in a wide, barren valley. As they moved towards it, it became clear it was a fortification. Perhaps sixty or seventy paces across in both directions, it was a walled fort made of stone and mudbrick, with enormous buttresses along each side and a single, heavily protected gate.

As they came closer, however, the native guides' manner changed. Bows were unshouldered, arrows drawn and nocked, the men stalking towards the place as though they were hunting mudbrick forts. They spread out and began to come from all sides. Densus cleared his throat to ask what was happening, but the only one he could communicate with simply held a finger to his lips, checked the level of his arrow, and moved on with his friends. Another of the Kushites motioned them to stop, and they did so, watching as their escort moved in like a closing noose on the small fort.

Three disappeared into the gateway, while two remained on guard there, arrows pointed within, and the others stayed in a loose circle, bows ready, watching the walls.

The tension seemed to free almost explosively as the three men reappeared, bows lowered, motioning for their friends to stand down. Without waiting for an invitation, Densus hurried over to the entrance. The one who spoke reasonable Greek saw him coming and, though his friends headed back to their own men, he waited.

Densus walked inside, through the gate, hand on his sword hilt, as the man fell in beside him.

'Tell me.'

'Empty,' the man said. 'All gone.'

'Dead?'

'Gone,' the man corrected. 'No body.'

Inside, there were only four buildings, all of light construction, and the centurion ducked into the nearest two on the way in, confirming that they appeared to be barrack blocks, but were resoundingly empty. A cistern stood to one side, buckets nearby, where it was presumably filled regularly from some nearby source. The main building at the centre was just as deserted as everywhere else, but there were a plate and cup on the table of the principal room, as though the owner had just stepped out for a moment. He felt tense.

As they left the room, he noted once again the symbols of the king's name, and once again scratched out and difficult to read.

'What is this?'

'Nothing for Romans to worry about,' the man said.

But as they returned to the men and then set about making camp for the night he did anyway.

23

MEROË

SIX DAYS AFTER THE IDES OF OCTOBER AD 61

'Cart no,' the warrior said, holding up a warning hand.

The tribune bristled for a moment, looking past the man into the compound. There were already two wagons inside, of a light, native design.

'The cart comes. It contains gifts for your king.'

'Unload here. Cart no.'

Faventinus could feel the frustration emanating from the tribune as he gripped and ungripped his hands, a habit the centurion was coming to recognise. Finally, aware that he was unlikely to change the guard's mind, the tribune turned to his officers.

'Unload the royal gifts from the cart, and have the slaves bear them inside. Half the men remain here with the cart, the rest with us.'

Faventinus saluted and, along with Densus, turned and relayed the orders. As the sixteen guardsmen and the six slaves worked, removing chests and sacks from the vehicle, the centurion looked about.

He could still feel eyes on them, and not just the obvious ones from all around. It was a feeling that had followed them all the way from that deserted fort on the desert path. The moment Densus had returned from searching the interior, they had set up camp for the night, and the next morning moved on. And from sunrise that morning, Faventinus was certain they were being watched by someone. Neither Densus nor the tribune felt it, the few scouts they sent out found nothing, and the native guides had been tight-lipped and claimed to know nothing of it, yet he would be prepared to wager that they were lying. They *were* being watched.

That feeling had been with him for the past six days, never letting up. They had arrived at Meroë a little after noon, finding themselves trapped on the west bank, looking across at the city on the far side, a sprawling place. Had they been alone, Faventinus was certain that the ferrymen would have fleeced them for every coin they could, but with the presence of the military escort from Napata, they were given transport across the river free of charge. In three trips, the entire column was moved to the east bank, using all the vessels that could be mustered.

There, they had reassembled, moving through a narrow belt of rich farmland fed by the Nile's waters, climbing the dusty slope beyond to reach Meroë. A huge mass of small mudbrick houses covered the land, the larger shapes of temples and public buildings rising among them. In the distance, outside the city, there were visible clusters of pyramids, though the Romans' goal stood apart from most of the city. Above it, on a rise sat a walled enclosure. This, their guides had informed them, was the royal enclosure. The escort had seemed to have a short dispute with the guards at the gate and while they were all admitted to the great enclosure, the Romans and their escort were directed to different places within.

Faventinus had felt another flicker of alarm at that. It seemed odd, and worrying, and after a terse farewell, he watched the men who'd escorted them from Napata disappear among the smaller walled compounds within the great enclosure. No longer with anyone to rely upon for advice or support, the Romans had approached the compound to which they were directed, carts creaking, animals rumbling, men complaining.

And that was where Faventinus now waited. Finally, everything was ready, and the guard gestured for them to enter. The tribune led the way into the palace compound, and Faventinus looked around as they followed some royal lackey, in just a pleated blue kilt and sandals, across the dusty ground towards the palace proper. The compound contained three buildings, each of different size and design. A low, basic place with many doors seemed to be a barracks, from which various servants or slaves came and went. A slightly better-quality place, with several doors and many windows, was clearly a barracks for the guards visible around this compound and in other parts of the enclosure. The large building, though, had to be the palace, a white-walled structure full of windows painted red, small balconies, plants in hanging pots, and even palm trees in their own containers.

More guards stepped in, alert, as they approached the palace, but the lackey they followed waved them aside, and led the Romans to the door. There was a short, very linguistically difficult, conversation then, but with some wariness on the Kushites' behalf, the soldiers were also admitted, though more of the royal guard appeared with every other heartbeat, until they had enough of an escort to overcome them, should the need arise.

The throne room, when they reached it, was impossible to mistake. The room was huge, light and airy, thanks to the large windows all around, but also thanks to the seven slaves who constantly wafted huge fans, swirling the air, making the heat much more bearable. The walls were white, and painted with patterns and images in bands high and low, and heavy columns similarly painted stood in rows to left and right. The only furnishing, though, was a single large chair, made apparently from solid gold, on a low dais. Upon the throne sat a man of middling years, in rich garments of blue and white, fair dripping with gold and gems, an elaborate skullcap of gold and lapis lazuli atop his head. He also held some sort of golden staff.

He looked bored.

A rangy servant stepped forward and addressed them.

'His greatness Nebmaatre, the Nedjeh of Great Kush and the gold lands, master of the two kingdoms, greets the embassy of his brother, Nero Augustus of Rome.'

As they came to a halt, Faventinus almost chuckled at the sight of the tribune, twitching, hands balling into fists at the suggestion that this barbarian southerner might think himself the emperor's equal. Indeed, the tribune's voice failed him as he tried to answer, coming out cracked and inaudible. Before he could clear his throat and start again, however, a new voice behind them cut across the room in the native tongue, a female voice with the most commanding tone Faventinus had ever heard.

The tall, thin servant blanched, and shuffled speedily back into the shadows. Faventinus couldn't help noticing how the hand of every Kushite guard in the room went to the hilt of their weapon, though as he turned to look at the new arrival, their reaction was entirely understandable.

The woman in the doorway was tall and muscular. She wore a long white dress and trod barefoot. Though she was clearly noble, and bore a marked resemblance to the king, she was unadorned with jewellery, and, apart from her dress, bore only one other item of apparel: a wide red belt from which hung a wicked-looking, gleaming sword with a slight curve to the blade.

She was an impressive sight, but that was probably not what had the soldiers on their guard. Next to the woman was a lion, standing almost to her armpit height. The monstrous animal seemed perfectly tame by her side, until you looked into its eyes, which held death and mayhem caged within. The damn thing was not even on a leash, just padding along at the woman's side.

Suddenly, Faventinus could understand the trouble the Roman general had found in Kush at the hands of its warrior queen. If that Kandake was anything like this one, she'd have been a truly terrifying character. And that was clearly who this woman had to be: the Kandake, the king's sister.

The interpreter dismissed, the woman strode past the Romans without even a hint of nerves at the presence of armed and armoured foreigners. She strode to the throne and sat. Faventinus was hugely impressed, for there wasn't a chair there, but before she could fall to the floor, a slave was suddenly there with a golden seat, which he slid underneath her descending posterior.

The woman spoke to the king in her own language without turning to him, her eyes on the visitors. The king responded, and his tone sounded oddly petulant and huffy. Whatever they had said, she won out, for he fell silent and glared at her, while her expression remained unreadable as the huge lion dropped down and lay beside her.

'My brother wonders why I dismissed his man.'

'I am wondering the same, my lady,' the tribune said.

'You are the spokesman for a god, are you not?'

The tribune bowed his head. 'Nero Augustus, emperor of Rome, beloved of Jupiter and Venus. Pharaoh of Aegyptus,' he added, dangerously in Faventinus' opinion, given the history of the two nations.

'Then it is not fitting for such an embassy to be addressed by a slave, no matter the reason. I am Kandake of Kush, Amanikhatashan, daughter of kings, mother of princes, light of Amun. *I* shall speak for the king.'

Faventinus looked across at her brother, and privately wondered just how much of what she said to the visitors was what she relayed to the king. He doubted the man was even allowed an opinion, looking at the two of them. If there *was* a hint of civil war in the air, he was fairly sure who would win.

'Greetings, then, to the great king of Kush, and to his beautiful and formidable sister.'

The woman bowed her head slightly in acknowledgement. Without passing that on to her brother, she placed her hands on the chair arms and leaned forward a little.

'In eighty-five winters, this is the first official visit to Kush of the emperor of Rome's men. That is what this is, yes? An embassy, and not a precursor to a repeat of the last time. We may have sued for peace, but I doubt even Rome has forgotten how much she also paid for that peace.'

The tribune's fists went again at that, clenching and unclenching, yet his tone was clear even as he replied. 'We are neither an invasion force, nor an embassy, in truth. The emperor has commanded an expedition to seek the source of the great river and to pay homage to its gods and spirits. As such, our path takes us through Kush and beyond. In the spirit of the great friendship of our peoples, we seek your goodwill in our passage, as well as any information and aid you can provide in our onward journey.'

There was an odd silence, then, and the Kandake's left eyebrow rose quizzically. The king muttered something. Asking what had been said, Faventinus thought, but her reply was short and sharp, and the king looked annoyed at the response, though he made no move to rebuke her.

He is frightened of her, Faventinus decided, and probably rightly so.

'My teachers,' she said suddenly, 'always told me that Rome is a beast of war. That she trades and she builds and she explores, but that whatever else she might do, she will *always* be at war with *someone*. Is this true?'

Yes, thought Faventinus, though the tribune's answer was more measured. 'That is perhaps a simplification and exaggeration. But I will say that Rome never shrinks from war if it is required for either the defence of the empire or for the good of the world entire.'

The Kandake's eyes gleamed as though she were

unwrapping the tribune's words and finding something of value within. 'Our warriors grow fat and idle,' she said. 'Barring encounters with wildlife or occasional raiders, they have no war on which to sharpen their teeth. Constant war is, I think, why your soldiers look like fighting men. We lack a great enemy against whom to harden our armies. To the west lies open desert with scattered nomads. To the south: swamp and jungle with minor tribes. To the north is your emperor's lands, with whom we have pledged peace. To the east lie Axum and the kingdom of Zoskales, but we cannot go to war there, for they hold the key to trade with India, and we have been told in no uncertain terms that any move by us against Zoskales and Axum will result in the cutting of Indian trade, which would be crippling. So as you can see, we can have no war, and our warriors wane.'

Faventinus' already impressive opinion of this woman shot up at the discovery that not only did she think like a general, but also like a king.

'What are you suggesting, Kandake?' the tribune asked carefully.

'Let our warriors make war with you. *For* you. Let them fight great enemies and become warriors of whom my ancestors would be proud.'

The fists stopped clenching. The tribune straightened. 'I am certain that were I to take such a proposal back to the emperor, he would be more than happy to agree. It is heartening to see the alliance between our peoples only strengthening.'

But Faventinus was watching the king. Two things struck him at once. Firstly, from the look on the king's face as she spoke, he was of an entirely different opinion. He wanted nothing less than to go to war, for Rome or for anyone. And secondly, thanks to that realisation, Faventinus suddenly knew that the king spoke perfectly good Greek, for he had to be able to understand every word.

As the centurion continued to watch, and the tribune and the queen spoke, the expressions on Nebmaatre's face confirmed that he could understand every word. Was he so frightened of his sister that he allowed her to speak for him even when he disagreed?

Faventinus could just imagine some veteran Kushite commander up in Kerma scratching out the king's name in aggravation and mobilising his men to march to the side of the warlike queen. The troubles in Kush were no longer an unknown thing. But perhaps those he had spoken to had been correct in saying that there was nothing for the Romans to worry about. The king held to the treaty, but should he be replaced by his sister, it was fairly clear that Rome could only benefit from it.

By the time he'd stopped musing on what was happening under the surface of the conversation, and started concentrating once more, the subject had moved on.

'...supplement your supplies,' the Kandake was saying. 'In addition to filling your carts with food and water for the journey, we have excellent iron smiths here. We would be happy to replace any damaged armour and weaponry before you leave the city.'

'We had not planned to stay long,' the tribune said, apologetically.

'It will not *take* long,' she replied. 'Stay one day, long enough to supply, and you should visit the temples of the city, for our priests are learned and know much of the lands and peoples that will lie ahead in your travels. And during that time, my brother will draw up letters for you with his seal. There are several tribes upriver with whom we have good relations, and letters from the king could ease your passage considerably.'

The tribune, all signs of tension having vanished from him now, smiled warmly. 'That is most kind. And in return, I have brought gifts from the emperor.'

At a snap of his fingers, the slaves brought forth their heavy burdens, straining and sweating. Faventinus watched with only half an interest as baubles and offerings sufficient to turn the head of even a rich man were produced and given, laid upon the floor before the king. The centurion's mind was elsewhere again, now. Surely those eyes he'd felt watching them on that last leg of their journey had been working for the queen. Since she now knew there was no danger from these Romans, would the silent surveillance end?

His unease, which had almost disappeared during the exchanges, returned, then, as he watched the emotions drifting across the king's face like clouds scudding across the moon. He did not fear interference from a usurper in Kush now, for clearly that usurping, when it happened, would be a boon. What he now feared was what the king might do to stop her.

24

MEROË

FIVE DAYS AFTER THE IDES OF
OCTOBER AD 61

'What is this place?' Densus asked their guide.

The man, a palace servant with a good command of Greek assigned to them by the Kandake, looked over his shoulder at the three men following him. 'This is temple of Amun. Temple of victory,' he added, and there was a slight tremor of nerves in his voice. The centurion's eyes narrowed at that. Victory over whom? He wondered, a suspicion there.

Behind him, the tribune wore his usual stern, aloof expression, while Faventinus looked twitchy.

'What is it?' he asked his fellow centurion.

'I still feel like we're being watched.'

'Of course we are. We're Romans in the royal compounds of Kush. *Everyone's* watching us.'

'Not like that. You know what I mean. Someone out of sight. Someone following us.'

'The Kandake has no reason to suspect us now. She sees us as allies.'

'And that means the king probably doesn't. We may have swapped one lot of watchers for another.'

'It matters not,' the tribune interrupted. 'We are here for one day only and then we begin to move out of Kush. We have their goodwill and promised aid for the onward journey. Let them watch us while we are here.'

The temple was much like the Aegyptian ones Densus was used to. The differences were stylistic and minor, and they were led through a courtyard surrounded by colourful columns and into a chamber with insufficient light, that there was given off by four elaborate bronze braziers in the room's corners. There they were asked to wait for a few moments, and Densus squinted, willing his eyesight to adjust, picking out details. Ahead, a set of four steps led up to another large room, while doorways led off left and right. The walls were decorated as Aegyptian ones were, but it took only moments for Densus to confirm his suspicions.

The victory the temple celebrated was clearly over Rome. In reliefs and paintings on the wall, figures on thrones looking mighty as they gazed down upon rows of bound captives wearing what were clearly Roman military tunics.

'Back home, we're taught that we won the war in Kush,' he murmured. 'That we forced them to sue for peace.'

'And that is the case,' the tribune said confidently.

'This temple tells a different story.' He shivered.

As they waited, a temple servant, barefoot and naked but for a skirt, shaven-headed and lean, bowed to them as he strode past, reaching the steps, where he paused to spit on the middle one, stamping both feet on it before reaching the top and disappearing into the room above. Densus watched with suspicion again, and when a priest, identifiable by his white skullcap, paced into the room with a bow of the head, the centurion saw the man's eyes flick to the steps momentarily before coming up to meet those of the tribune.

'Greetings, soldiers of Rome. I have been requested to make myself available and to answer any questions of yours of which I am capable, to aid you on your journey.'

'Any question?' Densus put in, earning an irritated glance from the tribune, who had opened his own mouth to speak.

The priest frowned. 'Yes.'

'Tell me about the steps.'

'Sir?'

'Those steps,' he clarified, pointing. 'What is their meaning? Their significance?'

The priest looked mighty uncomfortable, suddenly. 'They are a symbol of the Kandake Amanirenas' victory over the forces of Governor Petronius, many years ago.'

'Victory?' the tribune asked, archly.

The priest shuffled his feet. 'What's buried there?' Densus asked, pointing at the stairs.

'War booty.'

Densus wracked his brain, going over the stories again. No eagles had been taken in the campaign, and any loot taken would be negligible, just the equipment of an army at war. Unless he meant the loot from the Kushite invasion of Aegyptus that had started it all. He scratched his chin.

'A number of imperial statues were taken away in that campaign. Some were recovered, but not all. It's a statue of Augustus under there, isn't it?'

The priest's expression confirmed it. Densus half expected the tribune to explode and angrily demand that it be removed and restored, and from the sudden balling of the man's hands, it was clear he was fighting that very urge. Thankfully, he remained silent. The peace with Kush was useful, and had to be maintained, if for no other reason than that the column had to get out of here alive. Demanding they tear up one of their temples was unlikely to help.

'Tell us of the lands to the south,' the tribune said, with a cleansing breath.

'Come,' the priest said, and strode off into one of the side doors. At his heel, the three Romans followed, through a series of rooms and passages, seemingly out of the main temple and into some side structure or complex. They passed through the edge of a room filled with wooden desks and chairs in ordered rows, where young men bent over parchments, carefully painting their arcane symbols, through a room filled with racks of such scrolls, and finally into a room with just one stone table and chair, several rolls of parchment and pens and ink pots stood waiting.

'It is my understanding,' the priest said, dropping into the seat, 'that you intend to follow the Mother River beyond Kush.'

'This is true.'

'Which one?'

The three Romans all leaned closer now, brows furrowing. 'What?'

'In the very south of our lands, the river divides. Two flows create the river, there.'

Densus blinked. 'Shit. Which one, sir?'

The tribune, similarly thrown, scratched his head. 'Tell us what you know of both. Diodorus and Herodotus both tell of a land of rich cultivation and endless wild animals along the river.'

The priest nodded. 'Of the eastern river, much is known, for its length lies within Kush and within the neighbouring lands of Zoskales. To follow it takes perhaps a month and a half. It curves wide to south and east, and originates at a lake in the territory of Axum. Should you wish to follow it, you would be wise to seek an introduction through the king, for Zoskales is not a man to welcome strangers in his land.'

As he spoke, the priest drew two rough circles on a piece of parchment, and placed a small hut shape in the middle of one. He then drew a line that had to be the Nile, winding through that circle and then arcing off east, where it entered the other.

'This is here,' he said, pointing to the hut. 'This is where the rivers meet,' he added, drawing another hut to the bottom of the circle. He then started to draw another line from there, heading south and then west, which he gradually petered out into mere dots. 'The western river passes through the lands of small tribes who pay tribute to Kush. Many days away, it moves into green lands with many wild animals. It is of this place, I think, that your friends spoke. The river then reaches a great marsh, and of the lands beyond, we have no further knowledge.'

'It is this river we must follow,' the tribune said confidently. 'If it is the greater one, and the other is fully known, then clearly it is this western branch that the emperor expects us to explore.'

Densus nodded, resigned to the fact. He listened as the man told everything he could think of regarding the journey onwards, which was really not that much. The tribune continually asked questions, most of which found no answer. When they finally thanked the priest and returned to the compound where the men were quartered, Densus was still uncertain about the journey to come, though he had to admit he would be grateful to leave Meroë.

PART 4

AETHIOPIA, AD 61

περιμάχητος οὗτος ὁ τόπος γίνεται τοῖς τε Λίβυσι καὶ
τοῖς Αἰθίοψι, καὶ πρὸς ἀλλήλους ὑπὲρ αὐτοῦ πολεμοῦντες
διατελοῦσι.

his region is contested by the Libyans and the Ethiopians,
who wage unceasing warfare with each other for its
possession.

Diodorus Siculus, *Library of History*

25

UPPER NILE
LATE OCTOBER AD 61

'Are we out of Kush, then?'

Densus looked across at his friend and shrugged. 'I've only been here as much as you, but I'd guess so.'

Faventinus nodded. A small mudbrick fort perhaps a mile back had held a small Kushite garrison, but they'd not paid a visit. There was little chance of border guards this far south speaking Greek, and the difficulty of communication would make any visit troublesome to say the least. The place did have all the hallmarks of a border, and a rough estimate of distance travelled would make it about right.

They had left Meroë with the vocal good wishes of their hosts, though their eyes had spoken volumes more. The king's had been full of mistrust and uncertainty, the queen's full of hunger and belligerence. Even the soldiers and the slaves seemed to heave a collective sigh of relief as Meroë disappeared behind them, fading into the horizon. After all, perhaps what had been their final taste of civilisation had also been their last taste of politics and duplicity, and that at least would be a relief. Faventinus was half convinced that by the time they returned, the Kandake would be the one sitting on the throne, nothing to see of the king but a suspicious stain on the floor.

They had moved fast to begin with, supplies plentiful, animals and men rested, and with reasonable trails to follow. Mainly, though, they had moved fast to get away from the capital and to somewhere where the dangers would be easier to spot, usually running at you and full of sharp teeth, rather than watching surreptitiously from shadows.

They'd travelled upriver, only stopping when requested to by garrisons of Kushite warriors, where on each occasion an inscribed amulet the tribune had been given by the Kandake seemed to get them through with no trouble. They had passed one particularly large garrison at the confluence of two rivers, confirmed as the paired branches of the Nile by the commander there.

Following the western branch, they'd moved into the very south of Kush, and Faventinus had begun to note changes to the world with every day of travel. Firstly, the terrain itself was changing. The far bank, to the west, looked dusty and golden, as it had since the day they had first set foot in Aegyptus, with little of note. But the sand and grit of the eastern bank along which they travelled gradually gave way to greenery, to cultivation and fields, and even small areas of trees and undergrowth. Faventinus had not realised just how much he'd missed green. Everything had been brown for at least two months.

Another change had been the weather. It was still hot, *uncomfortably* hot. The men had been allowed to march on in simple tunic and boots, the bulk of their kit in the carts, but the searing, dusty, dry heat of the north was fast becoming a sultry, warm heat that made men sweat like never before.

Despite all discomfort, though, there was a strange and tenuous air of positivity about the men that no one could have expected. The column had been attacked by monsters and bandits, had faced fever, thirst and starvation, had marched into what was almost a civil war, and marched back out without a sword drawn. They were weathering the storm, and for now at least, the predictions of doom and the sacrifice of Urbicus seemed to have slid from the men's consciousness. Even those rattly sistrums had disappeared from general view. Faventinus hadn't seen a man shake one since Napata.

Of course, he also knew that when things appeared their calmest was when you started to look in the shadows for disaster waiting to strike.

The next few days saw even greater changes. With their leaving Kush, it seemed the world of towns and cities was behind them. Even the smaller agricultural villages along the riverbank had now petered out. The only sign they saw of settlements now were minor hamlets of small mud huts with grass roofs, their occupants even darker skinned, almost ebony, with fascinating hairstyles, decorations painted on their bodies, some carrying spears.

One thing that Faventinus decided might soon be of concern was the fact that these natives seemed to live entirely naked, which was fine in principle. Each to their own, in his opinion. Faventinus himself had a cousin from Carthage who'd undertaken ritual castration to join the priesthood of the Galli. But on a practical level, parading a bouncing pair of breasts in front of a soldier who's not seen a naked woman for a third of a year might be asking for trouble.

Three days of travelling in the sweaty green world, with occasional glimpses of these naked tribes, and they met their first potential problem. Though there was no such thing in this world as a paved road, the trail they were following, running within sight of the river and close enough to the bank, was probably what passed for a thoroughfare. It had been worn bare and flat by the passage of many over time, which suggested that it was used as a main trade route. So when the scouts ahead reported back that the road was blocked, Faventinus and the other officers shared a look and hurried out ahead.

Six warriors stood across the road, blocking it. Each was powerfully muscled, dark skinned, naked as the day he was born, and each had a wicked-looking spear in hand, as well as an animal-hide shield. Glancing this way and that, the Romans could see the river and its cleared bank, presumably where people came to wash clothes or fish, as well as another worn path leading off into trees away from the river. No simple way past without confrontation.

'Anee. T'way!' snapped one of the men in the road.

Faventinus sucked on his teeth. This was going to be difficult. At least through Aegyptus and Kush, there had been a chance of communication, thanks to the universality of the Greek tongue. Now, they had moved out of such lands. Densus looked at him helplessly. The man shrugged.

'Na. Ngusi u!'

Before the tribune could formulate an answer, the warrior

illustrated his incomprehensible words by jabbing out with his spear, pointing at the Romans, then at the path into the greenery.

'Well, that at least is fairly clear,' Faventinus said.

'The carts won't get through there,' Densus pointed out.

'Agreed,' the tribune acknowledged. 'You stay here with your men and guard them. Faventinus, you bring yours with us. I'll be damned if I'm going to walk off alone into the jungle with naked natives without an armed escort.'

The men of Faventinus' century swiftly hurried forward, settling into ranks. They may be unarmoured and wearing straw hats or felt caps, but they were at least uniformed and armed, their swords at their sides. The six natives watched this with suspicion, murmuring among themselves in their own tongue. They held a short debate, and then the one who'd first spoken did so again.

'S'miti.' To clarify, he pointed to the lines of men, then passed his spear and shield to a friend and held up eight fingers.

Faventinus turned and glanced a question at the tribune. The senior officer did not look entirely happy, but he gave a short nod. At least they would outnumber the natives. Faventinus held up eight fingers to the man and nodded.

The spokesman grabbed his spear and shield back and marched off up the side path. The others waited until Faventinus called for the first contubernium of his men to follow, and he and the tribune joined them, disappearing into the green with the other five natives following on.

The path wound for some way through the greenery, scrub [brush and dry, unhealthy looking trees, and then the landscape opened out once more, away from the river and beyond the woods, into a world of open fields and grassland, with small knots of trees here and there.

Their destination, however, was clearly the village that stood nearby. Larger than the ones they'd seen so far, it consisted of maybe thirty or forty of those circular mud and straw huts around a dusty barren central area. An old man was busy hooking a donkey to a cart filled with large jars of river water, while at the far side, two women were busy manufacturing bricks, mixing straw, cow excrement and river mud, and pushing it into moulds. Sheep roamed, children played and laughed, men sat tapping sticks on the ground. Such mundane sights, however, were overshadowed somewhat by the men standing around with spears, all across the village, but in particular close to the largest hut at the centre.

All, of course, were naked, from the warriors, to the workers and the children.

'Be ready for anything,' the tribune commanded, rather unnecessarily in the circumstances, given how every man had travelled with a hand on his sword hilt since the Kushite capital. As they reached the centre of the village, the man leading them stopped, turned and pointed his spear at the two officers, and then to the hut doorway, uttering 'Anee. Anee.'

'Assessment, Centurion,' the tribune said quietly.

'I think we're at the mercy of politics, sir. I'm not the biggest fan of stepping into the lion's mouth, but unless you're ready to start a war with them, I don't see an alternative.'

'And if we did?'

Faventinus blinked. Surely the man was jesting? 'Well,

sir,' he replied carefully, 'our men have to be better trained and equipped, but even with the men back at the carts, we're not a huge force, and there have to be more warriors around than these. We might well win if it comes to a fight, but we'd certainly lose enough men to make going on with the mission foolish.'

The tribune nodded. As if to support the centurion's words, other warriors began to appear in the village, stepping out of the woods and from among the huts. All the workers, hunters, children and so on had now stopped what they were doing to watch the new arrivals.

'Lead on,' the tribune said to the warrior, gesturing at the door with an open hand. The warrior watched him for a moment, and then slipped inside.

The hut was surprisingly light within, small gaps around the edge of the straw roof allowing in light, illuminating three men standing to one side with their spears, a small group of civilians opposite, and the man whom they were clearly here to meet, sitting proud in a chair draped with animal pelts. He was naked also, barring a circlet around his brow, which seemed to be made from the teeth of some animal. That he was the leader was clear from his position and air of authority. A king, perhaps.

The other five spear men had followed them in.

'M'nehee,' the king croaked at them. 'M'ni felik?'

Whatever it was, it was a question, and given the circumstances, its nature seemed fairly explicable. The tribune straightened. 'We come from the north,' he said, pointing to what he probably thought was that direction. 'We go to the south,' he added, pointing off that way. 'Along the river,' now making wobbly watery motions with his hand. The king gave him a baffled look that slid into a suspicious frown. 'We have come from Kush,' the tribune tried again. 'From Meroë. From King Nebmaatre. We are friends.'

He reached into the pouch at his belt, and the sudden activity had every spear in the room moving suddenly, pointing at the tribune. But in that moment, he held his hand out towards the king, proffering one of the tablets – the introductions – that had been delivered to them by the king's lackey in Meroë just before they left.

One of the warriors, lifting his spear away again, snatched the tablet from his hand and passed it to the king, who took it, turned it, opened it and looked at it for a while. Just when Faventinus had decided perhaps things were turning around, the king threw the tablet hard, the thing hitting the tribune in the arm and bouncing off, falling away into the dust. As the officers stared, the king followed this outburst by spitting at the tribune, missing by only a fraction.

'Centurion?' the senior man hissed.

Faventinus felt panic clawing at the edge of his senses now. How could they explain anything to this man when they could not understand one another? And he couldn't even say what was on the tablet, since he didn't speak the Kushite language either. In here were nine warriors, too, so their chances of fighting their way out were minuscule. All spears were now levelled at them.

Faventinus' mind whirled. Somehow the tablet had offended the king. The first thing to do, then, was to distance themselves from the tablet, and to try and make peace with the king. Knowing that any single step could bring spear-borne death, he took a breath and then two steps, bringing his heel down hard on the tablet, smashing it. He turned to the king, who was frowning deeply now.

What did he have that could mollify a king? A few coins in his purse, his dagger, his comb, a few Artemisia leaves. Not a lot. His searching hand found a bulge in one pouch, and he looked down. It was a stretch. His questing fingers pulled open the pouch, and drew from it the stone amulet of a scarab, painted rich blue and gold. The beetle amulet he'd been given by the seer all the way back in Syene. Densus had assured him that the scarab was a sacred thing there, but what it might mean here, he had no idea. Still, he held it out on a flattened palm, as gently as he could, and took another two steps towards the king, head bowed.

Again, the nearest warrior took it from him and passed it to the king, who looked at it carefully, turning it over and over, round and round. Then he smiled, brilliant white teeth between ebony lips, and nodded to Faventinus. The centurion almost exploded with relief, then tensed again, as the king turned to the tribune and gestured to him.

'Antisi?'

'Give him a gift,' hissed Faventinus.

'All the gifts are on the carts.'

'It doesn't matter if you have to pull it out of your arse, sir, find something nice and give him it, fast.'

The senior man glared at him, then huffed and began to pat his pouches and belt. He lifted out a small silver mirror and a bronze knife just two inches long, holding them aside while he ferreted around in the pouch, looking for something. The warrior stepped closer and snatched the two things from the tribune's hand.

'Wait. Not them, I was going—' he began, but it was too late. His prized possessions were in the king's hand now, and the man was staring in astonishment at the mirror. He grinned, then laughed, and showed it to the warrior, who stared in shock.

'They were a gift from my father,' the tribune grumbled.

'And now they are a gift to a king, sir.'

The natives seemed content, for all the spears had been raised, away from their threatening posture. The king began to discuss something with one of his warriors, and Faventinus took the opportunity to step closer to the tribune. 'I get the feeling we might not want to make use of the introduction tablets the king gave us. I think his falling-out with his sister has led to us being cursed.'

The tribune nodded. 'At least things seem to be going well, now.'

He had clearly spoken too soon, though, for as he fell silent, the quiet was broken by the sound of raised voices and a clash of some sort outside. All the warriors were suddenly alert again, spears ready. The king rose from his throne and pointed to the door.

'Come on, sir.'

The two Romans spilled out into the morning air once again, native warriors at their heel. The sight that greeted them was not encouraging. Seven of their eight-man escort had their swords out and were clustered together while a group of natives held them at bay at spear point. A few paces away, the other soldier was on his knees, three more spear points pressing into the flesh of his neck from different angles. They had not yet broken the skin, but one move and the man would be a corpse.

'What is the meaning of this?' demanded the tribune.

Presumably similarly summoned by the fuss, two dozen more Praetorians now emerged from the path to the river. As they arrived, led by Optio Gallo, more swords were drawn, and they began to fan out. However, more native warriors were also arriving, spears at the ready, their whole visit here balanced on the edge of a coin. Faventinus glanced back at the king, who was following the warriors out, a spear in his own hand now. He barked something at the scene, and everything became clear. As one of the warriors from the village square answered his king, he illustrated his words, pointing at the captured guardsman, then at a young woman nearby who looked horrified, and then miming grabbing his breast.

Faventinus winced. He'd seen that sort of thing coming, but he assumed his men bright enough at least not to try anything lascivious here and now. The timing couldn't have been any worse.

He didn't have to explain to the tribune, for the man had seen the gestures and was nodding to himself. The village was at an armed stand-off.

'Did you assault this girl?' the tribune demanded of the captured man, who said nothing, terrified to even open his mouth in case his throat was torn open.

'Assault, sir?' another soldier called. 'No, sir.'

'He did not?'

'Well, he only grabbed her tit, sir. He was complimenting her.'

'He may well have undone any good we have achieved here.' The tribune turned to the newly arrived soldiers. 'Back to the carts.' Then to the seven men nearby with their

swords out, 'You too. Sheathe your blades and get back to
the carts.'

No one moved, though a few swords were put away.

'Now!' the tribune barked, and as men began to back
away, he turned to the man on his knees. 'You brought this
on yourself, you fool.'

'Sir? No!' cried out one of the other soldiers.

The tribune turned to the king and nodded. The king
seemed to understand, flicked his hand with a single word,
and in front of all, the three captors drove their spear blades
into the guardsman's neck, deep enough to meet in the
middle. Then, as the man gurgled and screamed, they lifted
him off the ground on a tripod of gleaming points, where
he hung by the tattered neck for a long moment, blood
sheeting down him and pooling in the dirt below, before he
died, sagging, in agony, and they let him drop.

The men had not gone. They had stopped at the entrance
to the path, watching in horror and anger. Faventinus took
a breath. Trouble was brewing afresh here. He turned to the
men. 'Go now. Get ready to move out. We want to be out of
this man's lands within the day.'

The soldiers began to slowly make their way back to the
river, grumbling and murmuring their anger, and once they
had gone, Faventinus watched the tribune turn, bow his
head to the king, then to the offended girl, and then spit on
the body of the soldier who lay in the dirt.

The king nodded, and then pointed back towards the
river. As they left the village clearing, Faventinus cleared his
throat.

'I'm not sure that was a good idea, sir.'

'You do not think he deserved punishment?'

'Of course he did, sir, but not *execution*. And by his own, not by the natives. There could have been another way. More gifts. Any way to buy his life. Now, the men will remember all this, and it'll sit badly with them.'

'No. No more delays, no more gifts. We leave here immediately.'

26

UPPER NILE
END OF OCTOBER AD 61

Three days had passed since the incident at the village. They had continued to see naked warriors here and there on their journey, but fewer with each passing mile, and there were no more road blocks. Faventinus had related the incident to Densus, who had winced throughout, picturing the disaster unfolding.

'I didn't trust that king in Kush,' he agreed. 'I think he saw us not as neutral but as on his sister's side. I think he hoped a few hastily written tablets might get rid of us and remove us from the equation. Quick thinking with your scarab.'

Faventinus nodded. 'I'd been disappointed with a carved beetle, but in the end I was glad to have it.'

Since then, Densus had kept his eye as much on their own people as on the terrain around them. Briefly, after leaving Kush, the men had seemed happier, but this event had changed everything for the worse once more. The story had circulated among everyone in the column, and even the slaves were now glaring at the tribune with distrust and unhappiness. The atmosphere in the column had plummeted. It was not exactly mutinous, but it certainly marched forthrightly in that direction. The centurions and their juniors were going to have to do something to rein it all back in, and soon.

The tribune had held a command meeting this morning and suggested that perhaps a small ceremony with offerings to the gods might help calm matters. Fortunately, Faventinus had managed to persuade him otherwise. Densus could hardly imagine anything the tribune did as priest having a positive effect on the men, after last time. Indeed, seeing less of him, rather than more, was more likely to have a useful outcome.

This morning, also, they had apparently passed from the lands of the king they had met, for they started to see other tribesfolk in the distance, and these ones were clad in bright colours. The column halted at around noon, in a wide grassy area near the riverbank, though not too close, for they could see the shapes of crocodiles by the water. Men with pila sat guard, watching the water while food was prepared. Some sort of bean and fish stew cooked up by the men from the supplies they'd gained in Meroë turned out to be a great deal tastier than it looked. The unit's designated cooks were beginning to get the hang of these southern herbs and spices at last.

'I can't think of anything,' Faventinus sighed, spooning stew, the two centurions eating a little away from the men.

'We could throw the tribune to the crocodiles,' Densus snorted. '*That* would cheer everyone up.'

'For fuck's sake, Sempronius, don't even joke about that.

If comments like that get back to him, you could be beaten to death for it.'

'I'm touched by your concern,' Densus grinned.

'Fuck that. I just don't want to be left to deal with him on my own.'

'None of the traditional things will work,' Densus said. 'Extra rations, pay bonuses, promotions, and the like. None of that really means much out here, where rations rely on what we can get, promotions are pointless, and there's nothing to spend money on anyway. Only some sort of great gesture is going to bring the men back on-side. I just don't know what.'

Faventinus nodded his agreement, and the two men went back to their food.

Densus chewed thoughtfully, then looked up. For a moment, he didn't realise what he was seeing over his friend's shoulder, then it moved and he focused in an instant.

'To arms,' he bellowed as he dropped the half-eaten meal and rose, drawing his own sword. Faventinus, caught by surprise but quick to react, followed suit.

The figure Densus had caught sight of in the undergrowth at the edge of the clearing had now fully emerged into the open, two more appearing behind him. He was of a very dark skin, black hair braided into tight locks that were kept tight to his head, jammed beneath a headdress of feathers, but surprisingly little of his black flesh was on show. He wore a kilt of bright blue and red materials, but much of his flesh was painted a sort of pottery orange-red, possibly with some variety of mud or clay, and the painting was fashioned into designs, including a sort of skull motif over the face.

The first man carried a short spear with a long, narrow head, one of the men behind him similarly armed, while the third had a long wooden club with a wicked-looking knobbly end.

The three men pulled close together at the sight of the Romans, and now soldiers all across the camp were reaching for swords and hurrying over. Two more red-painted natives joined the three already visible, and they had all taken up a warlike stance.

Suddenly, the tribune was there, hurrying up to the centurions as the men converged.

'What happened?'

'Native warriors, sir,' Densus replied, pointing at the five painted men.

'Did they attack you?'

'Not yet.'

The tribune made exasperated noises and then turned, waving his hands at the soldiers hurrying over. 'Stand down. Stand down, I say.' Then, back to the centurions. 'We need to try peaceful relations with these people.'

'Easy for you to say, sir, when they didn't jump you with spears during dinner.'

'Watch that tongue, Centurion.'

Densus fought the urge to say something acidic, then stood and watched, as the tribune approached the tribesmen with both hands empty and raised.

'Peace,' he said, calmly.

There was a pause, and then the natives' weapons were lowered a little. Not gone, but less threatening, at least. A sixth man appeared then from the undergrowth, and his social superiority over the others was displayed in his rich skirt, extraordinarily ornate feather headdress, and the fact that they all made way for him.

'Oza nani?' the man asked in an imperious tone, pointing at them.

The tribune bowed. 'I am Lucius Curtius Lupus, a tribune in the Praetorian Guard of the emperor of Rome, the blessed and divine Nero.' He straightened, pointed back the way they had come, then made walking motions with his fingers, and pointed on south, along the river. He gave the native an easy smile and bowed again, briefly.

The noble warrior looked them up and down for a few moments. Then he frowned, rolled his shoulders, and spoke. 'Tolukaka nkosi. Omoni nkosi?'

'Any ideas?' the tribune called across to the others.

'Not a clue.'

The native frowned. 'Tolukaka nkosi,' he repeated, but this time mimed stalking through the undergrowth with his spear raised.

'You're hunting?' The tribune mimed hunting, Roman style, and the native frowned for a moment, but then nodded. 'Nkosi,' he said again. He dropped to all fours and padded around, then rose and bared his teeth, pointing at them.

'Whatever they're hunting, I don't think it's crocodiles or hippos,' Faventinus said.

'At least it doesn't appear to be us,' Densus added.

'A lion,' the tribune said. 'I think they are hunting a lion. I think they want to know if we've seen it.' He shook his head and tried 'No nkosi. No.'

The native sighed and sagged a little, seemingly confirming they were on the right track.

'We help?' the tribune said.

'Nini?' the native asked, brow furrowed in confusion.

The tribune smiled. 'Help,' he said again, miming stalking through the undergrowth with weapon raised, pointing at himself and then the man.

This seemed to break the language barrier and the native gave a cautious smile and nodded.

'Sir,' Densus said, 'is this a good idea?'

'We want to be on good terms with the natives this time. It is but a hunt. I have hunted many times. Once even with the divine Claudius.'

'Not a lion, though, sir. They're fucking big and dangerous. The bestiarii in the arena are trained for months to hunt the bastards, and still more often than not the lion wins.'

'Point crudely made, Centurion, but taken nonetheless. Bring me a tent party of men. We will help this chieftain hunt his lion.'

Densus waited until he had turned away from his commander to roll his eyes. Great. 'Picens, bring your lads up. The tribune's going hunting and he wants some lads to help.' He was not hugely encouraged by the look the soldiers gave him as they wandered over, arming up, so he waited until the tribune was busy, and pulled the leader aside. 'Go steady, and go careful. Don't put yourself in danger, but try to stop the silly old sod getting himself killed.' Again, the look he got alongside the nodded reply suggested that the men might come down on the side of the lion if it came to a choice. 'Just bear in mind the trouble we could all face if we get back to Rome without the tribune.'

Another nod, and the man scuttled off before Densus could get a good look at his expression.

'Oh bollocks,' he sighed to himself, and gestured to Faventinus. 'Look after the lads. I think I'll go look after the tribune.'

His fellow centurion gave him a wry smile and then wandered back through the camp. The tribune had gone for a moment, and now came back with his horse, gripping a pilum taken from one of the guardsmen. He was just pulling himself up into the saddle when the native spoke urgently.

'Te!' he called. 'Te. Mpunda moko te.' He pointed at the horse and waved his hands, shaking his head, then mimed stalking on foot once more.

The tribune chewed his lip in thought for a moment, then dismounted and wandered over, joining the men assigned to go with him. He looked at Densus for a moment, noting the man's presence but not commenting, then cleared his throat. 'Very well, men. It would appear that we are about to hunt a lion. I have only two rules for you. Firstly, any man who even accidentally harms one of the natives will answer to me. Secondly, you will help and support, but this man is a king to his people, I think. He must be the one to kill the lion. If any of you beat him to it, I might let him kill you instead. Understood?'

Densus noted once again the less than supportive looks the men threw at the officer, but they saluted nonetheless. The centurion decided that he might just need to keep an eye on Curtius Lupus and make sure a Roman pilum didn't end up in him instead.

A few moments later, the natives gestured for the Romans to join them and pushed back into the undergrowth. With the tribune and the other eight men, Densus followed. They swiftly found themselves on a narrow trail between greenery, which soon opened out into a wide, gently sloping meadow of chest-deep grass, dotted with trees and patches of thicker undergrowth.

Now that the ground was clearer, the leader of the natives gave a series of staccato commands, and his five warriors moved off ahead. The leader then dropped to a crouch and moved from one patch of undergrowth to the other, almost hidden in the deep grass. Densus watched, fascinated, as the other natives began to make plaintive calls, gently rapping their spears or clubs with their free hands.

'Fuck me, they're trying to lure the thing out.'

'Centurion?'

'The warriors aren't here to hunt the lion, sir. They're here to flush it out so that their chief can attack it alone. Holy fucking Minerva, but the man's mad.' He turned to the tribune, wincing. 'I think you offered to hunt the thing with him alone, sir. Me and the others are like those men down there. We're supposed to flush the lion out and drive it to you.'

He was gratified to see the tribune's face falter for a moment, a look of panic crossing it before being forced down. 'If the gods will us on, they will protect us,' he said, taking two steps towards the chief and dropping to a crouch. 'You know what to do, then.'

Densus nodded. Watching the tribune move off with his pilum, nearly disappearing into the grass, he turned to the others. 'Same as the natives. We move out and flush the bugger out.'

'And what do we do when we find it?' one of the lads asked.

This was a good question. Densus hadn't yet thought

of that. 'Drop and hide. Let the tribune and the chieftain attract its attention then.'

It seemed a sensible answer.

He moved off with his men, taking an arc not covered by the five native warriors, and lifted his sword. As they closed on the scrub and knots of trees, he started slapping the flat of his blade with his hand, and doing his best to mimic the noises the natives were making, off across the flat land, almost out of sight. His men followed suit with pila and swords. Three of them had thought to bring shields, but the others hadn't. That was the problem with the currently rather lax arms and armour rules on the journey: there was no automatic standard.

For the first half hour, Densus was experiencing the strangest mix of being tense, expecting to come across the beast at any moment, and yet bored with the constant nothing. They moved in various directions, and the men had fanned out such that they were just within sight of one another, heads and chests protruding from the high grass, Densus at one end so that he could make sure he could still see the two main hunters and some of the native bait.

When the lion came, it was a shock.

He had no idea they had found it until there was a crunch and a scream, and the furthest of his men disappeared downwards into the grass. The next two men started howling in panic and ran towards Densus, arms in the air. He tried to wave them to silence, and when he finally succeeded, wished he hadn't for he could just hear the crunching and tearing noises as the unseen lion tore one of his guardsmen apart.

'You've found it?' came the very distant call of the

tribune, and Densus bit down on the heavily sarcastic reply that leapt to mind. He had his own troubles. Even as the crunching and tearing went on, there was a soul-trembling roar, and another man disappeared with a scream.

Two of the bastards!

Then the other six of his men were running past him, shouting and screaming, hurtling back in the direction of the tribune. A moment later, Densus was with them. It occurred to him that it might have been more noble to have stood his ground and tried to rally the men, but standing alone near two lions while the others ran away did not sound appealing. In a heartbeat he was passing the terrified men. He could see the tribune, now, up the gentle rise.

'That's it,' the man shouted, 'bring it to me.'

'I'll fucking bring it to you, alright,' Densus growled under his breath as he ran.

'Mibale kati na bango,' shouted the native chief near the tribune, pointing out at two positions behind Densus.

'*Two* of them?' the tribune bellowed, and his voice cracked a little with fear.

Densus turned as he ran, and wished he hadn't. The grass was parting slightly not a long way behind them, in a similar manner to the waters of the Nile when a just-submerged crocodile approached. The analogy did not improve matters.

'Run,' he cried as he bore down on the tribune. A scream behind him told him he'd lost another man, but he didn't stop to look. With the rest still running, they converged on the two nobles atop the slope. The rest of the natives were coming now, too, racing back to their master.

The other lion appeared as suddenly as the first, and

this time Densus saw it. An immense creature of dusty brown suddenly leapt from the grass and one of the natives vanished beneath it with a scream.

'Now,' Densus called. 'Now. You know where it is!'

The native chieftain and the tribune both hurtled off towards where the latest attack had taken place, and Densus turned, knowing there was a second lion out there, still. His other five men were coming to a halt now, white-faced and wide-eyed, weapons held tight in their grip as they looked this way and that, trying to spot the danger.

Densus saw it coming with just sufficient time to leap. The brown shape was suddenly springing from the long grass directly at him and the soldier by his side. He yelled a warning as he dropped to his left, but it had not been fast enough. The lion slammed into the other man and drove him to the ground, massive jaws closing on his neck. There were a series of crunches and gurgling screams that the centurion knew he would remember in the dead of night for the rest of his life, and the man was done for.

'Kill it,' he bellowed. 'Kill it now!'

And with that, he was up and leaping. It was, he would later admit, the most idiotic thing he had ever done in his life. As the lion devoured the screaming Praetorian beneath it, Densus was suddenly landing in turn on the lion's back, astride the damn thing, gladius in one hand, dagger in the other, both rising and falling, stabbing and chopping, stabbing and chopping, trying to finish the thing.

But the lion was made of sterner stuff, and rose with a furious roar, leaping off the bag of bones and meat it had been enjoying. As it reared up, Densus found himself thrown backwards into the grass, winded. Two more men were there now, stabbing the monster, hacking and screaming, bellowing and chopping.

One was knocked aside with the swipe of a massive paw, but by then the other two were there, adding their own blades to the desperate fight. Densus clambered to his feet, knowing there were bruises and pulled muscles there that would trouble him for a week or so. Then he was in the fight again, as the lion, now mortally wounded, its hide little more than a network of deep cuts and stab wounds, fought to take them with it. It writhed and fought back even as they all took part now, five of them stabbing and chopping, even the man who'd been swatted aside, nursing a broken and shredded arm.

By the time it was over, Densus knew he'd lost another. One of the men had taken two swipes to the belly and had dropped his sword in order to use both hands in an attempt to hold in the coils of intestine that were constantly trying to slide free through the vicious rents in his flesh. Densus walked wearily round behind the man, and delivered him a mercy blow, putting him out of misery and agony. He stood, then, over the body of the lion, trembling and panting, three of his eight men still with him, one carefully cradling his broken arm.

'*What* a hunt!' shouted the tribune, suddenly hoving into view with a wide grin.

Never in his life had Densus been closer to killing a man with his bare hands. He held in his fury at the blasé comment and the ridiculousness of this heavy loss. The feathered chieftain was coming along behind the tribune, and at least *that* man's face bore a more solemn expression, as the three remaining native warriors joined him.

'It appears that we are in the favour of the local king,' the tribune said, rolling his shoulder and wincing at some unseen pain.

'I hope it was worth it,' Densus replied, looking down at the beast. Five men. *Five men* just to win some goodwill they might not even need.

The tribune's popularity was hardly going to rise when the tale was told repeatedly back at the camp.

'I hope it was worth it.'

27

UPPER NILE
END OF OCTOBER AD 61

The natives had gone. There had been a brief exchange between them and the tribune, in which they had, despite the difficulty of translation, seemed to greet the Romans into their lands, and it seemed likely the column would now travel through the world of these red-painted warriors without trouble.

But then the Romans had been left to their own devices. The surviving natives had borne their dead aloft, two to each body, the leader taking part. They had adopted a strange, clearly ritual, walk, and taken their dead back to their own homes.

That had left the Romans. The tribune had been almost euphoric, pleased with his success at diplomacy and with the killing of not one, but two lions.

The men had been less effusive, but now was not the time to argue. The soldiers had five compatriots to bury, after all. Even though they were from one or the other of the two centuries on the mission, the bond between them had become solid enough over the past few months that such things as individual century pride was more or less a thing of the past, and all the guardsmen took the losses equally personally.

There had been a discussion over whether the use of funeral pyres to render the bodies down to ash would be the best method of burial. That was what the men overwhelmingly, and quite vocally, favoured. They had plenty of pots they could use in the carts, after all. The tribune, in his latest bid to become the least popular Roman since Cato the Censor, had refused this, however. Cremation would take ten times as long as inhumation, and would send up columns of smoke visible for many miles. Were the men so sure of the new alliance with the red-painted men that they wanted to risk drawing all life for ten miles to their location?

It was not popular, but even Faventinus had to privately admit that there was a certain logic in the tribune's decision. If it had been him, though, he'd have risked it, in order to give the men something they wanted, to try and de-escalate the growing rift between the Praetorians and their commander.

It was not to be. At the tribune's order, they dug five graves on the hillside overlooking the site of the fight where they had died. While the work was carried out, Densus and a tent party of his men disappeared for a while, which intrigued Faventinus, but he was kept busy with the work.

While the soldiers dug, their task difficult with the hard, stony ground, the capsarii from the two centuries worked with assistants, preparing the bodies. They were washed with water from the river, most of the blood having drained now anyway, through their horrific wounds. Spare tunics and other minor apparel were produced from the carts, and the bodies re-dressed without the bloody rends. Their eyes were closed, their hair combed, and finally they were wrapped in their cloaks like shrouds. As they worked, the three surviving men from their tent party went through the dead men's possessions, marking some to be placed in storage for return to their families, some to be buried alongside the men, and others for the soldiers who knew the dead to keep as mementoes.

All tasks complete, the entire column gathered, and such was the solemnity of the occasion and the growing fraternity of men in danger that no one even complained about the slaves attending the funeral alongside the soldiers.

The bodies were brought in one at a time by their friends, and lowered with care into the holes. The two unit musicians had forsaken their great military horns for the occasion, Venator playing a quiet, sad melody on a simple pipe while Genialis kept up a slow, stately rhythm on a small drum. Other than the music, the breeze rustling the leaves, and the distant babble of the river, there was silence as the five men lay in their graves, the others looking on with reverence.

What Densus had been up to was made clear, then, as the small group of soldiers reappeared at a slow march, in time with the drum beats, bearing a stone torn from the ground perhaps two feet across and freshly carved with a crude inscription commemorating the struggle, and bearing the names of the dead. The monument was placed on the highest point of ground behind the graves, a small hollow scraped out with hands to rest the stone's base in.

It was a relatively pitiful memorial for five men, but Faventinus had to remind himself that it was considerably more than they had managed for those men eaten by hippos and crocodiles, or that soldier whose head had been taken at the deserted fort. At least these men had had a burial, and bore a marker.

As the stone was settled, and the men returned to their ranks and pulled their cloaks up over their heads in respect, Faventinus glanced at Densus. In the absence of Urbicus, the entire unit was looking at the dead men's centurion to give a short eulogy. Which is why, when Tribune Curtius Lupus pulled his own cloak over his head and stepped up beside the memorial, the centurion winced and held his breath. The tribune perhaps thought that he could appeal to the men through the camaraderie of loss, bring the men back to him by showing his respect for their peers.

No, Faventinus decided. The tribune was clearly still largely unaware of the depth of feeling against him among the men, and that was a subject the two centurions were going to have to bring up soon. So, in fact, the man just thought he was doing the appropriate thing. Faventinus looked out across the gathered ranks, packed into tight rows and columns before the graves, and one look at the assembled faces told him that anything the tribune said would be wrong. The best thing he could do right now was to step down and be silent. But there was no way to issue him a warning. It was too late.

'In the sight of Venus Libitina, and of Mercury, bearer of the dead, and of Mars, lord of combat and war—'

The next words were lost. Somewhere in the press of men, unseen, several bronze sistrums had begun to rattle furiously.

The tribune frowned, looking out over the gathered men,

then raised his voice a little. 'In the name of Rome, of the emperor—'

But the shaking became more furious, more and more rattles joining in, until it was almost deafening. Faventinus closed his eyes. He knew what was coming, and the very last thing he needed now was to be the man standing between the tribune and the soldiers, but that was clearly his fate.

'Belay that rattle,' he bellowed across the men, so loud that his voice cracked with the effort.

He was not entirely sure it had been enough to be heard, but even if it was, it made no difference. The men had always liked Faventinus. He'd one of the best reputations with the men among the Praetorian centurionate, and he knew Densus to be well-liked too. It took a lot to make a guardsman disobey an officer, particularly one they liked. Such was the negative feeling towards the tribune right now.

Trouble lay ahead, for all of them.

The tribune tried once more to speak over the top of the noise, but this time he couldn't even make one word heard. Faventinus could see the warning signs. The man had gone almost puce, trembling, veins in his temple thumping proud, hands repeatedly balling into fists. Densus had also seen, and hurried over to the senior officer, shouting something at him, the words lost beneath the deafening metallic rattle. Faventinus was rooted to the spot, uncertain what to do. The men were not listening to their officers, and until that rattling stopped, he was unlikely to be heard. He saw the tribune reply angrily to Densus, following which the centurion actually reached out and gripped his commander's bicep as he shouted something desperate. Whatever the exchange was, it was unheard of for a centurion to lay a hand on a senior officer. He watched the tribune tear himself free of Densus' grip, and actually push him aside as he took two steps towards the tightly packed lines of men.

The rattling was coming from somewhere in the middle, and the tribune was bellowing at them, face almost purple. He grabbed two soldiers in the front line and tried to pull them apart, to see between them into the press, but the two men actually closed ranks, keeping him out.

Never had Faventinus seen a unit closer to open mutiny.

He had to do something.

Bracing himself, taking a breath in preparation for a move that could end his career, he strode across the ground to the tribune, and pulled him back from the men. The officer turned, eyes bulging, realised who it was that had so roughly manhandled him, and pulled back his hand, delivering a ringing slap around Faventinus' face.

The centurion's head snapped painfully to the side, but the act had done what was needed.

The rattling had stopped.

Every pair of eyes across the funeral audience was on Faventinus, eyes wide, breath held.

The tribune stared at the centurion, then brought his hand round and stared at that as though it had been under the control of someone else.

'I...' the man said, then faltered into silence.

Faventinus, cheek pulsing with pain, leaned a little closer and hissed something quiet enough not to reach the lines of soldiers only a few paces away. 'Sir, the men are ready to rebel. Let me handle this.'

The tribune, still visibly stunned, looked at his hand again, then at Faventinus, then nodded sharply. He tried to say something, though it came out as little more than a croak. He tried again, this time finding his voice.

'Deal with it, Centurion. I want the men disciplined for this. And when you find the ringleaders, I want them crucified.'

With that, the officer threw a furious glare at the gathered ranks, turned and marched away. Faventinus turned to his fellow centurion, who was staring at him in shock. He walked over to Densus. 'Follow him. Calm him. Make sure he stays out of earshot.'

Densus nodded, eyes still wide, turned and followed the retreating shape of the tribune. Faventinus waited until the pair were well out of sight, on their way back to the camp nearer the river, then waited a while longer, to be sure.

The gathered ranks were silent. They looked at him, to a man, still stunned by what he'd done. They had defied a senior officer, an act that carried extreme punishment, but Faventinus had actually manhandled him, which was unthinkable.

'Alright. Who's responsible for that little display?' It was not spoken with an underlying threat, but with a sort of resigned weariness. It didn't entirely surprise him when the entire unit took a step forward. 'So that's how it is. Nice to see such unity and fraternity in the Guard.'

He scratched his head, then walked around the still-open graves and sank onto the new stone monument, resting his elbows on his knees.

'I've known most of you for the majority of your careers. Some of you joined under me. And those I don't know of old, I've known well these past few months. And *you* know *me*. And you know Sempronius Densus. If any man has the intention of standing against his centurion, raise your hand now.'

It was a risk, and he knew it, even in the short silence that followed. All it would take was for one man to raise a hand, and they would go up in a wave. And if that happened, then they had lost control of the unit for good. To his immense relief not one hand shot up.

'Good. Because you know that Densus and I are *your* centurions. *Yours.* We've spent every day on this ridiculous journey doing everything we can to keep you all alive, and as comfortable as we can manage. And we'll keep doing that.'

He sighed deeply and scrubbed his curly hair, which really needed a cut. 'I know. I really do. We *both* know. The man is a knob of the highest order.'

A small ripple of chuckles was audible somewhere in the press. Silently, Faventinus thanked the gods for the gift of oratory and negotiation that came with the mercantile success of his family. 'I doubt that without our help he would find the right opening in his underwear.' Another chuckle. He straightened, and his voice took on a serious tone. 'But he is also a tribune in the Praetorian Guard. Above him come only the Praetorian prefects and then the emperor. Let that sink in for a moment. In the whole empire, as far as we are concerned, there are only three people with more authority than Curtius Lupus, and one of those is a god.'

The silence then was uncomfortable. In all their time in Aegyptus, in Kush, in Aethiopia, the rules had become somewhat relaxed, and they had lost a little of the formality of the Guard back in Rome, much more resembling a legion on hard campaign. Harking back to their true origin was something rare now.

'Just like Densus and me, you all took an oath when you joined up. Do you all remember that oath? You took it to three things. To Rome, to the Emperor, and to the Eagle. Well, Curtius Lupus represents all those things. He is the voice of the emperor out here, he is the most senior man for thousands of miles, so the eagle is his to bear, and he represents Rome. I, for one, am no oath-breaker. *Nothing* will make me deny that oath I took in the sight of the gods, with my hand on the altar of Apollo. If there are oath-breakers among you, it saddens me, and it cheapens the Guard, but I cannot say I don't understand.'

Now he stood. 'So, I give you this choice. You stop this disobedience, and act like soldiers. You hold to your oaths and respect the chain of command, no matter how stupid the links in the chain might seem. You do as we say and let us try and get you back home, alive and victorious. Or you choose to break your oath. If you choose to walk away you may do that now, and until the sun next rises. You will be allowed to take three days' food and water, enough to see you back to our naked king friend, and you will have to barter and beg your way from there. *After* sunrise, any man who chooses to leave will be dealt with as a deserter.'

There was a tense silence again.

'Any man who walks away, walks away from his rank, his place in the Guard, his pension, and any hope of peaceful life in Rome. You know how Rome looks on military deserters. If you choose to leave, and you make it as far as civilisation, my advice is to find a quiet corner of the empire and live your life there, without making waves.'

Still, that silence remained.

'And one more thing: the sistrums end now. We've been letting you all get away with it, out of respect of the memory of poor, idiotic Urbicus. No more. Get rid of the things tonight. From sunrise tomorrow, any man I find shaking one will be flogged.' He reached down, pulling his vine stick of office from his belt and smacking it against the stone, which had every man's head jerk back straight, eyes on him. 'Decide tonight. You're either a fugitive, or a member of the *Praetorian fucking Guard*!'

With that, he turned and walked away, pointing at the graves.

'And bury those poor bastards before you decide.'

He was halfway back to the path that led to the river when Gallo, his optio, caught up with him.

'Jove, Minerva and Hades' balls, that was brave, sir. Well fucking done.'

Faventinus gave him a shaky smile. 'I am trembling like a leaf, mate. I need a drink. Oh, and Minerva doesn't *have* balls.'

'This one does, sir. I will be very surprised if even one man walks away,' Gallo said. 'But I think you've only bought time. Unless the tribune changes completely, this won't be the last trouble.'

Faventinus sighed. 'I know. I appealed to their duty, and it worked, but it won't work twice. We're just going to have to do what we can and pray things work out.'

'Never mind,' Gallo grinned. 'Maybe the source of the river is right around the corner.'

28

UPPER NILE

TWO DAYS AFTER THE KALENDS OF NOVEMBER AD 61

Densus slapped his neck with his palm, lifted his hand, examined the flattened bug on it, then wiped it on the log on which he sat. 'It is my fear that the further south we go, the hotter and wetter it gets and the more bugs there are. If it keeps increasing at the rate it's going, within two hundred miles we'll have to use an axe to cut our way through the bugs, though it won't matter, because we'll all be underwater anyway, drowning in our own sweat.'

Faventinus laughed. 'I've got two new bites today, in just the right shape to add the Aventine and the Palatine to the red lumps on my leg. I only need the Viminal and Quirinal now to collect the set.'

'I wish I was so perky about it. Every time I find a new one, I expect to come down with fever.'

His fellow centurion could only nod at this.

Three days had passed since the funeral of the lions'

victims, and each day had been a little less comfortable than the last. 'Come on. Let's do the duty,' Densus sighed, rising.

A tour of the camp had become a thing they did either individually, or together, at least every couple of hours, now. Things had settled after his friend's little speech, and miraculously, no one had left that night. Perhaps even more miraculously, they had found a small pile of sistrum rattles near the burial site. But it was, as Gallo had noted, far from over. There was a tangible undercurrent of discontent. Men talked quietly, then stopped when an officer came near them. The centurions had taken to walking about the camp, gauging the situation and, to some extent, showing themselves to still be 'one of the lads'.

On this particular occasion, however, they had an extra visit to make. One of the slaves had dropped across with a message from the two capsarii, asking them to visit the 'hospital'. Of course, it wasn't really a hospital. As the two centurions passed outside the main camp, leaving behind the flickering firelight and the subdued conversation of the men, they approached the medical section.

Due to the potential of the little-understood illness to be spread among the men, those who were suffering were not only being kept separately during travel, but were quartered in their own little camp at night, as well.

Two tents stood close together, both separated from the camp by some twenty paces. Two slaves – drawn from the group of six that had been assigned to the two medics – sat on watch, eyes on the surrounding landscape.

As the centurions approached the small sub-camp, their arrival coincided with one of the capsarii stepping out of a tent and coming over to wash his hands in a bucket of water covered with a scarf to prevent bugs landing in it. The combat medic looked up.

'Ah, sirs. Thank you for coming.'

'Good news, I hope?'

'Good and bad in equal quantities, I'm afraid. I'll give you the good first. Come with me.'

Shaking the excess water from his hands, the medic turned and made for one of the tents. Densus and Faventinus followed, making their way inside, ducking beneath the flap. The room smelled of sweat, warm moisture, and a hint of vomit, as well as a number of acrid tinctures that stood open on a chest. The room held four sleeping pallets, each with an occupant. Densus glanced across the men, and recognised them, two from his unit, two from the other century, but all familiar faces after many days of travelling as sick men. To him, they looked the same as they had before, waxy and faintly grey.

'Tell me.'

'Believe it or not, this is the good news,' the man said. 'As you know, we really don't understand the swamp fever, but we're starting to recognise early signs, various stages, and more. So...' he said, crossing to the two men at the left side. 'These are the men who we think picked up the illness at Thebes, who were already suffering by the time we entered Kush. I reckon they've been running this illness for maybe a month and a half now. But I can tell you this, and hopefully it will make you smile. They're getting better, and rapidly.'

'Really? They look half-dead.'

The capsarius narrowed his eyes. 'I'd take it as a favour if you kept sentiments like that away from my patients, sir. Words can heal or hurt, too.'

'Sorry,' Densus sighed. 'You say they're well?'

'Not too far off. Two days ago, I thought I'd noticed their symptoms fading. I brought Titus in to check, and he concurs. We've watched them ever since, and they are most definitely improving. The reason they look so drained and ill now is that we had them doing a little exercise today. First time in a month they could even have hoped to do a push-up. Now that they're improving, we need to give them regular exercise and an increased food ration, trying to bring them sufficiently up to strength to rejoin the unit properly.'

'And then they'll be well? No relapses?'

The man shook his head. 'Some of the Greek physicians of note are of the firm belief that once a man recovers from such an illness, his resistance to a second infection is greatly increased, and I have noted similar in my time. I think that once these two men are hale and back with the unit, they will end up being the healthiest men here.'

'Gods, but that *is* good news,' Faventinus breathed.

'And further to that,' the medic added, turning and gesturing to the other side of the room, and its two occupants, 'I reckon these two have been suffering for half a month. But already, their descent into the many associated symptoms seems to have halted. In short, they are far from well, but they do not appear to be getting any worse, which means they are not suffering as badly as the last ones. We may find that in eight or ten days these two also will be at a place where we can begin building up their strength once more.'

'So we're looking at the end of it? Maybe the Artemisia leaves are the cure the man said they would be.'

The medic nodded but looked uneasy. 'I would certainly say the Artemisia has helped keep the worst at bay, and has probably saved countless other men from coming down with the illness. I am all for the continued consumption of Artemisia leaves, though I also note that we are starting to run a little short of them.'

'Well maybe we're away from where you catch this fever now?'

'That is a possibility. But sadly, that is where the *bad* news comes in.'

A lump arose in Densus' throat. 'Uh oh.'

'Quite. Follow.' With that, the capsarius led them out of the tent and across the small encampment to the other identical shelter. The moment the flap opened, Densus noticed the difference, both he and Faventinus reaching up to cover their mouths and noses. The smell was appalling.

'You see?'

The medic nodded a greeting to his fellow capsarius who was working in there, decanting some liquid from one phial to another, then gestured to a man lying on a pallet.

'All this smell is coming from *him*?' Densus said.

'It is. He started showing signs of the swamp fever last night, and we removed him from the main body of men. However, over today and this evening, he has become worse and worse. His symptoms are similar, but much more pronounced, and there are other symptoms, too.'

'What are you saying?'

The medic straightened. 'I'm saying that we have a second illness here. We may have left behind the source of the swamp fever the men already had, perhaps, contracted at the cataracts, where there is lush vegetation and eddying water. But we have moved into the world of a new disease. This one is faster acting, more virulent, and evidence thus far suggests that chewing Artemisia does nothing to prevent it. We've tried everything we have with us, and he's still getting worse.'

The man gestured back to the tent door, and they emerged into the open, breathing the night air deeply and with relief. The capsarius rolled his shoulders. 'This might be just the start. At the moment, we have one sick man, but only the gods know how many others might have it. We'd got to the point where we could identify the warning signs of the swamp fever, but this comes on much faster, and separating out the men will be more difficult. As of this moment, that man is in isolation. I will be dealing with all medical matters, and no one goes in or out of that tent, other than Titus or the man or men he's treating.'

'Shit.'

'Exactly. So I need you and the other officers to keep a close eye on the men. I'll try, but there's only one of me. Any remote sign of illness of any sort, short of arse grapes, send them to me, and I'll check them over. We need to jump on any new cases the moment we find them. In the meantime, we'll start playing around with mixing things up and see if we can brew something that makes a difference.'

'Should we put out an announcement?' Faventinus mused. 'Make sure the lads are watching each other?'

Densus shook his head. 'No. In addition to them already being close enough to the edge over the tribune, if you tell them about this, they'll start seeing the signs of it everywhere, even when it's not real. You know what hypochondriacs soldiers can be.'

Nodding their thanks to the medics, the two centurions strode back towards the camp. 'I know what Urbicus would say,' Densus sighed.

'Oh?'

'That this new plague was sent by the gods.'

Faventinus sagged. 'And that means that the moment all his little disciples hear about it, they'll think exactly the same. We'll have to keep this under wraps as long as possible.'

'Shouldn't be too hard. The sick travel separately anyway. Come on. Let's tour.'

The two men moved into the camp, separating, taking different routes in an effort to come into contact with more of the men. Densus found himself looking into the face of every man he came near, not just trying to judge his mood, but also his wellbeing, his general state of health. At one of the camp fires, he found three men busily repainting their shields, and approached, dropping to a crouch.

The shields, unchanged since leaving Rome, were the standard design of Praetorian infantry, a long oval with bronze edges and boss, painted blue, decorated with gold lightning bolts of Jupiter and wings of Mercury, white stars and crescent moons. The blue was looking sun-bleached on every shield by now, and the gold was flaking in places. There was little the men could do about that, but they were replacing the white, carefully going over the lines with small brushes. It was a heartening sight after recent events, and suggested that perhaps Faventinus' plea to their oaths had taken hold.

'Where did you find white paint out here?'

One of the men shrugged. 'Terentius bought it back in Syene. Blue and yellow, too. They make them for the wall paintings they do. He used all the blue and yellow on his own tent party's shields, but white's cheaper and he had some spare.'

Densus nodded, smiling. It was nice to see something so normal… so military. He moved around, exchanging in small talk with the men, admiring their handiwork and steady grips. It was only as he was looking at the last of the three that he noticed a design on the inside of the shield. That in itself was not uncommon. A soldier would usually paint their name in the shield to prevent mixing them up, and would often adorn that with religious symbols, or even pictures of phalluses or rude comments. This was different, though. A rather expertly done cartoon showed a man lying on a couch with a sword hanging, point first, above him, a thin white line to the top of the shield suggesting the sword hanging by a single hair.

'What is this?' he demanded.

The soldier tried to look innocent, but the guilt that quickly flashed across his face first made a mockery of what followed. 'It's Damocles, sir, and the sword hanging over him.'

'Does Damocles look familiar to you?'

'I wouldn't know, sir. I've never met him.'

'Don't get smart with me, Bibulus. That's a picture of the tribune. Very clever. Very smart. Get rid of it now. If word of that gets back to the tribune, you'll be beaten.'

'Sir, it's—'

'I know, Damocles. I'm not stupid, man. You are, though, if you think you can get away with that. Clean it off.'

As he stood and strolled off to find something else to do, he sighed. Clearly suppressing the men's rebellious tendencies had only made them emerge in different, more inventive, ways. He just hoped it would go no further than painted slogans and pictures.

29

UPPER NILE

IDES OF NOVEMBER AD 61

'A market?' Faventinus frowned at the scout.

'Certainly seems to be, sir. It's like a village made of tents. Quite a big one, on a road of sorts, and with a bunch of local trails leading to it. We skirted round it and looked from a distance, but there seem to be stalls and boxes of food at all the tents, and animals in pens, and all sorts.'

'Are they locals, you think? Or traders from afar? Kushites, maybe?'

The soldier shook his head. 'They're all very dark skinned, and I haven't seen wagons, just small hand carts or donkeys with baskets over their backs. There might be other encampments nearby though, sir. We thought it best to report back before checking further.'

Faventinus nodded. 'Well, well. A market. And we were starting to look low on a few essentials. I wonder if they accept actual coins out here, or whether it's all done with barter. I suppose we'd better find out.'

He turned and waved to Densus, and saw past him. To

his dismay, the tribune was riding forward from where he'd been checking on his own cart. He braced himself. No conversation with the senior man was easy these days. Fortunately, Densus got to him first.

'The scouts have found a native market. Looks like only locals, but they said there's a sort of road, so there might be a few foreigners there too. We need a number of supplies, and they might have Artemisia.'

Densus nodded at that. The bitter leaf was in extreme demand these days. With supplies now short, the daily consumption to help build a resistance had dropped such that a single leaf was being shared between four men, not that it was looked on as a cure any more anyway. Five men were now down with that second, more virulent, strain of the illness, and the Artemisia seemed to have little, if any, effect on them. Still, it was better to at least try.

'We need to check it out, make our deals, and if all is safe, it might do morale good to let the men have a wander in the market.'

Densus agreed to that with a hearty nod, and the two men waited for the tribune to rein his horse in. 'What is it?' the man demanded.

Faventinus explained what lay ahead, the scout having returned to his duties. The senior officer's nose wrinkled. 'You have my authority to deal with all resupply. I see no reason for my presence.'

The centurion tried to hide his relief well, and moments later the tribune was riding off again. Gesturing for a contubernium of men to follow, the centurion turned and strode off ahead, taking the opportunity, away from the bulk of the men, to raise his arms and let the warm, sweat-drenched armpits of his tunic unstick from his flesh. Since the funeral, even he and Densus had forgone the wearing of armour. It simply was not practical in this sticky heat. Indeed, he was fast approaching the moment he might exchange his thicker military tunic for a light, airy one of local manufacture. He was trying to hold off from going too native, but practicality was definitely driving him in that direction.

The scouts were still circling ahead, but Faventinus felt himself relaxing a little as they walked on, for the riders looked calm and unhurried, and their weapons were still sheathed, clearly having encountered nothing that concerned them.

They made their way along the track, between two stands of acacia trees, their umbrella-like canopies allowing room for shrubbery and undergrowth beneath, and as the men emerged into the open, Faventinus whistled through his teeth.

The market was huge.

A clearing large enough to race chariots around led up from the bank of the river, paths and tracks leading off in many directions, and the place was home to enough tents to create a network of streets, each of the shelters formed by what looked to be rugs draped over simple wooden frames, the interiors cast into deep shade. The noise was interesting, without the yelling and din of a Roman market, for negotiations at the many stalls seemed to be performed in low, soft-spoken tongues, and even the gathered animals seemed calm. As the ten Romans approached, centurions at the head, no one armoured, no shields or helmets in evidence, just swords belted at the side, the various stall holders seemed neither stand-offish, nor perturbed by their appearance. Without shouting, the many traders beckoned with wide smiles, calling them over in low tones and unintelligible words.

Faventinus walked among the stalls with the others, impressed at the huge variety of goods on sale, though well over half of it was foodstuffs of one sort or another. By the time they had done the third street of tents, he turned to Densus. 'What you reckon? No danger here, I think.'

Densus nodded. 'Seems safe. Don't think we need the escort.'

Faventinus turned back to the soldiers who'd accompanied them. He took a tablet from his belt pouch and quickly scribbled some instructions, tongue poking from the corner of his mouth. 'Orders for the optios to send the men to the market two contubernia at a time,' he said as he wrote. He handed it to the men. Take this to the optios and return to the column.

The soldiers left them, with smiles – the first smiles he remembered seeing since that disastrous hunt. The opportunity to peruse the market off duty would lift everyone's spirits. As the others vanished, Densus had produced his own tablet and was beginning to list what they could do with locating, reeling off the list aloud as he wrote. Faventinus half-listened, looking about at the stalls around them. It was then he heard words he understood.

He held up a hand to Densus, who blinked in surprise and fell silent.

It was neither Latin, nor Greek, nor Kushite, nor even the languages they'd been hearing in this southern region. It was a language from his youth. Many moons ago, he'd had a passable command of the tongue, at least enough to engage in basic trade. It had been a requirement for any member of the family who expected to take part in mercantile activity in the region.

'What is it?' Densus whispered.

'Follow me,' Faventinus breathed, and moved towards the sound of the voice. He found the source in the next street of tents, and his eyes widened at what he saw. The man was of a different skin colour, still dark, but more resembling the desert nomads in the north. He wore a tunic of silk, a material they had not seen since Aegyptus, but it was what lay on his table that truly stunned the centurions. Jars of Roman manufacture, as well as pottery that Faventinus would be willing to bet was made not far from his home. There were hides from other regions, and some local fruit, and other items, but in among them were most definitely goods that had come from within the empire. The trader had now switched to some local dialect to call across to another stall holder.

'What in the name of blessed Mercury?' Densus gasped. 'Is that... wine?'

'That or garum. Or both.' Faventinus looked up at the merchant. 'Garamantian, yes?' he asked in that long-ago language.

The man's head snapped round at the words. When he spoke it was also in that familiar tongue. 'You know of the Garamantes?' Then his eyes widened and he grinned. 'Soldier of Rome? Sha'adab, but you are a long way from home, my friend.'

'You too.'

'Who you here to conquer, Roman?' There was an amused twinkle in the man's eye.

Faventinus laughed. 'No conquest today. We are exploring the great river on an imperial commission. And we need supplies. Are you happy to take sestertii?'

'I will take *any* coin, my Roman friend.'

'In that case, we want every jar you have, whether it's wine or garum!'

Now, the trader chuckled. 'I travel a thousand miles southeast, only to sell Roman goods to a Roman from the north. But yes, take, though it will not be cheap.'

Faventinus gave in to the tugging at his sleeve and turned to Densus. 'What?'

'How do you speak his language?'

'He's of the Garamantes, a tribe from southern Libya. We used to trade with them south of Carthage. If you wanted anything that came north across the desert, it came via the Garamantes. My father would be astonished to hear I was at the other end of that trade route.' He looked about at the other stalls.

'Do you know these other people?' he asked of the Garamantian.

'Some of them,' the man replied. 'I am here every autumn, following the desert routes, buying and selling as I go, and even beyond this place, to the coast. I have more, with my slaves and guards, in another place not far from the market.'

'I don't suppose you can tell us whether anyone here sells Artemisia.'

The man frowned. 'In this land, for medicines, you do not want a merchant. You want a magic man. But as it happens, there is one here.'

'Will you take us to see him?'

The man thought about this for a moment, dropped into the local tongue for an exchange with the trader at the next tent, and then nodded to the Romans and beckoned, walking out into the street. He led them around several corners, and at one point Faventinus smiled to see the first group of soldiers, freshly arrived from the column, perusing the nearby stalls.

He was not at all sure about the wisdom of the move as they arrived at the stall, and the Garamantian gestured at the owner. The new man stood behind a table, his face painted in white and red stripes, feathers and beads projecting like a halo around his face. He leaned on a staff that clattered with small bones and feathers, and wore some sort of long robe made from several different animal pelts. But more disconcerting than the man himself was the table behind which he stood. As well as many plants, bowls of powders, and squat pottery jars, the table held a number of dead creatures, several live ones, including snakes tethered with twine, and several bowls of things that must have come out of recently living creatures. He stopped looking when he came across the bowl of eyes, and focused on the man.

'You want Artemisia?' the Garamantian said to him.

'We have men sick with the swamp fever. I know of no other potential solution. I think that is Artemisia, yes?' he asked, pointing to a basket of leaves. 'I'll buy it all.'

The Garamantian slipped once more into a native language and spoke to the magician, who stood, stony-faced, pondering what he was being told. In the end, he shook his head with a barked syllable, and slapped Faventinus' hand away from the basket. The centurion was somewhat taken aback, but recovered as the magic man sorted through the pots at the back of the table, selected one, lifting the lid and checking the contents before nodding, replacing it, and holding it up on display.

'What is that?'

Again, there was a short and incomprehensible exchange between the two traders, and then the Garamantian turned to him. 'He says leaves are not enough for your illness.'

Faventinus felt a tingle of hope. The capsarius had said much the same thing about this new strain. 'What else?' he asked, urgently. 'What does he suggest?'

'The jar,' the Garamantian said. The magician clearly decided that more clarification was needed from the expression on Faventinus' face. He spoke rapidly to the Garamantian, who translated and paraphrased. 'He says that the leaves can be combined with other elements – I'm not sure whether he means real substances or some sort of magic – and ground into a paste that can then be mixed with the juice of the pawpaw. The resulting liquid is far more effective against the illness than the leaves alone.'

'Shit,' Faventinus said, eyes wide. 'Tell him we'll take everything he's got. And if he can tell us how to make it, he can name his price.'

There was another brief exchange, and the Garamantian shook his head. 'He will not tell his secrets. But he is happy to sell you what he has.'

Faventinus ground his teeth. The secret to health might lie in this man's head, but the Romans were hardly in a position to demand the knowledge, and he doubted that force would help. He looked around in frustration and spotted four of his men perusing a nearby stall, purchasing soft, light tunics of colourful materials. The capsarius, on a break from his duties, seemed to be buying acres of clothing. Faventinus told the others to wait, and scurried over.

'Something for the summer?' he asked, indicating the pile of light cloth.

The capsarius rolled his eyes. 'We're throwing out and burning all the blankets and tunics that might be infected. I need replacements.'

'Come with me.'

Grabbing the medic, he dragged him over to the magician's stall. Grasping the pot, he showed it to the man. 'This is a solution made from Artemisia and something called a pawpaw, which I'm guessing is a fruit, although it sounds more like something that might try to eat you. The sorcerer here says it will help with the fever, where Artemisia doesn't. He won't tell me how it's made, but since you're in the business, he might discuss it with you.'

The medic, suddenly interested, dropped his pile of cloth into the centurion's arms as though he were a servant, took the pot and lifted the lid. He examined it. Sniffed it. 'Bitter-sweet. The former will be the Artemisia. The latter is likely this fruit, which could be a binding agent, or possibly even just to make it more palatable. There are other things I smell, though. The Aegyptians, I learned in Memphis, brew a mould with their beer that helps prevent infections. I was shown the mouldy compound, made from rotting grains, and I'm not sure what I'm smelling is not that same thing.'

He fixed Faventinus with a look. 'Can you ask him, sir, whether he adds rotten plants to his mixture.'

Faventinus relayed this to the Garamantian, who passed it on to the magician. Though the reply that came back was another flat refusal to explain the process, there was something about the man's manner that strongly suggested the capsarius was onto something.

'He will say no more,' the trader announced, and Faventinus nodded. 'That's all you'll learn,' he told the capsarius. 'But I'm going to buy all he has. If you examine it, can you work it out?'

'I'll certainly try,' the man said. 'And Titus will help me. Thanks, Centurion.'

Faventinus blinked and sighed as the man ran off, carrying the pot, leaving the centurion holding an armful of folded linens. Two voices cut in, and he looked back and forth to realise that the magic man was asking for payment, as was a cloth merchant across the way, waving and pointing at the pile in his arms.

'This is getting ridiculous.' He looked at the colourful tunics. 'The prefect back in Rome would have a fit if he saw what his soldiers were wearing out here.' He dumped the clothing on Densus, and fished in his pouch, producing a handful of coins, ready to pay.

'They're alive,' reminded Densus, struggling to hold the linen. 'Alive, and not mutinying. I'll take that as a win.'

'And soon,' Faventinus added, eyeing the pots on the stall, 'hopefully, healthy too.'

30

UPPER NILE
LATE NOVEMBER AD 61

'You think you've got it then?'

The capsarius made a so-so motion with his hand. 'The problem is that so far everything is theoretical. It has the right odour and consistency, and everything that's gone into it should be fine. But it's not been tested. And when it comes down to it, sir, I'm only a combat medic. I get my pay bonuses and immune status from stitching wounds and treating knob-rot in garrison. This sort of medicine is way beyond my expertise. I'm learning as I go.'

'And I think you'll be set for a very lucrative private practice in the city when you retire,' Densus suggested. 'But do you think it's safe to test?'

'I can only answer that by testing it, sir.'

Densus sucked his teeth and looked across at Faventinus. 'What d'you think?'

'We'll never know if we don't try. And some of the men are sick enough that I keep expecting to see the ferryman hovering behind them, waiting for payment. What have we got to lose?'

'We'll still need permission from the boss,' Densus sighed. 'You and I are already on thin ice with him. If we feed a soldier a compound and he dies from it, the tribune will tear us a new arsehole each.'

'The tribune *is* an arsehole,' said the capsarius, quietly. Both centurions snapped round to look at him.

'Stow that shit, soldier. No matter how accurate it might be, it never gets said out loud, remember?'

'Sorry, sir.'

'Alright,' Densus said, stretching his arms, 'I'll go ask his imperial pompousness whether we have permission to test random cures on the sick. I suggest you go get set up ready. The moment I get the go-ahead, we might as well start.'

Leaving Faventinus and the capsarius, he stretched, climbed to his feet, and adjusted his uniform. Even now, late in the night, it was hot and damp. His clothes clung to him as though he'd gone into a bath-house steam room fully dressed, and it took some tugging and shuffling to look like anything other than a drowned rat, but when he was at least remotely comfortable and passable for presentation to a senior officer, he belted on his sword and left the tent.

He was not alone in his apparel. Every soldier he passed, though most were already abed, wore only a sword to indicate that he had any military connection at all. Other than that, every man now seemed to be dressed in different materials and different colours. They looked more like a theatre audience than an army on expedition. He nodded to the occasional soldier as he passed, and realised with surprise that he was also nodding politely to the slaves and getting the same in return. That made him smile. When... *if...* they ever got home, over-familiarity with slaves was going to be only one habit he would have to kick.

The tribune's tent sat twenty paces away from the camp, on the far side to the medical section, as though he had deliberately positioned himself as far from the illness as possible, which was quite likely. Two soldiers stood on guard outside as always, though these men at least looked remotely like soldiers. One thing the tribune insisted on was that the men guarding his tent still wore Roman military tunics. The men were unarmoured and bare-headed, but had swords at their sides and stood with pila, using them more as a staff to lean on than a weapon. They straightened as he approached. Both were men from his century, and they made the effort to salute.

'I'm here to see Curtius Lupus.'

The two soldiers looked at one another, and there was something odd in that visual exchange. Densus' eyes narrowed as they turned back to him. 'The tribune is asleep, sir.'

'I'm sure he is. But this is important. Wake him.'

'Wake him, sir? I...'

Something odd was going on here, and Densus took a couple of steps forward. He noted the two men glance momentarily at the tent door before looking back at him, nervously.

'Stand aside.'

'Centurion, I...'

He stepped towards the door. The two soldiers shared another sharp look and one made to stop him. Densus had seen the last look, though, and knew something was wrong. As the soldier stepped in the way, the centurion grabbed the out-thrust arm, bent it back almost enough to break it, and as the man yelped, hooked a leg behind his calf and shoved him, sending him falling backwards into the dirt.

The other guard reacted quickly, but not quickly enough. Already prepared, Densus spun and punched him resoundingly in the face, the man staggering back, grunting as he dropped his pilum and reached up to his nose, from which blood was gushing. Densus leapt forward, into the tent.

He didn't pause. He had more than an inkling what was going on, from the fact that the guards outside knew something was happening in the tent and were insistent on keeping him out, and from the fact that there was no sound issuing from within.

He hit the man just a few feet short of the tribune's bed, diving onto the back of his legs, his arms wrapping around the would-be assassin's knees. The man grunted and fell face first across the sleeping tribune, the dagger in his hand slamming down and hammering into the wood at the far edge of the tribune's bed.

The officer awoke with a start, a soldier lying full across his middle, armed and cursing. Densus had not let go his encircling grip of the man's knees, and before the attacker could recover, rammed his heels into the dirt and pulled. With a squawk, the man was dragged back from the pinned tribune. He made a desperate attempt to slam the dagger into the senior officer's chest as he slid backwards, but the tribune was awake now, even if acting on instinct only, and he rolled out of the way of the blow.

Aware that he had failed, the soldier twisted in Densus' grip and lashed out with the knife. The blade cut a thin line across the centurion's chin, drawing from him some very un-officer-like language. Densus had but moments to react before another blow came. He knew he had insufficient time to draw one of his weapons, and the man's arm was out of immediate reach, with his own around the man's knee. All he could do was pick a local target to incapacitate the attacker. In a heartbeat, he let go with his right hand, which slid up underneath the man's tunic hem. There was no need to negotiate complicated underwear, for, like most of the men, he had foregone underwear for the comfort of circulating air. Densus closed his hand on the man's testicles and squeezed with all his might.

The dagger had been coming round for a second blow, but the attack never happened. Instead, the dagger skittered off into the dark recesses of the tent as the assailant screamed a piercing wail, arms coming down to try and save his ruined manhood. Densus knew in an instant that the man would never recover, that he had crushed the dangling pair for good. He let go and scrabbled back.

The tribune had pulled himself up and was trying to clamber out of bed without coming anywhere near the scuffle, while the failed assassin had forgotten anything but his unbearable agony, as he gently coddled his flapping remnants, tears streaming from his eyes as he made hoarse keening sounds.

There was no time for Densus to enjoy his victory, though, for even as he struggled to his feet, breathing heavily, the tent door was thrown aside, and the two men he'd waylaid outside came barging in. He threw himself to one side just as the man he'd tripped dived for him. The man with the broken nose, blood still pouring down his face, was snarling, white and pink teeth on show, and he advanced on the tribune, sword out.

There was nothing Densus could do to help there right now. For a moment he considered bellowing a call to arms, to draw aid to the tribune's tent, but given that the men he was fighting were already his own faithful guardsmen, he could hardly guarantee that anyone else who came to their aid wasn't just as likely to join the assassins.

The man who had dived for him staggered, righting himself, and turning. He stopped, sword in hand, and pointed a finger at the centurion.

'Stay out of this, sir. I don't want to hurt you.'

'Then you should have stood by your fucking oath,' Densus snarled, rising and drawing his own sword. The two men faced one another, each with a gladius ready. Past the man, Densus could see the tribune fighting off the other attacker. The senior officer was no gladiator, clearly, but his lack of practice with his weapon was very much counter-balanced by the fact that his opponent was already in pain and struggling to see properly. All he had to do was hold the man off.

'Drop your sword now, and I'll let you die like a soldier,' Densus told the man before him.

'You know I can't do that, sir. What we're trying is for the good of everyone, even you.'

Densus sighed. He was just the width of a whisper away from agreeing with the man at times, but he was a soldier. He'd taken an oath. There had to be discipline. Even with all the allowances they'd made to keep the soldiers comfortable, there still had to be discipline. Without it, there was no hope.

'Then you are an oathbreaker, a mutineer, and I cannot help you.'

As though with that he had signed the man's death sentence and removed all hope of a peaceful resolution, the soldier struck. He leapt forward, lancing out with his gladius. It was a reasonable attack, but the man's gait was clumsy. As his left foot came down, the leg wobbled slightly, and Densus realised the man's fall had strained or pulled some muscle. He ducked back out of the way of the blow, and found himself against the wall of the tent. Decided upon a course of action, he turned slightly and shuffled sideways to his right, heading towards a low table and stool, and the tribune's bed. The soldier turned to follow him, and cursed as his knee almost gave way with the movement.

The centurion's foot touched the leg of the stool that went with the table, and he smiled. He steadied himself, blade in his grip, and used his free hand to beckon the soldier, taking one more step to the right. In response, the guardsman had to turn again slightly, his damaged left leg used to pivot upon. He had barely come to face Densus before the centurion kicked out, flicking the stool forward. The small wooden seat smacked into the attacker's leg at around knee height, and the man bellowed in pain, struggling to stay upright.

Densus was on him in a heartbeat. His sword came down in a chopping motion onto the soldier's right forearm. The blow struck hard, breaking the bone, and cleaving a deep cut. The enemy's sword fell from his grip and he screamed, still staggering on his bad leg as he reached round to grip his wounded wrist.

Densus stepped forward, then, and was taken rather by surprise when the soldier suddenly snarled and lashed out with his good arm. The punch was good enough to land hard on the centurion's cheek, just below his left eye. He floundered for a moment. He'd thought the man out of the fight. Next time he'd have to make sure.

His attack was neither careful nor graceful, however. Densus hit the guardsman like an angry bear, driving him to the ground. The soldier made a valiant attempt to fight him off, but with a ruined knee and a ruined wrist, he was struggling. The centurion hit him in the face, then again, and again. When the man was groaning, eyes unfocused, arms limp, Densus gripped him by the temples, and lifted his head, slamming it back against the hard dirt of the ground. The man slid into unconsciousness in a heartbeat.

For a moment, Densus considered finishing him, but forced himself not to. These men had mutinied and attacked two senior officers. There would be no easy end for them. The latest attacker was out for good, and the original was still sitting near the bed, gently holding his lost manhood and weeping endlessly. Only one man remained.

The last of the three was busy with the tribune. He'd managed to land one blow, for the officer had a red line along his outer elbow, but the senior man was still holding him off. Densus, in no mood to deal with any of this right now, suffering with pain in the eye and the chin, simply padded quietly across the room, lifting his own gladius. He was right behind the soldier when the man realised he was there far too late. The sword's pommel came down on the last assassin's head, slamming into the back of his skull and driving him into the black in an instant.

As the soldier slumped to the ground, there were shouts.

Densus turned to the door, bleakly aware that anyone arriving was just as likely to try and kill him as to save him. Two more men suddenly burst into the tent. The guardsman, he didn't know, but Gallo, Faventinus' optio, was a welcome sight. Neither man made any move to attack, the soldier instead stepping to the side, sword in hand, surveying the scene, the optio looking back and forth between the tribune and the centurion, eyes wide.

'Fuck me, but your officer parties are wild,' he said.

31

LATE NOVEMBER AD 61

'I want examples made of them. I want them to suffer as no man has ever suffered,' the tribune snarled, jabbing a finger.

Faventinus looked across at Densus. The centurion, still sporting blood that had belonged to both he and others, stood, stony-faced, nodding slowly.

The commotion had stirred the camp, all the shouting and the screams, starting with those who were on watch, and those on various duties, then those preparing for sleep, and then even those already wrapped in the arms of Somnus. Faventinus had been early on the scene, for once Densus had left to speak to the tribune and the capsarius had gone to prepare his tests, at a loose end, Faventinus had done his rounds of the camp, listening to the general air of dissent, and had happened to be in the rough area of the tribune's tent when the noise began.

Gallo and half a dozen trustworthy lads had got there first, only to discover that they were too late and that it was all over anyway, but Faventinus had been close behind.

The tent had been a sight. The tribune, shaking, leaning against a piece of ornate furniture dragged all the way from Rome; Densus propped against the table, nursing his injuries; two men flat out, unconscious and bloody on the floor, with a third moaning and coddling his privates.

Realising that Densus was still in that slightly stunned, inattentive state that a man experiences once the fight is over and the danger passed, Faventinus stepped forward. 'We'll see to it, sir.'

He turned to Gallo. 'Have these three men taken outside and bound, then wait for me. And have two of the slaves come in and clean away the blood and tidy up.'

The optio nodded and began to give out orders. The tribune simply stood there, shaking, as it was all carried out, but Faventinus saluted, grabbed Densus, and turned. His fellow centurion looked up in surprise, defocused eyes now zeroing in on him as he returned to the present from wherever he'd been. Densus let him lead the way and the pair left the tent into the sultry, sweaty night. Looking around to take stock of the situation, he nodded to himself and drew his fellow centurion away, out of earshot of the others.

'That was some work, overcoming three of them. That's the sort of thing that gets medals. I'm starting to see why you were decorated so often.'

Densus shivered. 'I was lucky. I realised something was up before they knew I was onto them. I managed to put two of them out of the fight quickly while I went inside and dealt with the third. Then, when the other two reappeared, I had the tribune to help. If it had been just one on three, I wouldn't have fared so well.'

Faventinus snorted. 'If you say so. You need to have the capsarius look at that.'

'It's just a scratch,' Densus said, touching the red line on his chin, gingerly.

'Not that. The eye.'

The other centurion reached up and touched his cheekbone, just below his eye, hissed and flinched. He probably wasn't aware that the eye had already blackened impressively in just that short time. 'Can you see straight?'

'Yeah. No permanent damage. Hurts like a bastard, mind.'

'I'll bet. I think we have a problem, Sempronius.'

'I think the problem is three men smaller now.'

Faventinus sighed. 'Two of those men were yours, but the other was one of mine. That means this was something widespread. If men from two centuries were in on it, I doubt this was limited to three. Others knew, even if they weren't directly part of it. Men were probably employed distracting guards and suchlike.'

'Hopefully we've taught them a lesson,' Densus said.

Faventinus rather doubted that. 'Yes. I think we'll have taught them to find a better way, next time.' Densus looked across at him, fresh worry lining his face. Faventinus shrugged. 'It's going to happen again, unless the tribune starts to work on this, to mollify them, and I can't see that happening. He's more likely to wind them up more. The next time, it might not be a knife in the night, but a full-on mutiny, storming the tent by force.'

Densus shivered again. 'Do you not wonder whether I did the right thing there?' he said in little more than a whisper.

'Shush. Don't say that. Don't even *think* it.'

'*You're* thinking it.'

There was nothing Faventinus could say to that. He was. He was starting to wonder whether maybe this whole escapade should be stopped, even in defiance of the tribune. 'You know what we should have done.'

'What?'

'Stopped somewhere in Kush for half a year, written a really detailed story about what might lie to the south, made it look like it was not worth conquering, then gone home and delivered the report, telling the emperor we met the spirits and they told us to piss off.'

Densus laughed, darkly. 'You're a dangerous man, Claudius. If we'd done that, and word somehow got back, the palace torturers would peel us.'

The two men fell silent, breathing loudly in the dark. 'What are we going to do with those three?' Faventinus asked, pointing back towards the tent, where the three prisoners, bound, were being hauled out into open ground. A fair crowd had grown at the edge of the camp, watching.

'They have to die.'

'I know that,' Faventinus rolled his eyes. 'And it can't be a clean execution. The tribune won't have it. But anything else is going to sit badly with the men, even those who *weren't* part of it. Somehow we have to find a middle ground.'

Densus chewed his lip, and hissed in pain, as the move tugged at the cut on his chin. 'They're a superstitious lot,' he said.

Faventinus nodded. 'If we did this right, we might be able to make it look like the gods punishing them, rather than us. That might put off any fresh attempt, for a while, at least. Take the death itself out of our hands.'

'If only we had a hippo or a croc to do it for us.'

'We do,' Faventinus replied with a dark look. 'This place is crawling with wildlife. There are still crocs on the river, and lions in the wild, remember. Let's leave it to the gods.'

'Tether them and wait?'

'Exactly.'

Gesturing for his friend to follow, Faventinus turned and strolled back towards the scene of the crime. Slaves were now entering the tent with cloths and a bucket of water, and one of the two unconscious men had woken, and was groaning in pain, while the newly castrated man had gone silent and was staring, glassy-eyed, into nothing. Gallo and his men remained protectively close, but a glance at the watching soldiers at the edge of the camp confirmed it for Faventinus. Others had been in on it. His hand danced lightly down to his sword hilt for reassurance. It felt disturbingly as though the night's violence had only paused, and that these men might take up the banner at any moment.

'Follow my lead.' He straightened, putting on his most authoritative visage as he marched over to the watching guardsmen. Coming to a halt in front of them, he drew his vine stick from his belt and gripped it in both hands, holding it across his pelvis. 'Take careful note,' he said to the men, loud enough for them to hear even at the back. 'These men are hereby condemned. They have broken their military oath, and stand accused and guilty of the attempted murder of their commander. You all know that the punishment for such a grievous crime is death.'

There was a rumble of discontent from across the gathering, confirming how close they were to trouble breaking out once again. Faventinus took a deep breath, with a silent prayer to Minerva. 'You have your grievances, I know. Many of you sympathise with these men, and would have us commute their sentence. But even the gods are against a breaker of sacred oaths. If you would have these men live, then you would have us defy the gods.'

He really hoped this was going to be enough. There was, at least, an air of uncertainty about the gathering before him, now. He had to capitalise on that before it faded.

'So we will leave it to the gods to decide.' The men frowned. Good. He had them. 'These three criminals will be taken to the nearest clearing and there tethered and left alone for the night. If the gods favour them, they will survive unharmed, and their sentences will be commuted with the dawn. If the gods confirm the need for death, then they will not survive the night. Thus the gods decide, and no man here will interfere. Do you all understand?'

There was a brief, tense, pause before a murmured affirmative rippled across the gathered watchers. Faventinus allowed himself the smallest breath of relief. He turned and passed those orders on to Gallo and his men, and as the three prisoners were dragged away and chains fetched from one of the carts, Densus crossed to him. 'Clever. If they die, the men will think the gods have spoken. The chances of a repeat performance will be pretty small.'

'And you've heard what it's like out there beyond the firelight at night,' Faventinus replied. 'The land is crawling with things that want to eat us.'

As the captives and their escort disappeared into the darkness, many of the gathered observers followed at a distance, and soon the two centurions were all but alone, barring the sentries dotted about a short distance away. He braced himself at the sight of the tribune marching their way from the tent.

'Did I hear you correctly, Centurion?' the man demanded angrily, coming to an imperious halt nearby.

'Sir?'

'I gave the order for those men to be tortured to death. To be an example. Instead, you disobey my orders and hand over their fate to chance. That is unacceptable. Tell me why I shouldn't have you join them?'

Faventinus fought down the irritation, deliberately keeping his voice steady and calm. 'Sir, this was not an isolated incident. Unless we do something, it will not be the last knife you face. But if the men see the gods condemn them, they will think twice about trying to do the same thing.'

The tribune frowned. He had not thought about that, clearly.

'And if they survive? What then?'

Faventinus shrugged. 'I would be more than surprised to see any of them make it through the night. I've done the rounds of the sentries in the dark out here. Things with fangs are never more than fifty paces from the camp. Those three men are going to die tonight, and horribly, just as you asked, but because of the way we've done it, the men will see the gods protecting you and condemning the criminals.'

Curtius Lupus drummed his fingers on crossed arms. 'I hope you're right, Centurion.'

'He will be,' Densus put in. 'He always is. He's a clever bastard, is Faventinus.'

The tribune sniffed deep, and then gave a curt nod, turned and stomped back towards his tent.

'I wish he would piss off back to Rome and leave us to it,' Densus grumbled once he was out of earshot.

'*I* wish *he'd* stay here and send *us* back to Rome,' added Faventinus. 'Come on.'

They followed the path taken by the prison party, their position through the scrub visible by the torches carried by three of the men. The two officers walked out into the clearing to see that Gallo, efficient as ever, was already hard at work. The centurions found a place to stand and watch, slightly apart from the rest of the spectators. Over the ensuing quarter of an hour, all was made ready. Any undergrowth was cut away from the clearing, leaving it wide open and bare, barring three narrow tree stumps turned into posts by men hacking off the branches. The criminals were chained twice each, one ankle and one wrist encased in a steel cuff that was attached to the post. This done, they stepped back and saluted to the two centurions.

Faventinus was pleased to note that, unnoticed by the casual observer, Optio Gallo had had the forethought to make sure that the chaining treatment was rough, scraping skin and drawing blood, for fresh blood would only help draw hunters. The prisoners left at their execution posts in the centre of the clearing, and the centurions turned to the others. 'I realise you will want to witness this,' Faventinus said, 'but we need you rested in the morning to press on. Thus your centurions and your optios will take turns in shifts watching the prisoners, and for your own peace of mind, two men may stay and watch with us, to be certain it is the will of the gods that is done tonight. The rest of you will return to camp.'

This seemed to satisfy the rebellious element among the

men, and two men were chosen to stay. Faventinus looked at Densus and Gallo. 'I'll take the first shift. After two hours, I'll come and wake one of you. When you get back to camp, let Flaccus know what's happening and that he's part of the rota.'

The two men nodded and Densus clapped his hand reassuringly on his friend's shoulder before the rest left the clearing. In moments, Faventinus and the two other observers were left alone with the prisoners.

'Back,' he said, pointing to the cleared path to the camp. 'Away from the clearing. We must observe from a distance, and not interfere.'

With a little reluctance, the pair joined him, and the three men padded back from the clearing to where a fallen tree provided a natural bench. There, they sank to the wooden seat and waited in silence. For a while, Faventinus wondered whether he should strike up a conversation, but decided against it. As well as having nothing really to say, any conversation might deter predators from approaching. Their own position was still close enough to the camp that the faint glow of the fires danced on their backs. Their view of the clearing was not good, distant and dark, and they could only see the middle of the three prisoners from here. They sat in silence and waited.

They did not have to wait long.

Faventinus' mind had started to wander a little, when there was a distant rustling. One of the men beside him made to rise from the log, but the centurion reached out, gripping the man's wrist and pushing him back down, silently. The canine-looking shape that had crept from the clearing's edge, out into silhouetted view, was moving carefully, nervously, and anything the three observers might do now could spook it. They held their breath. The creature moved into view, the moonlight catching it as it turned, and bathing it momentarily in silvery light. It was definitely canine, but with a slightly stunted head, a rough mane of hair faintly resembling a lion's, and a mottled hide of black stripes on brown.

It looked familiar. He was sure he'd seen such creatures on display in the imperial menagerie, but he couldn't put a name to it. Maybe Densus would have, had he been here. As he watched, he realised the creature was not alone. Other identical shapes were appearing now, the whole pack pacing around the edge of the clearing, making sure they were alone and that the prey was helpless, that this was not some sort of elaborate trap. One of the creatures paused and looked their way, along the path, pausing, tense. The three men were silent and still as statues, a combination of anticipation and nervousness gripping them.

Some signal seemed to go out among the animals, for that one turned, leaving the three watchers alone, and returned to the others. Screams of fear began to arise from the three men, aware that they were helpless and that the creatures were bold enough in a pack to come for them.

The first attack went unseen, as the animals surged forward to one of the prisoners out of sight. There was a cacophony of screams, snarls and the sounds of tearing and cracking loud enough to cut through the night. The man's screaming didn't last long, but it was compensated for by the other two, who were now screeching twice as loudly and desperately, as they watched their companion being torn to shreds and swallowed in bloody lumps.

The animals were efficient, finishing off their first victim while he was still fresh and tender.

Soft footsteps announced that the three watchers were no longer alone, and Faventinus turned quietly to see Densus approaching, more and more men behind, all coming slowly, reverently, silently, drawn by the screams.

Thus it was that by the time the first meal was done and the creatures moved on to the second, the man in clear view of the path, there was a considerable audience. Faventinus watched, made himself do so, silent witness to the lawful death of a man who had taken it upon himself to kill a tribune of the Praetorian Guard. It was not pretty. One of the creatures made the first attack. As the man thrashed about, unable to move too far for the chains that held him secure, that flailing free arm fell prey, the thing's jaws snapping shut around the wrist. As the man howled in agony, the creature gnawed on his wrist, snapping and crushing the bones to minimise resistance. Two more leapt, then, one on his free leg, the other taking a bite from his side. The screaming was intense as the animals chewed and bit, a fourth and fifth joining in, and the wails only ended when the sixth closed its jaws about his throat, the weight of the first four having dragged him down within reach. Even then, the man screamed silently through his destroyed throat as the animals tore him to pieces, eating their prizes in great swallows as they went. By the time he died, he was already half gone.

Faventinus felt faintly ill at the spectacle, and knew damn well that he was not alone. Violence, blood and death were the stock in trade of a soldier, but there was something indescribably different and unpleasant about watching a man being eaten alive. Soon, the creatures moved off out of sight, the panicked screams of the third captive rising until the attacks began. Faventinus waited until they had stopped, rose, and turned to the gathering behind him.

'The gods have made their will known,' was all he said, but his memory was replaying a scene from the tent of a seer back at Syene, a thousand miles and a lifetime ago. Seven smooth, round stones on the ground in the shape of an animal.

'Is Fisi.'

'No idea,' Densus had said with a shrug.

'Fisi. Fisi,' she repeated, making shapes with her hands that looked like they might be suggesting a dog of some kind.

'And Fisi is bad?'

'Fisi bad.'

He tore himself away from the memory. Yes, he decided, Fisi was most *definitely* bad.

32

SOMEWHERE

THE DAY BEFORE THE IDES OF DECEMBER AD 61

Densus looked along the column of men as the whole thing ground to a halt. He'd only dropped back to speak to the tribune, a task that was still required daily, no matter how irritating and pointless it generally turned out to be. It seemed as though the attempt on the man's life had cut through the last bond between the commander and the rest of the unit. He now travelled separately, if in the same column, riding alongside the wagon that held his personal effects, surrounded only by his personal staff, while the centurions and their deputies carried out the duty of keeping the column on track. The man seemed to have stopped taking any interest in the intricacies of their journey, maintaining only the position that the mission would be completed at any cost, and any man who got in the way would be punished. Densus and Faventinus took it in turns to take any questions to the man, as the chain of command required, despite the fact that the answer was now always a variant on the theme of 'do what you feel you must, as long as the mission remains our only goal'.

Densus was getting mighty tired of it.

And now, with the column halting for some unknown reason, the tribune would undoubtedly demand to know what was happening, although when told, his response would surely be 'then deal with it'.

As he made his way forward, content that the cause of the delay was nothing important, else there would be considerably more shouting, Densus looked at the men and sighed.

Another half month of travelling upriver had changed the Praetorians under his command again. It was no surprise, really, given the fact that it was almost mid-winter, Rome would probably be snowed in, yet here there was only that same sticky heat and lack of a breath of moving air that had become the norm the moment they left Kush. Such changes in the world were going to change the men in it.

He glanced back. The rear-guard looked like a bunch of Aegyptian levies, in their long, flowing white dresses, hair grown long and often bound up in knots on their heads, beards tied with thongs so that they became long and narrow things, like the fake ones the Pharaohs had worn, the only military equipment visible a sword at their waist and a pilum over their shoulder.

And they were probably the most Roman looking of the lot.

In front of them came the tribune and his wagon, he riding far enough to one side to be out of any dust cloud kicked up, though that was a rare thing in this warm, damp world. In front of the tribune came the rest of the carts, less laden with supplies now than at any time since they were on reduced rations before Kush, and at the head of that: the medical wagons. Two of the vehicles now no longer carried supplies, but rather those men suffering with the sickness.

That was another worry. The liquid the magician had sold them at the market had been the first thing to have a noticeable effect on the fever victims, and reasonably quickly. It had, over several days, brought the first men to succumb to the new illness back to a semblance of health. It would still be some time before they could be properly called 'well', but at least they were now getting there. The problem was that every few days, another case would crop up, and they would have to stretch the supplies. The version of the medicine that the capsarii had cooked up from studying the original did have a noticeable effect, but was not as efficacious as the magician's variant. Thus they were getting lower and lower on supplies while having to use it on more and more patients. Densus prayed they found another market soon, where they might find someone who knew the curative.

He strode forward, nodding to the capsarius, and past the lines of men. There were no traditional declarations of the unit's nature on display. The vexillum flag with its scorpion and cohort number was packed away in the cart, along with the standards of both centuries, the image of the emperor on its staff, and both the large, heavy musical instruments.

In fact, the expedition looked more like a gathering at a marketplace than a unit on the move. He shook his head as he walked. Hardly any contubernium of men wore the same clothes as each other. Some were clad in short tunics, some in long, voluminous robes, others in some sort of loosely tied-together thing of the men's own design that allowed the greatest access to air, although also to the bugs that brought the fever. One man, the previous day, he'd even found marching naked. He'd been astonished, and had told the man in no uncertain terms that if he wanted to keep his cock and balls, he had to keep them hidden beneath something. And every item of clothing all along the line seemed to be a different colour. Gone was Praetorian white and blue, with most men wearing bright colours and woven designs of eye-watering hue combinations, picked up at villages or that great market over the past days.

Three and a half months, now, in this world. Four and a half, if you included the voyage. In truth, time had become a negligible thing, since every day seemed to be the same. The only reason anyone even knew what month it was was because the tesserarius Milo had been keeping count, scratching it into a tablet since the day they'd landed in Alexandria. It was easy to see how border garrisons far from the heart of empire 'went native', stationed at the arse end of nowhere, year after year. His own men were almost there after only four months. If they were still out here when they reached a full year, they'd probably be animals, rather than men.

He passed a small group of men who were very different, and paused in his walk. He looked the five of them up and down. Each wore only a short skirt, like an Aegyptian peasant, and sandals, otherwise entirely naked. Moreover, they had shaved. Not just their chins and cheeks, either. Their heads were as smooth as hens' eggs, and he could see not a single body hair. He wasn't willing to delve into their sweaty underwear, but he reckoned there was a good chance they were smooth and bald down there too.

'Why?' he asked in a bored, tired tone, indicating their shiny scalps and tugging at his own, wild, wiry locks.

'It's not as hot, sir,' one answered.

'And you don't get bugs trapped in your hair, biting, if you don't have any.'

All he could do was nod. There was nothing to say. They looked more like Aegyptian catamite oil-wrestlers than Rome's elite soldiers, but there was also unarguable sense in both explanations. Certainly more sense than those long beards and top-knots among the rear-guard.

He walked on.

He blinked.

He stopped.

He turned to the soldier beside him, frowning, and pointed at the man's head. 'Explain.'

The soldier's eyes rolled upwards and he realised the centurion was referring to his hair, which was a solid thing, the man having rubbed wet red clay into it, then let it dry to a hard carapace. It looked ridiculous. Densus had seen similar on natives in the region, but it somehow looked normal on them. On Plautius Drusus, on the other hand, it looked bloody stupid.

'That's impractical, soldier.'

'Why, sir?'

'How will you get your helmet on?'

The man frowned. 'Sir, we haven't worn helmets for months. I don't even know where mine is, except that it's in a cart somewhere.'

Densus sighed again and rolled his eyes. 'You look

ridiculous. Like one of those treats you get at the races – the strings of lamb's meat wrapped round a stick.'

'At least it's red, sir. Good military colour, colour of Mars, sir.'

'For fuck's sake,' Densus muttered to himself, walking on, not bothering looking back.

At the front of the column, he found Faventinus and the cause for the hold-up. The men, including the scouts, were standing around a tall stone at the side of the path. As he approached, some of them parted to allow him access, and his fellow centurion turned to him.

'What do you think of that?'

Densus followed his pointing finger and stared in shock. The stone was carved, which, in itself, was a surprise. They'd seen no such thing since Kush. But it was what it was carved with that surprised him. 'Is that…?'

Faventinus shrugged. 'You're the expert. You tell me.'

'Hieroglyphics.'

'Exactly.'

And they were. They were most definitely hieroglyphics, though since Densus didn't know how to read the language, and could only translate a handful of sequences, he had no idea what it said.

'Why are they out here?' Faventinus asked. 'We're months out of Aegyptus, and even out of Kush for more than a month. What the fuck are hieroglyphics doing here?' He grabbed Densus by the bicep and turned him away from the others, before whispering in his ear. 'Tell me we haven't somehow done a huge circle. Tell me we're not back in Aegyptus.'

Densus shook his head. 'I can't explain it, but I saw the

river this morning and we're still going upstream. We've not changed course. We're still heading roughly south.' He shrugged. 'Maybe some pharaoh in years past sent men to do what we're doing? It might say "Shit, I wish we were still home in Memphis where there aren't all these bastard flies".'

Faventinus gave a humorous snort. 'I suppose. Whatever it means, it's the first sign of proper civilisation since Kush. Where there's writing, there's a people with a cause. I think we need to proceed carefully. Maybe we should get the men back into armour?' he mused.

Densus immediately pictured the man with the mud in his hair trying to pull a helmet down over it. He shook his head. 'Good luck with that. I think so long as the men are armed and alert to potential danger, that's the most we can realistically do.'

But as he marched back to report this to the tribune, he looked at the men, and wondered how likely they were to survive a proper fight out here if they were suddenly pushed into one.

He hoped the hieroglyphics meant friends, not enemies.

33

UPPER NILE

THE DAY AFTER THE IDES OF DECEMBER AD 61

It was civilisation, of a sort. Had Faventinus stumbled across this place straight from a sojourn in Rome or Carthage, he would have thought it had less sign of civilisation than the trench beneath a latrine, but after so many days of slogging through the sticky heat, up the Nile in this land of naked tribes, painted warriors and ferocious animals, frankly anything not made of mud and grass was starting to seem almost Virtuvian.

'It doesn't *look* Aegyptian,' he said, dubiously.

'But there are hints,' Densus replied.

That was true. The scouts had come back almost breathlessly enthusiastic over what they had found, mumbling that what they had stumbled across was no native village, but an actual town.

And it was. In fairness, it was. The buildings had roofs of mudbrick and timber, rather than just woven grass. The buildings were squared, with corners, rather than simple circular huts. There were deliberately placed streets, and two buildings at the centre that stood out, palatial by comparison. Moreover, for the first time since Kush, there was a man-made dock of sorts at the river side, where small coracles were tethered, signs of either fishing, or trade, or perhaps both.

Most telling of all, there were the ruts of carts in the dry mud streets, and not just the little hand carts they'd seen at the market, but proper animal-drawn ones, not dissimilar to their own, judging by the axle-width.

And they were not, apparently, enemies.

The scouts had met the locals in the bush at the edge of the settlement and, though there was no hope of an easy linguistic exchange, through the judicious use of smiles, sign language and gifts, had managed to open friendly relations with them. Thus they had ridden back, full of hope, and reported in. For the first time in days, the tribune had even taken an interest. He had joined the two centurions and the small honour guard as they went ahead of the column. It did not escape Faventinus' notice that the soldiers glared malice at the tribune whenever he came close, nor that Curtius Lupus carefully positioned himself so that the two officers were between him and the men, but any interest shown was at least a tiny hope that there could be a rebuilding of trust.

'Maybe they're not the ones who wrote the inscription?' Faventinus mused.

Densus sighed. 'It wasn't a recent one. Maybe it *was* a left-over from an old Aegyptian exploration, after all.'

Faventinus was not convinced. 'But they also don't look like the other locals.' And they didn't. Densus nodded sagely at that. They were not ebony-skinned like the other tribes they had found. Their flesh was a lighter, brown tone with a hint of olive, more reminiscent of the Aegyptians or the northern Kushites.

'There's a story here.'

They made their way to the heart of the place, to those two great buildings, and noted with interest two men guarding one of them. The figures wore colourful clothes and sported spears, their hair braided tight atop their heads, styles reminiscent of other locals, but their very presence spoke of something different. The native tribes the Romans had met down here had warriors, for sure, but men standing guard at a doorway was something different. That spoke of an ordered hierarchy with a military aspect. More civilised, certainly. The locals simply went about their own business, as though Roman explorers happened by every few days, which was curious. More curious was that Faventinus saw not a single sign of a cart, which led him to wonder where the wheel ruts had come from. They nodded politely, and in a friendly manner, to anyone who looked their way, and those people uniformly responded in a similar manner, to the relief of all.

'Let's check out the one without guards,' Faventinus urged and, in the absence of a plan of any kind, the others agreed and followed.

The building was larger than all but the guarded one, rectangular, some twenty paces across the front, perhaps sixty long, and two and a half times the height of a man. It was plain mudbrick, with a single doorway leading onto the village square, and no windows.

A few locals turned to look their way curiously as

they entered the doorway, but no one made to stop them. Faventinus went first, with the tribune at his heel, and then Densus, telling the eight soldiers to stay outside and keep watch.

What they found inside left them in no doubt.

The building had been divided into two parts. The first, into which they strode, was open-roofed, a simple courtyard, with heavy timber poles holding up a veranda, in a crude facsimile of a colonnade. Images had been etched into the mudbrick walls, and among them were hieroglyphics, though the state of them suggested they were decades old, if not centuries. Basic, and but a shadow of the real thing it might be, but what it clearly *was*, was a temple, of similar construction, in principle, to those of Aegyptus and Kush. Almost breathless with anticipation, they moved into the second room. This was the holy of holies, and Faventinus had learned way back in Memphis that only priests went into this part. Whatever these people had drawn from Aegyptus, that had not translated with it, for no priest came forth, telling them to keep out, and they entered a dark chamber that took time for them to see, as their vision adjusted. When it did, the revelation was confirmed. The walls were again carved with images and hieroglyphics, and in the centre, on a plinth, stood the statue of a man with the head of a dog.

Faventinus' memory raced. Not only Anubis, the Aegyptian god of the dead, who this surely had to be, but those ancient writings they had perused back in Rome, in preparation, when they had heard tall tales of the *kynokefaloi*, the dog-headed men to be found along the Nile. Several things fell into place.

'Whoever they are, they at least had cultural contact with Aegyptus,' Densus mused.

Behind them, the tribune gave an uninterested harrumph and strode back out. Faventinus ignored him, and looked at the statue. 'Look at their skin. These people are Aegyptians. Or they were, maybe. Everything here looks over a century old, and even then that may have been maintained from an earlier time.' He thought back, nodding. 'There are places in Carthage that were sacred to Baal and Tanit that were ravaged in the great wars, but are still maintained now. Every few years, devotees go round them, touching up the carvings and the paint. I reckon that's what's happening here.'

'Then they could have been here for centuries,' Densus breathed. 'Maybe even millennia.'

'Come on,' Faventinus grinned. 'I want to find out what the soldiers are guarding.'

They emerged into the square once more to mild interest from the locals, and took the tribune and the eight men across to the slightly larger building with windows.

The guards barked something in a strange tongue, and as the Romans came to a patient halt outside, there was a brief pause before a servant of some sort emerged from the doorway and beckoned for them to follow. They did so, but as the guardsmen made to follow, Curtius Lupus turned and waved them away. Any hope that the man might be trying to heal the divide crumbled, as Faventinus realised the man trusted the unknown quantity of a foreign world more than the dubious safety of his own men.

'Wait here,' the man said, unable to stop his lip curling in distaste. The soldiers glared, but stayed, and the three officers followed the man inside. This building was richly appointed, compared with the structures they had thus far found south of Kush. More guards stood here and there, watching them, making no move to halt the Romans, but also making it clear that any sudden move could result in violence. Faventinus, like his fellow centurion, made sure to keep his hands well away from the weapons at his belt as they followed. They were led to a large chamber, past the doorways to several smaller ones, and it appeared, as they entered, that they had arrived at meal time.

Seven figures, both men and women, sat on cushions and rugs at low tables around the room, though one stood out, seated on the pelt of a great spotted cat, a step higher than everyone else. As their guide approached the leader, bowing deeply and rattling out something in their foreign tongue, Faventinus sniffed. There was a strangely familiar smell. It could be the spicy food being served, but there was something there he definitely knew. Along with the other officers, he bowed deeply to the man at the head of the room.

'Observe, gentlemen, something unique,' the tribune said quietly as he came out of his bow, a new interest, absent for so long, in his voice.

Faventinus frowned at the display in the room, trying to spot whatever Curtius Lupus had seen. It was definitely a meal, the attendees either the leader's family or perhaps courtiers of some kind, given the way the servant who had led them in appeared to be introducing them to the head man. The meal was served in simple wooden bowls and cups, and the people were dressed not dissimilarly to others they had seen in the region, a nod to practicality. The leader was more ornate, for sure, wearing jewellery, and richer clothes, and a headdress of feathers…

He stopped. He looked at the feathers.

'Juno…'

'Quite.'

They were peacock feathers.

'Maybe peacocks live here?' suggested Densus.

The tribune shook his head. 'The peacock comes from India. Rome imports them from there. If they lived south of Africa, Libya or Aegyptus, do you not think we would import them from here, without risking trouble from Parthia?'

'Maybe they've not been found here before, sir? *We've* never been this far south, after all.'

Another shake. 'But our trade reaches this far, Centurion. Lions, cameleopards, rhinoceros, all for spectacle in Rome, brought from south of the African deserts. If peacocks lived here, we would import them from here, not over the expensive trade routes from India.'

Faventinus goggled. 'That means, then, that these people trade with the Indians.'

The tribune nodded. 'Which means there is a trade route from here to the Indian Sea. Seneca was right, after all. Aethiopia may offer an alternative trade route to India, which would allow us to bypass powerful, troublesome Parthia. This discovery alone has made our journey worthwhile. I must make careful notes of this in my journal this evening.'

Faventinus caught Densus' look and knew what his friend was thinking. It did indeed make their journey worthwhile, because now they might have a faster, safer, way back to

Rome that did not take them along the crocodile-and-hippo-infested Nile, and through a Kushite civil war. For a moment, hope blossomed. Hope of an end to this disastrous expedition.

'Perhaps we can take this knowledge back to Rome, sir?' he hazarded. 'Cut short our journey south and libate to the river spirits here, then trace the trade route to the sea for a way home. Surely that will be enough for the emperor? Surely he'll not be bothered about incorporating other lands to the south, if this far grants us alternative trade routes.'

Hope shattered with one glance at the tribune's face. 'No,' Curtius Lupus said. 'The emperor himself tasked us with reaching the Nile's source. I will not disobey an imperial command, and neither will you or the men.'

'I think we're being invited to the meal,' Densus interrupted, pointing to the servant, who was making a space and adding a low table and some cushions, while others were bringing forth bowls of food. 'Do we join them, sir?'

Curtius Lupus nodded. 'We must foster relations here. If the emperor wishes to add these lands to the empire, and this place in particular is some sort of hub for trade, then it is of prime importance.'

Faventinus followed as they were seated. It did not escape his notice that four more guards moved to stand some six paces behind them, protecting their king, while far enough back to be only a vague threat. As they tested the food gingerly, and then tucked in, joining the locals, Faventinus let Densus and the tribune lead the way in negotiation, for his fellow centurion had the most localised knowledge, while the tribune had the authority of the emperor. Faventinus, on the other hand, was quiet, enjoying the spicy-sweet food and piecing things together in his head. The Garamantian trader they had met back at the market had said that not only did he cross the desert roads from Carthage to this exotic land, but also 'I am here every autumn, following the desert routes, buying and selling as I go, and even beyond this place, to the coast.' Faventinus had missed that, at the time, so grateful were they to find supplies, and someone with whom they could communicate. But that trade route had to pass through here. The wheel ruts they'd seen did not seem to belong to any vehicle from the village, and so they had to come through it from elsewhere. And there were boats, too, and a dock, which meant that goods could cross the river here. This was a nexus for trade.

Indeed, as he tucked in to the food, he realised there were two other signs pointing to the trade with the Indian Sea. One was the smell. It was not just the food, but also burning myrrh, an incense from the southern Arabian lands, which Rome usually traded through the east, and which could surely have only come here from the coast. The other was the food. Faventinus had had meals flavoured with black pepper rarely since reaching Rome, but it was one of the small luxuries his rich mercantile family had indulged in back in Uthina and Carthage. And black pepper was most definitely imported from India.

He only half listened to the conversations going on around him. They were troubled, for these people may have links with the culture of Aegyptus, but had absolutely no knowledge of Greek, and translation and understanding were troublesome at best. His mind drifted back along their journey thus far, instead, and he almost jumped at the next connection. The merchant they had spoken with, so many months ago in Syene, who bought ivory from the south. He had said something about 'swamp town', and from there a road going far to the east. Half a month or so to the Indian Sea.

They had found the trade route, and a safer way home.

But that only highlighted what else the man had said. This place, then, was the last known location before the swamps began. And if desert and river had brought swamp fever to the men, what awaited them in the coming days?

PART 5

TERRA INCOGNITA, AD 61

Μέχρι μέν νυν τεσσέρων μηνῶν πλόου καὶ ὁδοῦ γινώσκεται ὁ Νεῖλος πάρεξ τοῦ ἐν Αἰγύπτῳ ῥεύματος· τοσοῦτοι γὰρ συμβαλλομένῳ μῆνες εὑρίσκονται ἀναισιμούμενοι ἐξ Ἐλεφαντίνης πορευομένῳ ἐς τοὺς αὐτομόλους τούτους. ῥέει δὲ ἀπὸ ἑσπέρης τε καὶ ἡλίου δυσμέων. τὸ δὲ ἀπὸ τοῦδε οὐδεὶς ἔχει σαφέως φράσαι· ἔρημος γὰρ ἐστὶ ἡ χώρη αὕτη ὑπὸ καύματος.

To a distance of four months' travel by land and water, then, there is knowledge of the Nile, besides the part of it that is in Egypt. So many months, as reckoning shows, are found to be spent by one going from Elephantine to the country of the Deserters. The river flows from the west and the sun's setting. Beyond this, no one has clear information to declare; for all that country is desolate because of the heat.

Herodotus, *Histories* 2.31.1

34

DECEMBER AD 61

'You're sure?' Densus squinted at the tablet. Frankly, he was willing to take it on trust rather than count the many, many lines.

'Not entirely,' Faventinus admitted. 'I mean, I like Milo, and he's bright enough, but could anybody keep track this long without losing count at some point. And since the illness...'

Densus nodded. His third in command had started showing the clear signs of the swamp fever yesterday morning, and by night was raving and sweating with the others in the sick wagon. It was entirely possible the man had missed out a day's mark or even two as he slid into the sickness, not to mention, as Faventinus had noted, the possibility that he'd simply lost count at some point anyway. The tablet was covered in hundreds of marks.

'Will the god be angry if we miss the festival and then celebrate it late?'

'Would you?'

Densus pursed his lips and nodded. 'Probably not.' He turned and looked at the column, coming to a halt in the late afternoon light. They needed a rest, something to lift their spirits. He turned and waved to his optio, who came ambling forward from where he'd been overseeing the emptying of a wagon. 'Gallo, you know those pig-like things we saw half a mile back? The ones with the big tusks that the lads wanted to hunt?'

The optio nodded. The men had seen the creatures and immediately pictured them steaming on a platter, but the tribune had refused to halt the journey there, in thick undergrowth, when they could see an open area ahead, safer for camping.

'Take a tent party back and grab a couple. It turns out... it's Saturnalia!'

Gallo broke into a wide grin and hurried back to the men he'd been working with. In moments they had pila and were jogging off into the wild to hunt the pig-things. That pigs were Saturn's sacrifice of choice, and that they seemed to abound in this strange land, could only be serendipity at work. He turned to Faventinus. 'Best go see the lads and let them know it's party night. We can only really afford one night, but let's make it a good one for them, eh? Gods, but they need it. Can you grab a couple of them and start up the cook fires ready?'

'And you?'

'I'm going to see the boss.'

Faventinus nodded, and Densus set himself ready. The tribune was bound to be difficult, but today he could go stick difficult up his arse. Today was about the men. Today was Saturnalia, even if it was late. He marched along the line, noting the atmosphere as he went, hoping to see a lifting of spirits. Here and there, a smiling face told him that news was spreading along the line faster than he could walk, but he was dismayed to still see a majority of stony downcast expressions, despite supposed tidings of merriment.

The tribune was standing some twenty paces from the activity. His secretary was busy scribbling on his tablet as the officer dictated his journal for submission to the emperor upon their return. Densus took a deep breath as he approached.

'Sir.'

'Centurion?' the tribune said, brow rising as he broke off his dictation.

'Sir, your last act as commander for the evening is to select a King of Misrule.'

The tribune's brow lowered again, right down to a frown. 'What?'

'It appears that we have entered Saturnalia without seeing it coming, sir. I have sent men off to find pigs for sacrifice and for feasting. The men will arrange gifts, and as tradition holds, the lowliest rule tonight. The slaves will get preference, the men next, while the officers and I shall prepare the feast. I think there is still a need for you to officiate at the sacrifice, mind, before you step down.'

'I shall do no such thing.'

Densus fixed the commander with a hard look. 'This is Saturn's time, a sacred feast. The gods will not be denied. And more importantly, neither will I. The men need this. They are close to breaking point. We found the perfect way to go home at swamp town, and the perfect excuse to do so, too, but, instead, we press on into potential disaster. The men are only coming with you because of what happened with the assassins, because they think the gods demand they do so. But if you flout the gods' festivals, you remove the only thing that's currently stopping them rebelling. It's Saturnalia. That makes the men my boss, and that makes me yours. Get yourself ready for sacrifice and then serving the men.'

Curtius Lupus' eyes glittered dangerously. His finger jabbed at Densus. 'Frankly I don't care what you and your officers have to do to keep the men in line, though personally I favour punishing those who step out of it, rather than rewarding rebellion. I, on the other hand, will have nothing to do with such antics. We are far from Rome, here, and I will not take part in such hedonistic lunacy. Begone.'

He turned back to his secretary, who threw Densus a long-suffering, apologetic look for a moment before going back to work. Densus stood for a heartbeat or two, quivering with anger, almost ready to insist. He bit down on the retort that arose and turned, marching away. Somehow he knew the tribune was not going to back down from this, and any attempt to force him would end with them at a dangerous impasse.

Instead, he returned to the head of the column. Faventinus already had the men at work. Gesturing to him, Densus pulled his fellow centurion aside. 'The tribune won't do Saturnalia, and I can't see any way we can force him that'll end well. Maybe the best thing is for him to stay away and out of sight for the duration.'

Faventinus, expression hard, nodded. 'Who'll officiate?'

'You or me.'

'You do it. You look more sacred.'

Densus snorted at that, but nodded anyway. The King of Misrule, a Saturnalia tradition, saw one man given licence to become a cavorting fool. In a perfect world, the role would go to Gallo, who was already halfway there at the best of times, but as one of the officer class, Gallo would be working to serve the men tonight. In the end, as things were made ready, Densus moved among the column looking for the jokiest man. It was hard enough finding someone even smiling, but in the end, he selected one of the men from Faventinus' century, who was telling a somewhat crude joke as they emptied sacks of food from a cart. The soldier went off, expression uncertain, to prepare.

Densus then joined in the preparations for dinner, something he'd not done since being raised to the centurionate many years earlier. By the time the sun was setting, Gallo and his men were back with three of the tusked, pig-like creatures. Two were immediately set roasting, while the third, which was still alive and tethered, was taken to a spot that had been cleared ready.

There, as the men gathered in a generally sullen mood, Densus sacrificed a pig with appropriate prayers to the great god as the King of Misrule, almost naked and painted red, danced the fool beside him. It was the first time Densus had ever performed a sacrifice, and it surprised him just how much blood it involved. He contemplated removing the pig's liver, poking it a bit and then pronouncing good omens for the coming days, but quickly decided against it. Any reading from him would be a sham, and the men would know that and resent him for it. Instead, he limited the ritual to a simple sacrifice to the god, following which he gave his hands a good wash and sent the carcass off with a couple of the lads to add to the meat on the camp fires.

He then joined the other officers in cooking the meal and serving it up to the men, following which they joined the soldiers and the slaves at the huge banquet. The appointed king cavorted sort of half-heartedly around the celebration, painted red as tradition demanded, smacking people on the head with one of the pigs' bladders inflated on a stick. In Rome, such attire as the king's was an outlandish thing. Here, in this strange world, red-painted people were not entirely unusual. In one of his last moments of authority, Densus freed up an extra ration of wine for the men, and then he, Faventinus and Flaccus hurried out to the edge of the camp and relieved the sentries so they could enjoy Saturnalia while the officers stood their watch. Gallo was not assigned such a duty, though. Given recent events, and as one of the few men on whom Densus felt he could rely, the optio stood guard near the tribune's tent, away from the festival, making sure that there was no repeat attempt on the commander's life.

Thus, Densus found himself sitting on a fallen log, eyeing the undergrowth and the trees, watchful for wild animals or angry natives, imagining every rustle and flutter to be a lion coming for him. The night was as warm as usual, even at Saturnalia, in the middle of winter, and his tunic clung to his sweaty frame uncomfortably as he sat in the dark, listening to the distant sounds of subdued socialising in the camp behind him. He'd hoped to engender an improved mood among the men with the unexpected festivities, but even this seemed unable to dent the sense of doomed discontent that blanketed the expedition now.

The three officers sat at intervals around the camp's perimeter, not quite able to see one another, but after the first hour or so, his musings were interrupted. Faventinus appeared from the darkness, waving ahead to show he was a friend. As he came to a halt, Densus frowned. 'Abandoning your post?'

'For a few moments. The men are all giving gifts. It's a bit far from here to the stalls on the Via Sigillaria, but I have something for you anyway.' He reached into his tunic neck and withdrew a small gleaming figurine on a leather thong, which he unfastened, handing the thing to his fellow centurion. Densus took it with a frown.

'That's too generous, Claudius.'

'Crap. What it is, is a figure of Tanit. The Carthaginians worshipped her as a sort of Minerva or Juno. She's a goddess of war, and I've carried her since I left Africa and joined the Guard. She's served me well. Now let her serve you.'

Densus smiled. 'I have only one thing worthy in return.' He dug into his pouch and produced the hooked blade covered with symbols that he'd been given back in Syene.

'I can't take that.'

'You would have done when I got it. You complained about being given a stone insect instead,' grinned Densus.

Faventinus shrugged, with a strange smile, and accepted the offering. 'I supposed I'd best get back to...'

He stopped, mid-sentence, and frowned. Densus was about to ask why, when he heard it, too. It was faint, muted by distance and foliage, but there was no mistaking the sounds of combat.

'What the fuck?'

'Shouldn't have left my post,' swallowed Faventinus,

and the two men broke into a jog, running in the direction whence the noise came. For a moment, as they passed, Densus wondered whether to issue the general call to arms, but struggled with it, and in the end decided against it. He was trying to relax the men and rebuild a little of their confidence and good nature, and until he knew the source of the noise, he could hardly afford to undo all his good work.

He and Faventinus reached the edge of the circle of firelight and a quick glance at the ground revealed the footprints of a number of people, all facing one way, heading away from camp. Heart lurching, he peered through the lit area, expecting the worst, but was relieved to see the distant shape of Gallo standing near the tribune's tent across the camp, looking bored. Whatever was happening, at least it seemed the tribune was safe.

As they pushed their way along the winding track between lush green vegetation, the sounds became clearer. Whoever it was had taken their unknown event far enough from the camp that the sounds would be masked by the crackle of camp fires and the murmur of conversation, but it had been audible at the sentry posts on the edge. There were three, maybe four, voices, as well as the furious sounds of two figures engaged in combat. Rounding a corner, the two centurions emerged into a clearing, and stumbled to a halt, staring.

Two almost naked men were busy sparring, a gathering of three slaves behind them looking terrified, roped together. Four guardsmen were there, too, a pair in conversation as they observed the fight, a third standing by the slaves with a bared blade out, threateningly, and a fourth busy jamming a freshly severed head onto a stick, lined up beside two that already stood there, grisly and open-mouthed in disarticulated horror.

'What is the meaning of this?' bellowed Densus, ripping his vine stick of office from his belt, and using it to indicate the display. The paired fighters faltered at the sudden interruption, the weapons in their inexpert hands lowering. He knew there was more than just a little trouble brewed up here, for he saw shock in those two men's faces, desperate hope in those of the roped slaves, but only belligerent defiance in the four guardsmen.

One of the four did manage a half-hearted salute, though as he did, the head he'd been securing on the stake fell with a thud to the ground.

'A word of advice, sir,' another said quietly but forcefully. 'Turn around and go back to camp.'

'Tell us,' Faventinus added, his own vine stick coming out now, slapped into his palm as a warning sign.

'Old Saturnalia traditions die hard, sir. We don't want trouble. You know we're yours even into the mouth of Hades,' the man said, then looked past them towards the camp. 'We're just not *his*.'

'Gladiator *munera*?' Densus snapped, narrowing his eyes. He'd never memorised their faces, and their sistrums of office had been left in a heap way back north, but he'd be willing to bet his right ball at that moment that these four were among those disciples of Urbicus back in the north. 'Really? Haven't we already had this discussion in Aegyptus? Human sacrifice is banned by decree of the senate.'

'How's that relevant out here?' one man demanded, as another, simultaneously, said 'This is not sacrifice. This is ritual killing.' The two men glared at each other, both aware they had undermined one another's point.

'What are you trying to do? Saturn has had his sacrifice. He had a pig. His favourite.'

'But what of his consort?' hissed the fourth man from by the slave line. 'What of Mother Destruction? She demands sacrifice, too, and you know this is how to appease her. Our forefathers did this. It's time-honoured tradition.'

Faventinus cut in at this point, jabbing his vine stick at the man. 'Don't think I don't know you, Marcus Julius Proculeius. Your ancestors were Gaulish wine merchants, if I remember rightly, from Aventicum. So that's bollocks. Your forefathers were more likely to be the ones in the ring with the swords.' He turned to one of the other four. 'And as for you, I know you damn well only scraped into the Guard on my recommendation, because your father had been accused of shagging a senator's wife, and was the subject of a rather infamous court case. Think your forefathers are something noble to live up to, do you?'

Densus could almost have laughed at the sheepish looks that crossed those men's faces, but that contrition was so swiftly replaced once more by defiance that he knew even Faventinus' wit was not helping.

'You know,' Densus tried, 'that sacrifice to Mother Destruction ended centuries ago, and if anyone tried this in the city, they'd be in the shit.'

'Not over slaves,' argued one man.

'They're not *your* fucking *slaves*!' Densus was getting angry now. 'They belong to the expedition, and therefore to the emperor. When we get home, you'll owe Nero for each man you kill. And until then, you should remember that these men have been promised their freedom if they make it, and that without them you will be doing twice the work. You're being stupid.'

'We're being careful. If we want to live to see Rome again, we need *all* the gods on our side. Better to have half as many of us live, with divine support, than all of us struggling alone. The gods protect that shit-head tribune and we can't stop him. And he's not going to turn us around. So what other hope *is* there for us?'

'You've killed three men,' Faventinus snapped, pointing at the heads on poles, or in one case *next* to a pole. 'Let that be enough.'

'No.'

'It's a trinity. Trinities are important to the gods. Look at the Capitol and its temples.'

'No,' said the defiant man by the slaves again, taking a step away from them, sword still raised. 'This is going to happen, Centurion. Don't interfere.'

Densus stepped forward next to Faventinus. 'No other slave dies tonight. That's my final word.'

It was bravely spoken, despite his suspicion that they were in trouble, and it had an effect. The two men who'd been watching the fight began to back away, and the man struggling with the head was now looking more like he was trying to hide behind his handiwork. The fourth, though, the man who'd been guarding the slaves, and who Densus now decided was the ringleader, was still advancing on them, sword in hand.

'It doesn't *have* to be your final word,' the soldier hissed, ominously, still advancing, sword coming up. Densus stepped past Faventinus, who looked at him with a frown.

'No centurion should have to kill his own man,' Densus explained with a resigned sigh. This simple statement seemed to further disarm the other three who were already backing down, but the one defiant, advancing man faltered not. As Densus advanced to meet the man, Faventinus began dealing with the rest of this mess. The man jabbed his vine stick at the fighting pair, who both dropped their swords in an instant. 'Go untie your friends,' he said.

Densus left the others to it. He had his own problem. The man facing him was no career soldier, no veteran legionary forged in the crucible of war in the east or north, drilled and run in the blistering sun or the pounding rain for years to toughen him, taught the every in and out of the Roman soldier's weapons. He was a Praetorian. Trained by the best, yes, but untested until this very expedition, inexperienced. Despite that, it would not do to underestimate him. The journey from Alexandria and the few small scuffles they'd had had changed the men.

Still, Densus knew what he himself was made of. He was a hard man, and like any who accepted the centurion's crest, he'd had to be utterly unafraid of death. A legionary was taught early on the three guaranteed kill zones: the neck, the armpit and the groin. Any one of those and your enemy was done for. In true war, they were usually hard to achieve. Most chain shirts these days had sleeves protecting the armpits, and came to the thighs with the addition of a cingulum of straps to protect the nethers. And between the collar of a chain shirt and the cheek pieces of a helmet was a hard target to hit.

This soldier, though, Marcus Julius Proculeius, was in just a long tunic of green and red, without helmet or armour.

For a moment, Densus wondered if he could get away with some sort of lesser punishment for the man. Put him down and then let him rejoin his unit? After all, they needed every man they had. But he glanced at the others, and saw how despite their backing away, they still looked to the fourth, watching, hoping.

No. One of them would not walk away from the clearing.

Proculeius came to a halt some six paces from Densus. The slaves were now busy unroping each other under Faventinus' protection, while the other three guardsmen had gathered together near the heads.

'I thought we'd left all this foolishness behind with those rattles of yours,' Densus said quietly.

'Draw your sword, Centurion.'

'I don't need a sword to deal with a little prick like you, Proculeius,' he said dismissively, swishing his vine stick back and forth. The centurion's vitis was not just a symbol of office, used occasionally to clout idiots across the back when they were doing something wrong. It was made of vine wood partially for the religious significance, but partially because aged vine might as well be made of iron for its weight and hardness. And a vitis was never a new, fresh thing, commissioned when a man became a centurion. They were passed down through the ages. Densus had no idea how old his was, but rumour had it that it was the same one that had been carried into Kush when the legion was first assigned to Aegyptus, all those decades ago. It had passed from the hands of one hard bastard to another over the years until it came into his possession, and today he would use it to teach a hard lesson to three other men.

He watched the soldier, saw the glint in his eyes, saw the

muscles bunching, knew already what the man's opening move was going to be.

Proculeius leapt forward in a blur, sword stabbing out in his right hand, aiming for Densus' midriff, his left arm coming out as though holding a shield, whether out of habit or in the belief it could do the same job, he couldn't decide. Whatever the case, the centurion had anticipated it all. As the sword lanced out, Densus made a simple and easy step to his right, taking him out of line of the blow. As he did so, he brought the vine stick down with as much force as he could muster.

The crack of bone would have told him that he'd broken the man's left arm even had the wrist and hand not suddenly dropped and sagged as though held onto the arm only by skin and drooping muscle. Not just a broken bone, but broken so hard as to almost sever the damn thing.

The man screamed, his bravado gone in a heartbeat.

To give the soldier his credit, he did stagger back and bring the sword up again, eyes brimming, teeth clamped on his lower lip to stifle his own whimpering. He stepped forward, trying to tuck his broken arm in so it didn't flap about. His sword was not aimed in a killing blow this time, but swished back and forth almost defensively even as he advanced.

The problem with such a move was that it looked better than it actually was. A man whipping his weapon back and forth sends the pointed tip at speed through quite an arc, but the base of the blade, near the hilt, is only moving slowly, and in short sweeps. So, when Densus took a step forward and slapped his vine stick into the flurry of blurred sword, it simply stopped the blade from swishing this way and that in an instant, while sending a painful jolt up the man's arm. Proculeius stared down at his disarmed hand in surprise as Densus twisted his vine stick, expertly prising the sword from the man's hand, where it fell to the ground.

The soldier stared at his fist, which was shaking with pain and effort. He was done. Densus hardened that part of himself that sympathised, for he truly did. These men had not been like this in Rome. It was the madness of what they were being forced to do that had driven them to abandon civilisation, and that was purely down to the tribune. For a moment, Densus cursed that all-powerful oath that made him obey the chain of command, and similarly now demanded that this man die. But it was that same oath that had made him a centurion, had earned him glory, and had made Rome an empire from a small collection of huts on a hill.

'Sir...?' Proculeius said, voice shaking, terrified, the certainty of his position shattered and scattered to the winds in two blows.

'No. You stand against your commander as an enemy. You broke an oath given before Apollo, on the eagles of Rome and the standards of the Praetorian Guard. You are no longer a member of that Guard. You are no longer a citizen of Rome. You are no longer even a free man. Your crimes have been witnessed by all here. You are a criminal, condemned by your own words and actions. The only sentence can be death.'

The man stared at him helplessly, knowing it was true, and that he had brought it all on himself. For a moment he glanced at his friends, and Densus was satisfied to see all three of them shake their heads slightly and look away. Good. There was still hope for them, then.

Knowing he was doomed, the soldier suddenly dropped forwards, reaching down for his fallen sword. Densus had known that was coming, too, though, and with a short step back, he brought his vitis round in a hard swing. The knotted, age-hardened wood slammed into the side of the man's head, smashing his eye socket and cheek. The soldier fell the rest of the way, collapsing in a painful heap.

Densus paced to one side, stooped and swept up the abandoned sword, swapping his vine stick to his left hand. 'Nice weapon,' he said appreciatively, holding up the sword and looking it up and down. 'Be grateful I'm me and not the tribune, for I'm still willing to give a man a soldier's death,' he said quietly, as he took a step forward and dropped, driving the sword down into the man's back, where it slid between ribs, punched through the man's heart, and then exited his chest into the dirt below.

As Proculeius died, quickly and with little fuss, face down in the murk, Densus rose once more, leaving the sword transfixing him.

'You three have had sufficient warning, I think,' he said, gesturing with his vine stick at the remaining guardsmen, who were still gathered together near the heads. 'I have all your faces memorised now, and that was my last mercy killing. From here on in anyone who breaks their oath gets crucified. Now get out of my fucking sight.'

The three men bolted in the direction of the camp. The last of the three slowed for a moment as he neared Proculeius' body, clearly intending to pick it up. Densus simply shook his head, eyes locked on the man, and the soldier hurried past, failing to meet his gaze. Once they were gone and out of earshot, Densus crossed to the surviving men in the clearing. Faventinus looked at him. 'You really going to let them go?'

He shrugged. 'What else. Killing three more soldiers won't improve our chances. Let's just hope what happened here helps deter any repeat of this. I lied when I said I remembered their faces, but I do remember *one*, as he's one of my engineers. The other two are yours, so you might have to keep an eye on them.'

Faventinus nodded and turned to the slaves. 'And remember, you lot, *that* was justice for your companions, what Densus here did. I don't want any budding Spartacus here, rising up and seeking revenge by hunting guardsmen in the night. It's over. Bury your friends and then mourn them, and rejoin us at the camp.'

Leaving them to it, the two centurions turned and strolled back towards the camp, along that winding path. As they went, Faventinus sighed. 'Human sacrifice? How low do we have to sink before Lupus gets it and turns us back?'

Densus snorted. 'He'll never turn back. You and me are career military, Claudius. We don't have to worry too much about success or failure. If we fail, it means we're dead. He's a tribune, though. In a year or so, he'll move on, looking for high office. If he's successful now, all he has to do is learn to smile at nothing and pretend the emperor's poetry is good. But to get that far, he needs to succeed here.'

'Then we'd best hope this swamp is not too wide, and the river rises on the other side, cos I don't know how much more of this the men will stand.'

35

JANUARIUS AD 62

Claudius Faventinus scratched his head as he looked out over the terrain ahead.

It was not a simple proposition.

The river had gradually opened up throughout the afternoon following the disastrous Saturnalia, the green strip at the margin slowly changing from grass and shrubbery to reeds and black, sucking soil. They had found that with every mile, they were moving further and further from the river itself, forced to stay on more solid land because of the carts, and the belt of thick green reeds between them and the water widened continually.

The trend had continued the next morning, at an accelerated rate. In the first hour of travel, they had almost lost sight of the main river, though it had split into several meandering sub-channels that wandered through the reeds. The days that followed brought more of the same. The river slowly turned in a westerly direction, as far as they could make out, but the green mass that marked the Nile, which had widened over one hundred and fifty miles to maybe three or four miles across, had changed again this morning.

Now, no one could see across it, the river and its channels and reed beds was that wide.

'How far, d'you reckon?' Faventinus asked, shading his eyes and peering north across the green.

'No idea,' Densus replied, 'but it's at least ten miles across, probably a lot more.'

'We need to find an accessible river channel. Supplies are running low.'

His friend could only nod at that. Since swamp town, they had travelled far, with an increasing number of fever victims crammed into two of the wagons. All supplies were running low, especially the Artemisia paste they were now eking out, and even the basic foodstuffs were now waning, for the constant damp heat had ruined the emergency grain they carried and accelerated the ripening and then rotting of everything else. Most troubling, though, was the water. They were down to just a few days' emergency supplies of water, and the few forays they had attempted to get to a channel of the river had been disastrous. The terrain, forging a path through reed beds and sucking mud, was bad enough, but it turned out also to be the perfect hiding place for both crocodile and hippopotamus, as well as many other animals. They had lost two men in attempting to reach water safely before the centurions had decided they would just have to keep eking it out and wait until a branch of the river came close.

A shout of alarm drew their attention, and the two men hurried on ahead. The sight that greeted them was far from heartening. One of the wagons' wheels had slipped into the greenery, coming a little too close with a distracted driver. The wheel had dropped into the murk and the whole thing had tipped to the right, sending what critical supplies it contained into the reeds and water, and the wheels on that side had broken in the process. Faventinus did not need the expertise of an engineer to tell him the wagon was done for.

He waited a while as the vehicle was emptied of anything that could be saved and then pushed further into the reeds to be out of the way of everything that followed. The driver was brought before him, and Faventinus prepared to tear a strip off the man for his carelessness, but one glance was enough to tell the centurion that the man was already near delirious with the fever. No wonder he'd strayed, and it could hardly be blamed on him now.

'Get this man to the sick wagons and the capsarius.'

That was another worry that consumed him as the column began to move again. When they had set off from Alexandria, the column had thirteen officers, one hundred and sixty men, and fifty slaves, as well as a dozen of the tribune's entourage. Between crocs, hippos, raiders, lions, illness, misadventure and random stupidity, that number had dropped drastically. There were now twelve officers, but only ninety-two active soldiers, just over a century's worth formed from two, with a further twenty-nine in the sick wagons, several of whom may not make it past a few more days. They were down to seventeen slaves, now, too. How many of the tribune's people remained, he couldn't guess, for the man travelled almost separately these days, and they never saw most of his people, who were either in the covered wagon during the day, or his tent at night.

The numbers were not looking good. And starvation and illness were likely to thin them out even more in the coming days.

That afternoon, they found a channel of the river that meandered tantalisingly close to the solid ground, but the shapes of numerous crocodiles put everyone off getting too close.

Another night of camp, another subdued evening of worried, grumbling soldiers, of hopeless slaves, of the tribune locked away in solitude with his secretary, of Faventinus and Densus prowling the camp, checking for trouble and listening for the men's mood, which was universally bad.

The next day: more of the same. Less food, less water, more misery, the going ever slower, the great river barely visible now through the difficult green. Then: something new.

For the first time since swamp town, late that morning, they stumbled across humans. They were, Faventinus decided at first sight, the least civilised humans he had ever met, but even the least civilised human was a welcome sight now. As the centurions hurried forward, a man went to make the tribune aware of the reason for the halt, though even this did not bring the senior officer from his wagon.

These natives were different from the many tribes they had already met. For one thing, they were all tall, *very* tall. Even the shortest among them towered over Faventinus by more than a foot. They were dark skinned, like the other local natives, and wore simple shabby tunics of brownish red, their heads shaved and their faces marked with deliberate scars in lines and patterns and whorls. Despite their fearsome appearance, though, they were clearly farmers, for in the background, across the muddy, dusty landscape, he could see more of them with their cattle herds.

'Oklamussa,' the nearest, tallest specimen said, as the two centurions approached, slowly, carefully keeping their hands away from their weapons.

'No speak your language,' Faventinus replied, gesturing to his mouth and shaking his head.

'Kweel,' the man replied with a nod.

'Can we buy some of your animals?'

A frown. Faventinus pointed to the cattle across the flat ground, made a mooing sound, pointed at their wagons, then opened his purse and showed a little jingle of coin. There was a frustrated, confused pause, and then three of the scarred giants went into a huddle in their language, before turning back to the visitors.

'Osobola okuba n'essatu,' one said, holding up three fingers.

'Three?' Faventinus felt a flutter of relief. Whatever else they might struggle with, at least there would be meat for a few days. He started to fish out coins, but the man shook his hand and his head, and pointed to Faventinus' sword, then held up three fingers again. In most circumstances, he would never relinquish weapons from the Guard to strange barbarians, but the simple fact was that they had lost enough men now that weapons were plentiful. At his instruction, one of the soldiers fetched four swords from the carts, which were handed over to the native, who smiled, apparently very pleased with the exchange. Not pleased enough to release four cows, mind, but at least the three that were brought forward and handed over to the Romans seemed to be good, healthy specimens.

The relief at having forged a relationship with them led to an opening of the floodgates. Members of the tribe came forward and began to speak to other Romans, and Densus turned and gave blanket permission for everyone to fall out of line and speak to the natives. Within fifty heartbeats, men were trading all along the column, and Faventinus felt a glimmer of hope. Not only would it seriously improve the morale of the men, but just possibly it might solve their supply problems.

With a little difficult exchange, the two centurions and three of the tribe's leaders sat in a circle a little away from the impromptu market that had kicked off.

'We need water,' Faventinus said, pointing to the skin he had brought and miming drinking from it.

The man opposite frowned, nodded, and then let forth a swift stream of syllables that Faventinus did not understand. Realising he'd failed to explain, the native nodded, thought for a moment, then clapped his hands. He mimed drinking. Faventinus nodded. He pointed in the direction of the river. Faventinus nodded. He pointed to the west, then up to the sky. Faventinus mused for a moment, then realised the man was pointing at the sun. He nodded. The man's finger drew a line down from the sun and stopped just above the horizon. Then he mimed drinking again.

The centurion laughed with relief. 'Half a day. By sunset, water?' He repeated the mime and the man nodded with a broad smile.

'Thank the gods. Access to water by the end of the day.' He turned to Densus. 'By late afternoon we need to have every man we have scouting ahead, looking for the water.'

Faventinus looked back to the man and rubbed his head.

How did he ask the next question? He took a deep breath, and tried. He pointed to the river, then picked up a stick and began to draw in the dirt. He traced a map, showing the line of the Nile, travelling south from Kush, then angling to the west here. He pointed at it, and then across at the river. The native nodded. He then began to expand the Nile in this area, drawing a series of channels, expanding it to be the great marshy expanse. He paused and looked up at the tribesman, hoping for a glimmer of understanding. The man nodded, sagely, and Faventinus was content he'd put his point across. He then gestured around them, at himself, at the man and so on, and then jabbed the stick into their assumed current position on his crude map. Again, the native nodded. This was it. Faventinus held his breath and pointed to the undisturbed dirt ahead, to the west. The man understood, much to his relief. Faventinus realised he was still holding his breath as the native took the stick and began to draw. He also realised that a small crowd had gathered around them now, a few more natives and quite a few men from the column. One of the scarred giants had a polished buccina horn over his shoulder, and Faventinus decided that he might have to have words with Genialis later. Selling their signalling equipment was maybe going a little too far. He turned back to the expanding map with his heart in his mouth.

The man had drawn their future. The river curved ahead, back to the south, though the swamp was clearly enormous. The man had drawn many days' worth of further travel, and then tapped his stick beyond it and gave Faventinus a look that made it clear he had drawn to the extent of his knowledge. Faventinus sighed. All he knew, after all that, was that the swamp went on for a very long way, turning south with the river once more. Still, it was more knowledge than he'd had before. And now they had fresh meat for days and the promise of water. Whatever they still did not know, they were in a better position than they had been.

With gestures and maps, he and Densus spent the next hour discussing the swamp with the natives. It took some time and effort to explain that they needed to follow the river, and even longer for the natives to mime rowing boats and explain that, in this swamp, the only real way to follow the river was to be on it.

Within an hour, the tribe had said their farewells and taken their herd back to the east. Densus got the column moving again, the mood of the men temporarily lifted, and then joined Faventinus as they visited the tribune's wagon.

He realised, as the secretary gave them a worried look and then disappeared inside, that he'd not actually seen the tribune in person for over a day, now, and as the wagon flap was thrown back and Curtius Lupus stepped into the light, he realised why.

The tribune's face was waxy and running with sweat, and he had something of a greyish pallor. He was not well. The man displayed symptoms of the swamp fever. He noted one of the jars of the Artemisia compound in the senior officer's hand. The man was medicating himself, and had secured, from what Faventinus could estimate, probably a quarter of their surviving stock of medicine just for himself.

'What is it, Centurions?' he said, a slight slur to his tone as he slumped into the wagon seat.

'Sir, the natives here have told us what lies ahead.'

'Good. And?'

Faventinus glanced at Densus, who gave him a very slight nod. It was a small lie, but in a good cause. 'Sir, the locals say the swamps go on forever. They have never found the far side.'

'Nonsense,' the tribune sneered. 'Nothing goes on forever, except perhaps the emperor's recitals.'

'Sir, we have to face the very real likelihood that this swamp *is* the source of the Nile. Remember what Herodotus said? There is a belief that the Nile flows from the encircling ocean that surrounds the world. Perhaps that is what we've found? The ocean? Like the Delta of the Nile near Alexandria where it flows out into the sea, this is the other end, *another* delta, where the river flows *in* from the great ocean. It makes sense, sir. We can libate and appease the spirits here, and we can return to Rome and the emperor with honest success.'

He closed his eyes for a moment, hoping. When he opened them, the hope melted away. The tribune was shaking his head. 'Herodotus thought that belief unlikely, almost as unlikely as the one involving the Etesian winds. He believed that the Nile came down from a place of snow and meltwater. Until we find that, we cannot say we are sure, and I will not take a lie to the emperor.'

Faventinus sagged. The tribune was still plenty lucid, for all the madness of their mission. 'You are decided, sir? We press on across the swamp?'

'We do.'

He glanced at Densus, and the man's narrowed eyes carried just a tiny hint of defiance, even a glimpse of promised violence, before he blinked it away. Faventinus filed that away to discuss later.

'Sir, if we want to follow the river, the natives made it clear that the only way to do that is in boats, along the river itself.'

'Then that is what we shall do.'

'Sir? We can travel until sunset and find a place where the river comes close enough to get water, but that is all. We have no boats. We *have* to turn back.'

'No. Back at the town... the trade post. They used coracles. Small, two-man boats. They can be made from reeds. They even do that in Aegyptus, so it should not be too hard for our engineers. We make such boats and use them to follow the river from here.'

Another glance at Densus, and Faventinus could see that his friend was barely controlling himself, forcing himself not to snap.

'What of the supplies? The wagons? The animals?'

'Leave them here. Set a guard if you like. If I can abandon my own wagon and trust to such a vessel, then so can every man here. And if the men complain about their burden, remind them that they are Marius' Mules. That a Roman soldier carries all he needs.'

Faventinus began to marshal his arguments, his hand shooting out to grasp Densus, who was making to rise angrily, but it appeared their audience was over. 'See to it,' was the tribune's final word as he rose, swayed a little, and then tottered back into the wagon.

'Come on,' Faventinus said with a sigh, drawing his friend away.

'He's changing,' Densus said as they walked.

'What?'

'He's losing it. Did you hear him? He even made a joke

openly about the emperor. Three months ago he'd have crucified one of us for doing that. And he's prepared to sit in a coracle and sail the swamp? We've dragged half his home furnishings halfway across the world so he can travel in comfort.'

'So he's becoming more of a soldier?' Faventinus said, though he already saw what his friend meant.

'No. He's losing his grip on things. He never had a particularly good grip in the first place, I'll admit, but he's slipping out of the tree now.'

Faventinus didn't like to admit it, but, as they walked away, he knew there was a strong possibility that his friend was right.

36

THREE DAYS LATER, JANUARIUS AD 62

Somehow Densus knew it was a dream even though he was in it, still, and it felt very real. Dog-headed men clawed and bit at him as he struggled to pull himself free. He felt their teeth and their raking claws catching in his flesh, but when he looked down, instead of the dog-headed men, what he now saw hooked into his skin was that hook-ended knife of the seer's from Syene. He looked up from the weapon to the hand that wielded it, then up the arm, and finally into his own face.

He woke with a start, even sweatier than usual.

There was uproar outside. He didn't bother to dress carefully, pulling the sweat-sodden tunic away from his skin for a moment, then fastening on his sword belt, and slipping his feet into his boots without bothering to lace them up. He realised he'd already blamed the tribune in his head before he even knew what he was blaming the man for. Pulling aside his tent flap he ran out into the pre-dawn light. Soldiers were hurrying this way and that, amid the chaos. The camp was little more than a construction yard with some habitable tents, for they had been camped here two days now, manufacturing small reed boats ready for the next leg of the journey.

The centurions had met resistance from the men initially, but pointing out a few salient facts had turned it around. On the river they would have constant access to water. They had all seen the abundant bird life over the swamps from the periphery, and there would undoubtedly be plentiful fish, too. Fresh food and water on hand at all times, and only a little rowing instead of the constant trudge through the dust. That had clinched it. The men were not keen to go any further, of course, but at least on the water it sounded an easier proposition.

What, then, was the cause of this fresh commotion?

He grabbed a passing soldier, one of Faventinus', and pulled him to a halt. 'What's happened?'

'Men have gone, sir.'

'Men? What men?'

'Dunno, sir. Quite a few.'

Let go, the man ran on, and Densus, fresh concern assailing him, scanned the camp until he spotted Faventinus, then hurried over.

'What's happened?' he said again.

His fellow centurion turned a weary look on him. 'I'm having a count done now, but we had a desertion during the night. A big one.'

That made Densus look around. Certainly there seemed to be a lot fewer men in camp than there should be, now that he was paying attention to the numbers. 'Tell me.'

'They killed the men on watch, including my optio,'

Faventinus said darkly, anger lining his face at the revelation. Densus could understand that. Gallo had become something of a fixture among the men, and Densus had come to rely on the irreverent, irrepressible officer.

'Shit.'

'Yes. I reckon we've lost some forty men and a small number of slaves. They took all the butchered meat and all the stored water jars, four of the wagons, including the tribune's, about which he'll spit teeth when we tell him, as it still had a lot of his stuff in it.'

Densus scrubbed his head and looked about. 'I presume they've been gone some hours.'

'Looks like it.'

'We'll never catch them.'

'No.'

'They'll probably be able to make it back to swamp town if they have all the supplies and the river to follow,' Densus said. 'And there they can trade all the tribune's stuff for more. I wouldn't be at all surprised if they reached the Indian Sea. After that, they could go anywhere. We've seen the last of them.'

Faventinus nodded. Densus ran through every possibility in his head, but nothing worked. If they took the scouts' horses and chased the men down, they might catch them, but they wouldn't be able to do anything against forty or so deserters. It was a fool's errand to give chase. He stood with his fellow centurion for the next quarter hour until Flaccus came over with the updated figures.

'Forty-one soldiers, including Venator, and five slaves, plus the dead sentries. Our expedition now numbers ten officers, forty-six soldiers capable of walking or rowing, twenty-four in the sick-tent – two more died of fever in the night – and twelve slaves. The supplies are negligible, and the carts—'

Densus waved him to silence. The carts were immaterial if they were going on by boat, anyway. 'Seventy-eight men, I reckon, including the tribune's staff, not counting the sick. That's considerably less than half what we set out with. Any sane man would call a halt here.'

Faventinus nodded. 'Sanity is no longer in play at command level. You know that. Ambition and bloody-mindedness are all that drive the expedition now.'

Densus looked around. The men were all busy and out of immediate earshot. He lowered his voice. 'When do we admit that those fuckwits with a knife in the night were right?'

'Shut up, Sempronius.'

Densus sighed. 'I know. Army. Oaths. Officers. Romans. But for all that, surely you know there's going to have to come a time when we stand up and say no. We're losing men all the time, and our hope of reaching the source is gone. We'll never find it. Urbicus was right.'

Faventinus shook his head. 'The seer said we could find it, but we'd regret it.'

There was an uncomfortable silence.

Finally, Faventinus sighed. 'We'd best tell the tribune.'

As they walked towards that tent, as always set apart from the main camp, Densus eyed his fellow centurion. Densus was a loyal soldier. His oath had always meant everything to him, but that faith had been eroded over the preceding days. It was always the unwritten law of the army that a centurion held to his oath like every soldier, but his second duty, after that to Rome and his commander, had to be to his men. He had to do the best for the men under his command. And that was now becoming a conflict. He could not look after his men and continue to hold to his duty with the tribune. Faventinus seemed to be having less trouble with it. A thought struck him.

'There is provision in the rule book for removing an unfit officer from command,' he noted quietly.

'What?'

'No matter how mad he is, what's important is that he's got the fever now. The more it takes hold, the less he'll live in the real world. The moment we can get the capsarii to officially determine that he can't do his duty, you and I can take command.'

'Sempronius, that's mutiny.'

'No it isn't. Not if he can't command.'

Faventinus looked troubled now. 'That would be extremely hard to prove back in Rome. Even with the testimony of the medics, you'd struggle to persuade the prefect it was necessary. Don't do anything you regret, my friend.'

They had reached the tent, now, and that dangerous conversation ended sharply. The tribune's door was answered by his secretary, and the air that wafted out as he opened the flap was little more than a putrid warm blast of sickness. The tribune emerged a moment later, still in his sleeping tunic. Densus looked him up and down. His colour had improved a little, and Densus might have thought him on the mend were it not for one thing. Not the waxy, sweaty look, for in this heat and just risen from bed, many a man might look the same. No. It was his eyes. They were pink and defocused, even as he tried to look at the centurions. They betrayed his poor condition.

'Yesss,' he slurred.

'Sir, we have had further desertions,' Faventinus said. The tribune seemed to have to think about this, translate it somehow in his head, then frowned. 'Who?'

'Almost half, sir. They took four wagons, including your own, and all the supplies. They killed the sentries, including an officer.'

Densus actually thought for a moment that the tribune was going to explode. He seemed to inflate, breathing in hard, eyes bulging, arms twitching, fists balling. 'Unacceptable,' the man snapped suddenly.

'Sir?'

'Round up the men. Hunt them down. They'll die for this. And slowly.'

Densus felt the anger rising again. The man was delusional. 'Sir, you know how this works. Just like the slave deserters all that way back on the border of Kush. We'll never catch them, and if we do, it'll be because we've ridden the horses to death, at which point we'll be outnumbered by deserters. We can't follow them.'

The tribune continued to vibrate, to clench and unclench, to breathe through the bars of his teeth. Finally, seeming to gain some mastery over himself again, he drew his figure up straight. 'We will succeed. We will achieve our goal. We will do our duty to the emperor, and when we return to Rome, I will have the name of every man who left our column added to the rolls of deserters. I will personally release a fortune to the fugitivarii to hunt them down, to the very ends of the empire if they must. Every last man will be found, no matter where he hides, and they will be nailed to a cross in the forum.'

Densus fought down the anger, aware that Faventinus was giving him urgent looks.

'Your commands, sir?' he said in a tense hiss.

The tribune wobbled for a moment, then righted himself. 'Finish the boats and the column moves out onto the water. This swamp is the furthest known part of the Nile. After this, somewhere, the source awaits us.'

A salute. Turning. Leaving.

As the two centurions stomped back across the camp, Densus still fighting the anger, Faventinus gave him a weary smile. 'At least now there are fewer of us, we need fewer boats.'

'Very comforting.'

'And you know, despite everything, that there is still the possibility of success. The tribune might be right, and if we do succeed and get home to report to Nero, your career's made. You'll get any position you want. And the seer at Syene said we could do it.'

'She also said we'd regret it many times over.'

'So long as we live long enough to regret it some more.'

37

SWAMP
JANUARIUS AD 62

It took three days to get the boats ready, and two more to launch them and secure everything on land. Despite arguments from ranks both above and below, it was decided to leave the sick where they were. The logistics of piling them into two-man coracles and expecting them to row were just too complex. One of the capsarii would stay with them on dry land, along with three slaves. They had ready access to drinking water and plenty of meat, by way of fish and birds, to survive, as long as they could bring them down with the one bow and sling they had.

The two capsarii had drawn lots as to who would go on with the expedition and who would wait for the rest to return. Needless to say, neither man thought he had the better deal when the lots were drawn. Faventinus had caught the capsarius' expressions and had recognised both. The man accompanying them knew that fresh troubles, dangers and illness awaited, and that there was a strong possibility he would not return. The man staying knew he had his work cut out keeping the fevered sick alive long enough for the expedition to return, but also knew that that might never happen, in which case they would slowly decay where they waited until nature or madness took them. No one got the better deal.

But at least there was progress of a sort. The tribune put in an appearance only as the boats were readied. He held himself upright, and had mopped his face and combed his hair. Unless you knew he was ill, it would be hard to tell, he hid it so well. The first completed boats were put into the water with a certain trepidation, expecting little more than an elaborate sinking device. A legion contained certified units of engineers who could build, change or deconstruct almost anything. Nominally, the same was true of the Praetorians, but on the whole, being city boys with little military experience, the Guard's engineers were usually capable of making a nice water feature for a garden, but little more. It had been the advice of Densus, as a man who had served in Aegyptus and had seen and used such boats at times, which had helped put together the reed boats, and it was, from his expression, a surprise even to Densus that they worked.

As the boats were slid into the water one by one, each occupied by a pair of men who would take turns with the rough oars hacked and shaped from the scrubby trees thereabouts, all eyes were on the reeds just thirty paces from the landing area both up and down stream. The shapes of crocodiles were clearly visible, hovering on the periphery, waiting for the foolish and the unwary to stray too far from the herd, and the great grey shapes of hippos had been seen in the distance twice in the past two days, as well.

'Keep mid-channel,' Faventinus called from the bank, as the first rather inexpert sailors paddled their two-man coracles out into the water. It was somewhat redundant advice, given the yellow reptilian eyes watching them from the reeds. Seventy-four men, crammed into thirty-seven small boats that bobbed out into the channel like chaff on the wind of the Nile. Their numbers were whittled down before they were even out of sight of the camp, by which time three of the vessels had proved non-river-worthy and had disappeared swiftly beneath the water with all six men, who had then swum like Olympic competitors to reach the safety of dry land where the sick party made camp. They would stay with those others, for there was no time to manufacture more boats. Thus it was that by the time they were mid-channel, and the camp sliding away behind them, the expedition had dropped to sixty-eight men. The tribune, starting to look waxy and sweaty already, shared a vessel with his secretary, who was now learning how to handle a new tool of his job as he rowed badly against the current. Faventinus and the other officers had each shared a boat with one of the guardsmen, trying to spread authority out across the flotilla as much as possible.

Faventinus felt any hint of positivity drain as he watched the fleet begin to move. Not a man among them was a natural sailor, and some seemed physically incapable of timing their oar strokes to make it work, several boats going comically round in circles for a time. Others were struggling to make any progress at all and, despite rowing like maniacs, were drifting back downstream away from the fleet, in the wrong direction. It took a full two hours for the coracles to gather together into a group and begin to journey upstream, the men swapping places so that the better oarsmen had the first shift.

By noon, they were out of sight of the sick-tents they had left behind on the bank.

They were officially moving on by river, through the apparently endless swamp.

Densus dropped back early on, as agreed, each of the centurions playing to their strength. Densus, being the more martial of the pair, would bring up the rear of the flotilla, making sure no one was left behind, keeping an eye on the stragglers. He carried a long rope with a grapple at the end, with the plan to use it like a lasso should any other boat hit trouble, throwing it, and hauling on the rope to pull the beleaguered vessel back within reach. Meanwhile, Faventinus, as the quicker of wit among them, was to take the lead, navigating as best he could. The boats of the tribune and the capsarius were somewhere mid-fleet, safe and sound.

Perhaps an hour into the afternoon, Faventinus had to make his first decision. The channel they were following, clearly not the main flow of the river despite its width, suddenly divided between great banks of green reeds. Water seemed to flow from both channels into this one, at the confluence, in roughly equal amounts, at equal speeds, and as such it was impossible to even guess which of the two led to the main river flow. In the end, reasoning that they had set off west from the southern bank, he chose the right-hand, northern channel as most likely to take them further out.

His decision might be borne out, but there was no way to confirm his choice, as they followed this new flow between thick green worlds.

The going was noisy, to say the least. Thirty-four sets of oars dipping and rising with splashes, none of them in time with any other, men shouting to one another, over one another, at one another, or seemingly just shouting, thousands of birds wheeling, dipping, swooping, each adding its cry to the cacophony.

It was late in the afternoon, after hours of struggling upstream, the men slowly finding their way with the oars, when the next choice came upon them. This one was less easy to make. Logic said that they still had not found the main channel, and that it therefore had to be to the right, further away from where they started, yet the left-hand channel seemed to be the one from which the greatest flow came, the right-hand slower and lighter. Faventinus sucked his teeth in thought as he threw up an arm and the coracles paused, using the oars only lightly to stop themselves being dragged back downstream.

He looked back and located Flaccus. The various officers and immunes among the men were so positioned that a message could be carried across the flotilla from one voice to the next, though every now and then they had drifted away and needed to hurry back to position.

'Decision time,' he called to Flaccus, hands cupped to his mouth as the man in front of him dipped the oars to hold his position. 'Right is the likely direction, but low flow. Left is a strong flow, but likely away from the main river. Thoughts?'

Flaccus passed this back to the capsarius, to Genialis, to Densus, having reached the tribune somewhere in the middle. Faventinus listened to distant shouting, the details reaching him as the message was relayed back.

'The tribune says follow the gods' will.'

'Well that's fucking useful,' Faventinus grumbled quietly, making the man opposite him smirk.

'And Centurion Densus asks what the point is in putting you in charge of navigation if you have to ask other people.'

Faventinus sighed and rolled his eyes. Was the water moving faster now from the right than before? Perhaps there had been an obstruction? His mind furnished him with the image of a hippo as a blockage in the channel, which made him shiver. Taking a deep breath, he pointed to the right and gestured to his companion, who began to row, using the oars at different paces to effect a slight turn. The flotilla followed suit, and the expedition moved slowly, inexpertly, into the right channel.

That the flow was slower was confirmed by the fact that as they moved into that channel, the going became easier, the men rowing cursing less and making better headway. Faventinus prayed he'd made the right choice, his decision based on geography over science, though he could as easily have gone the other way.

The light began to fade, and Faventinus prepared for the worst. They had all hoped to be able to find areas of riverbank like the one they'd left to settle in for the night, but they had all equally known the likelihood of that happening was extremely low. They were going to have to spend the night mid-channel. At least they were well prepared for that, the plan formed before they'd left. Every boat carried a length of rope, and every boat had a strong loop of hard reed through which that rope could be passed.

Faventinus, as the foremost boat, began the process as the sun touched the green, vegetative horizon. He tied the rope to the loop in his boat, then threw it to the next, where the man fastened the two vessels together, then did the same with another boat. Over the space of a quarter of an hour, the entire flotilla fastened themselves to the next vessel, creating a giant web of boats. Meanwhile, Faventinus, who carried a second rope with a grapple, just like the one Densus had, managed on the third throw to get the grapple to sink into the reeds and anchor, holding them fast. He checked this by having his companion ship oars and wait, and since they remained in position and did not drift back downstream, he was content it had worked.

The expedition tucked into the meagre supplies they had brought. No one had had the time to fish or bring down birds yet, but each boat carried sufficient supplies for two days. Once the meal was done, with little else to do in these weird, waterborne confines, and limited to pairs, the men slept.

The sun arose early, the men only partially rested, and it brought with it two extremely disheartening realisations. Firstly, they had lost a boat. Whether it had sunk or disappeared downriver, they could not tell, for there was no sign, just the rope to which it had been fastened, dangling off into the water, no longer anchored to anything. The second realisation was, if anything, worse. As Faventinus stood carefully, the boat rocking beneath him, shading his eyes and peering off into the distance, nothing looked familiar.

He felt a rising panic. He knew what the channel had looked like at sunset, for he'd scanned it carefully for the best anchor point for his grapple. Nothing looked the same.

He turned, risking capsizing, and confirmed his fears. The

world around them had changed. Somehow the channel was differently shaped, and, he was sure, the flow was now faster and stronger. Tufts of green were in different places.

'Shit.'

As the men prepared, lamenting the loss of two friends and accepting gloomily that the swamp was capable of shifting around them, Faventinus fretted. He wondered momentarily whether to speak to the tribune, but the man was still looking distinctly ill, and hardly spoke at all now, and thus Faventinus was not at all sure disturbing his superior was a good idea. Anyway, no matter how much he worried, there was nothing he could do about it. All he could do was continue to follow the channel they were on, and hope that it led to the main flow. The possibility that he might not even recognise the main channel of the river when they found it occurred to him, but he fought that one down as well, as another thing over which he had no control.

The ropes were untied and brought in, and men began to row, the flotilla setting off upstream once more.

Late morning, the channel they were in converged with another to form a single river with a strong flow. It was possible they were now out in the middle of the Nile, though Faventinus had no idea how he could tell. At the confluence, he did note a certain murkiness of water, and signs among the nearby reed beds that they had been somehow torn apart, which led him to the fascinating, if disturbing, conclusion that this had been a dead end when they'd set off up it, but had opened up in the night, which would account for the increased flow. The fact that the swamp had changed shape and geography overnight started to make sense.

As they approached noon, they found a lagoon of sorts

within the reeds, an area where the beds had formed a wide pool, and they used this to prevent drifting back downstream while they employed the two nets and five rods, that had been manufactured before they embarked, to haul fish from the water, while those men with bows and slings did what they could to bring down some of the birdlife.

The results were impressive. One good thing about the swamp, at least, was its abundant wildlife. The major snag then hit them. No cook fires, and, in small boats, no hope of starting one, either. They had hoped for landing sites where such activity could occur, but since thus far no landing site had appeared, they were stumped. Thus every boat fell back once more on their emergency rations, hoping for a good site for fires at sunset.

They pressed on in the afternoon. Three times, Faventinus was faced with channel decisions, and each time, he now chose the one with the stronger flow. The second day's sun began to close on the horizon while they were still distinctly far from any hope of a riverbank landing. Disaster hit them too late in the day to do much about it, as the channel they were following closed in ahead to nothing, a solid bank of green shoots and brown tangled roots blocking their way. The channel was a dead end! The water had to be coming between reed beds, or possibly even beneath them, for there was still a reasonable flow, but above the surface no way for a boat to pass.

With a sigh, Faventinus acknowledged the inevitability of this. It'd had to happen at some point, when they chose routes largely at random, and the world shifted constantly around them.

As the flotilla rowed gently to maintain position,

Faventinus and his companion made their way to the reed banks. Perhaps there was one advantage to their dead-end discovery. Perhaps they could dare to land and light fires for a tasty meal. Reaching the reed beds, the soldier kept the oars going, maintaining the boat's position against the bank as the centurion stood, slowly, carefully, gingerly. Once the boat stopped rocking, he stepped out and onto the reeds.

His foot disappeared alarmingly deep into the murk, and the whole reed bed moved, drifting away from the boat. Faventinus shouted in alarm, but the man behind him wasn't fast enough to react, and the centurion felt his crotch straining as his legs were pulled apart, one on a boat drifting back away from him, the other lodged deep in muck. Left with no choice, he leapt forward into the reeds, and for a moment panicked afresh as he sank to his knees in the black mud. Yelping, he struggled to pull himself up, but the motion caused only fresh disaster, as the section of reeds he was trapped in tore away from the bank and began to drift downstream.

'Fucking fuck,' he shouted in panic, as the reed patch drifted towards the nearest boats, but away from his own. With considerable effort and a lot of cursing and struggling, he managed to free himself from the reeds, and launched into the open water, swimming hard for his boat. He reached the coracle and clambered aboard with help from his companion, almost capsizing it in the process, falling into the bottom and shaking, sodden and exhausted, heaving in deep breaths.

As he returned to calm, slowly, the reality of this discovery hit him. Many, if not all, of these reed beds in the swamp were not attached to anything, but were free-floating, the water current flowing beneath them. That meant that the flow of no channel could be relied upon to indicate where it led, that no reeds could be trusted as a sign of land, that anything that disturbed the reeds could see them separate and then clump together with others, likely what was causing the changes all the time.

Nothing in this damned place could be trusted.

He relayed back to the other officers his thoughts. Densus had nothing of use to add, and the tribune sent back no reply at all. A new gloom settled all across the flotilla as they roped together for a second night. The rations had almost been used up now, and what remained was shared out among the boats, the men going hungry, worn out from their day's efforts.

Stupidity led to the next disaster, which occurred during the dark evening as the expedition largely settled in for sleep. Some fools in one of the outlying boats, driven by hunger and desperation, started a small fire in their coracle, resting combustible material on his sword sheath and striking stone and steel until sparks leapt. The wisdom of doing such a thing in a boat constructed of dried reeds was instantly brought home to the pair as the vessel rocked, burning cloth fell to the interior and caught the reeds. The outer surface was wet, of course, but inside, the reeds were dry as old parchment.

The men tried to stop the small fire becoming an inferno, but in less than a dozen heartbeats they'd had to throw themselves overboard to get away from the growing conflagration. They watched from the river, treading water, as their boat disappeared with an immense hiss, taking all their worldly goods with it. The principal fool made it to one of the other coracles, where friends reached down and pulled him aboard, though the boat now carried too much weight and sat deep in the water, the river's surface almost up to the edge. The second man never made it. What happened to him no one could say. They were all busy watching the first man climb to safety and when they looked back there was no sign of his companion, just the unbroken surface of the water.

Faventinus and Densus put out a general order that no fires should be lit, though after the example everyone had witnessed, there was little chance of a repeat.

The second night was subdued, though on waking, at least they had lost no further boats. Sadly, though the shape of their dead end had changed slightly in the night, a dead end it remained. Thus, hungry, tired and demoralised, without breaking their fast, thirty-two boats began to row and drift easily back the way they had come until they reached the next confluence. Some halfway back along the channel, the overloaded boat with three men ran into difficulty and almost sank, and only a hurried redistribution of all the goods stored in their vessel among the others made them river-worthy again.

Faventinus now threw caution to the wind and put their fates into the hands of the gods, tossing a coin to choose their next path. By noon, as he'd taken over his turn at the oars, they were lost once more among the ever-changing flow of interconnecting channels.

The lack of a noon meal brought spirits to a new low, and by mid-afternoon, men were struggling with the effort of rowing in their weakened state. A shout of alarm drew Faventinus' wandering attention later in the afternoon, and he looked around at the next boat, where a man was pointing off to the left. 'What the shit is that?'

Faventinus peered across the reeds to a great grey shape in the distance, towering over the green.

'That's an elephant, you prat,' he sighed, then turned back. Elephants had been a not unusual sight in Uthina and Carthage in his youth, traded across the desert and destined for show in Rome. He'd seen few in the capital, but there were at least a pair in the emperor's keeping – Caligula and Claudius had both had a thing for the magnificent beasts. He was content the thing posed no risk. Elephants on their own were rarely dangerous, for they were placid animals by nature, the gravest danger lying in stampedes, which at least couldn't happen alone and in water.

Four more decisions that afternoon led to no further dead ends, at least. The sun began to set for the third day on a truly disconsolate gathering of exhausted, starving men. Faventinus listened to them as they roped the boats together yet again, the only faint hope issuing from the lips of any man being that soon they would reach the end of the swamp and hopefully the river's source, or at least solid land. Faventinus hadn't the heart to tell them the truth that he kept silently in his heart. They were still ending their days rowing into the sunset, which meant they were still heading west. The tribesmen they'd met had showed the swamp turning south and going on that way for some distance. They were probably nowhere near even halfway.

He listened, and he watched, and he came to the early conclusion that only the lack of dry land for a night was saving the tribune's life. The feeling against the waxy-faced officer who had forced them into this predicament had reached new heights, such that men were openly criticising Curtius Lupus, probably even within earshot. No one, however, wanted to swim between boats to confront the man. Besides, there might be no point, with the growing suspicion that the senior officer was staggering weakly towards the gates of Hades now anyway, given his visible illness. At this stage, three days upstream and starving, every man knew there was at least the possibility of dry land and food ahead, while to turn back would definitely mean at least three more days of hunger.

Nevertheless, the next morning, a number of men decided they could manage it no longer. Fully half the boats that dawn, before they departed, displayed men tucking into their catches, hungrily devouring the meat of bird and fish raw, spitting out the bones as they could, grimacing at the taste and consistency, yet favouring it over weakness and starvation. In the still air of the swamp, the stench of raw fish and fowl being torn apart and consumed threatened to make Faventinus gag. He wouldn't be alone if he did, though, for half the men who'd eaten the raw meals threw it all back up over the next hour, the rest only holding down their food with difficulty. He sent a message back to the capsarius asking whether it was dangerous for the men to eat such raw meals, but the man had no answer to that, reminding the centurion once more that he was a combat medic, trained to stitch wounds and set bones, not a physician of note.

They set off once again, ever westward up the great river or one of its sub-channels, Faventinus taking the first turn at rowing this time. Late morning, they found yet another division of flows, and in desperation, Faventinus once more came to the bank and tested the ground, prepared for a repeat. This reed bank was a little more solid than the one that had almost crippled him, and he stepped onto it, managing to lurch and squelch through the green. A little exploration confirmed that the 'island', such as it was, was relatively stable. He soon found the weaker areas where it might tear away from the main mass, and carefully avoided them, remaining at the centre, where the root system beneath was deep, and thick enough to support his weight.

The plan formed, and within half an hour the boats were all tethered close and men were passing things to him via his own co-sailor, who had tied their vessel to that greenery with the grapple rope. Faventinus used clothes and weapons and whatever he could find to build a small platform above the sucking mud, then used six swords to create a surface of woven steel. Upon this he built a small fire and struck sparks to start it. For the next two hours, he kept the fire burning with anything the men could pass him, roasting fish and birds over it on the end of pila, passing them back across the flotilla, boat-to-boat, once they were done. It was long, hard work, for little recompense, but by early afternoon, every man had eaten cooked game or fish, and though it was only a small quantity, it felt like a banquet to every man after the days of hunger.

He did note that the tribune refused meat, passing it on to the men in a most uncharacteristic gesture of generosity. Whether that was because he was less tired, since he felt his rank saved him from rowing, and so the whole day's work came down to his secretary, or possibly because he had a hidden stock of emergency rations in his boat about which no one else knew, or most likely because his illness had robbed him of appetite, Faventinus couldn't say. The display may well have saved his life from the more angry of the men, but it only went a small way to countering the immense and bloodthirsty bad feeling among the unit.

The afternoon was a little less miserable now, though the gloom had begun to settle in at sunset as the boats were roped together for their fourth night. Some of the men had had the foresight to save a little of their cooked meat from the earlier meal, and in the spirit of shared hardship, these surviving morsels were divided up and passed among the boats to grateful friends. None, Faventinus noted, came anywhere near the tribune, who sat, silent and looking slightly sweaty.

The night, though far from comfortable, was an improvement on the last few. Still, Faventinus drifted into slumber pondering on the fact that they were still sailing west, yet even to find the point the river turned south.

The dream that came to him that night was troubling. His dream-form was bound to a shrub that kept moving when he took his eyes off it, while a few paces away men with dog heads rammed Roman heads onto spikes, laughing as they did so, and casting the rest of the bodies into water that simply eddied in circles, bringing the bodies back moments later, somehow sporting fresh heads that the dog men could remove and display.

He woke before dawn, sweatier than usual from the nightmare, and sat back in his end of the boat, breathing the warm, fetid air, slowly surfacing, letting the tatters of the dream fade. Shouts of alarm came with the sun, and he struggled to see the source of the commotion across the flotilla. Men were lurching upright in their boats, risking tipping them over, pointing and yelling. The murmured tidings that flowed across the fleet reached him even as, now untied, Faventinus' companion rowed him back towards the commotion.

Another boat had gone.

The reason was, however, quite clear this time. What had happened during the night was eloquently announced by the half-eaten body bobbing around in the water, caught up in the rope that still tied what was left of his boat to the next. Of his companion there was no sign, but the fact that their boat was one of the peripheral ones and had strayed towards the nearest reed bed gave Faventinus a sequence of likely events that played out in his imagination. Coming too close to one of the more solid beds, they had drifted from the main flotilla. When the crocs came in the night, they caught the men close enough to the bank to reach with ease, and fast asleep. The men would have woken to find themselves already in the mouths of crocodiles, and Faventinus now knew enough to know that one of the crocodile's first attacks was often the neck, to remove all possibility of resistance. The men were probably silenced with their throats torn even as they woke, the rest of the fleet sleeping, blissfully unaware that two of their friends were being eaten just a few paces away.

He shuddered. From now on, they would have to make sure that the flotilla overnighted more securely, with a watch set. However, as his gaze played across the greenery where the attack had taken place, something occurred to him. Crocs could swim, but they tended to prefer bathing in the muck on the riverbank, where they could easily get in or out of the water, and where the undergrowth gave them the greatest advantage in hunting. Thus far he'd not seen the beasts out in the reed beds amid the channels of the river, which suggested they preferred the solid banks, and not these troublesome, floating lands. That, in turn, suggested that the reeds where the attack happened were at least distantly connected to the bank itself.

With a grim smile, he put out the order that the ruined boat be cut adrift and all others made ready to row on. If what he reasoned was actually the case, somewhere nearby they might be able to reach solid land, and even though they'd have to press on eventually, everyone would relish one night ashore, with the corresponding camp fires and cooked meals.

Whatever the next day held, today he would find respite for the men.

38

SWAMP

JANUARIUS? AD 62

The following day and night would be one they'd remember for a while. An almost normal day, camped on dry land, eating real food and not watching the world change around them. A day that served to at least slightly lift the spirits of the sixty-three remaining men of the expedition. The tribune had clearly taken note of the murmurs of dissent the previous day, for as he made camp in his small, ordinary tent on the edge of the area, his secretary and two other attendants had been armed, and slept outside the tent as sentries, at least one awake at all times. He was taking no chances now. The precautions did little to endear him any further.

Densus had engaged his fellow centurion in a subdued conversation, out of earshot of all that evening, under the pretence of heading out to use a makeshift latrine.

'There will never be a better place to turn back,' Densus had urged his friend.

Faventinus shot him a dark, warning look, but Densus

shook his head. 'The man's gone too far now. Pushed us all too far.'

'You break your oath and even the gods will turn on you,' his friend whispered.

It *was* a worry. Densus knew nothing but the army life. He was career military. His father had served in the legions before him, and had also managed to reach the centurionate. He had retired to Crete and passed away there a respected veteran, by which time Densus was with the Twenty-Second. Even transferring to the Praetorian Guard, Densus had planned to follow his father's example, to the comfortable life of a respected retired centurion.

To turn on the tribune was to turn his back on his oath, and therefore on the army and his entire plan for life. He had struggled with this now for around a month – he couldn't be sure, for time and seasons had become more or less meaningless out here. Mutiny was never an easy thing, even when you were one among many. To *lead* a mutiny was far worse. He needed Faventinus on his side in this, because he was struggling with the need to turn his back on everything he knew in the name of sanity. To turn on Curtius Lupus would probably make it impossible even to return to Rome, let alone remain in the army.

'I'm amazed no one's tried to plant a knife in him since that first time,' he said quietly.

'The gods,' Faventinus replied. '*We* did that, you and I. We showed the men that the gods had punished his would-be killers, and now no one wants to be the next example of divine justice.'

'You and I know that was the will of wild animals, and nothing to do with gods.'

'Do we?' Faventinus said quietly. 'You can't turn your back on your oath, Sempronius Densus. I *know* you.'

Damn it, but it was arguments like that which would undermine the willpower he'd built to do this. 'How far do we have to go before it becomes a necessity?' Even he would admit that he was starting to sound whiney now.

Faventinus sat back. 'Alright, I'll say this: We need to find the end of the swamp.'

'If it even has an end. Or this could *be* the end of the swamp if we decided.'

'No,' his friend said. 'I've been thinking about this. If we turn round and sail back downriver now, we will get lost and turned around in the changing channels. There's a good chance we'll completely miss the camp of our friends, the wagons and animals. But if we disembark here and try to make our way back across solid land, we leave the water and its sources of food. We cannot guarantee food or water once we leave the river. Going back is not feasible. Not yet.'

'Damn you and your wit,' Densus grunted. 'So the alternative is to go on?'

'At least until we find the end of the swamp. Then, we can make the decision. We might find the source there. We might not. But then at least we know where we stand. I say the tribune stays in charge until then.'

'As if he's in charge anyway,' Densus snorted. The man was clearly permanently on the edge of fever and madness from the sickness, and only his hoarding of what medicine they had left was keeping him lucid, in Densus' opinion.

'At least on the river we have food and water.'

'Claudius, we're losing men all the time. Two the first night, and we don't even know what happened to them.

One to the fire. Two to the crocs. And half the men are still green and sickly from the raw meals they ate.'

'But we know how to do it now. I made that fire in the reeds. If I could do it once, I can do it again. It'll slow our progress, but roasted fish and meat every day, with plenty of water? I don't like the alternative.'

He fixed Densus with a firm expression. 'I can't turn my back on my oath, Sempronius, and neither can you. If the man dies of his fever, we have our own decisions to make, and they will be justified and with divine support, but standing against the tribune? No. Put such thoughts out of your mind, my friend.'

He tried. Over the ensuing days, Densus did so time and again, every time the notion of rebellion occurred to him.

He failed.

But the simple fact was that following their departure from that place the next morning, any hope of finding a route back on solid land was lost anyway. Once they returned to the main channel, the days became a seemingly endless tedium of troubles. Every day held the same problems. Dead ends, troublesome eddies and lagoons, long delays in order to find somewhere solid enough to build a fire and cook food. Even after so long with borderline starvation, the fish and bird flesh for every meal began to pall remarkably quickly. A little experimentation proved that the reeds were edible, though tough and not very tasty, and they palled quicker than the meat.

Men began to show symptoms of the swamp fever, and the boats were regularly rearranged to keep sick men separated from the healthy. The tribune continued to cling on to a rough facsimile of life, drifting in and out of consciousness half the time, always grey and running with sweat, yet always behind three devoted servants with swords, prepared to sell their lives for their master.

When one afternoon Faventinus noted with some relief that the river had definitely taken a generally southward turn, Densus had greeted the information with less enthusiasm than his friend had clearly expected. It was a landmark moment, but they had no idea how long the swamp went on for to the south.

One morning, while the boats made ready to sail and Densus was trying to decide whether it was still Januarius, or had flipped over to Februarius by now, one of the men who he recognised as a former sistrum shaker called for offerings to the river gods. The men each tossed overboard whatever they could find of value. Densus, unwilling to give the only thing he really valued – the figurine his friend had gifted him at Saturnalia – dug into his meagre pack and found one of his phalera, the medals worn over his armour, gathered during his days in the legion. Gazing at the silvery face of Medusa that stared unblinking back, he made a silent prayer to the gods and spirits of the Nile, and cast the disc into the water. It stared back at him, still, accusingly, for some time, until it sank from view. He glanced at Faventinus and then the tribune, feeling slightly guilty over what he had asked for in that silent prayer, but concluded that he would not have been alone in his plea. He even heard a man openly musing on the value of a tribune as an offering to the water.

The days wore on. Three men died: one of the fever, one from some form of food poisoning, and one who simply opened his own veins during the night. Their funerals were brief and mechanic, tipping the bodies overboard into the water and watching them float away downstream.

The river continued to meander in a southerly direction.

Some night, who knew how many days into the voyage, Densus was awakened in the darkest hours of night by a commotion, and, untying his boat and rowing over to the trouble, he found two guardsmen clinging on to the side of the tribune's boat with desperate white knuckles while swinging swords with their other hands, the tribune's secretary parrying them with surprising ease.

For a moment, Densus struggled with his decision. Joining in on the side of the men attacking the boat would be very easy. Leaving them to it and hoping they succeeded would be even easier. It was only when he saw Faventinus coming towards him, rowing furiously, hard eyes flitting back and forth between the fight and the other centurion, that he resigned himself. The two men had given up trying to fight their way aboard the tribune's small coracle now, and were, instead, heaving on the side, trying to capsize it. The secretary fought back like a mad man, hammering at their fingers carefully with the pommel of his sword, unable to risk using the blade in case he cut through the reeds of the boat. Somehow, in his fevered state, the tribune seemed to be sleeping through the whole thing, oblivious even as he was thrown this way and that with the action.

Densus, swallowing down the dark desire to see the tribune tipped in, knew there was little time. The boat would go over any moment. He handed the oars to the other occupant of the vessel to keep them in place, then lifted his rope and grapple and threw, hard. The metal grip slammed into the nearest of the two assailants and, as Densus yanked hard on the rope, the claws bit into the man's arm and pulled him from the side of the boat, back into the water. The man screamed, but Densus continued to pull, hauling him back towards his own vessel. At the fresh din, the tribune briefly opened his eyes, but failed to react further, closing them once more.

The secretary, apparently no fool with his weapon, succeeded in smashing the fingers of the remaining attacker, who fell back into the river with a cry. Densus did not see what happened to him after that, for a few more heaves on the rope brought the remaining assailant to the edge of his own boat. He looked into the man's eyes for a moment and saw a soul-destroying mix of desperation and regret, and knew in that look that the moment he turned on the tribune and broke his oath, his expression would be exactly the same. He mouthed an apology to the soldier, for in the depth of his heart he both empathised and sympathised with the man. He drew the dagger from his belt with his free hand, still pulling the man with the other, grapple claws embedded in the soldier's bicep. With growing regret, he reached down and stabbed out, hard, into the man's neck, a quick kill, a soldier's death.

It was a struggle, as the man seized and died, to free the grapple before the body fell back and floated away, and he dipped it in the water to wash the gore from the tines, before coiling the rope once more. Of the other would-be assassin there was no sign, though he had not made it back to his own boat, for that bobbed empty nearby.

The rest of that day, Densus paid careful attention to the men around him as they travelled. There was a sense of resignation, now. Twice, men had sprung a surprise attack on the tribune, and yet twice he had survived and the assassins had not. Clearly the gods were protecting him, and it seemed unlikely there would be a repeat attempt for some time. He found the odd resentful look thrown his way for his part in saving the commander once again, but still most of the men displayed nothing more than respect when they glanced his way. They may not agree with his actions, but there was something timeless, unchanging, and most importantly, comforting, in the dependability of the centurionate.

If only they knew the turmoil inside. Had Faventinus not showed up when he did, things might have worked out very differently.

The day ended with a quiet sullenness.

The next one was much the same as any other... until mid-afternoon. A message was shouted back with an air of excitement from Faventinus at the front of the flotilla.

Land.

Not the endless, green, murky, shifting land that drifted around them on the river. *True* land.

It was distant, yet, but the southern horizon held a thin strip of blue-grey that rose above the reeds and was topped with the jagged line of peaks and dips. Somewhere, many miles to the south, hills or mountains rose, and where there were hills, there was not swamp.

Better still, of all the theories of the source of the Nile they had read in Herodotus and other ancient sources, the one most favoured and most likely was that of the meltwater from the snow of mountains, the only realistic source for such a quantity as the Nile boasted. Distant mountains meant not only an end to the swamp, but just possibly the very thing for which they were searching: the source.

A weird thrill ran through Densus, then. Maybe the gods *were* protecting the tribune, even if they were using the centurion as a proxy.

They were going to do it. They were going to find the source.

As the day wore on, and the mood of the men became a little less grim, a thread of hope beginning to surface, Densus found that the struggle and turmoil of his indecision was fading, too.

What had he been thinking? He had almost crossed a line that could not be uncrossed.

That night, as the sun set, far to their right, confirming once again their southerly direction, Faventinus came to find him.

'We're almost there.'

'I saw the mountains.'

'More than that,' his friend said. 'The flow is faster, the channels narrower. And when was the last time we saw a split in the river?'

Densus thought back. 'Maybe two hours ago.'

'No. That was a confluence… our channel joining another, not splitting into two. All day that's been happening: the channels from all over the swamp converging. That means the swamp has to be narrowing, returning to a single flow of river. And with the proximity of the mountains and the increased flow rate, I think we're closing on the source.'

'And a decision,' Densus said, turning and glancing back at the boat, which was being rowed as always by the secretary, the tribune unconscious opposite him.

'Do you think he even knows what's happening any more?'

'We'll have to consult the capsarius when we land.'

Both men turned, then, to look longingly at the distant band of grey peaks.

39

SOMEWHERE
POSSIBLY FEBRUARIUS AD 62

It took another two days. As the afternoon wore to an end, they looked for a landing spot, for the channels had narrowed all the time until they were now but one great river, with the occasional mud bank or reed bed mid-flow. It was the narrowest any of them had seen the river, perhaps just five or six hundred paces at times.

The coracles were rowed one after another across to the east bank of the river. Should the decision be made to return by land, and try and reconnect with those men they'd left at the far end of the swamp, then at least they would be on the correct side of the great flow by the time it widened immensely. Faventinus, as the lead boat, was the first to set foot on dry ground, and could not underestimate the relief he felt at the sensation.

He stomped around, enjoying the feel of the land beneath his feet as behind him, men disembarked. He turned with interest as the tribune's boat neared the shore, and then hurried over, aware that men were gathering around where it would dock. He reached them, grabbing shoulders, turning them.

'You four, run a scouting perimeter. Go out to just within sight of the river, no further, and report back from those positions with signals.' He pulled others aside. 'Bring all the goods ashore, and pile them up according to their nature. I want to know what we still have with us now.'

To the remaining men: 'Pull these boats up far enough into the grass that they won't end up back in the water, even in a storm. Find branches, sticks, or whatever, use the ropes and peg them down. Secure them.'

The men grudgingly departed, leaving Faventinus alone, watching the tribune and his secretary close on the shore. The next boat behind held his other two men, all of his staff armed and ready for trouble, all the more so after the attack on the boat. Faventinus presumed the tribune still unconscious until the boat touched the bank and the man unfolded like some gangly contraption of poles and parchment, and lurched out of the coracle and onto the grass. He half-tottered, half-staggered up the gentle slope and to open ground, where he stood, turning slowly, blinking, as though freshly woken from slumber.

'We have so few men,' the tribune said, looking out across the water. 'How have you been so careless?'

That he was directing the accusation at Faventinus was undeniable, for he turned to look at the centurion as he spoke.

Faventinus was about to reply, keeping a careful and tight hold on his anger, when the tribune's secretary, busily carrying a bag from their boat turned and stormed towards his master.

'No!'

Curtius Lupus turned, with a confused frown, to his staff, looking at the secretary the way one might at a pet puppy that just threatened a lion.

'What?'

'The centurion here and his friend saved so many lives, Tribune, including your own.'

The commander turned narrowed eyes on Faventinus. They were, the centurion noted, still defocused, and the man was swaying slightly. He'd appeared to be well again just for a moment, but that was the optical illusion borne of the man actually moving and speaking after so long unconscious. In truth, he was still far from better.

'I...' he faltered. 'I forget... I don't know.'

He turned back to the secretary, who was angry, still, now only a few paces away. Faventinus was grateful the young clerk had his sword sheathed, for he was clearly in the mood to do something precipitous. 'I have had enough.'

Faventinus winced as the tribune took a slightly wobbly step back.

'What?'

'I have served you faithfully, even saved your life when you were unaware it was in danger.' Every syllable or two was a step forward, the tribune backing away, but unsteadily, slower. 'I've watched your men, even your officers, over *months* now, and only their professionalism, their devotion to duty, and their oath, has stopped them rebelling time and again. Well now it is *my* turn, and *I* shall rebel.'

'Get back to your post,' snarled Curtius Lupus.

Faventinus watched in fascination. Had the confrontation been from almost any other man on the expedition, he would already have stepped in, given his rank and seniority over them. The tribune's secretary, though, was no Praetorian. He was a civilian, answering solely to Curtius Lupus. By the letter of the law, Faventinus actually had no authority over this man at all, and so instead of intervening, he watched.

'It's time to turn back, sir,' the secretary said.

'No.'

'Sir...' the man began, now but a pace away from his master. Faventinus blinked as the tribune's hand suddenly shot out with the speed and accuracy of a striking asp, his fingers and thumb wrapping around the man's throat. The secretary gagged, made an 'urk' sound, and reached up to the hand round his neck.

'As Mars and Apollo are my witness,' the tribune bellowed, the sound loud enough to echo back from the eaves of the woods, 'I will not let this expedition fail. *Never.*'

The centurion was stunned. He watched, helpless, too far away to do anything, as the tribune simply squeezed his hand, crushing his secretary's windpipe and throat-apple. The man made a hoarse rasping noise that would have been a scream were such a thing possible, and, as the tribune let go, fell to the grass, the hands that had been clawing at the attacking hand now clawing at his own throat.

Faventinus turned. Everyone was staring, motionless, silent. Even Densus, in the rearmost boat, was watching impotently from out in the water. All eyes were on the tribune, none on the man writhing and dying at his feet.

'The gods are with me,' Curtius Lupus bellowed. 'Does anyone else wish to stand against me?'

Faventinus winced again. He was fairly sure that at least

half of them did, and half expected a rush of men. No one stepped forth. The tension in the air crackled. A sudden movement caught Faventinus' eye and he turned to see one of the men, face filled with unresolved hate, start to move. The man whose arm shot out to keep him in place was, Faventinus was surprised to note, that same former cultist of Urbicus and shaker of sistrums that had led the offerings to the river gods in the swamp. The angry soldier looked at the man beside him in surprise, and the acolyte gave a barely perceptible shake of his head.

Interesting.

'There will be no further challenges to my authority,' the tribune shouted, and it was well done, the strength of his tone only cracking at the very end, a tell-tale sign he was still suffering, if you were listening for it. It sounded like a flat statement, though it was in fact, clearly, a challenge. The tribune remained motionless, looking about him. The whole landing site was still and silent. 'Make camp here,' Curtius Lupus demanded, then gestured to his other two staff, who were staring, ashen faced. 'Get rid of this,' he told them, nudging the body with his foot, 'and then raise my tent.'

Faventinus could see Densus closing on the dock now, his face dark with anger, and was glad his friend had not been present. The centurion was the very soul of honour and military discipline, but he was close to breaking point with the tribune. Faventinus had decided some time ago that it was his job to save Densus from doing anything stupid. In essence, to save Densus from himself.

He turned to see the tribune walk away, and noted again the slight sway that revealed he was still not well. That being said, he had suffered worse than some of the men in the depths of his fever, and a few days ago Faventinus would have put money on digging his grave before the month was out, and yet he seemed to be recovering, and fast.

He hurried after the commander, who stopped when he was out of easy earshot of the gathering, and turned to the centurion. 'Are they following?'

Faventinus glanced back and shook his head. 'I think you shocked them into obedience, sir, for now, at least. You sound like you're on the mend, sir.'

'My fever broke this morning, I think. I am a little disoriented. It may have been yesterday. Yes, my mind is clearing fast. I still feel weak. My legs... also my arms.'

'It didn't look it, the way you strangled the man.'

Curtius Lupus glanced sharply at him, perhaps hearing an accusation in the words. 'I will not be disobeyed. We are soldiers of Rome. Praetorians. The best of the best. What value is a Praetorian who cannot stand by his oath? We are the bodyguard of emperors, servants of the divine Nero. A bodyguard who breaks oaths is worthless. I *will* find the source, and make offerings to the spirits, if I lose every last man in the process and have to climb the mountains on my knees. *That* is what it means to keep a promise. To stand by an oath.'

Faventinus nodded. In some circumstances, such an oration would be a stunning piece of work. Here and now, it felt dangerous.

'Your orders, sir?'

'How many healthy men do we have, and what is the supply situation?'

Faventinus sighed. 'We're down to fifty-seven men,

ourselves included, sir. Of them, two are your staff and nine are slaves. Of those men, five slaves and thirty-one men are showing at least some sign of the swamp fever. Perhaps half of them are going to have trouble going any further. Of course, we have no carts or animals, for they were left back before the swamp. Any scouts now will have to be sent out on foot. So, if you're talking healthy, active men, I'd say twenty-six guardsmen, four slaves, and your staff, are good to go. As for supplies, we have the usual pots and pans we brought with us, a bunch of waterskins that we can still fill, but we'll be following the river anyway, and sufficient bird and fish meat, salted, to last thirty-odd men five or six days on full rations.'

The tribune sighed and slumped a little, the effort of holding himself straight and strong in front of the men now too much. He dropped to a rock and sat there. 'We camp here tonight, Centurion. It is my belief that the source of the river cannot be far away now. We leave the sick, and the capsarius to tend them. They can also keep guard on the boats for our return, as well as trying to stockpile supplies in our absence. From here, the men will have to carry what they need. They will truly be Marius' mules like the legions of old. We travel by foot, following the river along this bank until we have completed our mission, appeased the spirits, and then we will return to Rome by the safest and shortest route possible. I expect the mission to begin again in earnest at dawn.'

Faventinus saluted, turned, saw Densus halfway back to the river, stalking this way, and made his excuses. Leaving the recovering officer to regain what strength he could, the centurion hurried off across the grass. Densus had a thunderous look on his face, and Faventinus planted himself firmly in his friend's path.

'Leave it.'

'That fucking lunatic strangled his own man, just to push the rest back into line.'

Faventinus nodded sadly. 'That may well be the case, but it makes no difference. No one is going to stand against him now.'

'*I* am.'

Faventinus reached out and grasped his fellow centurion's shoulder, preventing him marching off. 'No you're not. Look, we are almost there, Sempronius. Almost there. And whether the man has gone off his mental wagon or not, I have to admit that now I want to know. This close, I want to know. And all we have to do is make it that bit further and when we get back to Rome we'll be bloody *heroes*, man.' He sighed. 'We've come this far, lost so much, and we're so near. We have to finish it, now.'

Densus rolled his eyes. 'You're too soft for the centurionate, Claudius. You're too nice.' He let out an explosive breath. 'Alright. We go on. But only until that man crosses the next line. Every time he steps over one, we draw a new line for him and accept whatever mad shit he's done. No more. The next line is the last one. You want him to make it through this, keep him from doing anything stupid, cause my sword is starting to thirst for noble blood.'

With that, he spun and walked away. Faventinus heaved a sigh of relief and turned, taking it all in. The site was deceptively calm and efficient as camp was being set, the boats secured, the supplies stockpiled, fires lit and sentries posted. For just a moment, one might think nothing was wrong. He watched Densus getting into a conversation with the capsarius, and hurried off in a different direction.

He found the man he was looking for cutting branches from a tree, for firewood. He had a slightly wide and flat nose, which had been broken at some point in his youth, and sharp eyes beneath a short forehead and hair that he had cut short enough to bristle. His beard was now longer than his hair. He was very familiar, for Faventinus had been watching him on and off since Aegyptus, in the company of Urbicus, then later with the rattle-shaking lunatics, and most recently taking charge in the boats.

'Probus?'

The man stopped chopping, turned, rubbed the sweat from his forehead, and saluted.

'Why did you stop it?'

'Stop what, sir?'

'The men were going for the tribune. You held them back. Why?'

Probus dropped his axe to the ground and rubbed his hands. 'Divine providence, sir.'

'What?'

'With respect, sir, the commander's a fucking madman. He's dangerous, puts duty over everything, even his own welfare, and might well walk us straight into a lion's stomach.'

'So I ask again, why stop it?'

'Because the gods are with him. Shit, sir, but he's survived two assassination attempts now. He's managed the whole journey without losing that mad fucking streak that brought us all here. He's even recovered from the swamp fever. The man's fucking indestructible.'

'No man is indestructible, Probus.'

'*He* is, sir. It's not that I like him, or trust him, and certainly not that I want to go any further.'

'Then, again: why?'

'Because every man who stands in his way dies, sir. Every last one. I've lost enough mates. I don't want to lose any more. Following him does less damage than *not* following him, sir.'

And with that, he spat on his hands again, turned, picked up the axe, and began chopping.

Faventinus took a few steps away, and looked up at the distant mountains.

Could they do it?

Could they find the source?

40

NILE

AD 62

A single day had been enough to suppress once more any relief or excitement the men might feel at the presence of proper land. Though the vastly diminished expedition were only carrying light kit – their armour and anything unnecessary long since left back with the wagons – and were low on supplies other than meat and water, the men were now learning what it meant to be Marius' Mules, carrying all they had for the campaign on their backs. Of course, though they were less laden than most legionaries had been throughout the campaigns of the empire, the conditions they were slogging through were also far worse than most soldiers would expect to endure, for the heat never seemed to let up, the humidity was unbearable, the world filled with insects, and now that they were no longer mid-Nile, even what little breeze there had been was gone.

Densus and his fellow centurion, as officers, were not expected to bear a load, of course, yet both men carried their share, aware of the morale effects of 'mucking in with the lads'. The tribune, of course, did not. Despite still being in slow recovery from the fever, the man led the expedition from the fore, now, barring the scouts out ahead, and his stride, though it faltered at times through so many days of atrophy and weakness, was purposeful. Like his centurions, the commander could sense the end of their journey coming ever closer, and what had felt impossible at the other end of the great swamp now felt possible.

Indeed, even over the space of one day, Densus could swear he'd watched the river flowing past on their right become slightly narrower and slightly faster.

'Natives ahead, sir,' called one of the scouts, appearing from the scrubby trees.

'Friendly or not?' the tribune asked.

'Farmers, by the look of it, sir.'

Densus felt a sigh of relief whisper through him. The last thing he wanted right now was to meet a new enemy. Indeed, he worried greatly about any likelihood of military action. The men had not been in fighting condition for months, and though they carried their swords and a few pila, most of them didn't even have a helmet now, let alone their armour or shields, which were back with the wagons. He was not convinced his men could win a fight with a drunken vagrant, let alone the sort of hunters they'd met during that horrible day with the lions.

'Officers to me,' the tribune called.

Densus joined Faventinus and the two jogged ahead to meet the commander as the scout also converged on their position.

'Column, halt,' Densus shouted. 'Wait here.'

And with that, the three officers made their way with

the scout, ahead through the trees. The natives, when they found them, turned out to be a dozen men in dun-coloured skirts and tight-braided hair, with an immense herd of cattle. The tribune marched over to the nearest of them, with the other three hurrying along close at heel.

'How close are we to the source of the river?' Curtius Lupus asked, somewhat briskly. The farmer, utterly unfazed, simply looked at him and frowned, turned and babbled something to the rest, and the whole group chuckled.

The tribune, eyes glittering with irritation, turned to the centurions. 'Find out,' he demanded, then stepped back, gesturing to the soldier who'd been scouting ahead and pulling him aside to learn what he could of their surroundings. Without the commander paying attention to them, Densus and Faventinus smiled disarmingly at the locals and produced a small wrapper of salted meat, offering it up. The natives stared at it suspiciously, but one took it, chewed for a moment, seemed to like it, and then the rest took some. In a matter of a score of heartbeats three of the natives were seated in a circle with the two centurions, a sure sign of peaceful intentions on both sides.

Densus began. He knew that Faventinus was probably better suited to negotiation, but Densus could draw, at least. He pointed to the river not far away and then began to draw a map, not bothering with anywhere north of the great swamp, on the assumption that the natives would never have got that far. He drew the westerly line and the turn to the south, then added many channels that interconnected and gradually combined to one river, before pointing to the five of them in a circle and then tapping the map with where he thought they were.

The three locals muttered to one another for some time, gesticulating wildly and pointing in various directions and to the map. Finally, one shushed the other two, and began to draw in the dirt with his finger. The line was extended further south, in a wavy manner, then off slightly west, and then opened out into a circle.

'A lake?' Densus hazarded. This, of course, was of no help to the locals, so he tapped the river on the map, and then pointed off to the Nile, then tapped the possible lake, pointed to the Nile and made a large circular motion with his arms. After a further discussion, there was a nod.

'That's not too far,' Faventinus said, almost breathlessly. 'Hang on.'

The native had started to draw again. A new line issued from the lake to the southeast for a short distance before opening out into a second large oval.

'*Two* lakes.' He waited for a time, to see if there was to be any further embellishment. There was not. The man put down the stick and leaned back.

Densus leaned in. He pulled his waterskin from his belt and poured a gentle trickle of water into the dusty groove of the Nile map, so there was, for a moment, a line of water, looked up at the natives, to see them looking interested, and then tapped the new lake on the map and mimed pouring out water into the lake. They looked puzzled.

Faventinus joined in, then, taking the flask and repeating the gesture, but in reverse, trying to make it look like more of one continuous flow, with a source at the lake. He did the same twice more, and eventually shrugged a question. The natives conferred, and finally the spokesman nodded. What he mimed, then, looked like a fountain exploding up from the ground into the air, followed by repeated circles with his arms. Faventinus grinned. 'The water comes up from the earth and forms a lake. Gods, but that's our source. That's what we're looking for. We're not that far away, Sempronius.' He looked at the map for a while. 'If the scale is the same, that's maybe ten days, maybe fifteen.'

But while Faventinus was grinning and looking pleased with himself, Densus had noticed something else. The three natives were sharing a look he didn't like.

'What is it?' he asked, shuffling forward.

'What?' Faventinus frowned.

'There's something they've not told us.' He looked at the three men and shrugged. He used two fingers on the map to mime walking along the Nile to the lakes. Now, the locals seemed to understand, for the spokesman shook his head and swatted Densus' fingers away.

'Why not?' he asked, then started the walking again with a shrug.

There was some discussion once more, and even a little argument, and Densus had the idea that they were trying to work out how to explain something. He and Faventinus sat patiently, though twitching to know what was happening. It very much sounded like they were being told not to follow the river. He felt the skin prickle on the back of his neck. Finally, the lead native rubbed out an area of dirt near the map and began to draw.

Densus had to hand it to the man. He was good. All he drew was stick men, but they were artistic enough that Densus recognised them as Romans. He and his companions, clearly. They were walking in the image, and it seemed to be along the Nile. The man paused, looked up, pointed at them, and then the stick men. Densus nodded. 'That's us.'

Satisfied he was getting through, the man then drew some new figures facing the first group. They were carrying long sticks, possibly spears, and seemed to have oval shields. He then drew a larger figure behind them, and seemed to draw a circle on his head.

'A crown? He's a king?'

The artist, of course, had no idea what the word meant, but he mimed a circlet around his brow, then his friends all bowed to him, before he leaned back and pointed up to the sun. Back and forth his finger went between sun and crown while the others kept bowing.

'A sun king. A king of the sun? Something of the sort,' Faventinus said.

'And they're our enemies,' Densus added.

'Just because they're facing us?'

'Facing us, armed, driven by a king, and we're told not to go. This sun king has an army, and it lies somewhere ahead, up the river.'

Just in case they hadn't got the point, the man now drew a new enemy warrior with his spear stuck in one of the Romans. 'Alright, I guess that's fairly unambiguous,' Faventinus admitted.

'I'll go tell the tribune,' Densus said. 'Why don't you see if this lot are willing to trade with us? After so long on fowl and fish, I'd wrestle my own grandmother for one of their cows, or some fruit or something.'

Leaving Faventinus opening negotiations, he turned and marched back across the open ground to where the tribune stood, alone and looking around, the scout having been sent back to the column. He waited for the scout to be out of sight, and braced himself. He'd not spoken personally to the tribune since the man had murdered a clerk, and had not trusted himself to do so without comment.

'You've learned something?' the tribune asked.

Densus nodded. 'Probably *too* much. If the scale on the man's map was right we cannot be more than half a month away from the river's source. It rises and forms a great lake, which then empties via a river into another lake, before meandering up to here.'

'Great Jove, then we're close.'

'He also told us not to go.'

'Why?'

'From what I can gather, the lands in that direction are owned by some sort of sun king, with an army. The local gave us a fairly clear warning that if we go on, this sun king's army will stick spears in us.'

'Such nonsense. Two weeks, you say?'

Densus frowned. Nonsense?

'Yes. Two weeks. But in a kingdom where it appears we are not welcome.'

The tribune fixed him with a disbelieving look. 'They, and you, are assuming that because these locals are not welcome in this sun king's lands, then neither are we. Can you categorically say that is the case?'

Densus sighed. 'No, sir.'

'Precisely. Frankly, though in our current circumstances we are beholden to primitive natives and are forced by necessity to engage in polite conversation with the barbarian, were these people to continually stray across the border into *imperial* lands, I doubt they would be welcome there, either. It may be that this king does not like his precious arable land being consumed by his neighbour's cattle. There is little such land here, after all.'

That was, as far as Densus was concerned, utter crap. He'd looked into the eyes of those men when they'd done their pictures of warning, and he was under no illusion that this sun king was going to be most unhappy with a small force of armed foreigners stomping into this kingdom. But the problem was that, though he was privately convinced this was the case, there was no denying that it was at least possible that the tribune was correct, and that would be enough to be overruled. He straightened. 'Your orders, sir?'

'You said they had made a map. I wish to see it, though I would prefer not to involve myself with these people. I will have my...' his voice trailed off as he remembered that he no longer *had* a secretary. 'I need you to make a copy of it on one of my tablets.' He reached to the pouch at his side, which always held his current writing tablet, drew it out and handed it over.

'And then, sir?'

Curtius Lupus rolled his shoulders, which caused him to sway for a moment, his balance still not quite right. 'And then we march on upriver to find these lakes and their spirits, and fulfil our mission for the emperor.'

41

NILE

AD 62

It was the scout's fault. It had to be. The only people who had been with the natives for the conversation were the two centurions, and the information had then been passed on to the tribune. The only other person who could have known about the 'sun king' was the scout, if he had been slow in returning to the rest and had still been within earshot of the tribune, just on the other side of the trees. Yet by the time they were on the move again with the three cows they had managed to buy from the natives, who were shaking their heads in dismay, the rumour of a violent native army blocking their path was flying around the column.

When they'd stopped that night, Faventinus had done all he could to quell the rumour, but it did not seem to have had much effect. Privately, he put that down to the very real likelihood that Densus was accidentally supporting the notion even as he was trying to tell them it wasn't true, for the man clearly believed the same as them. For Faventinus, the truth lay undiscovered. Perhaps the locals and Densus were correct in being overcautious, but the tribune had been right that it was not a foregone conclusion. Time would tell.

'Time. And steel. And blood. And shit,' had been Densus' reply when he'd used that phrase earlier.

So, the next day, as they marched on along a river that was now most definitely narrower and faster the further they travelled, the men slogged on in a subdued, discontented silence. By the end of the second day, Faventinus was becoming concerned that any inclination to obedience among the men was rapidly being eroded by the fear of what they were now marching into. It did not help that the flat land was giving way to a valley as they finally moved into the higher land they'd been able to see from the swamp, the grey hills still awaiting them ahead.

On the third day, they came across a lake, and the men went almost wild with relief. If they were finally at the first lake, then the next must be close, and they had yet to bump into the dreadful nebulous foe they all feared. Faventinus sadly corrected them. The natives' map had shown the river turn east and then go for some way before reaching the lake, while their journey had been in a generally southerly direction thus far, with only a very recent angle towards the west.

His fears proved well-founded, for by the end of that day they had found a whole series of lakes and pools to both sides of the river as it tumbled towards them through the endless green scrubland.

The fourth day brought new tension. The scouts were now keeping within sight ahead, given the tactical danger of funnelling an army along a river in potentially enemy territory. Thus, anything they saw was usually within visual range of the rest of the men a few moments later. So, when the scouts waved and gave the signal, without a sound, for the column to stop, Faventinus felt his tension rise as he jogged out ahead with Densus.

The scouts had entered an area strewn with boulders of immense size, and rocks projecting from the ground like jagged, broken teeth, surrounded by tangled undergrowth and deep grass that swept from the riverbank up to the trees and the rising ground.

In truth, what the scouts had found could have meant anything. It could have been a political boundary of some sort, a religious sign, even just something personal for a local family or group. Yet Faventinus knew in an instant that it hovered somewhere between warning and threat.

Either side of the trail they were following stood a red post, which at first glance, Faventinus confirmed to be a branch hacked free of projections and stained, but it was what topped the posts that drew their attention. Each side held the skull of some bovine creature with wide, impressive horns, also stained red. The very sight of them sent a shiver up the centurion's spine, and from the expressions on Densus and the scouts, they felt it too. A definite warning. Thoughts and ideas raced through his head. One of the scouts had already spread the rumour of an enemy awaiting them. If this news reached the column, morale would take a further dive. He had to do *something*. Frowning, he prayed that Densus was quick enough to catch on and follow his lead.

'Jupiter Optimus Maximus!' he announced, trying to sound breathlessly excited and reverent. He came to a halt looking from post to post, with a quick sidelong glance at

Densus, who, to his relief, swiftly put aside his surprise and followed suit.

He saw the confusion in the eyes of the scouts, saw it slide into uncertainty and suspicion for a moment, but knew he could have them now. Humbly, he approached the left-hand post and, fumbling in his purse, produced a handful of coins, which he laid at the foot of the post. An offering to the greatest god of Rome, which he accompanied with a loud, clearly audible prayer to Jove as the god of this place. He repeated the procedure at the other post, and Densus began to do the same.

It was a little bit of a reach, out here, in truth. That anyone in this place could even know of Jupiter, let alone worship him, seemed farfetched, and yet the scouts would be taking it in. The skulls of oxen, the favoured sacrificial animal of the god, and red, the colour Jupiter's statue was painted in the great temple on the Capitol. Two unmistakable symbols of the god in a place where they should not be. That cattle seemed to be the main constituents of farmers' herds in the region, and that red was a colour seemingly used by many native tribes, became unimportant as the men absorbed what Faventinus had given them: the greatest of Roman gods in this inhospitable place.

In mere heartbeats the scouts were leaving their own offerings. Faventinus heaved a silent, private, sigh of relief. Had that gone the wrong way, it could have brought panic. Still, he prayed to Jupiter that the trend would continue, and as Densus sent the order for the column to move again, and the rest of the expedition followed on, he watched, tense, even though he was trying to hide it. Every man approached the twin columns, word of their nature having travelled back with the speed of which only rumour is capable, and each gave an offering. Though Faventinus was fairly certain Jupiter had never even looked this far south, and that the columns were, indeed, a warning from an enemy, he prayed to the great god anyway, and hoped that Jupiter heard their pleas and accepted their gifts, and perhaps that through him the gods of Rome might take an interest in what was happening here. Then they moved on.

Two more days saw them pass a particularly large pool connected to the river. By now, every pool they found was eyed with hope and desperation, wishing it to be the lake marked on the native map that signalled they were almost at the end.

Faventinus had resigned himself to the fact that the men's mood was in a perpetual decline, sliding towards hopelessness and desperation, and there was no hope now of fully turning that around without finding the river's source. All they could do was try and battle the decline, as they had been doing for some time. A small victory here, a hopeful find there, each time boosting morale by enough of a fraction to keep the column under control and together. He filled the boredom of hours of steaming, sweaty travel with the development of new ideas of how he could put a positive veneer on anything they found, as he had done with the skull posts. Anything he could do now, to keep the men going, so close to the end, to prevent the seemingly inevitable moment when they had simply had enough and turned on their officers once more.

He had a feeling the next time that happened would be different from the last three attempts on the tribune's life. Next time, it would undoubtedly involve the whole unit.

It was perhaps just over an hour before sunset on some unknown day – the expedition had long since now lost track of the date – that the next warning came, somewhat obliquely. As the scouts ranged ahead, looking for a site for the night's camp, a place with good visibility and suitable for defence, which in itself was a difficult proposition in this thick, green world, Densus fell into step beside him so suddenly and quietly it made Faventinus jump a little.

'Have you seen them?'

Faventinus frowned. 'What?'

'I can't say for sure, but I reckon we're being watched, followed even.'

With a frown, Faventinus turned.

'Not behind,' his friend said. 'To the sides.'

Now, he turned. The river did not so much carve a valley here, despite the fact that they were clearly climbing steadily, day after day, but meandered through rocky green lands, though there were distinct elevations to each side some distance away. Faventinus could see nothing moving for some time, and when he eventually did, it turned out to be the distant shape of a cameleopard, feeding among the trees in the distance.

'Nothing.'

'Keep watching. They're subtle. Clever.'

'The sun king's army, you think?'

'Seems likely. I'm trying to decide why they haven't confronted us yet.'

'Either they're still observing us, weighing us up, or there aren't enough of them, and they're waiting for others.'

'Quite.'

For the remaining hour of sunlight, he kept his eyes on

the horizon. He thought that perhaps he did see movement occasionally, but if it was warriors, then they moved with a stealth that would earn the envy of a cat. Densus must have damn sharp eyes if he was as sure as he sounded.

They found a place and set up camp for the night, and no one complained or questioned the decision when the number of sentries was doubled. With the exception of the tribune and the two centurions, everyone was now on the watch rota, including Mordanticus, the standard bearer, Genialis, the musician, and even the four slaves. The social difference between soldier and slave meant so little out here, where they were all Romans in an alien world, that the guardsmen no longer even complained that the slaves were regularly armed. That night, the unit did two-to-three-hour watches, with twelve men on duty at all times. Faventinus found it hard to sleep, and woke often, startled at every noise, of which there was a seemingly endless number in this hot, green world.

The dream he was having as the night drew towards a close was a surprisingly comforting one, in which he was back in Rome, a hero for his explorations, trying to decide to which impressed young lady he would devote his attention. The dream turned sexual rather suddenly, which oddly surprised him, even in the state of slumber, and that instinct saved his life. As the girl ran her hand up his thigh, some preternatural sense told him something was wrong, and he pulled back, shooting to his feet in his tent, backing away, blinking awake, looking around. He saw the snake quickly, still slithering towards him. It was clearly fast, and quite a size, the fangs suggesting poison, and he had little confidence of being able to leap around it and get out.

He watched it coming, took a deep breath, waited...

Timing was all.

He slowly lifted his foot as the creature slithered ever closer.

He slammed it down suddenly on the snake, right behind the head, pinning it. The head whipped this way and that with furious hisses, but Faventinus was not about to let it have any chance of slithering free. With just as careful timing, his other foot came down, slamming onto the snake's head. He had been sleeping in his boots against the possibility of snakes, scorpions or other horrors for a long time, now, and tonight it paid off, as the snake's skull crunched beneath his boot, and the thing shook and coiled and slithered for a time until it fell still. He remained in place, pinning it for fifty heartbeats before he let go, content that it was definitely dead.

He left his tent, grabbing his sword belt as he went, and stood for a time, outside, in the pre-dawn light, recovering from the fright. He remained there, watching, as the camp came slowly to life.

They marched on, the two centurions still watching the horizons.

Towards the end of the day, the scouts called them forward, and the column was halted once more. This time it was not cow skulls on posts awaiting them. He and Densus found three scouts, standing and looking at a strange scene. A single wide and flat rock lay amid the green, but the six small stone cairns that lay in an arc around it gave it a shrine-like feel. It took Faventinus some time to work out what the poor creature was that lay on the stone, for its limbs had been hacked free and were nowhere to be seen.

The neck had been opened wide like some sort of diagram in the office of a surgeon. Similarly, the chest had been cracked and split wide, and several organs seemed to be missing. Though Faventinus was no expert, he thought the heart and liver at least were missing.

It resembled a dog, though the shape was slightly distorted, and he realised soon that the last time he'd seen a creature that shape, it had been eating tethered prisoners in a clearing far to the north, following the attempt on the tribune's life. The stains all over the stone and around it spoke eloquently of some sort of bloody ritual. At least this one seemed not to be directly aimed at the interlopers. They had simply stumbled across some native practice.

His eyes leaving the animal's dismembered corpse, he now spotted the small pit that lay behind the stone. Something was gleaming within. He walked over to it and crouched, peering inside. He dipped his hand in, praying for a lack of scorpions. His fingers closed on something hard and smooth, and he lifted from the hole a diamond the size of an egg. He stared in surprise. He frowned in suspicion. He looked back at the hole. The earth around the edge had been disturbed, and not by him just now. He dropped the gem back in the pit and rose once more.

'Alright, whoever took anything, put it back.'

He eyed the three scouts warily. They all looked shifty. No one moved or spoke.

'This is a shrine. The people of this land have given to their gods. Are you so comfortable out here that you want to piss off their gods? Put them back, unless you want to be the next thing we find on your back on a flat stone.'

The guilty looks were shared by all three, and the

moment one broke, pulled the huge diamond from his belt and crouched, dropping it in the hole, the other two quickly followed suit. 'Now give them something of your own. I think an apology is in order, don't you?'

Coins and small valuables were added to the offerings, and with just a narrow-eyed look of warning, the scouts were dispatched ahead once more. Densus gave the order again, and the column began to move. As they passed the shrine, Faventinus made sure to stand close to it so that no man could come and disturb it in the name of diamond hunting. Once they were past, and moving on, Faventinus turned. Something had made that space between his shoulders itch, and his gaze raked the green landscape.

There was no mistaking the figure this time. There had undoubtedly been others, but this one had deliberately lingered in the open. Quite some distance away, the details were hard to make out, but the figure seemed to be wearing only a skirt of something white and protruding, and something around his neck and head that distinctly resembled a lion's mane. He held a spear, point down. There were no words, could not be at such a distance, but the man's very presence felt like another warning, and this time a more direct one. Faventinus had a distinct feeling that this sun king's forces were gathering, and that their advance along the Nile was not going to be uncontested for much longer.

'Brazen, isn't he?' Densus said, falling into position beside him.

'I'll tell you one thing,' Faventinus replied, quietly. 'They're not afraid of us.'

'Why should they be. We're just a few men, and not even particularly well equipped now, and this is their land.'

'Do you get the feeling that the closer we get to the source of the river, the more dangerous and more numerous the obstacles are becoming?'

Densus sighed. 'The seer said it; I can only repeat. We can achieve our goal, but we'll wish we hadn't, many times.'

'Or maybe Urbicus was right after all, and *no man* is meant to discover the source.'

They both turned to look at the column of men, focusing on the figure of the tribune.

Faventinus somehow doubted the man would be willing to stop now.

42

NILE

AD 62

'Twelve men do not fall asleep at the same time,' Densus snarled, eyes raking the sentries, who were all standing in a line, looking...

Not chastened, nor defiant. Looking terrified, in fact. He took a steadying breath and let the anger drain. Back in Rome, on duty around the Palatine, or even with the emperor on tour, if every man on sentry duty had managed to fall asleep and leave their charge unguarded, he'd have had them beaten until they were raw, then discharged without pension or benefits. He would be furious, and all culpability would be with the lazy bastards.

This was different.

It had happened in the mid-night watch. All the men on guard duty had somehow contrived to fall asleep at the same time. That seemed too much to be a coincidence, especially given what else had happened, but also he knew damn well that those men were very nervous about the lands into which they were now travelling, and would be more alert and careful than usual, not less.

They were not the only result of the incident, though.

'I want every one of you to reflect on what you've done. Get back to your posts.'

As they scattered, he turned and marched over to the centre of the camp, where Faventinus was examining the other thing that had happened.

A post driven into the ground right outside the officers' tents at the centre of the camp. A post stained red. A familiar sight, since the first warning they had come across back downriver. Atop the post was another bovine head, though this one still bore the flesh upon its bones, freshly hacked free and with tendrils of neck matter dangling beneath, the ground below soaked dark with blood.

'No witnesses?' he asked his fellow centurion as he neared the post. 'That seems unlikely even in the middle of the night.'

'As unlikely as a dozen sentries nodding off?' Faventinus countered, and Densus had no answer to that.

'And we're missing a man, too?'

A nod. 'His tent mates said he was up later than them. Extra duties because he pissed Flaccus off yesterday by complaining too much. He was doing the clean-up after the meal, cleaning the cook pots and the like, and no one saw him after that. We have to consider the likelihood that he was a witness, and that seeing what he saw cost him his life.'

'You think he's dead?' Densus asked. 'Not just captured?'

Faventinus gave him a bleak look. 'I have a feeling these people are not just fucking around, Sempronius. What would they do with a captive?'

Densus shuddered. He'd rather not think about that. Perhaps the next red post they found would have a different type of head.

'It's clearly another warning,' he said.

Faventinus nodded. 'And a clear one, at that. The last time was a general warning that we were entering the sun king's lands, meant for anyone who came across it. This one is telling us to turn back, but it's also making it very clear that they can stroll into our camp whenever they like and do whatever they like. That's the important message here. I think this is likely to be our last warning, though. We're going to have to work out what to do, now.'

'I think we're about to draw another line with the tribune. Will he cross it, d'you think?'

Faventinus ignored his question. 'I've been thinking about the sentries.'

'Oh?'

'Barring the possibility of magic, the only real reason I can see for them all dozing off at the same time is because they were drugged.'

Densus frowned. 'Drugged? How?'

'I don't know. We'd have to go back over the last day or so's movements, and check what they all ate and drank. Check the rest of the men now, too, see if anyone else has been knocked out.'

'Hard to tell, since they were all asleep anyway.'

'True. What about food?'

Densus waved over Flaccus. 'You were the last officer on duty last night. Last time you saw the sentries on your rounds, they were all awake and fine?'

'They were, sir.'

'We all ate a couple of hours before we retired. Were the sentries given extra rations later, for their shift?'

Flaccus shook his head. 'Not that I know of, sir.'

'Nothing in the food, then, because I ate the same things at the meal, and I'm fine. What about water?' Densus said, turning and eyeing the bucket in the middle of the camp that served as a water butt, from which the waterskins were filled.

Faventinus turned to him, brow furrowed. 'What?'

'The water bucket's not far off full. It was drained heavily at dinner. That means it's been refilled. I don't suppose that among our missing man's late-night jobs was refilling the water?'

Faventinus blinked. 'Gods, you're right, Sempronius. I can picture it. A man goes out with a bucket to fill from the river. He comes back in with the full bucket. The sentries probably didn't give him a second glance. And in pitch black they might not have realised he was dark skinned.'

Densus waved over a soldier, who crossed to him, eyes darting around nervously. 'Sir?'

'Drink this,' Densus said, scooping a cup into the water bucket. The man eyed him suspiciously. 'Sir?'

'Drink.' The man did as ordered. 'Now, wait there.'

As the soldier stood to attention, Densus and Faventinus moved closer, voices lowering. 'If you're right,' Faventinus said, 'then these bastards really are wily. Wish we still had one of the capsarii with us to test the water somehow.'

'How are you going to explain the post and head this time?'

Faventinus sighed. 'I can't. No one is going to believe it's anything to do with Jupiter this time. Especially with that,' he added, pointing. Densus' gaze followed the line to the rest of the cow they had bought from the farmers before moving into the sun king's land. One of the three had been butchered the first night, the meat salted and stored in packs for the journey, the other two kept with the column. The second had been butchered yesterday, when the meat had run out. The third, though, had been beheaded in the night, the corpse now lying in a huge pool of blood.

'What a fucking mess.'

As the two men stood there, silent and pensive, the soldier beside them suddenly collapsed in a heap.

'I think that clinches it,' Faventinus said, looking down at the unconscious man. 'The water was drugged somehow.'

Densus nodded. 'So, a man goes for water, is smacked on the head. A native drugs the water, changes into his clothes and sneaks the water back into the camp. He waits as the men drink the water, and they probably drank plenty and pretty quick. It's warmer than ever tonight. He waits for the sentries to pass out, then kills a cow and somehow puts this thing up before pissing off into the night. It's clever.'

Faventinus turned and gestured to a soldier. 'Take the water bucket and sling it out.'

'Do it yourself, sir,' the man replied, and turned away.

Faventinus threw a surprised look at Densus, but the centurion was already moving. He was behind the insolent soldier in a matter of heartbeats, his vine stick out and held in a white-knuckled grip. The gnarled end, wood as hard as iron, caught the man behind the ear and sent him sprawling into the grass. The soldier rolled over, shock blanching his face. He was surprised, and stunned, but he would be fine. Densus had had cause to hit soldiers with his vitis often enough over the years to be able to judge how to pull a blow just enough to hurt, but not to injure.

'Get up, Glaucus.'

As the man struggled to his feet, shaking, Densus thrust the vine stick out again, the end resting just under his chin. He pushed upwards, raising the soldier's face so that he was looking the centurion in the eye.

'We are all aware that we're so deep in the shit now, we're swimming to stay afloat, Glaucus. And Faventinus and Flaccus and I will do everything we can to keep everyone safe and well, and to bring this expedition home, but one thing I will not accept is disobedience in my men. You all know that we're on your side, but if I hear one word like that from you to an officer, *ever again*, I will personally beat you until your *in*sides are on the *out*side. Do you understand?'

The man saluted, with trouble, the vine stick remaining just below his chin. 'Yes, sir.'

'Mutiny out here will get all of us killed,' Densus said, tone calming a little, stick lowering, allowing the man to relax some. 'We are in enemy territory, in danger, and only by maintaining the discipline that allowed Rome to conquer the world are we going to make it home. Would you rather face what's out there on your own, or as a century of Praetorians?'

This seemed to get through to the man. He straightened a little.

'Sorry, sir. Won't happen again. Not to a centurion, sir.'

The man's eyes flicked momentarily to the tribune's tent. Densus considered disciplining the man further, but decided to let him go. The soldier may have qualified his obedience as to the centurionate and not the tribune, but

Densus was willing to go with that for now. Frankly, he was close to telling the tribune where to shove his mission himself, so could hardly blame the poor bastard. At least the man would obey his immediate officers. He turned to Faventinus, who was nodding his approval.

'Do we tell his majesty?' the man asked, indicating the senior officer's tent.

Densus glanced that way. The tribune had slept through the entire thing. Admittedly, it was not as though there had been a major commotion. Mordanticus had woken, left his tent to go for a piss and had found the head on the post, freshly made. He'd quickly gone to check on the scouts and found them all asleep. Bright as the man was, he'd not raised an alarm in case the enemy were still in the camp, and could overrun them as they arose. Instead, he'd woken the sentries he could, then scurried around the camp and checked it out to make sure it was safe, then woken the centurions. Densus and Faventinus had then roused sufficient men to secure the camp, but left the men who'd stood the first watch to sleep on, lest they be exhausted when the sun came up.

No one had woken Curtius Lupus. Densus knew deep down that he probably should have done, but the last thing they needed right now was the tribune's interference. 'Best not. Not until everything is settled. He'll have to hear, but only once everything is calm and the evidence removed.' He turned to Flaccus. 'Do me a favour. Take a couple of the lads and butcher that cow. We're not wasting the meat. Get it salted and stored for the next few days.'

Flaccus nodded and hurried off, and Densus turned to his fellow centurion. 'Best move around among the lads and give them a bit of support and encouragement. We're going to need every bit of nerve and strength they have, now.'

Leaving Faventinus to it, Densus marched over to the post at the camp's centre. With a grunt of effort, he pulled the head from the top, staggering under the weight. With a gesture to a nearby soldier, he pointed to the stake. 'Get that out of the ground and bring it.'

He waited long enough for the man to lever the thing free and lift it, and then the two men marched away. Densus led the way towards the latrine trench they'd dug the previous evening when setting up camp. Reaching the pungent hole, he swung his arms a few times, and then let go of the cow's head, which sailed out into the night and disappeared through the bushes beyond with a rustle and then a dull thud. Rubbing his hands together, he gestured for the soldier to do the same with the stake. The guardsman lifted the post and pulled back, but that was as far as he got. Before he could throw, his chest suddenly sprouted the shaft of a spear.

He let out a shocked noise and collapsed back to the ground.

It was pure instinct that sent Densus into a dive in the opposite direction, slamming to the ground as the second spear whipped through the air where he'd been, thudding into the turf and staying wedged there.

'Shit.'

He looked over to the dying soldier, who lay at a funny angle, gurgling and coughing up blood, unable to lie flat because of the impaling short spear. Even as Densus watched, the man gagged once more and then fell silent and still.

Densus listened. He could hear nothing. He rose slowly, carefully, drawing his sword. He was ready to jump again, but no fresh spear came. Eyes on the undergrowth, trying to spot any movement, he backed away, towards the camp again. Only when he was in the main inhabited area did he turn. He marched across the camp towards the tribune's tent. As he closed, Faventinus met him. 'What are you doing?'

'We just got attacked at the latrine trench. Never even saw them. Spears thrown. One of your men is dead. This has to end.'

With his fellow centurion in tow, he reached the tent and pulled the door open. Months back, there had been guards outside the tribune's tent, and then, as numbers declined, it had moved to the man's entourage to stand guard. Now, in these tense times, even that had changed, and the tribune's two men slept inside the tent doorway, where they could still protect him, but were out of the sight of any unruly, potentially rebellious, soldier. Densus kicked the man, who yelped and shot to his feet. The other attendant rose, groggily, nearby. 'Fuck off out for a moment,' Densus told them, thumbing over his shoulder. The two men looked at one another, uncertain, but one more glance at Densus' expression had them obediently ducking out of the tent. Faventinus hissed, 'Be careful, Sempronius.'

Densus ignored him. As his eyes adjusted to the dark, he realised the tribune was awake now, sitting up, a sword across his lap.

'What is the meaning of this?'

Densus took a deep breath. 'The expedition is over, sir.'

'What?'

'Over. Finished. Done. I know it, even if you don't, sir. I have fought in wars. You haven't. You have the rank, but I have the experience. In any campaign, it is the duty of the commander to weigh the odds at all times, and the moment there is no hope, to retreat.'

'No.'

Densus shook his head. 'If you ignore the odds, you end up with Crassus against the Parthians or Varus against the Germans. A disaster on an epic scale.' The tribune made to speak, but Densus levelled a finger at him. 'We are in the territory of a king with an army. They are hard warriors, and they are in their own land. They know it well. We don't. Any step further risks annihilation.'

'They will not get close enough to...'

Densus cut him off there. 'Don't be blind to our inferiority here, sir. They've already *been* close. Jove, but this very night they were in camp. They left us a present. Another warning. And myself and one of the men were just attacked at the latrine. Spears thrown, and we never even saw the men who did it. They can pick us off any time they like. Frankly, I'm grateful they've let us come this far. They won't let us go much further, though. If you want *anyone* to get home to report to the emperor, we have to turn back now.'

The tribune rose from his bed and stepped face to face with Densus. The man was taller than the centurion remembered. 'Never. We are Roman. The Praetorian Guard. Our duty is to obey the emperor's command, to the death if necessary. We were commanded to find the source of the river and, by all the gods, that is what we will do, even if every man falls along the way and I am alone at the end. I will *not* fail.'

'You're mad, sir.'

'What?' the man's face filled with ire in just a moment. He was getting dangerously angry, like he had been with his secretary.

'*Insane*,' Densus snapped. 'The fever robbed you of your wits. I thought as much when you strangled your own clerk, but it's never been clearer. You would sacrifice every last man on the altar of your vanity. No commander in his right mind would go on now. We're at the end. We're turning back.'

'No, we are not.'

Densus was suddenly acutely aware that he still had a bared sword in his hand, but that so did the tribune. Both men turned to look at Faventinus. The other centurion looked horrified.

'Claudius, you know I'm right,' Densus hissed.

Faventinus nodded, almost absently, but turned to look doubtfully at the tribune, who pointed at him. 'And are you an oathbreaker, too, Centurion Faventinus?'

Densus could feel the almost panicked indecision in his friend. He hated putting the man in this position, but there really was no other choice. Densus felt his spirits sink as Faventinus saluted the tribune, then turned back to him. 'I can't, Sempronius. I can't break my oath. Not even for this.'

The tribune turned to Densus. 'You are relieved of your command, Centurion.'

Faventinus snapped back to the commander, then. 'No, sir. *No*. You won't do that. Without Densus leading us, we're all fucked instantly. I won't turn on you, but Densus has to stay in charge.'

The tribune turned, then. 'Very well. But if there is a repeat of this insubordination, I will kill you myself, Centurion.' The man lowered his sword and turned back to his sleeping pallet. For a moment, as his back was turned, Densus was sorely tempted to plant his sword in it. He glanced at Faventinus, whose face was weary and saddened. The man gestured to the door, and the two centurions left.

Outside, Densus turned to his friend. 'You should have backed me up in there.'

Faventinus sighed. 'No. You shouldn't have challenged him. When that soldier outside disobeyed me, what did you do?' Densus didn't answer. He had, of course, disciplined the man. He knew where his friend was going with this. He couldn't be a man of double standards, expecting the soldiers to obey their centurions, and then refusing the tribune's orders himself. He sagged. Faventinus had him beaten, there. The man always had been clever.

'We can't do this much longer,' he sighed. 'We can obey the tribune, and we've just about still got the men with us, but much more of this shit and all three of us are going to wake up one morning staked out on the ground while the men load up to go home.'

'Eight days,' Faventinus said quietly. 'By my estimation, we're eight days away from the source – the second lake. We only have to survive that long. To the first lake, along the channel, then to the second. Then we're done and we can go home. We just have to be careful. Watch the water and food, camp far enough from the bushes to be out of thrown spear range. Eight days.'

Densus nodded unhappily. Eight days.

43

LAKE

AD 62

Four days had gone. To say Faventinus regretted having taken such a stand would be a *vast* understatement. He *hated* it. But the sad and simple fact was that, hate it or not, it had been the right decision, and he'd have made it again if he had to. To turn his back on his oath would be to deny who he was.

They were so careful. All water was checked, and so was all food. They only ate the salted meat and hardtack biscuits from their packs, knowing that to be safe. They only drank water drawn from the river in view of at least three or four men, to be certain it could not be drugged or poisoned. Each night, the size of the camp shrunk, all tents crammed in close together, in order to create a much-shorted perimeter to guard, and each man on guard was in clear sight of those to either side, each man required to check in by voice with the others every time he thought the quarter hour had passed. They were taking every precaution they could. There had almost been a mutiny the second day on from the 'incident'.

When a soldier had paused by the river to take a piss, his mates had taken their eyes off him for only moments, yet when they looked back, he was face down in the water, floating slowly away downstream.

The men had refused to go on. In a desperate attempt to hold things together and fend off a revolution, Faventinus had climbed onto a rock and slowly, in a loud voice, recited the oath of service and the oath to the emperor. When he'd finished, he asked them who among them was still Roman, still a Praetorian.

It had been a huge relief to him when almost two-thirds of the remaining men had crossed to join him. The rest of them, a short step from rebellion, looked about nervously.

'If you go back,' he shouted, 'then you go alone. You have to go all that way downstream without us, for we have just a few more days to travel, and we'll have held to our oath.'

There had been a short, tense silence, and then gradually the remaining soldiers had joined those expressing their loyalty with Faventinus. He'd won them round, and the mutiny hadn't happened, but he was also acutely aware of how close they'd come.

The next day one of the slaves disappeared. No one even saw him go. When they set out that morning, he was marching with the rest of them, sword at his side, and when they stopped to make camp that night, he just wasn't with them any more. Inexplicable.

Then, the next morning, only an hour into the march, they lost two more men, and learned horribly that they were going to have to be even more careful. They had strayed unknowingly into a trap. Worst of all, it had been a trap they might have anticipated, since Roman defences applied the same damn things. The legions called them 'lily pits', holes in the ground a foot across and a foot deep, with a sharpened point jutting up at the base, the whole thing covered with dried grass to hide it. Genialis had stepped into one, which had gone straight into the arch of his foot and right up into his ankle, but even as he shrieked a warning, the soldier at his left shoulder had fallen to the second one.

There had been discussion about what to do with the two men. The tribune had announced flatly that they could hardly be carried onwards. Densus had compromised, telling the two injured men that they were only a few days away from their goal. The two men could stay here with sufficient supplies to last them, and the others would pick them up on the way back. They were empty words, really. Even if they *did* come back, which was still a point argued among the men, Faventinus was fairly confident that the two men would be dead by then, killed by nature if not by the sun king's warriors.

In the end, the injured soldier was left there alone, for Genialis, the musician, knew his leg was done for, the ankle ruined. He knew his chances of survival were tiny, and that he would never be able to travel back to civilisation now. The best he could look forward to was an infection in the wound, then slow madness and death. At his plea, and despite the man being otherwise healthy, Densus had finished him with a swift blow.

It was a subdued and frightened column that found the lake towards the end of that day. Thirty-one men traversed the eastern edge of the lake, looking for a river that emptied into it from the east. Faventinus managed not to draw to the men's attention the figures he kept seeing at the edge of his vision.

'Why don't they attack?' he asked Densus that evening as the men went about building their camp on the lake's shore, with a good distance of open ground all around.

'What?'

'They're picking us off slowly, abrading us. Surely they must have enough men to take us on now? We've been seeing their warriors keeping pace with us for days, and sometimes I see even a dozen of them at a time. We're deep in their lands now. Why don't they just kill us?'

Densus snorted. 'Why bother? We've lost seven men in their lands already, and without them even having to put in an appearance. Why risk losing men when they can slowly peel us, day by day, without losing a man?'

That was a depressing thought. As they set the watches that evening, the unit's standard was found lying in the reeds at the lake's edge. Mordanticus' hand was still wrapped around it, torn from the arm at the wrist. No one had seen a crocodile for days, now, but the reed beds at the lake's edge looked like prime territory for them, and so now the watch was shuffled so that even the waters were under careful observation all night.

Faventinus slipped into his blanket that evening thoroughly troubled. He found that he was repeating the soldier's oath like a mantra, an almost inaudible whisper as he lay there, waiting for blessed sleep, using the oath like armour.

The dream that came that night was not encouraging.

In it, he stood on a field of green, surrounded by distant mountains, with less than two score men under his command. But every time he moved, one of them vanished. He blinked. Another one gone. Rubbed his eyes. Another. Turned. Another. Even as he tried desperately to keep his eyes wide, unblinking as they watered, and to see everywhere at once, his force was being whittled down to nothing by some unseen presence. And then he heard the laughter. He turned, which was foolish, for another man just out of his sight vanished. The laughter of many men, and he recognised them from their statues in Rome. Varus, who saw three legions under his command gone in Germania because he underestimated the danger. Crassus, whose vanity and greed had led him to the bloodbath at Carrhae. Terentius Varro and Aemilius Paullus, who had not learned from their defeats at Trebia and Trasimene, and marched their army into disaster against Hannibal. Sulpicius Longus, who marched against dreadful odds at the Allia and opened the door for the Gauls to invade Rome. Even Marcus Antonius, who divided the empire and lost everything, all for his infatuation with an Aegyptian whore.

He awoke, sweating even more than usual, just as the last man in his force vanished, leaving him alone on the field. Densus was watching him from across the tent they now shared in the interest of keeping the camp smaller, tighter, and everyone in sight of someone else.

'Bad dream,' he murmured.

'You should have supported me when you had the chance.'

Had he somehow seen into Faventinus' dream?

'What?'

'Now it might be too late. Was the seer right? Have you regretted going on often enough, yet?'

Faventinus blinked, but Densus lay back. 'Go to sleep.'

He couldn't. He tried, but sleep just would not come. Only the oath, his mantra, again and again. Without the oath, he was not Praetorian. Not a soldier. Without the oath, what would he be?

The clear answer to that was no comfort.

Alive.

44

TERRA INCOGNITA

AD 62

They'd managed one more day without mishap. One day from the lake, once they'd found the channel that led off in the correct direction to be the one indicated on the farmer's map. All the time there were more and more native warriors visible in the distance, keeping pace with them, or already ahead and waiting for them, always watching, threatening. Late that day they had passed what had to be another territorial marker, another pair of red posts with cows' skulls upon them. That they had left the territory seemed highly unlikely, and therefore Densus figured they had instead moved into a new and more important region of the sun king. That they were moving into the very heart of those lands now was supported by the increased manpower, and so they made camp early that night, some time before sunset.

It was a tense night with little sleep, for the sun king's men moved through the dark all around the camp, and every noise seemed to the Praetorians to be a signal of some sort. Though they had lost no further men that day, the constant danger preyed on every mind, and as the two centurions had moved around the camp that night, it was difficult to miss the fresh air of mutiny and rebellion. Densus and his friend had tried encouragement, speaking to the men as they went this way and that, but it had no appreciable effect.

It was nerve-wracking for the centurions. For months now, they had held the unit together and obedient to the chain of command, even when things had gradually become worse and there had been open stirrings of rebellion. Even when the men had almost turned on their leaders. Densus knew his men, and Faventinus was probably just as aware of his. The units had been pushed as far as they could go, now. There was no threat or encouragement that was going to drive them further. From this point on, they would go just as far as they felt like, and no more. Mutiny was a breath away, and that boded ill for the officers. If a Roman force mutinied, they would have to remove their commanders, including the centurions, whether they liked them or not.

A cataclysm was coming.

When they rose the next morning, that sense of approaching mutiny was all the stronger. Densus and Faventinus, who had always enjoyed the respect of their men, and who had played on those tight bonds to maintain discipline, were now receiving dark looks from even the quietest of the men. When the tribune emerged from his tent, his two armed attendants protectively at his side, Densus noted with unease how almost every hand in the camp went to the hilt of a weapon, then rested there, as though waiting for a signal.

'I think we are making excellent progress,' the tribune announced, as though this were some adolescent camping trip, and each of them an excited child. He stretched, apparently oblivious to the dark glares his words elicited from the men all around the camp. Densus saw half a dozen swords leave their scabbards by half a hand-width before sliding back once more, a threat unseen by their target. 'I should not be surprised if we discover the source by the end of this very day.' More glares.

Densus looked around. There was an air of tension so taut it felt as though the camp could snap. Glancing up from the sullen men, he could see the warriors of the sun king all around them, flitting between trees or just standing brazenly in the open, a ballista shot away, no more. He had a sense the enemy were gathering.

'Have you seen them?' Faventinus murmured, as though reading his mind.

'More than ever. Closer than ever.'

Faventinus huffed. 'I think we're getting too far into their lands. I think they're gathering to stop us going any further.'

Densus nodded. It certainly looked that way. He turned a slow circle, counting. He could see at least two score of them, and that was just the ones standing in the open. Judging by those he'd seen moving around between the bushes, he'd be willing to wager there was more than twice that number out there. Including officers and slaves, the expedition now numbered no more than thirty. A rough estimate put them at three to one, which was not an encouraging number for any strategist. Despite Roman military training, if it came to a fight, even one on one, Densus would lay his money on the sun king's men, who were clearly trained and experienced warriors, suited to the climate and terrain. So... outnumbered *and* outclassed.

One more day, the tribune believed. Densus was less convinced, but right now he would seize on anything he could to keep the men going. Scanning the camp, he spied Probus, a man both centurions had been watching carefully now for some time. The disciple of Urbicus, who had led the offerings in the swamp and had already once prevented men attacking the tribune. He seemed a good barometer for the mood of the men as a whole, and it was often to him before the centurions that the guardsmen looked when decisions needed to be made.

In moments, he was beside the man, who was busy packing his kit onto his furca, the ubiquitous military baggage pole.

'The men are not happy, Probus.'

The guardsman paused, turned, looked up at him. 'That cannot be a surprise, Centurion. Only self-preservation has stopped them gutting the tribune already.'

'Self-preservation?'

'The tribune is protected by the gods. We may all die horribly on this journey, but he will walk through it unscathed. Still,' he sighed and picked up a bag of salted beef, 'there are men here who intend to refuse to march further. More than half the lads will turn back this morning.'

'Actual mutiny?'

'Self-preservation.'

'The tribune believes we're less than a day away.'

'From death. We've all seen the warriors out there in the trees. By the end of the day we're more likely to be bleeding out than celebrating our success, Centurion.'

'Give us today.'

'What?'

Densus grabbed his shoulder. 'The lads will listen to you, even when they won't listen to me. Give us this one day. If the tribune is right and we find the source, all will be well. If not...' he turned and looked across the camp. 'If not, you won't be alone in turning your back on him.'

Probus frowned, looked him up and down. 'Really?'

'I could happily have broken his nose last night when he tried to remove me from office. Faventinus persuaded me to go on, but like everyone else I've had enough. If *you* can give *me* one more day, *I'll* give *him* one day. No more.'

The man paused for a time. 'I'll see to it that the men march upriver, not down, but the next time something happens, I don't think *I'll* be able to stop anyone, let alone you.'

Densus nodded. 'That's fair. Thank you.'

He turned and marched back over to Faventinus, to whom he relayed this information. His fellow centurion entirely failed to hide his relief.

Camp was broken and the tribune gave the order to move out. Densus and the others followed on, the centurion musing on how close the tribune had come to full mutiny this morning, yet remained totally unaware of it.

Still, as they moved in tight formation, all with weapons ready and eyes on their surroundings, Flaccus bringing up the rear, it was hard to miss the fact that those warriors in the trees at the edge of everyone's vision were growing in number with every step. Densus was forced to adjust his estimate constantly, and by the time they had been travelling for an hour, he had it up to either four or five to one. Insurmountable odds. Quite simply, if the enemy moved against them now, their only hope of survival was to flee, and fast. Any fight was a foregone conclusion.

By the second hour, they started to hear it.

'What the fuck is that?' someone asked, and the column paused for a moment, listening. From somewhere ahead, a distant din was reaching them, through the trees, along the river. Somewhere between a hiss and a roar, it sounded like the bellow of a monster from ancient legend. A number of the men went pale, their gazes drawn to the unseen source.

'The sun king,' someone breathed.

'My arse,' Densus replied.

'Then what is it?'

'What it *isn't* is a creature. The sound is constant. No breath taken.' He smiled. 'That, my friend, is a waterfall.'

Faventinus, nearby, grinned. 'Gods, but you're right. And if it's a waterfall, then that might be the lake. That's the source we're looking for. Fuck me, but the tribune was right.'

Densus gave the order to move once more, and this time there was little delay. After everything, it seemed they were within earshot of the end of their quest, and even those men who'd planned to turn away this morning were now moving with speed. They hurried through the long grass, the undergrowth, between trees and along the river. They had entered a stretch of valley without realising it, though it now became clear, for the sides of that valley drew in as they marched, closing to a narrow defile, filled with steamy green vegetation. The river was fast moving now, tumbling with white water. If they'd needed confirmation that there was a waterfall up ahead, one glance at the river would prove it.

There was still danger, though. As they walked, Densus' gaze kept returning to the heights along both sides of the valley, and each was now almost filled with warriors, massing like an army, looking down on the meagre force of Praetorians marching along between them. Tactically, what the Romans were doing was beyond foolish.

Expecting thrown spears or a whooping charge at any moment, Densus walked on, the sun slowly rising in this warm, damp world. Though the valley was narrowing, the bank along which they trod opened into an area of scrubby, sparser trees, and, as they crested a low rise, the sight that greeted them made every man in the column, the tribune included, stop dead in his tracks.

The falls were immense. Through a gorge between rocky crags, a torrent of white water larger than any Densus had ever seen poured over a series of drops before plunging into the river they followed. The noise was deafening. Suddenly, looking at the sheer quantity of water, it was quite easy to believe this to be the source of the great river they had been following since Alexandria.

They stood for a long moment, savouring this. This had to be their goal.

Then Densus saw the figures.

His breath caught in his throat. Just as the sun king's warriors lined the heights of the valley sides, they also stood atop the waterfall, and all around it, in an arc, sealing off any further journey as effectively as the rocks themselves. The forces gathered made it clear that they were not going to be allowed to travel any further.

'Go to the water,' Densus called to the tribune, shouting to be heard over the falls. It took two repeats for the man to hear and turn, frowning. Densus pointed to the bag, carried by one of the tribune's staff ever since the swamp, which contained the rich offerings they had brought from Rome for the river's spirits. 'It's time. Give the river its gifts.'

The tribune's frown deepened.

'We are not there yet.'

Densus blinked. 'Sir?'

'The water surfaces in a great lake. Your map-making farmer made that clear. It is the lake that is the source, not the falls. This is not the source. Our journey is not over, though we are close. Very close. Our goal lies beyond those falls, perhaps not more than a mile.'

Staring at the man, Densus shook his head. 'This is as far as we can go, sir.'

'Nonsense.'

Before he could argue more, though, Probus cut in. 'Look around you, Tribune.'

Curtius Lupus stared at the soldier who had so spoken out of turn, but Densus nodded. 'He's right. There is no path. Just rocks and falls. We would have to back-track for a while until the valley sides lowered and seek another way round. But it's not just the terrain stopping us, sir. Look at the sun king's men. They've closed the valley to us.'

'Half-naked barbarians with crude spears do not frighten me,' the tribune said, airily.

'Well they fucking frighten *me*,' Probus said, and despite the lack of discipline, all Densus could do was nod agreement.

'Beat that man,' Curtius Lupus snapped.

'Sir?'

'That insolent dog of a soldier has spoken thus to his commander for the last time. I want him beaten until he can do nothing but grovel. And he should be grateful I am not having him bound and thrown into the river.'

'No.' Densus set his hands on his hips.

'What?' demanded the tribune.

Densus could feel the presence of others. He could sense Probus now standing at his shoulder in support. Others from among the men were drifting close, too, backing up their centurion as he took a long-awaited stand.

'This has gone far enough, tribune. The mission is over. Call it a failure if you wish. Call it a success, and no one will argue. Give your gifts to the river and join us in running like fucking cowards before that lot on the cliff tops decide to start throwing spears, but this unit goes no further.'

He could feel their support behind him. Oath be damned, there came a time when simple common sense had to win out. He felt a twinge of dismay to see Faventinus move to stand by the tribune, arms folded, in much the same way as Probus had with him. He threw a pleading look at his fellow centurion, but then had to turn back to Curtius Lupus, as the tribune began to march towards him, hand going to the sword at his side, drawing it.

'You will do as I say, Centurion. This is still the army of Rome. The Praetorian Guard of the emperor. There is a chain of command, and you seem to forget your place in it. What this unit does is *my* decision. Mine, and mine alone. If I say we move on past the falls and find the lake, then we move on past the falls and find the lake. If I say you do it naked, you do it naked. If I say you fall on your sword, then you fall on your sword.'

'I said it back in camp the other night,' Densus declared, 'you're insane. The fever's rotted your brain. Simple common sense tells us this is as far as we go. Denying that is madness.'

He readied himself. The tribune was almost on him, now, Faventinus still alongside like a faithful hound. As the commander approached, he lifted his sword, threatening.

'I will not put up with insubordination. I have seen this unit slide too far from their duty. Clearly all those months ago in Rome I made poor choices. I chose a mutinous, rebellious centurion with insolent, disorderly men. *Look* at yourselves. I have seen captives from the Scythian hill-tribes in Rome's markets who have more discipline, who look more civilised. This is as far as your little rebellion goes, Centurion.' He looked over Densus' shoulder to the men behind him. 'You will all return to your ranks, silently and in an orderly fashion. Any man who does not will be beaten until he accepts orders like a soldier.' He focused back on Densus. 'As for you, you are hereby stripped of your rank. Should you accept this like a soldier, with no further argument, you may join your men in the line. If not, I shall have no choice but to take further steps.'

To illustrate his words, that sword dipped, pointing at the centurion's neck.

Densus was a career soldier. He'd fought in wars and endured hardships across the empire, and he damn well knew how to handle a sword. He'd seen the tribune fight, back when he'd been attacked in his tent that night. The man was no expert, but he'd managed to hold his own. In equal circumstances, Densus knew he could best the man. Right now, though, the tribune's sword tip was a hair's breadth from his throat, while his own sword was still sheathed, even if he had his hand upon the hilt. The man might not be an expert swordsman, but he had shown himself to be both fast and strong when he had crushed his secretary's throat. If Densus moved wrong now, Curtius Lupus could kill him, and he knew it.

But sometimes, a man has to take a stand, even in the face of death. The lives of every man here rested in the balance, not just his own.

'No.'

'Think carefully, Centurion,' the tribune hissed, his sword momentarily touching the flesh of Densus' throat.

'Kill me if you must, but this is over.'

He could feel the men behind him tensing, ready to act. They couldn't save him, but they could avenge him.

He stared in shock as Curtius Lupus suddenly snapped straight and gave an odd choking noise. The man's mouth opened, and instead of the stream of invective Densus expected, dark blood flowed down over his lip. He gave an odd whimper, and the sword fell from his hand. As Densus stared in shock, the tribune dropped to his knees, looked up plaintively, and then toppled over to the side, dead.

Behind him, Claudius Faventinus wore an expression Densus would remember as long as he lived. The man who had held to discipline as long as any man could hope, clinging to an oath that had become meaningless long ago, stared at his own blood-soaked hand, then at the body. Densus looked down, wide-eyed, to see the hook-pointed knife that he had been given by the seer at Syene so many months ago and then given to Faventinus, jammed to the hilt in the man's back, between the ribs, right into the heart.

The men behind him were barely daring to breathe.

Densus knew he had to take control. Faventinus had done the unthinkable, and right now he was struggling even to stand.

'Go,' he shouted to the tribune's staff, who stood, horrified and white-faced. 'Give the gifts to the river. To the spirits. Our journey is over.' Still, they stood, silent and pale. 'Go,' he barked, and this time they scurried off in a panic.

He turned to the others. 'Any man with a weapon bared, put it away. We're not out of danger yet. In the absence of the tribune, I hereby assume command of the mission. I say this torrent is the source of the Nile, and we have achieved our goal. If any man wishes to oppose that, they may.' They wouldn't, he knew. Anything to go home. A sense of profound relief echoed through the men, though it threaded through tangible shock that they still felt. 'Prepare to leave this place and retrace our route.'

'Do we bury him?' Faventinus whispered, voice shaky. 'Take him back with us somehow?'

Looking down at the tribune's corpse, Densus made a decision. He shook his head. 'The tribune sacrificed himself for the good of the mission. His body was lost to the waters.' Saying as much, and with gestures to his fellow centurion, Densus and Faventinus bent and lifted the body, carrying it across the grass towards the water. As they reached the bank, Densus used one hand to pull his scarf out and fold it over his head in the manner of a priest. He looked up at the gathered warriors on the heights.

'I know you can't understand me,' he bellowed, 'but we

are leaving in peace. This man we offer as a sacrifice to the gods of this place, to Nilus and Hapi, to Sat and Anuket, to Khnum and Satet, and to all the gods favoured by the sun king and his people. On behalf of Rome, I offer this man, his gifts, and a promise that the empire's eagles will never fly over this place.'

With that, he and Faventinus slung the body into the water, where it sank for a moment beneath the white, foamy surface, then reappeared some distance away, face down, knife handle still standing proud, as it bobbed downriver and out of sight.

Densus sagged for a moment, then straightened, and turned to his men. 'I want everyone to make it very clear that we are leaving, and that we are doing so in peace. It would be a bastard if we'd done all that only to be butchered by the locals.'

As the column began to move out, heading back the way they'd come, away from the falls, Faventinus' voice, recovering some of its strength, murmured weakly beside him.

'You realise that, ironically, there's a good chance what's left of Curtius Lupus will get back to Alexandria months before us.'

For the first time in as long as he could remember, Densus laughed.

45

VILLA ON THE EDGE OF ALBANUM, SOUTH OF ROME

IDES OF SEPTEMBER AD 63

'I am not entirely surprised the tribune would sacrifice himself for the good of the mission,' Seneca drawled, reaching down for his wine. 'The man had been living in the dark shadow of an earlier failure, and sought to redeem his name in the emperor's eyes. I was not convinced he had sufficient character, but it is good to know that he did.'

Faventinus bowed his head, praying that Densus kept his mouth shut.

Seneca took a sip. 'So that is what you have discovered south of Kush? Inhospitable deserts, impassable swamps, and a great torrent of water bursting from the rocks. The source of the Nile. Nothing but primitive tribes. And you say there is little in the way of resources.'

'Just cattle, really, sir,' Faventinus replied.

'So there is nothing of use to Rome?'

'I would say not, sir.'

'But tell me again of how you came back to civilisation? Surely that route is of value?'

Faventinus nodded again, and began to describe in reasonable detail their return journey. How they had left the falls, though with no mention of the sun king and his empire, for he and Densus had decided early on that their report could not include anything that piqued Rome's interest, either commercially or militarily. He told how they had skirted the great lake once more and moved down the river until they found the small force they had left behind at the end of the swamp. The medic had done a sterling job, and the losses had been few, miraculously. There, the expedition recombined, deciding not to risk the swamp once more. Instead, they skirted the eastern and southern edges of the great morass, checking every area of good ground in search of the rest of their unit.

They never did find them, though they stumbled upon a camp site long abandoned that may well have been where they'd built the boats so long ago. The fate of the men they had left there would probably never be known. Soon, though, the survivors had reached swamp town, and there, with the judicious exchange of gifts, had managed to secure a place with a merchant caravan bound for the Indian Sea coast. A month of travel had brought them to a small but very busy port, where they had managed to gain passage on two ships up the coast, which brought them, by mid-summer, to Clysma in Aegyptus. From there, their Praetorian status and documents secured them anything they needed without having to result to barter. A brief journey across the delta to Pelusium, and then a coastal vessel to Alexandria, and at the last, a month-long journey home.

Faventinus sat back, and Seneca tapped the table top. 'But you do not believe this trade road you followed to be viable for Rome?'

The centurion shook his head. 'To use the route, Rome would have to control not only Kush, but all that land down to the swamp. I suspect that the cost and danger of adding on a route of so many hundred miles through lands filled with disease makes paying Parthian taxes look favourable in the end, sir.'

Seneca nodded, sighed. 'Ah well. It was a nice idea. And what did the emperor say again?'

Faventinus couldn't help but snort. 'It wasn't the emperor, sir. We were shown to his secretary, Epaphroditus, who told us very apologetically that the emperor was not available. He'd taken a state visit to oversee the rebuilding of Pompeii after the earthquake. Apparently they're erecting an arch in his honour. Epaphroditus seemed surprised to see us, as if he'd forgotten we'd gone at all. He said that the emperor had changed his mind and given up the notion of Kushite conquest not more than a month after our departure. He'd sent a letter after us, calling us back, though it never reached us, obviously.'

'Well,' Seneca smiled, leaning back with glass in hand, 'your mission may have been of little value to the emperor or his court, and may not have opened up great trade or conquests, but to some of us, knowledge is more valuable than power or gold. You have brought us the knowledge of what lies south of Libya and Kush, and such information is never valueless. I, for one, salute you.'

The rest of the visit passed in small talk and platitudes, and Faventinus was grateful to get out of the villa. Their horses waited outside with the men who'd accompanied them. As Densus settled into his saddle, he looked across at Faventinus, and tapped the harness of medals across his chest. A new one, gleaming silver and bearing the emblem of a palm tree and crocodile, sat at the centre.

'At least you've got your first medal,' he laughed.

Faventinus looked down at the identical one on his chest. The others on his harness were just service discs, unlike the war trophies of Densus. Only that one in the centre told a tale of epic hardship and heroism.

He smiled.

'Come on. Let's go home.'

HISTORICAL NOTE

The source of the White Nile has still, to this day, never been definitively located, with the latest offering being found in the Nyungwe forest in Rwanda, only located in 2010. That means that even since the days of Livingstone and Stanley, who declared the source to be Ripon Falls at Lake Victoria, the known distance to a confirmed source has been extended by hundreds of miles. In fact, Nero's centurions may well have come closer to the Nile's source than any man until the mid-nineteenth century.

So, why this tale, and what do we know of its history?

Rome had always prized Egypt, that ancient kingdom that was the source of so much grain and gold, and knowing as they did that gold also came from south of the border would inevitably have had eyes looking that way. Relations between Rome and Kush had exploded in 25 BC, leading to the invasion of Kush and the sacking of Napata before Rome withdrew and set up border garrisons, achieving a nicely favourable peace deal with Kush. To learn more of that, I would direct you to another series of mine, and the novels *Capsarius* and *Bellatrix*, which tell that story. For the following eight decades, there was little of note in the region to record, connected with this subject, anyway. Reaching AD 61, we have only two short sources to go on for this second probe south of Egypt.

Seneca tells us: 'I heard two centurions whom Nero Caesar, great lover of the other virtues and especially of truth, had sent to search for the source of the Nile. They told how they made a long journey, when they were provided with assistance by the king of Ethiopia, were given recommendations to the neighbouring kings, and penetrated further inland. "Then," they said, "we reached interminable marshlands. The local people had not discovered where they ended, nor can anyone hope to do so: weeds are so entangled with the water and the water with weeds, they are impassable either on foot or by boat; only a small, one-man craft can manage on the muddy, overgrown swamp. There," he said, "we saw two crags from which a huge volume of river water cascaded down."'

Pliny gives us even less, and his account conflicts rather heavily with Seneca: 'the Praetorian troops that were sent by the Emperor Nero under the command of a tribune, for the purposes of enquiry, when, among his other wars, he was contemplating an expedition against Aethiopia, brought back word that they had met with nothing but deserts on their route.'

Moreover, our historical knowledge of sub-Saharan Africa during the Roman era is sketchy at best. Little can be said of the peoples of the Nile below Kush. Pliny,

Herodotus and others give us often fanciful accounts, including dog-headed people and other such monsters, but our confirmed knowledge is limited pretty much to the Bantu Expansion, and the tribes of the region have not left us written, constructed or archaeological evidence in the same way as those of Egypt and Sudan. So, in some ways, in coming to write this book, I was faced with similar problems to the characters in it. I was reliant more on fable, rumour and hearsay than on any confirmed facts. But then, as a writer, that is fertile ground from which to work.

Very little is known of the adventures of the Praetorians Nero sent to find the source of the Nile. We do not even know the names of the men chosen to lead this expedition. Indeed, the two sources cannot even agree on who commanded, one mentioning only two centurions, the other a tribune. Naturally, I combined the two. The principal characters in this work, then, are not historically attested as taking part. The tribune, Curtius Lupus, is entirely fictional. I needed a disposable character with no recorded history. My centurions, on the other hand, are a different matter. Sempronius Densus' history with the Twenty-Second Legion, and his part in this expedition, are my own additions, but the man would become independently famous some eight years later, when he sacrificed himself in the forum to save the emperor Galba from assassins. This episode is recounted in brief, though without naming the man, in my novel *Domitian*. My other centurion, Claudius Faventinus, is recorded by Tacitus (*Histories* 3.57) as the man who suborns the Roman fleet on behalf of Vespasian that same year in which Densus dies. Two real men, but brought into the tale by me. All the supporting cast are fictional.

My portrayal of the journey through Egypt is partially inspired by Roman accounts of the land, partially through my own journey up the Nile in that country as far as Aswan and Lake Nasser a number of years ago, and partly by other tales set in the region. One challenge I faced throughout this write was the military aspect. My characters are soldiers, and I have made my career writing about Roman wars and actions, yet this adventure, for all its military aspect, actually involves no recorded fights at all. That is not to say, of course, that there weren't any. Hence, I have animal encounters in Egypt. Though the Aswan High Dam and Lake Nasser put an end to crocodiles in the Egyptian Nile, their long history there is recorded, and we all know how dangerous these monsters could be. Nile crocs are some of the biggest and most dangerous reptiles in the world, and, though they generally do not attack humans on land, they are far from above taking stray figures in the water or close to the bank, and history is replete with such tales. Indeed, the 'Ambo' they visit is the site of Kom Ombo, a temple to the crocodile god. The hippopotamus attack is also hardly unrealistic. Hippos are known to be the fiercest killers of humans on the Nile even now.

In remote, southern Egypt, I have portrayed the Roman garrisons as rather ramshackle, gone largely native. We have little evidence of some of these units, and even less of their activity. However, as time marches on, the study of the Roman military is leading us to understand more and more that there was not the standardisation and homogeneity among the Roman army that had once been presumed.

Ethnic variation in unit personalities and equipment seems to have been more common than anyone might think, and long-term settlement in a region would naturally see the unit adapt to their locale as needs required. However, while the average soldier might 'go native' to some extent, given twenty-five years of service there, the officers might well have a different manner, being temporary appointees from Rome. My portrayal of these units is, I will admit, more than a little coloured by inspiration drawn from both *Apocalypse Now* and from the frontier outpost in *Dances with Wolves*.

Then, further south into Kush, our heroes are attacked by the Blemmyes. I can do no better on this subject than to quote myself from the historical note in *Capsarius*: 'The black-clad tribesmen that appear in the book are my own portrayal of the tribe known as the Blemmyes, which occupied the desert highlands east of the Nile, to the south of Egypt and the north of Kush. The Blemmyes are somewhat mysterious. All we know of them is from ancient writers, though they are now thought to be the ancestors of the nomadic Beja people. However, though they may have developed into a relatively peaceful tribe, there has to have been something frightening and martial in their past. Not only were they used as mercenaries by later Roman emperors, and they themselves invaded and occupied parts of Roman Egypt on at least two occasions, they must have been a powerful military force in their own right, for there is a somewhat telling hint that they terrified their Roman enemies. Of them, Pliny writes "The Blemmyes, by report, have no heads, but mouths and eyes in their chests" (author's translation), and Pomponius Mela echoes this peculiar and worrying image. What, then, were these monsters? I have made them human, at least.'

Moving into Kush itself, I devoted only passing time to Kerma and Napata, despite their historical importance, for I explored Napata quite thoroughly in *Capsarius* and *Bellatrix*, and this story is only 'passing through', so to speak. I have put Kush into the early stages of a civil war during their visit. This is my own extrapolation from two historical figures. Nebmaatre was the regnal name of the king Amanitenmemide. We know virtually nothing about this king, other than the pyramid at Meroë that held him, and that pyramid's form places him in the mid to late first century AD. Roman writers tell us that the treaties were holding well at this time. In around AD 62 the Kandake Amanikhatashan comes to the throne, possibly succeeding Nebmaatre. Queens in Kush inherited when the king died and the next king was not of age. This suggests that Nebmaatre actually died while the Praetorians were busy exploring the Nile, and that the Kandake took control immediately. I have simply embellished and given this a reason. We know that the queen, too, held to good relations with the empire, for she sent cavalry to support Rome during the first Jewish war only a few years later.

My descriptions of the tribes found south of Kush are a blend of those reported in such sources as Herodotus, and the modern tribes still to be found in the region, since they can largely trace their heritage back to the Bantu Expansion. The notable exception for this is the town I have labelled 'swamp town'. This is a fictional location, though based upon ancient sources. Herodotus tells a story of Egyptians in the reign of Psamtik III (526–525 BC): 'Now the Egyptians had been on guard for three years, and none came to relieve them; so taking counsel and making common cause, they revolted from Psammetichus and went to Ethiopia. [...] So they came to Ethiopia, and gave themselves up to the king of the country; who, to make them a gift in return, bade them dispossess certain Ethiopians with whom he was at feud, and occupy their land. These Ethiopians then learnt Egyptian customs and have become milder-mannered by intermixture with the Egyptians.' This tale, then, is the source of my surprisingly Egyptian tribe lurking in the wilds of South Sudan and guarding a trade route that leads from their lands to the coast in East Africa, one of the very things the expedition was hoping to find. Beyond swamp town, the Sudd is still one of Africa's most impressive landscapes, and the flora and fauna are abundant.

We then close in on the final area in the book, the Nile leading up to Lake Albert, then to Murchison Falls, which lies between that body of water and Lake Victoria and which could be the 'two crags from which a huge volume of river water cascaded down' of Seneca. Once again, it is worth reiterating the lack of recorded history in this whole region prior to the later Middle Ages. What we do have is another example of a tantalising legend, much like Psamtik's rebels in their swamp town. To this day, in Uganda there lies a Bantu kingdom named Bunyoro-Kitara. The recorded history of this people can be convincingly traced back to the fourteenth century AD. However, the oral history of the people goes back a great deal further, as far as the Bronze Age, and there is a suggestion that the Kitaran empire, as it has also been known, developed iron working early, learning it from the Meroitic Kushites.

Kitara is a legend. It may be that the whole thing prior to the Middle Ages is a fiction. *A History of Bunyoro-Kitara* by A. R. Dunbar tells us the legends. Prior to the fourteenth century, during which the brief dynasty of kings are referred to as 'demi-gods', the early leaders of Kitara are remembered as true gods, including Ruhanga, who created the sun, and his brother Nkya, who created the moon. What I have given you, then, in the lakes region, where that people's land would be powerful, is an empire of the sun god Ruhanga. 'Why put in a semi-fictional, legendary tribe?' you might ask. The simple answer is that if the expedition did reach Murchison Falls, I wanted a good reason for them not going further, for never finding Lake Victoria. A reason they gave up so close to the end.

In addition, given that Seneca and Pliny tell very different stories, yet should both have heard the results from the same people, it seemed to me that the centurions might have lied to one or both of the great writers, and the discovery of a powerful kingdom that would prevent any easy expansion explained that readily. That Pliny and Seneca were both interested in what could be gained south of Egypt might explain them receiving responses that flatly state further expansion would be pointless. Pliny? Oh, there's nothing there but desert. Seneca? Oh, just a swamp that goes on forever. It is a sad fact that by the time the expedition could have returned to Rome, Nero had dealt with the Boudiccan revolt and was building a new palace, which would probably have put him off the idea of expensive and unnecessary expansion for the time being. Thus the whole thing had been a colossal waste of time. And Seneca was no longer in Nero's good books, going into quiet retirement.

As you read the book, you may well have spotted aspects that brought other tales to mind. I had always seen this tale as something of a Roman *Heart of Darkness*, and so that might well have come across. In preparation, I watched many other such tales, including *Apocalypse Now*. *Too Late the Hero* and *The African Queen* both influenced my story to some extent, and the eagle-eyed may have noticed a flavour of the excellent *Ghost and the Darkness* in the lion hunt scene. And as far as the sun king's people (Kitara) are concerned, there is a touch of *The 13th Warrior* in there, I think. All these stories had their influence, not to mention the numerous documentaries on the Nile, from the 1970s BBC series to those accounts of more modern explorers, from Levison Wood to Joanna Lumley. And, of course, my own adventures as far as the edge of Sudan.

Indeed, one of the above-mentioned tales (*Heart of Darkness*/*Apocalypse Now*) gives this book one of its major themes. The idea that over so many months in a land completely alien, madness is never very far away, and 'going native' is a most natural phenomenon, surfaces repeatedly in the book.

Medicine naturally takes part in the story, too. It seemed extremely unlikely that any group such as this could travel through the marshy Sudd, and the green Nile lands of South Sudan and Uganda, without malaria at least raising its head. Malaria is still rife along the Nile valley, as far north as El Fayuum, not far past Cairo, which one still needs the jabs to visit now. These days, of course, malaria is well known and easily treatable. Things were different in AD 61. Even the name, though it comes from the Latin for 'bad air', is a later invention. But it was clearly known about and referenced by the Romans and Greeks. As such, I was led to wonder how it was dealt with then. After all, quinine is a relatively recent discovery and not from Europe or Africa. With some research, it turns out that one potential cure/prevention known about then was Artemisia, better known as Wormwood. It also seems that the native tribes of Africa have been using it for centuries, and it is even now being pursued as a natural deterrent. That there might be more than one strain of 'swamp fever' is only natural. My capsarii (combat medics) in this tale work hard, but struggle to deal with the illness. The compound produced by the magician (his description based on the Kikuyu witch doctors of Kenya) includes an antibiotic compound called tetracycline, which has been found in ancient skeletons unearthed in Nubia, and traced to the fermentation of ancient beer. There is a suggestion that this was done deliberately, and might have helped against malaria in the region. The combination therefore of the Artemisia and a tetracycline compound, along with a fruit to make it palatable, may well be the best pre-quinine defence against malaria. In fact, the most difficult piece of research involved in all of this was finding a fruit native to the region that was not imported by either the Portuguese or Islamic settlers.

Religion also takes a part in this book. I won't explore it deeply, but two things deserve pointing out. The first is Urbicus. We have no details of priests in the Roman army. In Rome, the priesthoods were eagerly sought by politicians, and their membership was for life. What of the army, then? Is it feasible that thousands of soldiers might be sent on campaign for years without the presence of a priest? The number of altars found at Roman military sites makes it clear that religion was important in the army, as indeed, to some extent it still is. There are, as the saying goes, no atheists in foxholes. My possibly inelegant solution is to have a member of the unit serve as priest. Most likely such duties were held by the senior officers, but then Urbicus is a tesserarius, the third in charge of a century. Secondly, I have to mention the sistrum. If men are going to get all superstitious about the evil eye in Egypt and Sudan, the sistrum is going to get shaken. This religious rattle came to Rome early on with the worship of Isis, but became more and more common. Examples now abound in museums. I've shaken one. They're noisy. I can only imagine what the shaking of twenty sounds like.

For the languages of my African tribes, I am somewhat limited, for there are not really dictionaries around for unnamed tribes only mentioned by Greek writers thousands of years ago. However, the successor languages of the Bantu people still exist in sub-Saharan Africa, as do pre-Islamic variants in East Africa. I have used a mish-mash of these tongues for my speakers.

Oh, and yes, by the way, the Romans did have umbrellas. It's not an anachronism.

So that's it. My soldiers went out and went home, as the original expedition must have done for Seneca to quiz them. This is the second standalone novel I've written with the excellent team at Head of Zeus, and I can only thank them for letting me have the opportunity to tell such amazing tales. I hope you've enjoyed journeying up the Nile with me. See you soon in other new works.

Simon Turney, July 2023

About the Author

SIMON TURNEY is from Yorkshire and, having spent much of his childhood visiting historic sites, fell in love with the Roman heritage of the region. His fascination with the ancient world snowballed from there with great interest in Rome, Egypt, Greece and Byzantium. His works include the Marius' Mules and Praetorian series, the Tales of the Empire and The Damned Emperors series, and the Rise of Emperors books with Gordon Doherty. He lives in North Yorkshire with his family.

Follow Simon at www.simonturney.com